There is nothing...
gorgeous alpha m...
wouldn't di... ...at...

ONE NIGHT WITH A
COWBOY

*A trio of passionate, powerful and
dramatic love stories.*

ONE NIGHT WITH A
COWBOY

New York Times bestselling author
Diana Palmer,
Annette Broadrick & Kathie DeNosky

M&B™ and M&B™ with the Rose Device
are trademarks of the publisher.
Harlequin Mills & Boon Limited, Eton House,
18-24 Paradise Road, Richmond, Surrey TW9 1SR

ONE NIGHT WITH A COWBOY
© by Harlequin Enterprises II B.V./S.à.r.l. 2009

Heartbreaker, Branded and *Lonetree Ranchers: Morgan* were previously published in Great Britain.

Heartbreaker © Diana Palmer 2006
Branded © Annette Broadrick 2004
Lonetree Ranchers: Morgan © Kathie DeNosky 2003

ISBN: 978 0 263 87541 6

24-0909

Harlequin Mills & Boon policy is to use papers that are natural, renewable and recyclable products and made from wood grown in sustainable forests. The logging and manufacturing processes conform to the legal environmental regulations of the country of origin.

Printed and bound in Spain
by Litografia Rosés S.A., Barcelona

HEARTBREAKER
Diana Palmer

To Tara Gavin and Melissa Jeglinski,
with love

The prolific author of over one hundred books, **Diana Palmer** got her start as a newspaper reporter. One of the top ten romance writers in America, she has a gift for telling the most sensual tales with charm and humour. Diana lives with her family in Georgia.

Don't miss Diana Palmer's new novel, *Heartless*, out in February 2010.

One

It had been a grueling semester. Tellie Maddox had her history degree, but she was feeling betrayed. He hadn't shown up for her graduation exercises. Marge had, along with Dawn and Brandi, her two daughters. None of them were related to Tellie, who was orphaned many years ago, but they were as close to her as sisters. They'd cared enough to be here for her special day. J.B. hadn't. It was one more heartbreak in a whole series of them in Tellie's life that J.B. was responsible for.

She looked around her dorm room sadly, remembering how happy she'd been here for four years, sharing with Sandy Melton, a fellow history major. Sandy had already gone, off to England to continue her studies in medieval history. Tellie pushed back her short, wavy dark hair and sighed. Her pale green eyes searched for the last of her textbooks. She should take them to the campus bookstore, she supposed, and resell them. She was going to need every penny she could get to make it through the summer. When the fall semester began, in August, she was going to have to pay tuition again as she worked on her master's degree. She wanted to teach at college level. No chance of that, with just a bachelor's degree, unless she taught adult education as an adjunct member of staff.

Once she'd thought that one day J.B. might fall in love with her and want to marry her. Those hopeless dreams grew dimmer every day.

J. B. Hammock was Marge's brother. He'd rescued Tellie from a boy in the foster home where she'd been staying since her mother's death. Her mother had been the estranged wife of J.B.'s top horse wrangler, who'd later moved out of state and vanished. Tellie had gone to a foster home, despite Marge's objections, because J.B. said that a widow with two children to raise didn't need the complication of a teenager.

All that had changed with the attempted assault by another foster child in care with the same family. J.B. heard about it from a policeman who was one of his best friends. He swore out a warrant himself and had Tellie give a statement about what had happened. The boy, only thirteen at the time, was arrested and subsequently sent to juvenile hall. Tellie had slugged the boy when he tried to remove her blouse and sat on him until the family heard her yelling. Even at such a young age, Tellie was fearless. It had helped that the boy was half her size and half-drunk.

J.B. had jerked Tellie right out of the foster home the night the boy was arrested. He'd taken her straight to Marge for sanctuary. Marge had loved her almost at once. Most people did love Tellie. She was honest and sweet and generous with her time, and she wasn't afraid of hard work. Even at the age of fourteen, she'd taken charge of the kitchen and Dawn and Brandi. The sisters were nine and ten at the time respectively. They'd loved having an older girl in the house. Marge's job as a Realtor kept her on the road at all sorts of odd hours. But she could depend on Tellie to keep the girls in school clothes and help with their homework. She was a born baby-sitter.

Tellie had doted on J.B. He was very rich, and very temperamental. He owned hundreds of acres of prime ranch land near Jacobsville, where he raised purebred Santa Gertrudis cattle and entertained the rich and famous at his hundred-year-old rancho. He had a fabulous French chef in residence, along with a housekeeper named Nell who could singe the feathers off a duck with her temper at ten paces. Nell ran the house, and J.B., to an extent. He knew famous politicians, and movie stars, and foreign royalty from his days as a rodeo champion. He had impeccable manners, a legacy from his Spanish grandmother, and wealth from his British grandfather, who had been a peer of the realm. J.B.'s roots were European, despite his very American cattle operation.

But he did intimidate people. Locally he was known more for chasing Ralph Barrows off his place on foot, wielding a replica fantasy sword from the Lord of the Rings movie trilogy. Barrows had gotten drunk and shot J.B.'s favorite German shepherd for growling at him and barking when he tried to sneak into the bunkhouse in the small hours of the morning during roundup. Drinking wasn't allowed on the ranch. And nobody hurt an animal there. J.B. couldn't get to the key to his gun cabinet fast enough, so he grabbed the sword from its wall display and struck out for the bunkhouse the minute his foreman told him what was going on. The dog recovered, although it limped badly. Barrows hadn't been seen since.

J.B. wasn't really a social animal, despite the grand parties he threw at the ranch. He kept to himself, except for the numerous gorgeous women he squired around in his private jet. He had a nasty temper and the arrogance of position and wealth. Tellie was closer to him than almost anyone, even Marge, because she'd taken charge of him when she was fourteen and he went on a legendary drunk after his father died. It was Tellie who'd made Marge drive her to J.B.'s place when Nell called in a panic and said that J.B. was wrecking the den and the computers. It was Tellie who'd set him down, calmed him, and made cinnamon coffee for him to help sober him up.

J.B. tolerated her interventions over the years. He was like her property, her private male. Nobody dared to say that, of course, not even Tellie. But she was possessive of him and, as she grew older, she became jealous of the women who passed through his life in such numbers. She tried not to let it show. Invariably, though, it did.

When she was eighteen, one of his girlfriends had made an unkind remark to Tellie, who'd flared back at her that J.B. wouldn't keep *her* around for much longer if she was going to be rude to his family! After the girl left, J.B. had it out with Tellie, his green eyes flaming like emeralds, his thick black hair almost standing up straight on his head with bad temper. Tellie didn't own him, he reminded her, and if she didn't stop trying to possess him, she'd be out on her ear. She wasn't even part of his family, he'd added cruelly. She had no right whatsoever to make any claims on his life.

She'd shot back that his girlfriends were all alike—longlegged, big-breasted, pretty girls with the brains of bats! He'd looked at her small breasts and remarked that she certainly wouldn't fit that description.

She'd slapped him. It was involuntary and she was immediately sorry. But before she could take it back, he'd jerked her against his tall, lean body and kissed her in a way that still made her knees weak four years later. It had been meant, she was sure, as a punishment. But her mouth had opened weakly under his in a silent protest, and the tiny movement had kindled a shudder in the muscular body so close to hers.

He'd backed her up against the sofa and crushed her down on it, under the length of him. The kiss had grown hard, insistent, passionate. His big, lean hand had found her breast under her blouse, and she'd panicked. The sensations he caused made her push at him and fight to get free.

She jerked her mind back to the present. J.B. had torn himself away from her, in an even worse temper than before. His eyes had blazed down at her, as if she'd done something unforgivable. Furious, he'd told her to get out of his life and stay out. She was due to leave for college the same week, and he hadn't even said goodbye. He'd ignored her from that day onward.

Holidays had come and gone. Slowly tensions had lessened between them, but J.B. had made sure that they were never alone again. He'd given her presents for her birthday and Christmas, but they were always impersonal ones, like computer hardware or software, or biography and history books that he knew she liked. She'd given him ties. In fact, she'd given him the same exact tie for every birthday and every Christmas present. She'd found a closeout special and bought two boxes of identical ties. She was set for life, she reasoned, for presents for J.B. Marge had remarked on the odd and monotonous present, but J.B. himself said nothing at all. Well, he said thank you every time he opened a present from Tellie, but he said nothing more. Presumably he'd given the ties away. He never wore one. Tellie hadn't expected that he would. They were incredibly ugly. Yellow, with a putrid green dragon with red eyes. She still had enough left for ten more years...

"Are you ready, Tellie?" Marge called from the door.

She was like her brother, tall and dark-haired, but her eyes were brown where J.B.'s were green. Marge had a sweet nature, and she wasn't violent. She had a livewire personality. Everybody loved her. She was long widowed and had never looked at another man. Love, she often told Tellie, for some people was undying, even if one lost the partner. She would never find anyone else as wonderful as her late husband. She had no interest in trying.

"I just have a couple more blouses to pack," Tellie said with a smile.

Dawn and Brandi wandered around her dorm room curiously.

"You'll do this one day, yourselves," Tellie assured them.

"Not me," Dawn, the youngest, at sixteen, replied with a grin. "I'm going to be a cattle baron like Uncle J.B. when I get through agricultural college."

"I'm going to be an attorney," Brandi, who would be a senior in the fall at seventeen, said with a smile. "I want to help poor people."

"She can already bargain me into anything," Marge said with an amused wink at Tellie.

"Me, too," Tellie had to admit. "She's still got my favorite jacket, and I never even got to wear it once."

"It looks much better on me," Brandi assured her. "Red just isn't your color."

A lot she knew, Tellie thought, because every time she thought about J.B., she saw red.

Marge watched Tellie pack her suitcase with a somber expression. "He really did have an emergency at the ranch," she told Tellie gently. "The big barn caught fire. They had fire departments from all over Jacobs County out there putting it out."

"I'm sure he would have come, if he'd been able," Tellie replied politely. She didn't believe it. J.B. hadn't shown any interest in her at all in recent years. He'd avoided her whenever possible. Perhaps the ties had driven him nuts and he'd torched the barn himself, thinking of it as a giant yellow dragon tie. The thought amused her, and she laughed.

"What are you laughing about?" Marge teased.

"I was thinking maybe J.B.'s gone off his rocker and started seeing yellow dragon ties everywhere…"

Marge chuckled. "It wouldn't surprise me. Those ties are just awful, Tellie, really!"

"I think they suit him," Tellie said with irrepressible humor. "I'm sure that he's going to wear one eventually."

Marge started to speak and apparently thought better of it. "Well, I wouldn't hold my breath waiting," she said instead.

"Who's the flavor of the month?" Tellie wondered aloud.

Marge lifted an eyebrow. She knew what Tellie meant, all too well. She despaired of her brother ever getting serious about a woman again. "He's dating one of the Kingstons's cousins, from Fort Worth. She was a runner-up for Miss Texas."

Tellie wasn't surprised. J.B. had a passion for beautiful blondes. Over the years, he'd escorted his share of movie starlets. Tellie, with her ordinary face and figure, was hardly on a par to compete with such beauties.

"They're just display models," Marge whispered wickedly, so that her daughters didn't hear her.

Tellie burst out laughing. "Oh, Marge, what would I do without you?"

Marge shrugged. "It's us against the men of the world," she pointed out. "Even my brother qualifies as the enemy from time to time." She paused. "Don't they give you a CD of the graduation exercises?"

"Yes, along with my diploma," Tellie agreed. "Why?"

"I say we get the boys to rope J.B. to his easy chair in the den and make him watch the CD for twenty-four straight hours," she suggested. "Revenge is sweet!"

"He'd just go to sleep during the commencement speech," Tellie sighed. "And I wouldn't blame him. I almost did myself."

"Shame on you! The speaker was a famous politician!"

"Famously boring," Brandi remarked with a wicked grin.

"Notice how furiously everybody applauded when he stopped speaking," Dawn agreed.

"You two have been hanging out with me for too long," Tellie observed. "You're picking up all my bad habits."

They both hugged her. "We love you, bad habits and all," they said. "Congratulations on your degree!"

"You did very well indeed," Marge echoed. "Magna cum laude, no less! I'm proud of you."

"Honor graduates don't have social lives, Mother," Brandi pointed out. "No wonder she made such good grades. She spent every weekend in the dorm, studying!"

"Not every weekend," Tellie muttered. "There was that archaeology field trip…"

"With the geek squad." Dawn yawned.

"They weren't all geeks," she reminded them. "Anyway, I like digging up old things."

"Then you should have gotten your degree in archaeology instead of history," Brandi said.

She chuckled. "I'll be digging up old documents instead of old relics," she said. "It will be a cleaner job, at least."

"When do you start your master's degree work?" Marge asked.

"Fall semester," she replied, smiling. "I thought I'd take the summer off and spend a little time with you guys. I've already lined up a job working for the Ballenger brothers at their feedlot while Calhoun and Abby take a cruise to Greece with the boys. I guess all those summers following J.B. and his veterinarian around the ranch finally paid off. At least I know enough about feeding out cattle to handle the paperwork!"

"Lucky Calhoun and Abby. Wow," Dawn said on a sigh. "I'd love to get a three-month vacation!"

"Wouldn't we all," Tellie agreed wistfully. "In my case, a job is a vacation from all the studying! Biology was so hard!"

"We don't get to dissect things anymore at our school," Brandi said. "Everybody's afraid of blood these days."

"With good reason, I'm sorry to say," Marge mused.

"We don't get to do dissections, either," Tellie told her with a smile. "We had a rat on a dissecting board and we all got to use it for identification purposes. It was so nice that we had an air-conditioned lab!"

The girls made faces.

"Speaking of labs," Marge interrupted, "who wants a nice hamburger?"

"Nobody dissects cows, Mom," Brandi informed her.

"We can dissect the hamburger," Tellie suggested, "and identify the part of the cow it came from."

"It came from a steer, not a cow," Marge said wryly. "You could use a refresher course in Ranching 101, Tellie."

They all knew who'd be teaching it at home, and that was a sore spot. Tellie's smile faded. "I expect I'll get all the information I need working from Justin at the feedlot."

"They've got some handsome new cowboys working for them," Marge said with sparkling eyes. "One's an ex–Green Beret who grew up on a ranch in West Texas."

Tellie shrugged one shoulder. "I'm not sure I want to meet any men. I've still got three years of study to get my master's degree so that I can start teaching history in college."

"You can teach now, can't you?" Dawn asked.

"I can teach adult education," Tellie replied. "But I have to have at least a master's degree to teach at the college level, and a Ph.D. is preferred."

"Why don't you want to teach little kids?" Brandi asked curiously.

Tellie grinned. "Because you two hooligans destroyed all my illusions about sweet little kids," she replied, and ducked when Brandi threw a pillow at her.

"We were such sweet little kids," Dawn said belligerently. "You better say we were, or else, Tellie!"

"Or else what?" she replied.

Dawn wiggled her eyebrows. "Or else I'll burn the potatoes. It's my night to cook supper at home."

"Don't pay any attention to her, dear," Marge said. "She always burns the potatoes."

"Oh, Mom!" the teenager wailed.

Tellie just laughed. But her heart wasn't in the wordplay.

She was miserable because J.B. had missed her graduation, and nothing was going to make up for that.

Marge's house was on the outskirts of Jacobsville, about six miles from the big ranch that had been in her and J.B.'s family for three generations. It was a friendly little house with a bay window out front and a small front porch with a white swing. All around it were the flowers that Marge planted obsessively. It was May, and everything was blooming. Every color in the rainbow graced the small yard, including a small rose garden with an arch that was Marge's pride and joy. These were antique roses, not hybrids, and they had scents that were like perfume.

"I'd forgotten all over again how beautiful it was," Tellie said on a sigh.

"Howard loved it, too," Marge said, her dark eyes soft with memories for an instant as she looked around the lush, clipped lawn that led to the stepping stone walkway that led to the front porch.

"I never met him," Tellie said. "But he must have been a lovely person."

"He was," Marge agreed, her eyes sad as she recalled her husband.

"Look, it's Uncle J.B.!" Dawn cried, pointing to the narrow paved road that led up to the dirt driveway of Marge's house.

Tellie felt every muscle in her body contract. She turned around as the sporty red Jaguar slid to a halt, throwing up clouds of yellow dust. The door opened and J.B. climbed out.

He was tall and lean, with jet-black hair and dark green eyes. His cheekbones were high, his mouth thin. He had big ears and big feet. But he was so masculine that women were drawn to him like magnets. He had a sensuality in his walk that made Tellie's heart skip.

"Where the hell have you been?" he growled as he joined

them. "I looked everywhere for you until I finally gave up and drove back home!"

"What do you mean, where were we?" Marge exclaimed. "We were at Tellie's graduation. Not that you could be bothered to show up…!"

"I was across the stadium from you," J.B. said harshly. "I didn't see you until it was over. By the time I got through the crowd and out of the parking lot, you'd left the dorm and headed down here."

"You came to my graduation?" Tellie asked, in a husky, soft tone.

He turned, glaring at her. His eyes were large, framed by thick black lashes, deep-set and biting. "We had a fire at the barn. I was late. Do you think I'd miss something so important as your college graduation?" he added angrily, although his eyes evaded hers.

Her heart lifted, against her will. He didn't want her. She was like a second sister to him. But any contact with him made her tingle with delight. She couldn't help the radiance that lit up her plain face and made it pretty.

He glanced around him irritably and caught Tellie's hand, sending a thrill all the way to her heart. "Come here," he said, drawing her to the car with him.

He put her in the passenger side, closed the door and went around to get in beside her. He reached into the console between the bucket seats and pulled out a gold-wrapped box. He handed it to her.

She took it, her eyes surprised. "For me?"

"For no one else," he drawled, smiling faintly. "Go on. Look."

She tore open the wrapping. It was a jeweler's box, but far too big to be a ring. She opened the box and stared at it blankly.

He frowned. "What's the matter? Don't you like it?"

"It" was a Mickey Mouse watch with a big face and a gaudy red band. She knew what it meant, too. It meant that his secretary, Miss Jarrett, who hated being delegated to buy presents for him, had finally lost her cool. She thought J.B. was buying jewelry for one of his women, and Miss Jarrett was showing him that he'd better get his own gifts from now on.

It hurt Tellie, who knew that J.B. shopped for Marge and the girls himself. He never delegated that chore to underlings. But, then, Tellie wasn't family.

"It's…very nice," she stammered, aware that the silence had gone on a little too long for politeness.

She took the watch out of the box and he saw it for the first time.

Blistering range language burst from his chiseled lips before he could stop himself. Then his high cheekbones went dusky because he couldn't very well admit to Tellie that he hadn't bothered to go himself to get her a present. He'd kill Jarrett, though, he promised himself.

"It's the latest thing," he said with deliberate nonchalance.

"I love it. Really." She put it on her wrist. She did love it, because he'd given it to her. She'd have loved a dead rat in a box if it had come from J.B., because she had no pride.

He pursed his lips, the humor of the situation finally getting through to him. His green eyes twinkled. "You'll be the only graduate on your block to wear one," he pointed out.

She laughed. It changed her face, made her radiant. "Thanks, J.B.," she said.

He tugged her as close as the console would allow, and his eyes shifted to her soft, parted lips. "You can do better than that," he murmured wickedly, and bent.

She lifted her face, closed her eyes, savored the warm, tender pressure of his hard mouth on her soft one.

He stiffened. "No, you don't," he whispered roughly when she kept her lips firmly closed. He caught her cheek in one big, lean hand and pressed, gently, just enough to open her mouth. He bent and caught it, hard, pressing her head back against the padded seat with the force of it.

Tellie went under in a daze, loving the warm, hard insistence of his mouth in the silence of the little car. She sighed and a husky little moan escaped her taut throat.

He lifted his head. Dark green eyes probed her own, narrow and hot and full of frustrated desire.

"And here we are again," he said roughly.

She swallowed. "J.B...."

He put his thumb against her soft lips to stop the words. "I told you, there's no future in this, Tellie," he said, his voice hard and cold. "I don't want any woman on a permanent basis. Ever. I'm a bachelor, and I mean to stay that way. Understand?"

"But I didn't say anything," she protested.

"The hell you didn't," he bit off. He put her back in her seat and opened his car door.

She went with him back to Marge and the girls, showing off her new watch. "Look, isn't it neat?" she asked.

"I want one, too!" Brandi exclaimed.

"You don't graduate until next year, darling," Marge reminded her daughter.

"Well, I want one then," she repeated stubbornly.

"I'll keep that in mind," J.B. promised. He smiled, but it wasn't in his eyes. "Congratulations again, tidbit," he told Tellie. "I've got to go. I have a hot date tonight."

He was looking straight at Tellie as he said it. She only smiled.

"Thanks for the watch," she told him.

He shrugged. "It does suit you," he remarked enigmatically. "See you, girls."

He got into the sports car and roared away.

"I'd really love one of those," Brandi remarked on a sigh as she watched it leave.

Marge lifted Tellie's wrist and glared at the watch. "That was just mean," she said under her breath.

Tellie smiled sadly. "He sent Jarrett after it. He always has her buy presents for everybody except you and the girls. She obviously thought it was for one of his platinum blondes, and she got this out of spite."

"Yes, I figured that out all by myself," Marge replied, glowering. "But it's you who got hurt, not J.B."

"It's Jarrett who'll get hurt when he goes back to work," Tellie said on a sigh. "Poor old lady."

"She'll have him for breakfast," Marge said. "And she should."

"He does like sharp older women, doesn't he?" Tellie remarked on the way into the house. "He's got Nell at the house, taking care of things there, and she could scorch leather in a temper."

"Nell's a fixture," Marge said, smiling. "I don't know what J.B. and I would have done without her when we were kids. There was just Dad and us. Mom died when we were very young. Dad was never affectionate."

"Is that why J.B.'s such a rounder?" Tellie wondered.

As usual, Marge clammed up. "We don't ever talk about that," she said. "It isn't a pretty story, and J.B. hates even the memory."

"Nobody ever told me," Tellie persisted.

Marge gave her a gentle smile. "Nobody ever will, pet, unless it's J.B. himself."

"I know when that will be," Tellie sighed. "When they're wearing overcoats in hell."

"Exactly," Marge agreed warmly.

That night, they were watching a movie on television when the phone rang. Marge answered it. She came back in a few minutes, wincing.

"It's Jarrett," she told Tellie. "She wants to talk to you."

"How bad was it?" Tellie asked.

Marge made a face.

Tellie picked up the phone. "Hello?"

"Tellie? It's Nan Jarrett. I just want to apologize…"

"It's not your fault, Miss Jarrett," Tellie said at once. "It really is a cute watch. I love it."

"But it was your college graduation present," the older woman wailed. "I thought it was for one of those idiot blond floozies he carts around, and it made me mad that he didn't even care enough about them to buy a present himself." She realized what she'd just said and cleared her throat. "Not that I think he didn't care enough about *you,* of course…!"

"Obviously he doesn't," Tellie said through her teeth.

"Well, you wouldn't be so sure of that if you'd been here when he got back into the office just before quitting time," came the terse reply. "I have never heard such language in my life, even from him!"

"He was just mad that he got caught," Tellie said.

"He said it was one of the most special days of your life and I screwed it up," Miss Jarrett said miserably.

"He'd already done that by not showing up for my graduation," Tellie said, about to mention that none of them had seen him in the stands and thought he hadn't shown up.

"Oh, you know about that?" came the unexpected reply. "He told us all to remember he'd been fighting a fire in case it came up. He had a meeting with an out-of-town cattle buyer and his daughter. He forgot all about the commencement exercises."

Tellie's heart broke in two. "Yes," she said, fighting tears, "well, nobody's going to say anything. None of us, certainly."

"Certainly. He gets away with murder."

"I wish I could," Tellie said under her breath. "Thanks for calling, Miss Jarrett. It was nice of you."

"I just wanted you to know how bad I felt," the older woman said with genuine regret. "I wouldn't have hurt your feelings for the world."

"I know that."

"Well, happy graduation, anyway."

"Thanks."

Tellie hung up. She went back into the living room smiling. She was never going to tell them the truth about her graduation. But she knew that she'd never forget.

Two

Tellie had learned to hide her deepest feelings over the years, so Marge and the girls didn't notice any change in her. There was one. She was tired of waiting for J.B. to wake up and notice that she was around. She'd finally realized that she meant nothing to him. Well, maybe she was a sort of adopted relative for whom he had an occasional fondness. But his recent behavior had finally drowned her fondest hopes of anything serious. She was going to convince her stupid heart to stop aching for him, if it killed her.

Five days later, on a Monday, she walked into Calhoun and Justin Ballenger's office at their feedlot, ready for work.

Justin, Calhoun's elder brother, gave her a warm welcome. He was tall, whipcord lean, with gray-sprinkled black hair and dark eyes. He and his wife, Shelby—who was a direct descendant of the founder of Jacobsville, old John Jacobs—had three sons. They'd been married for a long time, like Calhoun and Abby. J. D. Langley's wife, Fay, had been working for the Ballengers as Calhoun's secretary, but a rough pregnancy had forced her to give it up temporarily. That was why Tellie was in such demand.

"You'll manage," Justin's secretary, Ellie, assured her with a smile. "We're not so rushed now as we are in the early spring and autumn. It's just nice and routine. I'll introduce you to the men later on. For now, let me show you what you'll be doing."

"Sorry you have to give up your own vacation for this," Justin said apologetically.

"Listen, I can't afford a vacation yet," she assured him with a grin. "I'm a lowly college student. I have to pay my tuition for three more years. I'm the one who's grateful for the job."

Justin shrugged. "You know as much about cattle as Abby and Shelby do," he said, which was high praise, since both were actively involved in the feedlot operation and the local cattlemen's association. "You're welcome here."

"Thanks," she said, and meant it.

"Thank you," he replied, and left them to it.

The work wasn't that difficult. Most of it dealt with spreadsheets, various programs that kept a daily tally on the number of cattle from each client and the feeding regimen they followed. It was involved and required a lot of concentration, and the phones seemed to ring constantly. It wasn't all clients asking about cattle. Many of the calls were from prospective customers. Others were from buyers who had contracted to take possession of certain lots of cattle when they were fed out. There were also calls from various organizations to which the Ballenger brothers belonged, and even a few from state and federal legislators. A number of them came from overseas, where the brothers had investments. Tellie found it all fascinating.

It took her a few days to get into the routine of things, and to get to know the men who worked at the feedlot. She could identify them all by face, if not by name.

One of them was hard to miss. He was the ex–Green Beret, a big, tall man from El Paso named Grange. If he had a first name, Tellie didn't hear anyone use it. He had straight black hair and dark brown eyes, an olive complexion and a deep, sexy voice. He liked Tellie on sight and made no secret of it. It amused Justin, because Grange hadn't shown any interest in anything in the weeks he'd been working on the place. It was the first spark of life the man had displayed.

He told Tellie, who looked surprised.

"He seems like a friendly man," she stammered.

He lifted a dark eyebrow. "The first day he worked here, one of the boys short-sheeted his bed. He turned on the lights, looked around the room, dumped one of the other men out of a bunk bed and threw him headfirst into the yard."

"Was it the right man?" Tellie asked, wide-eyed.

"It was. Nobody knew how he figured it out, and he never said. But the boys walk wide around him. Especially since he threw that big knife he carries at a sidewinder that crawled too close to the bunkhouse. Cag Hart has a reputation for that sort of accuracy with a Bowie, but he used to be the only one. Grange is a mystery."

She was intrigued. "What did he do, before he came here?"

"Nobody knows. Nobody asks, either," he added with a grin.

"Was he stationed overseas, in the army?"

"Nobody knows that, either. The 411 is that he was in the Green Berets, but he's never said he was. Puzzling guy. But he's a hard worker. And he's honest." He pursed his lips and his dark eyes twinkled. "And he never takes a drink. Ever."

She whistled. "Well!"

"Anyway, you'd better not agree to any dates with him until J.B. checks him out," Justin said. "I don't want J.B. on the wrong side of me." He grinned. "We feed out a lot of cattle for him," he added, making it clear that he wasn't afraid of J.B.

"J.B. doesn't tell me who I can date," she said, hurting as she remembered how little she meant to Marge's big brother.

"Just the same, I don't know anything about Grange, and I'm sort of responsible for you while you're here, even though you're legally an adult," Justin said quietly. "Get the picture?"

She grimaced. "I do. Okay, I'll make sure I don't let him bulldoze me into anything."

"That's the spirit," he said with a grin. "I'm not saying he's a bad man, mind you. I just don't know a lot about him. He's always on time, does his job and a bit more, and gets along fairly well with other people. But he mostly keeps to himself when he's not working. He's not a sociable sort."

"I feel somewhat that way, myself," she sighed.

"Join the club. Things going okay for you otherwise? The job's not too much?"

"The job's great," she said, smiling. "I'm really enjoying this."

"Good. We're glad to have you here. Anything you need, let me know."

"Sure thing. Thanks!"

She told Marge and the girls about Grange. They were amused.

"He obviously has good taste," Marge mused, "if he likes you."

Tellie chuckled as she rinsed dishes and put them in the dishwasher. "It's not mutual," she replied. "He's a little scary, in a way."

"What do you mean? Does he seem violent or something?" Brandi wanted to know.

Tellie paused with a dish in her hand and rowned. "I don't know. I'm not afraid of him, really. It's just that he has that sort of effect on people. Kind of like Cash Grier," she added.

"He's calmed down a bit since Tippy Moore came to stay with him after her kidnapping," Marge said. "Rumor is that he may marry her."

"She's really pretty, even with those cuts on her face,"

Dawn remarked from the kitchen table, where she was arranging cloth for a quilt she meant to make. "They say somebody real mean is after her, and that's why she's here. Mrs. Jewell stays at the house at night. A stickler for convention, is our police chief."

"Good for him," Marge said. "A few people need to be conventional, or society is going to fall."

Brandi looked at her sister and rolled her eyes. "Here we go again with the lecture."

"Uncle J.B. isn't conventional," Dawn reminded her mother. "He had that football team cheerleader staying at his house for almost a month. And his new girlfriend was a runner-up Miss Texas, and she spends weekends with him…"

Tellie's hands were shaking. Dawn grimaced and looked at her mother helplessly.

Dawn got up and hugged Tellie from behind. "I'm sorry, Tellie," she said with obvious remorse.

Tellie patted the hands around her waist. "Just because I'm a hopeless case, doesn't mean you have to walk on eggshells around me," she assured the younger woman. "We all know that J.B. isn't ever going to get married. And even if he did, it would be some beautiful, sophisticated—"

"You hush," Marge broke in. "You're pretty. Besides, it's what's inside that counts. Beauty doesn't last. Character does."

"Her stock phrase," Brandi said with a grin. "But she's right, Tellie. I think you're beautiful."

"Thanks, guys," Tellie murmured.

She went back to her task, and the conversation became general.

The next day Grange came right up to Tellie's desk and stood staring down at her, wordlessly, until she was forced to look up at him.

"They say that you live with J. B. Hammock's sister, Marge," he said.

She was totally confounded by the question. She stared at him blankly. "Excuse me?"

He shrugged, looking uncomfortable. "I didn't come to Jacobsville by accident," he said, glancing around as Justin came out of his office and gave him a faint glower. "Have lunch with me," he added. "It's not a pass. I just want to talk to you."

If it was a line, it was a good one. "Okay," she said.

"I'll pick you up at noon." He tipped his wide-brimmed hat, nodded toward Justin, and went back out to the feedlot.

Justin went straight to Tellie. "Trouble?" he asked.

"Well, no," she said. "He wants to talk to me about Marge, apparently."

His eyebrows arched. "That's a new one."

"He was serious. He wants me to have lunch with him." She grinned. "He can't do much to me over a hamburger in town."

"Good point. Okay, but watch your step. Like I said," he added, "he's an unknown quantity."

"I'll do that," she promised.

Barbara's Café in town was the local hot spot for lunch. Just about everybody ate there when they wanted something home cooked. There were other places, such as the Chinese and Mexican restaurants, and the pizza place. But Barbara's had a sort of Texas atmosphere that appealed even to tourists.

Today it was crowded. Grange got them a table and ordered steak and potatoes for himself, leaving Tellie to get what she wanted. They'd already agreed they were going Dutch. So he must have meant it, about it not being a date.

"My people were all dead, and Marge and J.B. took me in," Tellie said when they'd given their orders to the waitress. She didn't add why. "I've known the Hammocks since I was a child, but I was fourteen when I went to live with Marge and her girls. She was widowed by then."

"Are you and J.B. close?" he queried, placing his hat in an empty chair.

"No," she said flatly. She didn't elaborate. She started to get the feeling that it was not Marge he wanted information on.

His dark eyes narrowed as he studied her. "What do you know about his past?" he asked.

Her heart jumped. "You mean, generally?"

"I mean," he added with flaming eyes, "do you know anything about the woman he tried to marry when he was twenty-one?"

She felt suddenly cold, and didn't know why. "What woman?" she asked, her voice sounded hoarse and choked.

He looked around them to make sure they weren't being overheard. He lifted his coffee cup and held it in his big, lean hands. "His father threatened to cut him off without a cent if he went through with the wedding. He was determined to do it. He withdrew his savings from the bank—he was of legal age, so he could—and he picked her up at her house and they took off to Louisiana. He was going to marry her there. He thought nobody could find them. But his father did."

This was fascinating stuff. Nobody had said anything to her about it, certainly not J.B. "Did they get married?"

His face tautened. "His father waited until J.B. went out to see about the marriage license. He went in and talked to the woman. He told her that if she married J.B., he'd turn in her brother, who was fourteen and had gotten mixed up with a gang that dealt in distribution of crack cocaine. There had been a death involved in a drug deal gone bad. The boy hadn't participated, but he could be implicated as an accessory. J.B.'s father had a private detective document everything. He told the woman her brother would go to prison for twenty years."

She grimaced. "Did J.B. know?"

"I don't know," he said uncomfortably. "I came here to find out."

"But what did she do?"

"What could she do?" he asked curtly. "She loved her

brother. He was the only family she had. She loved Hammock. She really loved him."

"But she loved her brother more?"

He nodded. His whole face clenched. "She didn't tell Hammock what his father had done. She did tell her father."

"Did he do anything?"

"He couldn't. They were poor. There was nothing he could do. Well, he did get her brother to leave the gang when she killed herself. It was all that saved him from prison."

She was hanging on his every word. "What about the woman?"

"She was already clinically depressed," he said in an odd monotone, toying with his fork, not looking at her. He seemed to be far away, in time. "She knew that she could never be with Hammock, that his father would make sure of it. She couldn't see any future without him." His fingers tightened on the fork. "She found the pistol her brother had hidden in his room. She shot herself. She died instantly."

The iced tea went all over the tablecloth. Tellie quickly uprighted the glass and grabbed at napkins to mop up the flow. Barbara, seeing the accident, came forward with a tea cloth.

"There, there, we all spill things," she told Tellie with a smile. "Right as rain," she added when she'd mopped the oilcloth-covered table. "I'll bring you a new glass. Unsweetened?"

Tellie nodded, still reeling from what Grange had told her. "Yes. Thanks."

"No problem," Barbara said, smiling at them both as she left.

"You really didn't know, did you?" Grange asked quietly. "I'm sorry. I don't want to hurt you. It's not your fault."

She swallowed, hard. It all made sense. Why J.B. never got serious about a woman. Why he refused to think of marriage. He'd had that death on his conscience all his life, when it wasn't even his fault, not really. It was his father's.

"His father must have been a horror," she said unsteadily.

Grange stared at her. "Have been?" he queried.

She nodded. "He died in a nursing home the year I moved in with Marge," she said. "He'd had a stroke and he never fully recovered from it. It left him in a vegetative state. J.B. paid to keep him in the facility."

"And the old man's wife?"

"She died long before I lived with Marge. I don't know how." He looked odd. "I see."

"How do you know all this?" she wondered.

"Her brother is a friend of mine," he told her. "He was curious about the old man. I needed a job, and this one at the feedlot came available. I like Texas. It was close enough that I could find out about old man Hammock for him."

"Well, now you know," she said, trying not to let the trauma show in her face.

He frowned. His hard face went even harder. He stared down into his coffee cup. "I didn't realize it would have such an impact on you."

"J.B. is like an older brother to me," she told him, lying through her teeth. "But nobody ever told me why he plays the field like he does, why he won't consider ever getting married. I thought he just liked being a bachelor. I guess he blames himself for what happened, don't you think?" she added, surprising an odd look on Grange's face. "Even though it was his father who did the real damage, J.B. surely realized that if he'd never gotten mixed up with the poor woman, she'd still be alive."

He winced. "You don't pull your punches, do you?"

"It's the truth, isn't it?" she added thoughtfully.

"So he doesn't want to get married," he said after a minute.

She nodded. "He has lots of girlfriends. The new one was a runner-up in the Miss Texas pageant."

He didn't even seem to be listening. He finished his steak and sat back to sip cold coffee.

Barbara came around with Tellie's new glass of tea and the coffeepot. She warmed Grange's in his cup.

"Thanks," he said absently.

She grinned at him. "No problem. You're new here, aren't you?"

"I am," he confessed. "I work for Justin and Calhoun, at the feedlot."

"Lucky you," she said. "They're good people."

He nodded.

She glanced at Tellie. "How's Marge?"

There was something in the question that made Tellie stare at her. "She's fine. Why?"

Barbara grimaced. "It's nothing, really."

"Tell me," Tellie persisted. It was her day for learning things about people she thought she knew.

"Well, she had a dizzy spell the last time she ate lunch here. She fell into one of the tables." She sighed. "I wondered if she ever had a checkup. Just to make sure. I never knew Marge to have dizzy spells."

"Me, either," Tellie said, frowning. "But I'll find out," she promised.

"Don't tell her I told you," Barbara said firmly. "She can light fires when she's mad, just like J.B."

"I'll ask her gently, I promise," Tellie said, smiling. "She won't get mad."

"If you do, you'll eat burned hamburgers forever," Barbara told her.

"That's just mean," she told the older woman, who grinned and went back to the kitchen.

"Well, it's your day for revelations, apparently," Grange observed.

"I don't think I know anybody anymore," she agreed.

"Listen, don't tell Hammock's sister about any of this," he said suddenly. "I'm not here to cause trouble. I just wanted to find out what became of the old man." His eyes darkened. "I suppose J.B. knew what his father did?"

"I have no way of knowing," she said uneasily.

He put cream into his hot coffee. He drew in a long breath. "I'm sorry if I shattered any illusions."

He had. He'd just put the final nail in the coffin of her dreams. But that wasn't his fault. Tellie always felt that people came into your life for a reason. She forced a smile. "I don't have illusions about J.B.," she told him. "I've seen all his bad character traits firsthand."

He searched her green eyes. "One of the boys said you're in college."

She nodded. "I start master's work in the fall."

"What's your subject?"

"History. My field is Native American studies. I hope to teach at the college level when I finally get my master's degree."

"Why not teach grammar school or middle or high school?" he wondered.

"Because little kids walk all over me," she said flatly. "Marge's girls had me on my ear the first six months I lived with them, because I couldn't say no. I'd make a lousy elementary school teacher."

He smiled faintly. "I'll bet the girls loved you."

She nodded, smiling back. "They're very special."

He finished his coffee. "We'll have to do this again sometime," he began, just as the café door opened and J.B. walked in.

J.B.'s eyes slithered over the patrons until he spotted Tellie. He walked to the table where Tellie and Grange were sitting and stared down at Grange with pure venom. His eyes were blistering hot.

"What are you doing here in Jacobsville?" he asked Grange.

The other man studied him coolly. "Working. Tellie and I are having lunch together."

"That doesn't answer the question," J.B. replied, and he'd never sounded more menacing.

Grange sipped coffee with maddening calm. "So the old man did finally tell you what happened, did he?" he asked with a sudden, piercing glance. "He told you what he said to my sister?"

J.B.'s big fists clenched at his side. He aged in seconds. "Not while he was alive. He left a letter with his will."

"At least you had time to get used to the idea, didn't you?" Grange asked icily. "I found out three weeks ago!" He forced his deep voice back into calmer channels and took a deep breath. "Care to guess how I felt when my father finally told *me,* on his death bed?"

J.B. seemed to calm down himself. "You didn't know?" he asked.

"No," Grange said harshly. "No, I didn't know! If I had…!"

J.B. seemed suddenly aware of Tellie's rapt interest and he seemed to go pale under his tan. He saw her new knowledge of him in her paleness, in her suddenly averted face. He looked at Grange. "You told her, didn't you?" he demanded.

The other man stood up. He and J.B. were the same height, although Grange seemed huskier, more muscular. J.B. had a range rider's lean physique.

"Secrets are dangerous, Hammock," Grange said, and he didn't back down an inch. "There were things I wanted to know that I'd never have heard from you."

"Such as?" J.B. asked in a curt tone.

Grange looked at him openly, aware that other diners were watching them. His shoulders moved in a curious jerk. "I came here with another whole idea in mind, but your young friend here shot me in the foot. I didn't realize that you were as much a victim as I was. I thought you put your father up to it," he added tautly.

Tellie didn't know what he meant.

J.B. did. "Things would have ended differently if I'd known," he said in a harsh tone.

"If I'd known, too." Grange studied him. "Hell of a shame that we can't go back and do things right, isn't it?"

J.B. nodded.

"I like working at the feedlot, but it's only for a few months," he said. "If it helps, I'm no gossip. I only wanted the truth. Now I've got it." He turned to Tellie. "I shouldn't have involved you. But I enjoyed lunch," he added quietly, and he smiled. It changed his dark eyes, made them deep and hypnotic.

"Me, too," she said, flushing a little. He really was good-looking.

Grange shrugged. "Maybe we can do it again."

She did smile then. "I'd like that."

He nodded at J.B. and left them to go to the counter and pay for his meal. J.B. sat down in the chair Grange had vacated and looked at Tellie with mingled anger and concern.

"Don't worry, J.B., he didn't spill any state secrets," she lied as she sipped tea. "He only said your father had done something to foil a romance years ago, and he wanted to know how to get in touch with the elder Mr. Hammock. He said he wanted to know for a friend of his." She hoped he believed her. She'd die if he realized she knew the whole terrible secret in his past. She felt sick at her stomach, imagining how he must feel.

He didn't answer her. He glanced at Grange as the younger man left the café, and then caught Barbara's eye and ordered coffee and apple pie.

Tellie was trying not to react at the surprise of having coffee with J.B., who'd never shared a table in a restaurant with her before. Her heart was beating double-time at just the nearness of him. She had to force herself not to stare at him with overt and visible delight.

Barbara brought coffee. He grinned at her and she grinned back. "Dating in shifts these days, huh, Tellie?" she teased.

Tellie didn't answer. She managed a faint smile, embarrassed.

J.B. sipped his coffee. He never added cream or sugar. Her

eyes went to his lean, darkly tanned hands. There was a gold cat's-eye ring on his left ring finger, thick and masculine, and a thin expensive watch above it on his wrist. He was wearing a lightweight gray suit with a cream Stetson. He looked expensive and arrogant, and seductive.

"I don't like the idea of your going out with that man," J.B. told her curtly.

"It wasn't a date, J.B., it was just lunch," she said.

"It was an interrogation," he corrected. "What else did he want to know?"

She knew she'd never get away with lying. "He wanted to know about your father," she said.

"What about him?"

"If he was still alive. I told him he wasn't. That was all."

"What did he say?"

"Not much," she returned. She searched his green eyes. They were troubled and stormy. "Just that a friend had asked him to find out about your father, over some romance of yours that went bad years ago. He didn't say anything specific," she added without looking at him. He usually could tell when she was lying.

His face tautened as he looked at her. "I never meant anyone to know about what happened except Marge and me," he said tightly.

"Yes, I know, J.B.," she replied, her voice weary and resigned. "You don't share things with outsiders."

He frowned. "You're not an outsider. You're family."

That, somehow, made things even worse. She met his eyes evenly. "You sent Jarrett out to get my graduation present. You'd never do that to Marge or the girls. And you lied about being at the graduation exercises. You were in the office with some businessman and his daughter. I gather that she was a real looker and you couldn't tear yourself away," she added with more bitterness than she realized.

His eyes almost glowed with anger. "Who told you that?"

"I took classes in ESP in college," she drawled facetiously, and with a bite in her voice. "What does it matter how I know? You lied to me!"

His indrawn breath was audible. "Damn it, Tellie!"

"Why can't you be honest with me?" she demanded. "I'm not a kid anymore. You don't have to protect me from the truth."

"You don't know the truth," he said curtly.

"Sure I do. I'm a liability you assumed because I had no family and you felt sorry for me," she replied.

"I felt sorry for you," he conceded. "But I've always included you in family activities, haven't I?"

"Oh, yes," she agreed. "I get to have Christmas and summer vacation and all the other holidays with Marge and the girls, I even get to go on overseas trips with them. I've never doubted that I was part of Marge's family," she said meaningfully.

He frowned. "Marge is part of my family."

"You're not part of mine, J.B.," she replied. Her heart was breaking. "I'm in the same class as your big-boobed blondes, disposable and unimportant. We don't even rate a handpicked present. You just send out the secretary to buy it, and to lie for you when you avoid events you'd rather not be forced to attend."

He glared at her. "You've got the whole thing upside down." He cursed under his breath. "Damn Grange! If he hadn't barged in…!"

Something was fishy here. "You know him!"

His lips made a thin line. "I know him," he admitted reluctantly. "I went to see him at the feedlot when I realized who he was. But I barely had time to say anything to him before Justin showed up. I didn't go back."

"Who is he, J.B.?" she asked, but she was sure that she already knew the answer.

"He's her brother," he said finally. "He's the brother of the woman my father kept me from marrying."

Three

The look in J.B.'s eyes was painful to Tellie, who loved him with all her heart, despite the knowledge that he was never going to be able to love her back. She could almost feel the pain that rippled through him with the words. The woman, the only woman, he'd ever loved had killed herself, because of him. It was a pain he could never escape. And now the woman's brother had shown up in his own town.

"Why is he here, do you think?" she asked.

J.B. sipped coffee. "Revenge, perhaps," he said tautly, "at first."

"Revenge for what?" she asked, because she knew the answer, but she didn't want him to realize how much Grange had told her.

He glanced at her appraisingly. "It's a story that doesn't concern you, Tellie," he said quietly. "It's ancient history."

She finished her own coffee. "Whatever you say, J.B.," she replied. "I have to get back to work."

She stood up. So did he. "How are you going to get back to the feedlot?" he asked abruptly. "Didn't you ride in with Grange?"

She shook her head. "It was Dutch treat."

"Are you coming to the barbecue Saturday?" he added.

It was the end of roundup, one that he gave for the ranch hands. Marge and the girls, and Tellie, were always invited. It was a comfortable routine.

Tellie had never felt less like a routine. "No, I don't think so," she said abruptly, and was pleased to see his eyelids flicker. "I have other plans."

"What other plans?" he demanded, as if he had the right to know every step she took.

She smiled carelessly. "That's not your business, J.B. See you."

She went to the counter and paid Barbara. When she left, J.B. was sitting there, brooding, his face like steel.

It wasn't until that night Tellie finally had time to digest what she'd learned. She waited until the girls went to bed and then cornered Marge at the kitchen table where she was piecing a quilt.

"Do you know a family named Grange?" she asked Marge.

The older woman blinked, surprised. "Grange? Why?"

That wasn't an innocent look Marge was giving her. Tellie folded her hands on the table. "There's a man named Grange who came to work at the feedlot," she said. "He's tall and dark-eyed and dark-haired. J.B. was going to marry his sister a long time ago…"

"Him! Here! Dear God!" Marge exclaimed. She put her hands to her mouth. "No!"

"It's all right, Marge," she said at once. "He came looking for your father, not J.B."

Marge's eyes were wide, frightened. "You know?" she asked huskily.

She sighed heavily. "Yes. Grange told me everything. J.B. doesn't know that," she added quickly. "I said that Grange only mentioned that there was a romance gone bad in the past."

Marge drew her hands over her mouth. "It was much worse than that, Tellie. It was a nightmare," she said heavily. "I've never seen J.B. like that. He went crazy after she died. For three months, he went away and nobody even knew where he was. We couldn't find him. Dad cried…" She took a steadying breath. "I never understood what happened, why she did it. J.B. thought it was because they'd had an argument about her giving up her house to live with us. They parted in anger, and he didn't know what had happened until her best friend called him and gave him the news. He blamed himself. He lived with the guilt, but it ate him alive. Dad was so kind to him afterward," she added. "They'd had problems, like some fathers and sons do. They were both strong willed and domineering." She sighed. "But Dad went out of his way after that to win J.B.'s affection. I think he finally succeeded, before he had the stroke." She looked up. "Did Grange have any idea why she did such a desperate thing?"

Now things were getting sticky. Tellie hesitated. She didn't want to destroy Marge's illusions about her father. And obviously, J.B. hadn't told his sister about his father's interference that had caused the tragedy.

Marge realized that. She smiled sadly. "Tellie, my father never cared one way or the other about me. I was a girl, so I was a disappointment to him. You don't need to spare my feelings. I would like to know what Grange told you."

Tellie took a deep breath. "All right. He said that J.B.'s father came to see the girl and told her that if she married J.B., he had enough evidence to put her fourteen-year-old brother in prison for the rest of his life. The boy was involved in drugs and part of a gang."

She gasped. "So that was it! Did he tell J.B.?"

"Yes," she said. "He did. Apparently Grange only just found

out himself. His father only told him when he was dying. I'm
sure he was trying to spare Grange. He'll go through his own
pain, realizing that he provided your father with the reason to
threaten his sister."

"So many secrets," Marge said, her voice thready. "Pain and
more pain. It will bring it all back, too. J.B. will relive it."

That was painful. But it wasn't all Grange's fault. "Grange
just wanted to know the truth." Tellie defended the stranger.
"He thought J.B. put his father up to talking to the woman."

"My brother doesn't have any problem telling people unpleasant things," she replied musingly. "He does his own dirty
work."

"He does," Tellie agreed.

She frowned at the younger woman's expression. "What are
you not telling me?"

She shrugged. "Jarrett let something slip."

"J.B.'s secretary? Did she? What?" she asked with a lazy
smile.

"J.B. wasn't at the graduation exercises, Marge," Tellie
said sadly. "He was in a meeting with a businessman and his
attractive daughter. He made Jarrett cover up for him. She was
really upset about what he said to her. She was more upset
when she found out that the present he wanted her to buy was
for me, for my graduation."

"Wait a minute," Marge replied, frowning. "He lied about
being at the stadium? He actually did that?"

Tellie grimaced. "Yes."

"I'll strangle him!" the older woman said forcefully.

"To what end, Marge?" Tellie asked. She felt old, tired,
worn-out. "Can you make him love me? Because that isn't ever
going to happen. I thought he was just a carefree playboy who
liked variety in his women. But it's not that at all, is it?" She
sat back in her chair, her face drawn and sad. "He blames
himself because the woman he loved died. He won't risk
feeling that way about another woman, setting himself up for

another loss. He thinks he doesn't deserve to be happy because she killed herself."

"And all along, it was our father who did the dirty work." Marge's eyes were thoughtful. "I noticed that he seemed haunted sometimes, absolutely haunted. And I'd ask him if anything was wrong. He'd just say that people had to pay for their sins, and he hoped his punishment wouldn't be as bad as he deserved. I didn't know what he was talking about, until today. I suppose he was afraid to tell the truth, because he knew he'd lose J.B. forever."

"You couldn't have blamed him. Whatever he thought of the woman, it was J.B.'s life, and his decision. The old man couldn't live his life for him."

"You didn't know him, honey. He was just like J.B. There's the wrong way, and there's J.B.'s way. That was Dad, too."

"I see."

Marge reached across the table and held her hand. "I'm sorry you had to find it out like this. I told J.B. we should tell you, but he said—" She stopped suddenly. "Anyway, he wouldn't hear of it."

Tellie knew what Marge had avoided saying, that it was none of Tellie's business because she wasn't family. She smiled. "Don't pull your punches. I'm getting tougher by the day since I graduated."

"J.B.'s helped, hasn't he?" she said with a scowl.

"He can't change the way he feels," she said wearily. "If he was going to fall head over heels in love with me, it wouldn't have taken him seven years, Marge. Even now, I'm just a stray that he took in. Well, that *you* took in," she corrected. "J.B. decided that both of you would take care of me, but you'd do the daily work." She laughed. "And it's just like him."

"It is," Marge had to admit. She squeezed Tellie's hand and then let go. "Maybe it isn't a bad thing that you know the truth. It helps explain the way he is, and why there was never much hope for you in the first place."

"Perhaps you're right," Tellie agreed. "But you mustn't ever let J.B. know. Promise me."

"I'll never tell him what you know, Tellie," Marge agreed. She hesitated. "What is Grange like?"

"Mysterious," she replied. "Dangerous. Nobody knows much about him. They say he was in Special Forces."

"Not in the Mafia?" Marge replied dryly, and she wasn't totally kidding.

"He said that his sister's death took him right out of drug use and gang participation, although he told me at first that it was a friend and not himself," she replied. "The tragedy saved him, in fact. He felt guilty, I'm sure, when he realized that she died partially because J.B.'s father threatened to put him in prison. The awful thing is that he didn't know that until three weeks ago. I expect he's hurting as much as J.B. did when he read the letter his father left him."

"That was another bad month, when J.B. got that letter attached to Dad's will," Marge said. "He got extremely drunk." She frowned. "That was the year before you graduated from high school, in fact. You came over and took a gun away from him," she added, shocked at the memory. "I yelled at you, and you wouldn't listen. You went right into his den, poured the bottle of whiskey down the sink with him yelling curses at you, and then you took away the pistol and popped the bullets out on the floor. I screamed…"

"You thought he'd hit me," she agreed, smiling. "But I knew better. J.B. would never hit a woman, not even if he was stinking drunk. Which he was, of course."

"You led him off to bed and stayed with him all night. The next morning he carried you into the living room where I was, and laid you out on the sofa under an Afghan. He looked very funny. When I asked him why, he said it was the first time in his life that he'd ever had a woman take care of him. Our mother wasn't domestic," she added quietly. "She was never very nurturing. She was a research chemist and her life was her work. Housekeepers raised J.B. and me. It was almost a relief for Dad, and us, when she died. I did admire her," she added. "She did a socially beneficial job. A dangerous one, too. She was working with a terrible virus strain, looking for a cure. One day in the lab, she stuck a needle, accidentally, into her hand through her rubber glove and died. I was sorry, and I went to the funeral. J.B wouldn't go and neither would Dad. They said she deserted all of us for her job."

"That sounds like him," Tellie agreed.

"J.B. never stopped fussing about the way you took care of him," she recalled on a laugh. "But then he'd lose his temper when you weren't around to do it. He was furious when you spent your summer vacations with those friends at Yellowstone National Park."

"I had a good time. I miss Melody. She and I were wonderful friends, but her parents moved overseas and she had to go with them."

"I don't think I have one friend left in Jacobsville, from my school days," Marge recalled.

"What about Barbara?"

"Oh. Yes. Barbara." She chuckled. "She and that café. When we were girls, it was what she wanted most of all, to own a restaurant."

"It's a good one." Tellie hesitated. "Now, don't get angry, but she's worried about you," she added.

"Me? Why?"

"She said you had a dizzy spell."

Marge frowned. "Yes, I did. I remember. I've had two or three lately. Odd, isn't it? But then, I'm prone to migraine headaches," she added carelessly. "You get all sorts of side effects from them. In fact, I see fireworks and go blind in one eye just before I get one. The doctor calls them vascular headaches."

Tellie frowned. "Why? Does blood pressure cause them?"

Marge laughed. "Not in my case, honey. I have the lowest

blood pressure in two counties. No, migraine runs in my family. My mother had them, and so did her mother."

"I'll bet J.B. doesn't have them," Tellie mused.

"That's a fact," came the laughing reply. "No, he doesn't get headaches, but he certainly gives them."

"Amen."

Marge went back to her piecing. "Maybe it's just as well that you know all about J.B. now, Tellie," she said after a minute. "Maybe it will save you any further heartache."

"Yes," the younger woman agreed sadly. "Maybe so."

Grange didn't ask her out again, but he did stop by her desk from time to time, just to see how she was. It was as if he knew how badly he'd hurt her with the information about J.B.'s past, and wanted to make amends.

"Listen," she said one day when he gave her a worried look, "I'm not stupid. I knew there was something in J.B.'s past that, well, that caused him to be the way he is. He never cared about me, except as a sort of adopted relative." She smiled. "I've got three years of college to go, you know. No place for a love life."

He studied her quietly. "Don't end up like him," he said suddenly. "Or like me. I don't think I've got it in me to trust another human being."

Her eyes were sympathetic. He was blaming himself for his sister's death. She knew it. "You'll grow old and bitter, all alone," she said.

"I'm already old and bitter," he said, and he didn't smile.

"No gray hairs," she observed.

"They're all on the inside," he shot back.

She grinned. Her whole face lit up.

He gave her an odd look and something in his expression softened, just a little.

"If you really want to look old, you should dye your hair," she pointed out.

He chuckled. "My father still had black hair when he died. He was sixty."

"Good genes," she said.

He shrugged. "Beats me. He never knew who his father was."

"Your mother?"

His face hardened. "I don't talk about her."

"Sorry."

"I didn't mean to growl," he said hesitantly. "I'm not used to women."

"Imagine a man ever admitting that!" she exclaimed with mock surprise.

He cocked an eyebrow. "You're sassy."

"Yes, I am. Nice of you to notice. Now would you mind leaving? Justin's going to come back any minute. He won't like having you flirt with me on his time."

"I don't flirt," he shot back.

"Well, excuse me!"

He shifted. "Maybe I flirt a little. It isn't intentional."

"God forbid! Who'd want to marry you?" she asked curiously.

He scowled. "Look here, I'm not a bad person."

"Well, I wouldn't want to marry you," she persisted.

"Who asked you?" he asked curtly.

"Not you, for sure," she returned. "And don't bother," she added when he started to speak. "I'm such a rare catch that I have men salivating in the yard, wherever I go."

His dark eyes started to twinkle. "Why?"

"Because I can make French pastry," she told him. "With real whipped cream and custard fillings."

He pursed his lips. "Well!"

"See? I'm quite a catch. Too bad you're not in the running."

He frowned. "Even if I were interested, what would I do with a wife?"

"You don't know?" She gave him such an expression of shock and horror that he burst out laughing.

She grinned at him. "See there? You're improving all the time. I'm a good influence, I am!"

"You're a pain in the neck," he returned. "But not bad company." He shrugged. "Like movies?"

"What sort?"

"Science fiction?"

She chuckled. "You bet."

"I'll check and see what's playing at the theater Saturday, if you're game."

Saturday was the barbecue at J.B.'s that she was determined not to attend. Here was her excuse to miss it. She liked Grange. Besides, no way was she going to sit home and eat her heart out over J.B., especially when she'd already told him that she had other plans. "I'm game."

"Your adopted family won't like it," he said slowly.

"Marge won't mind," she said, certain that it was true. "And I don't care what J.B. thinks."

He nodded. "Okay. It's a date. We'll work out the details Friday."

"Fine. Now please go away," she added, glancing at the door, where Justin was just coming inside the building. "Or we may both be out looking for work on Monday!"

He grinned and left her before Justin got the door closed.

Marge was less enthusiastic than Tellie had expected. In fact, she seemed disturbed.

"Does the phrase, rubbing salt on an open wound, ring any chimes?" Marge asked her somberly.

"But Grange didn't do anything," she protested. "He was as much a victim as J.B. was."

Marge hesitated, uneasy. "I understand that. But he's connected with it. J.B. will see it as a personal attack on him, by both of you."

"That's absurd!"

"It isn't, if you remember the way my brother is."

For the first time since Grange had asked her out, Tellie wasn't sure she was doing the right thing. She didn't want to hurt J.B., even if he'd given her reason. On the other hand, it was a test of control, his over hers. If she gave in now, she'd be giving in forever. Marge was her friend, but J.B. was Marge's brother. It was a tangled situation.

Marge put an arm around her. "Don't worry yourself to death, honey," she said gently. "If you really want to go out with him, go ahead. I'm just saying that J.B. is going to take it personally. But you can't let him run your life."

Tellie hugged her back. "Thanks, Marge."

"Why don't you want to go to the barbecue?" the older woman asked.

Tellie grimaced. "Miss runner-up beauty queen will be there, won't she?"

Marge pursed her lips. "So that's it."

"Don't you dare tell him," came the terse reply.

"Never." Marge sighed. "I didn't even think about that. No wonder you're so anxious to stay away."

"She's really gorgeous, isn't she?"

Marge looked old and wise. "She's just like all the other ones before her, Tellie, tall and blond and stacked. Not much in the way of intelligence. You know," she added thoughtfully, "I don't think J.B. really likes intelligent women much."

"Maybe he feels threatened by us."

"Don't you believe it," Marge scoffed. "He's got a business degree from Yale, you know."

"I'd forgotten."

"No, I think it has to do with our mother," she continued. "She was always running down our father, making him feel like an idiot. She was forever going to conventions with one of her research partners. Later, they had a serious affair. That was just before she died."

"J.B. didn't have a great respect for women, I guess."

"Not in his younger days. Then he got engaged, and tragedy

followed." She seemed far away. "I lost my first love to another woman, and then my husband died of an embolism after surgery." She shook her head. "J.B. and I have poor track records with happily ever after."

Tellie felt sad for both of them. "I suppose it would make you gun-shy, when it came to love."

"Love?" Marge laughed. "J.B. doesn't believe in it anymore." She gave Tellie a sad, gentle appraisal. "But you should. Maybe Grange will be the best thing that ever happened to you. It wouldn't hurt to show J.B. that you're not dying of a broken heart, either."

"He won't notice," Tellie said with conviction. "He used to complain that I was always underfoot."

"Not recently."

"I've been away at college for four years more or less," she reminded the older woman. That reminded her of graduation, which he hadn't attended. It still stung.

"And going away for three more." Marge smiled. "Live your life, Tellie. You don't have to answer to anybody. Be happy."

"That's easier said than done," Tellie pointed out. She smiled at Marge. "Okay. If you don't mind me dating Grange, J.B. can think what he likes. I don't care."

Which wasn't the truth, exactly.

Grange was good company when he relaxed and forgot that Tellie was a friend of J.B.'s.

The movie was unforgettable, a film about a misfit crew aboard a space-going freighter who were protecting a girl from some nasty authorities. It was funny and sweet, and full of action.

They came out of the theater smiling.

"It's been a good year for science-fiction movies," he remarked.

"It has," Tellie agreed, "but that was the best I've seen so far. I missed the series when it was on television. I guess I'll have to buy the DVD set."

He gave her an amused look. "You're nice to take around," he said on the way to his big gray truck. "If I weren't a confirmed bachelor, you'd be at the top of my list of prospects."

"Why, what a nice thing to say!" she exclaimed. "Do you mind if I quote you frequently?"

He gave her a quick look and relaxed a little when she laughed. "Quote me?" he asked quizzically.

Her shoulders rose and fell. "It's just that nobody ever said I was marriageable before, you see," she told him. "I figure with an endorsement like that, the sky's the limit. I mean, I won't be in college forever. A woman has to think about the future."

Grange stared at her in the light from the parking lot. "I don't think I've ever been around anyone like you. Most women these days are too aggressive for my taste."

Her eyebrows arched. "Like doormats, do we?" she teased.

He shook his head. "It's not that. I like a woman with spirit. But I don't like being seen as a party favor."

"Now you know how women feel," she pointed out.

"I never treated a woman that way," he returned.

"A lot of men have."

"I suppose so," he conceded. He gave her a smile. "I enjoyed tonight."

"Me, too."

"We'll do it again sometime."

She smiled back. "Suits me."

Grange dropped her off at Marge's house, but he didn't try to kiss her good-night. He was a gentleman in the best sense of the word. Tellie liked him. But her heart still ached for J.B.

Tellie assumed that Marge and the girls were in bed, because the lights were all off inside. She locked the door behind her and started toward the staircase when a light snapped on in the living room.

She whirled, surprised, and looked right into J. B. Hammock's seething green eyes.

Four

"What...are you doing here?" she blurted out, flushing at the way he was looking at her. "Has something happened to Marge or the girls?" she added at once, uneasy.

"No. They're fine."

She moved into the room, putting her purse and coat on a chair, her slender body in jeans with pink embroidered roses and a pink tank top that matched. Her pale eyes searched his dark green ones curiously. She ran a nervous hand through her wavy dark hair and grimaced. He looked like an approaching storm.

"Then why are you here?" she asked when the silence became oppressive.

His eyes slid over her body in the tight jeans and tank top and narrowed with reluctant appreciation. He was also in jeans, but his were without decoration. A chambray shirt covered his broad, muscular chest and long arms. It was unfastened at the throat. He usually dressed casually for barbecues, and this one didn't seem to be an exception.

"You went to a movie with Grange," he said.

"Yes."

His face tautened. "I don't like you going out with him."

Her thin dark eyebrows arched. "I'm almost twenty-two, J.B."

"Jacobsville is full of eligible bachelors."

"Yes, I know. Grange is one of them."

"Damn it, Tellie!"

She drew in a steadying breath. It was hard not to give in to J.B. She'd spent most of her adolescence doing exactly that. But this was a test of her newfound independence. She couldn't let him walk all over her. Despite his reasons for not wanting her around Grange, she couldn't let him dictate her future. Particularly since he wasn't going to be part of it.

"I'm not marrying him, J.B.," she said quietly. "He's just someone to go out with."

His lean jaw tautened. "He's part of a painful episode in my past," he said flatly. "It's disloyal of you to take his side against me. I'm not pushing the point, but I gave you a home when you needed one."

Her eyes narrowed. "*You* gave me a home? No, J.B., *you* didn't give me a home. You decided that *Marge* would give me a home," she said emphatically.

"Same thing," he bit off.

"It isn't," she replied. "You don't put yourself out for anybody. You make gestures, but somebody else has to do the dirty work."

"That's not how it was, and you know it," he said curtly. "You were fourteen years old. How would it have looked, to have you living with me? Especially with my lifestyle."

She wanted to argue that, but she couldn't. "I suppose you have a point."

He didn't reply. He just watched her.

She moved to the sofa and perched on one of its broad, floral-patterned arms. "I'm very grateful for what your family has done for me," she said gently. "But nobody can say that I haven't pulled my weight. I've cleaned and cooked for Marge and the girls, been a live-in baby-sitter, helped keep her books—I haven't just parked myself here and taken advantage of the situation."

"I never said you did," he replied.

"You're implying it," she shot back. "I can't remember when I've ever dated anybody around here…!"

"Of course not, you were too busy mooning over me!"

Her face went white. Then it slowly blossomed into red rage. She stood up, eyes blazing. "Yes," she said. "I was, wasn't I? Mooning over you while you indulged yourself with starlet after debutante after Miss Beauty Contest winner! Oh, excuse me, Miss Runner-up Beauty Contest winner," she drawled insolently.

He glared at her. "My love life is none of your business."

"Don't be absurd," she retorted. "It's everybody's business. You were in a tabloid story just last week, something about you and the living fashion doll being involved in some sleazy love triangle in Hollywood…"

"Lies," he shot back, "and I'm suing!"

"Good luck," she said. "My point is, I date a nice man who hasn't hurt anybody…"

He let out a vicious curse, interrupting her, and moved closer, towering over her. "He was Special Forces in Iraq," he told her coldly, "and he was brought up on charges for excessive force during an incursion! He actually slugged his commanding officer and stuffed him in the trunk of a civilian car!"

Her eyes widened. "Did he, really?" she mused, fascinated.

"It isn't funny," he snapped. "The man is a walking time bomb, waiting for the spark to set him off. I don't want him around you when it happens. He was forced out of the army, Tellie, he didn't go willingly! He had the choice of a court-martial or an honorable discharge."

She wondered how he knew so much about the other man,

but she didn't pursue it. "It was an honorable discharge, then?" she emphasized.

He took off his white Stetson and ran an irritated hand through his black hair. "I can't make you see it, can I? The man's dangerous."

"He's in good company in Jacobsville, then, isn't he?" she replied. "I mean, we're like a resort for ex-mercs and ex-military, not to mention the number of ex-federal law enforcement people…"

"Grange has enemies," he interrupted.

"So do you, J.B.," she pointed out. "Remember that guy who broke into your house with a .45 automatic and tried to shoot you over a horse deal?"

"He was a lunatic."

"If the bullet hadn't been a dud, you'd be dead," she reminded him.

"Ancient history," he said. "You're avoiding the subject."

"I am not likely to be shot by one of Grange's mythical old enemies while watching a science-fiction film at the local theater!" Her small hands balled at her hips. "The only thing you're mad about is that you can't make me do what you want me to do anymore," she challenged.

A deep, dark sensuality came into his green eyes and one corner of his chiseled mouth turned up. "Can't I, now?" he drawled, moving forward.

She backed up. "Oh, no, you don't," she warded him off. "Go home and thrill your beauty queen, J.B., I'm not on the market."

He lifted an eyebrow at her flush and the faint rustle of her heartbeat against her tank top. "Aren't you?"

She backed up one more step, just in case. "What happened to you was…was tragic, but it was a long time ago, J.B., and Grange wasn't responsible for it," she argued. "He was surely as much a victim as you were, especially when he found out the truth. Can't you imagine how he must have felt, when he knew that his own actions cost him his sister's life?"

He seemed to tauten all over. "He told you all of it?"

She hadn't meant to let that slip. He made her nervous when he came close like this. She couldn't think. "You'd never have told me. Neither would Marge. Okay, it's not my business," she added when he looked threatening, "but I can have an opinion."

"Grange was responsible," he returned coldly. "His own delinquency made it impossible for her to get past my father."

"That's not true," Tellie said, her voice quiet and firm. "If I wanted to marry someone, and his father tried to blackmail me, I'd have gone like a shot to the man and told him…!"

The effect the remark had on him was scary. He seemed to grow taller, and his eyes were terrible. His deep, harsh voice interrupted her. "Stop it."

She did. She didn't have the maturity, or the confidence, to argue the point with him. But she wouldn't have killed herself, she was sure of it. She'd have embarrassed J.B.'s father, shamed him, defied him. She wasn't the sort of person to take blackmail lying down.

"You don't know what you're talking about," he said, his eyes furious. "You'd never sacrifice another human being's life or freedom to save yourself."

"Maybe not," she conceded. "But I wouldn't kill myself, either." She was going to add that it was a cowardly thing to do, but the way J.B. was looking at her kept her quiet.

"She loved me. She was going to have to give me up, and she couldn't bear to go on living that way. In her own mind, she didn't have a choice," he said harshly. He searched her quiet face. "You can't comprehend an emotion that powerful, can you, Tellie? After all, what the hell would you know about love? You're still wrapped up in dreams of happily ever after, cotton-candy kisses and hand-holding! You don't know what it is to want someone so badly that it's physically painful to be separated from them. You don't understand the violence of desire." He laughed coldly. "Maybe that's just as well. You couldn't handle an affair!"

"Good, because I don't want one!" she replied angrily. He made her feel small, inadequate. It hurt. "I'm not going to pass myself around like a cigarette to any man who wants me, just to prove how liberated I am! And when I marry, I won't want some oversexed libertine who jumps into bed with any woman who wants him!"

He went very still and quiet. His face was like a drawn cord, his eyes green flames as he glared down at her.

"Sorry," she said uneasily. "That didn't come out the way I meant it. I just don't think that a man, or a woman, who lives that permissively can ever settle down and be faithful. I want a stable marriage that children will fit into, not an endless round of new partners."

"Children," he scoffed.

"Yes, children." Her eyes softened as she thought of them. "A whole house full of them, one day, when I'm through school."

"With Grange as their father?"

She gaped at him. "I just went to a movie with him, J.B.!"

"If you get involved with him, I'll never forgive you," he said in a voice as cold as the grave.

"Well, golly gee whiz, that would be a tragedy, wouldn't it? Just think, I'd never get another present that you sent Jarrett to buy for me!"

His breath was coming quickly through his nose. His lips were flattened. He didn't have a comeback. That seemed to make him angrier. He took another step toward her.

She backed up a step. "You should be happy to have me out of your life," she pointed out uneasily. "I was never more than an afterthought anyway, J.B. Just a pest. All I did was get in your way."

He stopped just in front of her. He looked oddly frustrated. "You're still getting in my way," he said enigmatically. "I know that no matter what Marge may have said, she and the girls were disappointed that you missed the barbecue. It's the first time in seven years that you've done that, and for a man who represents as much hurt to Marge herself as he does to me."

She frowned. "But why? She never knew Grange!"

"You told her what my father did," he said deliberately.

She grimaced. "I didn't mean to!" she confessed. "I didn't want to. But she said it wouldn't matter."

"And you don't know her any better than that, after so long in her house? She was devastated."

She felt worse than ever. "I guess it was rough on you, too, when you found out what he'd done," she said unexpectedly.

His expression was odd. Reserved. Uneasy. "I've never hated a human being so much in all my life," he said huskily. "And he was dead. There was nothing I could do to him, no way I could pay him back for ruining my life and taking hers. You can't imagine how I felt."

"I'm sure he was sorry about it," she said, having gleaned that from what Marge had said about the way he'd treated J.B. "You know he'd have taken it back if he could have. He must have loved you, very much. Marge said that he would have been afraid of losing you if he'd told the truth. You were his only son."

"Forgiveness comes hard to me," he said.

She knew that. He'd never held any grudges against her, but she knew people in town who'd crossed him years ago, and he still went out of his way to snub them. He didn't forgive, and he never forgot.

"Are you so perfect that you never make mistakes?" she wondered out loud.

"None to date," he replied, and he didn't smile.

"Your day is coming."

His eyes narrowed as he stared down at her. "You won't leave Grange alone. Is that final?"

She swallowed. "Yes. It's final."

He gave her a look as cold as death. His head jerked. "Your choice."

He turned on his heel and stalked out of the room. She watched him go with nervous curiosity. What in the world did he mean?

Marge was very quiet at breakfast the next day. Dawn and Brandi kept giving Tellie odd looks, too. They went off to church with friends. Marge wasn't feeling well, so she stayed home and Tellie stayed with her. Something was going on. She wondered what it was.

"Is there something I've done that I need to apologize for?" she asked Marge while they were making lunch in the kitchen.

Marge drew in a slow breath. "No, of course not," she denied gently. "It's just J.B., wanting his own way and making everybody miserable because he can't get it."

"If you want me to stop dating Grange, just say so," Tellie told her. "I won't do it for J.B., but I will do it for you."

Marge smiled at her gently. She reached over and patted Tellie's hand. "You don't have to make any such sacrifices. Let J.B. stew."

"Maybe the man does bring back some terrible memories," she murmured. "J.B. looked upset when he talked about it. He must…he must have loved her very much."

"He was twenty-one," Marge recalled. "Love is more intense at that age, I think. Certainly it was for me. She was J.B.'s first real affair. He wasn't himself the whole time he knew her. I thought she was too old for him, too, but he wouldn't hear a word we said about her. He turned against me, against Dad, against the whole world. He ran off to get married and said he'd never come back. But she argued with him. We never knew exactly why, but when she took her own life, he blamed himself. And then when he learned the truth…well, he was never the same."

"I'm sorry it was like that for him," she said, understanding how he would have felt. She felt like that about J.B. At least, she thought, she wasn't losing him to death—just to legions of other women.

Marge put down the spoon she was using to stir beef stew and turned to Tellie. "I would have told you about her, eventually, even if Grange hadn't shown up," she said quietly. "I knew it would hurt, to know he felt like that about another woman. But at least you'd understand why you couldn't get close to him. You can't fight a ghost, Tellie. She's perfect in his mind, like a living, breathing photograph that never ages, never has faults, never creates problems. No living woman will ever top her in J.B.'s mind. Loving him, while he feels like that about a ghost, would kill your very soul."

"Yes, I understand that now," Tellie said heavily. She stared out the window, seeing nothing. "How little we really know people."

"You can live with someone for years and not know them," Marge agreed. "I just don't want you to waste your life on my brother. You deserve better."

Tellie winced, but she didn't let Marge see. "I'll get married one of these days and have six kids."

"You will," Marge agreed, smiling gently. "And I'll spoil your kids the way you've spoiled mine."

"The girls didn't look too happy this morning," Tellie remarked.

Marge grimaced. "J.B. had them in the kitchen helping prepare canapés," she said. "They didn't even get to dance."

"But, why?"

"They're just kids," Marge said ruefully. "They aren't old enough to notice eligible bachelors. To hear J.B. tell it, at least."

"But that's outrageous! They're sixteen and seventeen years old. They're not kids!"

"To J.B., you all are, Tellie."

She glowered. "Maybe Brandi and Dawn would like to go halves with me on a really mean singing telegram."

"J.B. would slug the singer, and we'd get sued," Marge said blithely. "Let it go, honey. I know things look dark at the moment, but they'll get better. We have to look to the future."

"I guess."

"The girls should be home any minute. I'll start dishing up while you set the table."

Tellie went to do it, her heart around her ankles.

If she'd wondered what J.B. meant with his cryptic remark, it became crystal clear in the days that followed. He came to the house to see Marge and pretended that Tellie wasn't there. If he passed her on the street at lunchtime, he didn't see her. For all intents and purposes, she had become the invisible woman. He was paying her back for dating Grange.

Which made her more determined, of course, to go out with the man. She didn't care if J.B. snubbed her forever; he wasn't dictating her life!

Grange discovered J.B.'s new attitude the following Saturday, when he took Tellie to a local community theater presentation of *Arsenic and Old Lace*. J.B. came in with his gorgeous blonde and sat down in the row across from Tellie and Grange. He didn't look their way all night, and when he passed them on the way out, he didn't speak.

"What the hell is wrong with him?" Grange asked her on the way home.

"He's paying me back for dating you," she said simply.

"That's low."

"That's J.B.," she replied.

"Do you want me to stop asking you out, Tellie?" he asked quietly.

"I do not. J.B. isn't telling me what to do," she replied. "He can ignore me all he likes. I'll ignore him back."

Grange was quiet. "I shouldn't have come here."

"You just wanted to know what happened," she defended him. "Nobody could blame you for that. She was your sister."

He pulled up in front of Marge's house and cut off the engine. "Yes, she was. She and Dad were the only family I had, but I was rotten to them. I ran wild when I hit thirteen.

I got in with a bad crowd, joined a gang, used drugs—you name it, I did it. I still don't understand why I didn't end up in jail."

"Her death saved you, didn't it?" she asked.

He nodded, his face averted. "I didn't admit it at the time, though. She was such a sweet woman. She always thought of other people before she thought of herself. She was all heart. It must have been a walk in the park for Hammock's father to convince her that she was ruining J.B.'s life."

"Can you imagine how the old man felt," she began slowly, "because he was always afraid that J.B. would find out the truth and know what he'd done. He had to know that he'd have lost J.B.'s respect, maybe even his love, and he had to live with that until he died. I don't imagine he was a very happy person, even if he did what he felt was the right thing."

"He didn't even know my sister, my dad said," Grange replied. "He wouldn't talk to her. He was sure she was a gold digger, just after J.B.'s money."

"How horrible, to think like that," she murmured thoughtfully. "I guess I wouldn't want to be rich. You'd never be sure if people liked you for what you were or what you had."

"The old man seemed to have an overworked sense of his own worth."

"It sounds like it, from what Marge says."

"Did you ever know him?"

"Only by reputation," she replied. "He was in the nursing home when I came to live with Marge."

"What is she like?"

She smiled. "The exact opposite of J.B. She's sweet and kind, and she never knows a stranger. She isn't suspicious or crafty, and she never hurts people deliberately."

"But her brother does?"

"J.B. never pulls his punches," she replied. "I suppose you know where you stand with him. But he's uncomfortable to be around sometimes, when he's in a bad mood."

He studied her curiously. "How long have you been in love with him?"

She laughed nervously. "I don't love J.B.! I hate him!"

"How long," he persisted, softening the question with a smile.

She shrugged. "Since I was fourteen, I suppose. I hero-worshiped him at first, followed him everywhere, baked him cookies, waylaid him when he went riding and tagged along. He was amazingly tolerant, when I was younger. Then I graduated from high school and we became enemies. He likes to rub it in that I'm vulnerable when he's around. I don't understand why."

"Maybe he doesn't understand why, either," he ventured.

"You think?" She smiled across the seat at him. "I'm surprised that J.B. hasn't tried to run you out of town."

"He has."

"What?"

He smiled faintly. "He went to see Justin Ballenger yesterday."

"About you?" she wondered.

He nodded. "He said that I was a bad influence on you, and he wondered if I wouldn't be happier working somewhere else."

"What did Justin say?" she asked.

He chuckled. "That he could run his own feedlot without Hammock's help, and that he wasn't firing a good worker because of Hammock's personal issues."

"Well!"

"I understand that Hammock is pulling his cattle out of the feedlot and having them trucked to Kansas, to a feedlot there for finishing."

"But that's horrible!" Tellie exclaimed.

"Justin said something similar, with a few more curse words attached," Grange replied. "I felt bad to cause such problems for him, but he only laughed. He said Hammock would lose money on the deal, and he didn't care. He wasn't being ordered around by a man ten years his junior."

"That sounds like Justin," she agreed, smiling. "Good for him."

He shrugged. "It doesn't solve the problem, though," he told her. "It's only the first salvo. Hammock won't quit. He wants me out of your life, whatever it takes."

"No, it's not about me," she said sadly. "He doesn't like being reminded of what he lost. Marge said so."

Grange's dark eyes studied her quietly. "He didn't want you to know about my sister," he said after a minute. "I ticked him off that first day we went to lunch, by telling you the family secret."

"Marge said that she would have told me herself eventually."

"Why?"

She smiled. "She thinks I'd wear my heart out on J.B., and she's right. I would have. He'll never get past his lovely ghost to any sort of relationship with a real woman. I'm not going to waste my life aching for a man I can't have."

"That's sensible," he agreed. "But he's been part of your life for a long time. He's become a habit."

She nodded, her eyes downcast. "That's just what he is. A habit."

He drew in a long breath. "If you want to stop seeing me…"

"I do not," she said at once. "I really enjoy going out with you, Grange."

He smiled, because it was obvious that she meant it. "I like your company, too." He hesitated. "Just friends," he added slowly.

She smiled back. "Just friends."

His eyes were distant. "I'm at a turning point in my life," he confessed. "I'm not sure where I'm headed. But I know I'm not ready for anything serious."

"Neither am I." She leaned her head against the back of

the seat and studied him. "Do you think you might stay here, in Jacobsville?"

"I don't know. I've got some problems to work out."

"Join the club," she said, and grinned at him.

He laughed. "I like the way I feel with you. J.B. can go hang. We'll present a united front."

"Just as long as J.B. doesn't go and hang us!" she exclaimed.

Five

Grange liked to bowl. Tellie had never tried the sport, but he taught her. She persuaded Marge to let the girls come with them one night. Marge tagged along, but she didn't bowl. She sat at the table sipping coffee and watching her brood fling the big balls down the alley.

"It's fun!" Tellie laughed. She'd left the field to the three experts who were making her look sick with her less-than-perfect bowling.

"That's why you're sitting here with me, is it?" Marge teased.

She shrugged. "I'm a lemon," she confessed. "Nothing I do ever looks good."

"That's not true," Marge disputed. "You cook like an angel and you're great in history. You always make A's."

"Two successes out of a hundred false starts," Tellie sighed.

"You're just depressed because J.B.'s ignoring you," Marge said, cutting to the heart of the matter.

"Guilty," Tellie had to admit. "Maybe I should have listened."

"Bull. If you give J.B. the upper hand, he'll walk all over you. The way you used to be, when you were fourteen, I despaired of what would happen if he ever really noticed you. He'd have destroyed your life, Tellie. You'd have become his doormat. He'd have hated that as much as you would."

"Think so? He seems pretty uncomfortable with me when I stand up to him."

"But he respects you for it."

Tellie propped her elbows on the table and rested her chin in her hands. "Does the beauty queen runner-up stand up to him?" she wondered.

"Are you kidding? She won't go to the bathroom without asking J.B. if he thinks it's a good idea!" came the dry response. "She's not giving up all those perks. He gave her a diamond dinner ring last week for her birthday."

That hurt. "I suppose he picked it out himself?"

Marge sighed. "I think she did."

"I can't believe I've wasted four years of my life mooning over that man," Tellie said, wondering aloud at her own stupidity. "I turned down dates with really nice men in college because I was hung up on J.B. Well, never again."

"What sort of nice men?" Marge queried, trying to change the subject.

Tellie grinned. "One was an anthropology major, working on his Ph.D. He's going to devote his life to a dig in Montana, looking for PaleoIndian sites."

"Just imagine, Tellie, you could work beside him with a toothbrush…"

"Stop that," Tellie chuckled. "I don't think I'm cut out for dust and dirt and bones."

"What other nice men?"

"There was a friend of one of my professors," she recalled. "He raises purebred Appaloosa stallions when he isn't hunting for meteorites all over the world. He was a character!"

"Why would you hunt meteorites?" Marge wondered.

"Well, he sold one for over a hundred thousand dollars to a collector," the younger woman replied, tongue in cheek.

Marge whistled. "Wow! Maybe I'll get a metal detector and go out searching for them myself!"

That was a real joke, because Marge had inherited half of her father's estate. She lived in a simple house and she never lived high. But she could have, if she'd wanted to. She felt that the girls shouldn't have too much luxury in their formative years. Maybe she was right. Certainly, Brandi and Dawn had turned out very well. They were responsible and kindhearted, and they never felt apart from fellow students.

Tellie glanced at the lanes, where Grange was throwing a ball down the aisle with force, and grace. He had a rodeo rider's physique, lean in the hips and wide in the shoulders. Odd, the way he moved, Tellie mused, like a hunter.

"He really is a dish," she murmured, deep in thought.

Marge nodded. "He is unusual," she said. "Imagine a boy on a path that deadly turning his life around."

"J.B. said he was forced out of the military."

Marge gaped at her. "He told you that? How did he know?"

Tellie glowered. "I expect he's had a firm of private detectives on overtime, finding out everything they could about him. J.B. loves to have leverage if he has to go against people."

"He won't bother Grange," Marge said. "He just wants to make sure that the man isn't a threat to you."

"He wants to decide who I marry, and how many kids I have," she returned coolly. "But he's not going to."

"That's the spirit, Tellie," Marge chuckled.

"All the same," Tellie replied, "I wish he wouldn't snub me. I'm beginning to feel like a ghost."

"He'll get over it."

"You think so? I wonder."

Saturday came, and Grange had something to do for Justin, so Tellie stayed home and helped Marge clean house.

A car drove up out front and two car doors slammed. Tellie was on her hands and knees in the kitchen, scrubbing the tile with a brush while Marge cleaned upstairs. J.B. walked in with a ravishing young blond woman on his arm. She was tall and beautifully made, with a model-perfect face and teeth, and hair to her waist in back.

"I thought they abolished indentured servitude," J.B. drawled, looking pointedly at Tellie.

She looked up at him with cold eyes, pushing sweaty hair out of her eyes with the back of a dirty hand. "It's called housecleaning, J.B. I'm sure you have no idea what it consists of."

"Nell takes care of all that," he said. "This is Bella Dean," he introduced the blonde, wrapping a long arm around her and smiling at her warmly.

"Nice to meet you," Tellie said, forcing a smile. "I'd shake hands, but I'm sure you'd rather not." She indicated her dirty hands.

Bella didn't answer her. She beamed up at J.B. "Didn't we come to take your sister and your nieces out to eat?" she asked brightly. "I'm sure the kitchen help doesn't need an audience."

Tellie got to her feet, slammed the brush down on the floor and walked right up to the blonde, who actually backed away.

"What would you know about honest work, lady, unless you call lying on your back, work…!"

"Tellie!" J.B. bit off.

The blonde gasped. "Well, I never!"

"I'll bet there's not much you've never," Tellie said coldly. "For your information, I don't work here. Marge gave me a home when my mother died, and I earn my keep. When I'm not scrubbing floors, I go to college to earn a degree, so that I can make a living for myself," she added pointedly. "I'm sure you won't ever have a similar problem, as long as your looks last."

"Tellie!" J.B. repeated.

"I'd rather be pretty than smart," the blonde said carelessly. "Who'd want to give you diamonds?" she scoffed.

Tellie balled a fist.

"Go tell Marge we're here," he demanded, his eyes making cold threats.

"Tell her yourself, J.B.," Tellie replied, eyes flashing. "I'm not anybody's servant."

She turned and left the room, so furious that she was shaking all over.

J.B. followed her right into her bedroom and closed the door behind them.

"What the hell was that all about?" he asked furiously.

"I am not going to be looked down on by any smarmy blond tart!" she exclaimed.

"You behaved like a child!" he returned.

"She started it," she reminded him.

"She thought you were the housekeeper," he replied. "She didn't know you from a button."

"She'll know me next time, won't she?"

He moved closer, glaring at her. "You're so jealous you're vibrating with it," he accused, his green eyes narrowing. "You want me."

She drew in a sharp breath and her hands tightened into fists. "I do not," she retorted.

He moved a step closer, so that he was right up against her. His big hand went to her cheek, smoothing over it. His thumb rubbed maddeningly at her lower lip. "You want me," he whispered deeply, bending. "I can feel your heart beating. You ache for me to touch you."

"J.B., if…if you don't…stop," she faltered, fighting his arrogance and her own weakness.

"You don't want me to stop, baby," he murmured, his chiseled mouth poised just over her parted lips. "That's the last thing you want." His thumb tugged her lower lip down and he nibbled softly at the upper one. He heard her breath catch, felt her body shiver. His eyes began to glitter with something like triumph. "I can feel your heart beating. You're waking up. I could do anything I liked to you, whenever I pleased, and we both know it, Tellie."

A husky little moan escaped her tight throat and she moved involuntarily, her body brushing against his, her mouth lifting, pleading, her hands going to his hard upper arms to hold him there. She hated him for doing this to her, but she couldn't resist him.

He knew it. He laughed. He pulled away from her, arrogance in his whole bearing. He smiled, and it wasn't a nice smile at all. "She likes to kiss me, too, Tellie," he said deliberately. "But she's no prude. She likes to take her clothes off, and I don't even have to coax her…"

She slapped him. She was humiliated, hurt, furious. She put the whole weight of her arm behind it, sobbing.

He didn't even react, except to lift an eyebrow and smile even more arrogantly. "Next time I bring her over to see Marge, you'd better be more polite, Tellie," he warned softly, and the deep edge of anger glittered in his green eyes. "Or I'll do this in front of her."

Tellie was horrified at even the thought. Her face went pale. Tears brightened her eyes, but she would have died rather than shed them. "There aren't enough bad words in the English language to describe what you are, J.B.," she said brokenly.

"Oh, you'll think of some eventually, I'm sure. And if you can't, you can always give me another one of those god-awful dragon ties, can't you?"

"I bought boxes of them!" she slung at him.

He only laughed. He gave her a last probing look and went out of the room, leaving the door open behind him.

"Where have you been?" the blonde demanded in a honeyed tone.

"Just having a little overdue discussion. We'd better go. See you, Marge."

* * *

There were muffled voices. A door closed. Two car doors slammed. An engine roared.

Marge knocked gently and came into Tellie's room, her whole look apprehensive. She grimaced.

Tellie was as white as a sheet, shaking with rage and humiliation.

"I'll tell him not to bring her here again," Marge said firmly. She put her arms around Tellie and gathered her close. "It's all right."

"He's the devil in a suit," Tellie whispered huskily. "The very devil, Marge. I never, never want to see him again."

The thin arms closed around her and rocked her while she cried. Marge wondered why J.B. had to be so cruel to a woman who loved him this much. She had a good idea of what he'd done. It was unfair of him. He didn't want Tellie. Why couldn't he leave her alone? He'd brought his latest lover here deliberately. Tellie had refused to go to the barbecue, avoiding being around the woman, so J.B. had brought her over to Marge's to rub it in. He wanted Tellie to see how beautiful the woman was, how devoted she was to J.B. He was angry that he couldn't stop her from seeing Grange, not even by snubbing her. This was low, even for J.B.

"I don't know what's gotten into my brother," Marge said aloud. "But I'm very sorry, Tellie."

"It's not your fault. We don't get to choose our relatives, more's the pity."

"I wouldn't choose J.B. for a brother, after today." She drew away, her dark eyes twinkling, mischievous. "Tellie, the girls wouldn't let J.B. introduce them to his girlfriend. They gave her vicious looks, glared at J.B. and went to Dawn's room and locked themselves in. He's mad at them now, too."

"Good. Maybe he'll stay at his own house."

"I wouldn't bet on that," Marge thought, but she didn't say it aloud. Tellie had stood enough for one day.

* * *

Grange took Tellie with him around the feedlot the next week, explaining how they monitored statistics and mixed the feed for the various lots of cattle. He'd asked Justin for permission. The older man was glad to give it. He liked the strange young man who'd come to work for him. It was a compliment, because Justin didn't like many people at all.

Grange propped one big, booted foot on the bottom rail of one of the enclosures, with his arms folded on the top one. His dark eyes had a faraway look. "This is good country," he said. "I grew up in West Texas. Mostly we've got desert and cactus and mountains over around El Paso. This is green heaven."

"Yes, it is. I love it here," she confessed. "I go to school in Houston. It's green there, too, but the trees are nestled in concrete."

He chuckled. "Do you like college?"

"I do."

"I went myself, in the army."

"What did you study?"

He grinned at her. "Besides weapons and tactics, you mean?" He chuckled. "I studied political science."

She was surprised, and showed it. "That was your major?"

"Part of it. I did a double major, in political science and Arab dialects."

"You mean, you can speak Arabic?"

He nodded. "Farsi, Bedouin, several regional dialects. Well, and the Romance languages."

"All three of them?" she asked, surprised.

"All three." He glanced at her and smiled at her expression. "Languages will get you far in government service and the military. I mustered out as a major."

She tried not to let on that she'd heard about his release from the service. "Did you like the military?" she asked with deliberate carelessness.

He gave her a slow appraisal from dark, narrowed eyes.

"Gossip travels fast in small towns, doesn't it?" he wondered aloud. "I expect Hammock had something to do with it."

She sighed. "Probably did," she had to admit. "He did everything he could to keep me from going out with you."

"So he holds grudges," he remarked. "Lucky for him that I don't, or he'd be sleeping with guards at every door and a gun under his pillow. If it hadn't been for him, I'd still have my sister."

"Maybe he thinks that, except for you, and his father, he'd be happily married with kids now."

He shrugged. "Nobody came out of it laughing," he said. He looked down at her, puzzled. "If he wanted you to stop going out with me, why haven't you?"

She smiled sadly. "I got tired of being a carpet," she said.

He cocked his head. "Walked all over you, did he?"

She nodded. "Since I was fourteen. And I let him. I never disagreed with anything he said, even when I didn't think he was right." She traced a pattern on the metal fence. "I saw what I could have become last Saturday. He brought his newest girlfriend over to show me. She thought I was the hired help and treated me accordingly. We had words. Lots of words. Now I'm not speaking to J.B."

He leaned back against the gate. "You may not believe it, but standing up to people is the only way to get through life with your mind intact. Nothing was ever gained by giving in."

"So that's how you left the army, is it?" she mused.

He laughed curtly. "Our commanding officer sent us against an enemy company, understrength, without proper body armor, with weapons that were misfiring. ˙ took exception and he called me a name I didn't like. I deci˙˙d him, wrapped him up in his blanket and gagged him, and led the attack myself. Tactics brought us all back alive. His way would have wiped us out to the last man. The brass didn't approve of my methods, so I had the choice of being honorably discharged or court-martialed. It was a close decision," he added with cold humor.

She just stared at him. "How could they do that? Send you into battle without proper equipment… That's outrageous!"

"Talk to Congress," he said coolly. "But don't expect them to do anything, unless it's an election year. Improvements cost money. We don't have enough."

She stared out over the distant pasture. "What happened to your commanding officer?"

"Oh, they promoted him," he said. "Called his tactics brilliant, in fact."

"But he didn't go, and they were your tactics!" she exclaimed.

He raised an eyebrow. "That's not what he told the brass."

She glowered. "Somebody should have told them!"

"In fact, just last week one of his execs got drunk enough to spill the beans to a reporter for one of the larger newspaper chains. A court-martial board is convening in the near future, or so I hear."

"Will they call you to testify?" she wondered.

He smiled. "God, I hope so," he replied.

She laughed at his expression. "Revenge is sweet?"

"So they tell me. Being of a naturally sweet and retiring disposition, I rarely ever cause problems…why are you laughing?"

She was almost doubled over. He was the last man she could picture that way.

"Maybe I caused a little trouble, once in a while," he had to admit. He glanced at his watch. "Lunch break's over. Better get back to work, so that Justin doesn't start looking for replacements."

"It was a nice lunch break, even if we didn't eat anything."

"I wasn't hungry. Sorry, I didn't think about food."

She smiled up at him. "Neither did I. We had a big breakfast this morning, and I was stuffed. Wouldn't you like to come over for pizza tonight?"

He hesitated. "I would, but I'm not going to."

"Why?"

"I'm not going to provide any more reasons for Hammock to take out old injuries on you."

"I'm not afraid of J.B."

"Neither am I," he agreed. "But let's give him time to calm down before we start any more trouble."

"I suppose we could," she agreed, but reluctantly. She didn't want J.B. to think she was bowing down to him.

The weekend went smoothly. J.B. and his blond appendage were nowhere in sight, and neither was Grange. Tellie played Monopoly with Marge and the girls on Saturday night, and went to church with them on Sunday morning.

Monday morning, Marge didn't get up for breakfast. Tellie took her a tray, worried because she seemed unusually pale and languorous.

"Just a little dizziness and nausea, Tellie," Marge protested with a wan smile. "I'll stay in bed and feel better. Really. The girls are here if I need help."

"You'd better call me if you do," she said firmly.

Marge smiled and nodded. Tellie noticed an odd rhythm in her heartbeat—it was so strong that it was shaking her nightgown. Nausea and an erratic heartbeat were worrisome symptoms. Tellie's grandfather had died of heart trouble, and she remembered the same symptoms in him.

She didn't make a big deal out of it, but she did put aside her hurt pride long enough to drive by J.B.'s office on the way to the feedlot.

He was talking to a visiting cattleman, but when he saw Tellie, he broke off the conversation politely and joined her in the outer office. He looked good in jeans and a chambray shirt and chaps, she thought, even if they were designer clothing. He was working today, not squiring around women.

"Couldn't stand it anymore, I gather?" he asked curtly. "You just had to come and see me and apologize?"

She frowned. "Excuse me?"

"It's about time," he told her. "But I'm busy today. You should have picked a better time."

"J.B., I need to talk to you," she began.

He gave her slender figure in the green pantsuit a curiously intent scrutiny, winding his way back up the modest neckline to her face, with only the lightest touch of makeup, and her wavy hair like a dark cap around her head. "On your way to work?"

"Yes," she said. "J.B., I have to tell you something…"

He took her arm and led her back outside to her car. "Later. I've got a full day. Besides," he added as he opened her car door, "you know I don't like to be chased. I like to do the chasing."

She let out an exasperated breath. "J.B., I'm not chasing you! If you'd just give me a chance to speak…!"

His eyes narrowed. "I don't like treating you like the enemy, but I also don't like the way you spoke to Bella. When you apologize, to her, we'll go from there."

"Apologize?"

His face hardened. "You took too much for granted. You aren't part of my family, and you aren't a lover. You can't treat my women like trespassers in my own sister's house. Maybe we were close, when you were younger, but that's over."

"She started it," she began, riled.

"She belongs with me. You don't." His eyes were hard. "I need more from a woman than a handshake at the end of the evening. That's as much as you're able to give, Tellie. You're completely unawakened."

She wondered what he was talking about. But she didn't have time to ponder enigmas. "Listen, Bella's not what I came here to talk about!"

"I'm not giving up Bella," he continued, as if she hadn't spoken. "And chasing after me like this isn't going to get you anything except the wrong side of my temper. Don't do it again."

"J.B.!"

He closed the door. "Go to work," he said shortly, and turned away.

Of all the arrogant, assuming, overbearing conceited jackasses, she thought as she reversed out of the parking space and took off toward town, he took the cake. She wasn't chasing him, she was trying to tell him about Marge! Well, she could try again later. Next time, she promised herself, she'd make him listen.

She walked in the front door after work, tired and dispirited. Maybe Marge was better, she hoped.

"Tellie, is that you?" Dawn exclaimed from the top of the staircase. "Come on up. Hurry, please!"

Tellie took the steps two at a time. Marge was lying on her back, gasping for breath, wincing with pain. Her face was a grayish tone, her skin cold and clammy.

"Heart attack," Tellie said at once. She'd seen this all before, with her grandfather. She grabbed the phone and dialed 911.

She tried to call J.B., but she couldn't get an answer on his cell phone, or on the phone at the office or his house. She waited until the ambulance loaded up Marge, and the girls went with her, to get into her car and drive to J.B.'s house. If she couldn't find him, she could at least get Nell to relay a message.

She leaped out of the car and ran to the front door. She tried the knob and found it unlocked. This was no time for formality. She opened it and ran down the hall to J.B.'s study. She threw open the door and stopped dead in the doorway.

J.B. looked up, over Bella's bare white shoulders, his face flushed, his mouth swollen, his shirt off.

"What the hell are you doing here?" he demanded furiously.

Six

Tellie could barely get her breath. Worried about Marge, half-sick with fear, she couldn't even manage words. No wonder J.B. couldn't be bothered to answer the phone. He and his beautiful girlfriend were half-naked. Apparently J.B. wasn't much on beds for his sensual adventures. She remembered with heartache that he'd wrestled her down on that very sofa when she was eighteen and kissed her until her mouth hurt. It had been the most heavenly few minutes of her entire life, despite the fact that he'd been furious when he started kissing her. It hadn't ended that way, though...

"Get out!" J.B. threw at her.

She managed to get her wits back. Marge. She had to think about Marge, not about how much her pride was hurting. "J.B., you have to listen..."

"Get out, damn you!" he raged. "I've had it up to here with you chasing after me, pawing me, trying to get close to me! I don't want you, Tellie, how many times do I have to tell you

before you realize that I mean it? You're a stray that Marge
and I took in, nothing more! I don't want you, and I never
will!"

Her heart was bursting with raw pain. She hoped she
wouldn't pass out. She knew her face was white. She wanted
to move, to leave, but her feet felt frozen to the carpet.

Her tormented expression and lack of response seemed to
make him worse. "You skinny, ugly little tomboy," he raged,
white-hot with fury. "Who'd want something like you for
keeps? Get out, I said!"

She gave up. She turned away, slowly, aware of the gloating
smile on Bella's face, and closed the door behind her. Her
knees barely gave her support as she walked back toward the
front door.

Nell was standing by the staircase, drying her hands on her
apron, looking shocked. "What in the world is all the yelling
about?" she exclaimed. She hesitated when she saw the
younger woman's drawn, white face. "Tellie, what's wrong?"
she asked gently.

Tellie fought for composure. "Marge…is on her way to the
hospital in an ambulance, with the girls. I think it's a heart
attack. I couldn't make J.B. listen. He's…I walked in on him
and that woman… He yelled at me and said I was chasing him,
and called me horrible names…!" She swallowed hard and
drew herself erect. "Please tell him we'll all be at the hospital,
if he can tear himself loose long enough!"

She turned toward the door.

"Don't you drive that car unless you're all right, Tellie,"
Nell said firmly. "It's pouring down rain."

"I'm fine," she said in a ghostly tone. She even forced a
smile. "Tell him, okay?"

"I'll tell him," Nell said angrily. Her voice softened. "Don't
worry, honey. Marge is one tough cookie. She'll be all right.
You just drive carefully. You ought to wait and go with him,"
she added slowly.

"If I got in a car with him right now, I'd kill him," Tellie said through her teeth. Helpless tears were rolling down her pale cheeks. "See you later, Nell."

"Tellie…"

It was too late. Tellie closed the door behind her and went to her car. She was getting soaked and she didn't care. J.B. had said terrible things to her. She knew that she'd never get over them. He wanted her to stop chasing him. She hadn't been, but it must have looked like it. She'd gone to his office this morning, and to the house this afternoon. It was about Marge. He wouldn't believe it, though. He thought Tellie was desperate for him. That was a joke, now. She was sure that she never wanted to see him again as long as she lived.

She started the car and turned it. The tires were slick. She hadn't realized how slick until she almost spun out going down the driveway. She needed to keep her speed down, but she wasn't thinking rationally. She was hearing J.B. yell at her that she was an ugly stray he'd taken in, that he didn't want her. Tears misted her eyes as she tried to concentrate on the road.

There was a hairpin curve just before the ranch road met the highway. It was usually easy to maneuver, but the rain was coming so hard and fast that the little car suddenly hydroplaned. She saw the ditch coming toward her and jerked the wheel as hard as she could. In a daze, she felt the car go over and over and over. Her seat belt broke and something hit her head. Everything went black.

J.B. stormed out of the living room just seconds after he heard Tellie's little car scatter gravel as it sped away. His hair was mussed, like his shirt, and he was in a vicious humor. It had been a bad day altogether. He shouldn't have yelled at Tellie. But he wondered why she'd come barging in. He should have asked. It was just that it had shamed him to be seen in such a position with Bella, knowing painfully how Tellie felt about him. He'd hurt her with just the sight of him and Bella, without adding his scathing comments afterward. Tellie wouldn't even realize that shame had put him on the offensive. She had feelings of glass, and he'd shattered them.

Nell was waiting for him at the foot of the staircase. She was visibly seething, and her white hair almost stood on end with bridled rage. "So you finally came out, did you?"

"Tellie was tearing up the driveway as she left," he bit off. "What the hell got into her? Why was she here?" he added reluctantly, because he'd realized, belatedly, that she hadn't looked as if she were pursuing him with amorous intent.

Nell gave him a cold smile. "She couldn't get you on the phone, so she drove over to tell you that Marge has had a heart attack." She nodded curtly when she saw him turn pale. "That's right. She wasn't here chasing you. She wanted you to know about your sister."

"Oh, God," he bit off.

"*He* won't help you," Nell ground out. "Yelling at poor Tellie like that, when she was only trying to do you a good turn…!"

"Shut up," he snapped angrily. "Call the hospital and see…"

"You call them." She took off her apron. "You've got my two weeks' notice, as of right now. I'm sick of watching you torture Tellie. I quit! See if your harpy girlfriend in there can cook your meals and clean your house while she spends you into the poorhouse!"

"Nell," he began furiously.

She held up a hand. "I won't reconsider."

The living room door opened, and Bella slinked into the hallway, smiling contentedly. "Aren't we going out to eat?" she asked J.B. as she moved to catch him by one arm.

"I'm going to the hospital," he said. "My sister's had a heart attack."

"Oh, that's too bad," Bella said. "Do you want me to go with you and hold your hand?"

"The girls will love that," Nell said sarcastically. "You'll be such a comfort to them!"

"Nell!" J.B. fumed.

"She's right, I'd be a comfort, like she said," Bella agreed, missing the sarcasm altogether. "You need me, J.B."

"I hope he gets what he really needs one day," Nell said, turning on her heel.

"You're fired!" he yelled after her.

"Too late, I already quit," Nell said pleasantly. "I'm sure Bella can cook you some supper and wash your clothes." She closed the kitchen door behind her with a snap.

"Now, you know I can't cook, J.B.," Bella said irritably. "And I've never washed clothes—I send mine to the laundry. What's the matter with her? It's that silly girl who was here, isn't it? I don't like her at all…"

J.B. reached into his pocket and pulled out two large bills. "Call a cab and go home," he said shortly. "I have to get to the hospital."

"But I should go with you," she argued.

He looked down at her with bridled fury. "Go home."

She shifted restlessly. "Well, all right, J.B., you don't need to yell. Honestly, you're in such a bad mood!"

"My sister has had a heart attack," he repeated.

"Yes, I know, but those things happen, don't they? You can't do anything about it," she added blankly.

It was like talking to a wall, he thought with exasperation. He tucked in his shirt, checked to make sure his car keys were in his pocket, jerked his raincoat and hat from the hall coat rack and went out the door without a backward glance.

Dawn and Brandi were pacing the waiting room in the emergency room at Jacobsville General Hospital while Dr. Coltrain examined their mother. They were quiet, somber, with tears pouring down their cheeks in silent misery when J.B. walked in.

They ran to him the instant they saw him, visibly shaken.

He gathered them close, feeling like an animal because he hadn't even let Tellie talk when she'd walked in on him. She'd come to tell him that Marge was in the hospital with a heart attack, and he'd sent her running with insults. Probably she'd come to his office that morning because something about Marge had worried her. He'd been no help at all. Now Tellie was hurt and Nell was quitting. He'd never felt so helpless.

"Mama won't die, will she, Uncle J.B.?" Brandi asked tearfully.

"Of course she won't," he assured her in the deep, soft tone he used with little things or hurt children. "She'll be fine."

"Tellie said she was going to tell you about Mama. Why didn't Tellie come with you?" Dawn asked, wiping her eyes.

He stiffened. "Tellie's not here?"

"No. She had to go over to your house, because you didn't answer your phone," Brandi replied. "I guess the lines were down or something."

"Or something," he said huskily. He'd taken the phone off the hook.

"She may have gone home to get Mama a gown," Dawn suggested. "She always thinks of things like that, when everybody else goes to pieces."

"She'll be here as soon as she can…I know she will," Brandi agreed. "I don't know what we'd do without Tellie."

Which made J.B. feel even smaller than he already did. Tellie must be scared to death. She'd been with her grandfather when he died of a heart attack. She'd loved him more than any other member of her small family, including the mother she'd lost more recently. Marge's heart attack would bring back terrible memories. Worse, when she showed up at the hospital, she'd have to deal with what J.B. had said to her. It wasn't going to be a pleasant reunion.

Dr. Coltrain came out, smiling. "Marge is going to be all right," he told them. "We got to her just in time. But she'll have to see a heart specialist, and she's going to be on medication from now on. Did you know that her blood pressure was high?"

"No!" J.B. said at once. "It's always been low!"

Coltrain shook his head. "Not anymore. She's very lucky that it happened like this. It may have saved her life."

"It was a heart attack, then?" J.B. persisted, with the girls standing close at his side.

"Yes. But a mild one. You can see her when we've got her in a room. You'll need to sign her in at the office."

"I'll do that right now."

"But, where's Tellie?" Dawn asked when they were alone.

J.B. wished he knew.

He was on his way back from the office when he passed the emergency room, just in time to see a worried Grange stalking in beside a gurney that two paramedics were rushing through the door. On the stretcher was Tellie, unconscious and bleeding.

"Tellie!" he exclaimed, rushing to the gurney. She was white as a sheet, and he was more frightened now than he was when he learned about Marge. "What happened?" he shot at Grange.

"I don't know," Grange said curtly. "Her car was off the road in a ditch. She was unconscious, in a couple of inches of water, facedown. If I hadn't come along when I did, she'd have drowned."

J.B. felt sick all the way to his soul. It was his fault. All his fault. "Where was the car?" he asked.

"On the farm road that leads to your house," Grange replied, his eyes narrowed, suspiciously. "Why are you here?"

"My sister just had a heart attack," he said solemnly. "The girls and I have been in the emergency waiting room. She's going to be all right. Tellie came to tell me about it," he added reluctantly.

"Then why in hell didn't she ride in with you?" Grange asked, brown eyes flashing. "She must have been upset—she loves Marge. She shouldn't even have been driving in weather this dangerous."

That was a question J.B. didn't want to touch. He ignored it, following the gurney into one of the examination rooms with Grange right on his heels.

He got one of Tellie's small hands in both of his and held on tight. "Tellie," he said huskily, feeling the pain all the way to his boots. "Tellie, hold on!"

"She shouldn't have been driving," Grange repeated, leaning against the wall nearby. He was obviously upset as well, and the look he gave J.B. would have started a fight under better circumstances.

The entrance of Copper Coltrain interrupted him.

Copper gave J.B. an odd look. "It isn't your day, is it?" he asked, moving to Tellie's side. "What happened?"

"Her car hydroplaned, apparently," Grange said tautly. "I found it overturned. She was lying facedown in a ditch full of water. If I'd been just a little later, she'd have drowned."

"Damn the luck!" Coltrain muttered, checking her pupil reaction with a small penlight. "She's concussed as well as bruised," he murmured. "I'm going to need X-rays and a battery of tests to see how badly she's hurt. But the concussion is the main thing."

J.B. felt sick. One of his men had been kicked in the head by a mean steer and dropped dead of a massive concussion. "Can't you do something now?" he raged at Coltrain.

The physician gave him an odd look. It was notorious gossip locally that Tellie was crazy about J. B. Hammock, and that J.B. paid her as little attention as possible. The white-faced man with blazing green eyes facing him didn't seem disinterested.

"What would you suggest?" he asked J.B. curtly.

"Wake her up!"

Grange made a rough sound in his throat.

"You can shut up," J.B. told him icily. "You're not a doctor."

"Neither are you," Grange returned with the same lack of warmth. "And if you'd given her a lift to the hospital, she wouldn't need one, would she?"

J.B. had already worked that out for himself. His lips compressed furiously.

Tellie groaned.

Both men moved to the examination table at the same time. Coltrain gave them angry looks and bent to examine Tellie.

"Can you hear me?" he asked her softly. "Tellie?"

Her eyes opened, green and dazed. She blinked and winced. "My head hurts."

"I'm not surprised," Coltrain murmured, busy with a stethoscope. "Take a deep breath. Let it out. Again."

She groaned. "My head hurts," she repeated.

"Okay, I'll give you something for it. But we need X-rays and an MRI," Coltrain said quietly. "Anything hurt besides your head?"

"Everything," she replied. "What happened?"

"You wrecked your car," Grange said quietly.

She looked up at him. "You found me?"

He nodded, dark eyes concerned.

She managed a smile. "Thanks." She shivered. "I'm wet!"

"It was pouring rain," Grange said, his voice soft, like his eyes. He brushed back the blood-matted hair from her forehead, disclosing a growing dark bruise. He winced.

"You're concussed, Tellie," Dr. Coltrain said. "We're going to have to keep you for a day or two. Okay?"

"But I'll miss graduation!" she exclaimed, trying to sit up.

He gently pushed her back down. "No, you won't," he said with a quizzical smile.

She blinked, glancing at J.B., who looked very worried. "But it's May. I'm a senior. I have a white gown and cap." She hesitated. "Was I driving Marge's car?"

"No. Your own," J.B. said slowly, apprehensively.

"But I don't have a car, don't you remember, J.B.?" she asked pleasantly. "I have to drive Marge's. She's going to help me buy a car this summer, because I'm going to work at the Sav-A-Lot Grocery Store, remember?"

J.B.'s indrawn breath was audible. Before the other two men could react, he pressed Tellie's small hand closer in his own. "Tellie, how old are you?" he asked.

"I'm seventeen, you know that," she scoffed.

Coltrain whistled. J.B. turned to him, his lips parted in the preliminary to a question.

"We're going to step outside and discuss how to break it to Marge," Coltrain told her gently. "You just rest. I'll send a nurse in with something for your headache, okay?"

"Okay," she agreed. "J.B., you aren't leaving, are you?" she added worriedly.

Coals of fire, he was thinking, as he assured her that he'd be nearby. She relaxed and smiled as she lay back on the examination table.

Coltrain motioned the other two men outside into the hall. "Amnesia," he told J.B. at once. "I'm sure it's temporary," he added quickly. "It isn't uncommon with head injuries. She's very confused, and in some pain. I'll run tests. We'll do an MRI to make sure."

"The head injury would cause it?" Grange asked worriedly.

J.B. had a flush along his high cheekbones. He didn't speak.

Coltrain gave him a curious look. "The brain tends to try to protect itself from trauma, and not only physical trauma. Has she had a shock of some kind?" he asked J.B. pointedly.

J.B. replied with a curt jerk of his head. "We had a…misunderstanding at the house," he admitted.

Grange's dark eyes flashed. "Well, that explains why she wrecked the car!" he accused.

J.B. glared at him. "Like hell it does…!"

Coltrain held up a hand. "Arguing isn't going to do her any

good. She's had the wreck, now we have to deal with the consequences. I'm going to admit her and start running tests."

J.B. drew a quick breath. "How are we going to explain this to Tellie?"

Coltrain sighed. "Tell her as little as possible, right now. Once she's stabilized, we'll tell her what we have to. But if she thinks she's seventeen, sending her to Marge's house is going to be traumatic—she'll expect the girls to be four years younger than they are, won't she?"

J.B. was thinking, hard. He saw immediately a way to solve that problem and prevent Nell from escaping at once. "She can stay at the house with Nell and me," he said. "She and Marge and the girls did stay there when she was seventeen for a couple of weeks while Marge's house was being remodeled. We can tell her that Marge and the girls are having a vacation while workmen tend to her house. I'll make it right with Dawn and Brandi."

"You and Tellie were close when she was in her teens, I recall," Coltrain recalled.

"Yes," J.B. said tautly.

Coltrain chuckled, glancing at Grange. "She followed him around like a puppy when she first went to live with Marge," he told the other man. "You couldn't talk to J.B. without tripping over Tellie. J.B. was her security blanket after she lost her mother."

"She was the same way with Marge," J.B. muttered.

"Not to that extent, she wasn't," Coltrain argued. "She thought the sun rose and set on you..."

"I need to go back and check on Marge," J.B. interrupted, visibly uncomfortable.

"I'll stay with Tellie for a while," Grange said, moving back into the examination room before the other two men could object.

J.B. stared after him with bridled fury, his hands deep in his pockets, his eyes smoldering. "He's got no business in there," he told Coltrain. "He isn't even family!"

"Neither are you," the doctor reminded him.

J.B. glared at him. "Are you sure she'll be all right?"

"As sure as I can be." He studied the other man intently. "You said something to her, something that hurt, didn't you?" he asked, nodding when J.B.'s high cheekbones took on a ruddy color. "She's hiding in the past, when you were less resentful of her. She'll get her memory back, but it's going to be dangerous to rush it. You have to let her move ahead at her own pace."

"I'll do that," J.B. assured him. He drew in a long breath. "Damn. I feel as if my whole life crashed and burned today. First Marge, now Tellie. And Neil quit," he added angrily.

"Nell?" Coltrain exclaimed. "She's been there since you were a boy."

"Well, she wants to leave," J.B. muttered. "But she'll stay if she knows Tellie's coming to the house. I'd better phone her. Then I'll go back to Marge's room." He met Coltrain's eyes. "If she needs anything, *anything,* I'll take care of it. I don't think she's got any health insurance at all."

"You might stop by the admissions office and set things up," Coltrain suggested. "But I'll do what needs doing, finances notwithstanding. You know that."

"I do. Thanks, Copper."

Coltrain shrugged. "I'm glad she's rallying," he said. "And Marge, too."

"Same here."

J.B. left him to go back to the admissions office and sign Tellie in. He felt guilty. Her wreck was certainly his fault. The least he could do was provide for her treatment. He hated knowing that he'd upset her that much, and for nothing. She was only trying to help. Frustration had taken its toll on him and driven him into Bella's willing arms. The last thing he'd expected was for Tellie to walk in on them. He'd never been quite so ashamed of himself. Which was, of course, no excuse to take his temper out on her. He wished he could take back all the things he'd said. While her memory was gone, at least he had a chance to regain her trust and make up, a little, for what he'd done.

Tellie felt drained by the time Coltrain had all the tests he wanted. She was curious about the man who'd told her that he found her in the wrecked car and called the ambulance. He was handsome and friendly and seemed to like her very much, but she didn't know him.

"It was very kind of you to rescue me," she told Grange when she was in a private room.

He shrugged. "My pleasure." He smiled at her, his dark eyes twinkling. "You can save me, next time."

She laughed. Her head cocked to one side as she studied him. "I'm sorry, but I don't remember your name."

"Grange," he said pleasantly.

"Just Grange?" she queried.

He nodded.

"Have I known you a long time?"

He shook his head. "But I've taken you out a few times."

Her eyebrows lifted. "And J.B. let me go with you?" she exclaimed. "That's very strange. I wanted to go hiking with a college boy I knew and he threw a fit. You're older than any college boy."

He chuckled. "I'm twenty-seven," he told her.

"Wow," she mused.

"You're old for your age," he said, evading her eyes. "J.B. and I know each other."

"I see." She didn't, but he was obviously reluctant to talk about it. "Marge hasn't been to see me," she added suddenly. "That's not like her."

Grange recalled what J.B. and Coltrain had discussed. "Her house is being remodeled," he said. "She and the girls are on a vacation trip."

"While school's in session?" she exclaimed.

He thought fast. "It's Spring Break, remember?"

She was confused. Hadn't someone said it was May? Wasn't Spring Break in March? "But graduation is coming up very soon."

"You got your cap and gown early, didn't you?" he improvised.

She was frowning. "That must be what happened. I'm so confused," she murmured, holding her head. "And my head absolutely throbs."

"They'll give you something for that." He checked his watch. "I have to go. Visiting hours are over."

"Will you come back tomorrow?" she asked, feeling deserted.

He smiled. "Of course I will." He hesitated. "It will have to be during my lunch hour, or after work, though."

"Where do you work?"

"At the Ballenger feedlot."

That set off bells in her head, but she couldn't think why. "They're nice, Justin and Calhoun."

"Yes, they are." He stood up, moving the chair back from her bed. "Take care. I'll see you tomorrow."

"Okay. Thanks again."

He looked at her for a long time. "I'm glad it wasn't more serious than it is," he told her. "You were unconscious when I found you."

"It was raining," she recalled hesitantly. "I don't understand why I was driving in the rain. I'm afraid of it, you know."

"Are you?"

She shook her head. "I must have had a reason."

"I'm sure you did." He looked thunderous, but he quickly erased the expression, smiled and left her.

She settled back into the pillow, feeling bruised and broken. It was such an odd experience, what had happened to her. Everyone seemed to be holding things back from her. She wondered how badly she was damaged. Tomorrow, she promised herself, she'd dig it out of J.B.

Seven

Tellie woke up early, expecting to find herself alone. But J.B. was sprawled in the chair next to the bed, snoring faintly, and he looked as if he'd been there for some time. A nurse was tiptoeing around to get Tellie's vitals, sending amused and interested glances at the long, lean cowboy beside the bed.

"Has he been there long?" Tellie wanted to know.

"Since daybreak," the nurse replied with a smile. She put the electronic thermometer in Tellie's ear, let it beep, checked it and wrote down a figure. She checked her pulse and recorded that, as well. "I understand the nurse on the last shift tried to evict him and the hospital administrator actually came down here in person to tell her to cease and desist." She gave Tellie a speaking glance. "I gather that your visitor is somebody very important."

"He paid for that MRI machine they used on me yesterday."

The nurse pursed her lips. "Well! Aren't you nicely connected?" she mused. "Is he your fiancé?"

Tellie chuckled. "I'm only seventeen," she said.

The nurse looked puzzled. She checked Tellie's chart, made a face and then forced a smile. "Of course. Sorry."

Tellie wondered why she looked so confused. "Can I go home today?" she wondered.

"That depends on what Dr. Coltrain thinks," she replied. "He'll be in to see you when he makes rounds. Breakfast will be up shortly."

"Thanks," Tellie told her.

The nurse smiled, cast another curious and appreciative glance at J.B. and left.

Tellie stared at him with mixed emotions. He was a handsome man, she thought, but at least she was safe from all that masculine charm that he used to such good effect on women he liked. She was far too young to be threatened by J.B.'s sex appeal.

It was easy to see why he had women flocking around him. He had a dynamite physique, hard and lean and sexy, with long powerful legs and big hands. His face was rugged, but he had fine green eyes under a jutting brow and a mouth that was as hard and sensuous as any movie star's. But it wasn't just his looks that made him attractive. It was his voice, deep and faintly raspy, and the way he had of making a woman feel special. He had beautiful manners when he cared to display them, and a temper that made grown men look for cover. Tellie had rarely seen him fighting mad. Most of the time he had excellent self-control.

She frowned. Why did it sting to think of him losing his temper? He'd rarely lost it at Tellie, and even then it was for her own good. But something about her thoughts made her uneasy.

Just as she was focusing on that, J.B. opened his eyes and looked at her, and she stopped thinking. Her heart jumped. She couldn't imagine why. She was possessive of J.B., she idolized him, but she'd never really considered anything physical between them. Now, her body seemed to know things her mind didn't.

"How do you feel?" he asked quietly.

She blinked. "My head doesn't hurt as much," she said. She searched his eyes. "Why are you here? I'm all right."

He shrugged. "I was worried." He didn't add that he was also guilt-ridden about the reason for the wreck and her injury. His conscience had him on the rack. He couldn't sleep for worrying about her. That was new. It was disconcerting. He'd never let a woman get under his skin since his ill-fated romance of years past. Even an unexpected interlude with Tellie on the sofa in his office hadn't made a lot of difference in their turbulent relationship, especially when he realized that Tellie was sexually unawakened. He'd deliberately pushed her out of his life and kept her at arm's length—well, mostly, except for unavoidable lapses when he gave in to the passion riding him. That passion had drawn him to Bella in a moment of weakness.

Then Tellie had walked in on him with Bella, and his whole life had changed. He'd never felt such pain as when Grange had walked into the emergency room with an unconscious Tellie on a gurney. Nothing was ever going to be the same again. The only thing worse than seeing her in such a condition was dreading the day when her memory returned, because she was going to hate J.B.

"I'm going to be fine," she promised, smiling. "Do you think Dr. Coltrain will let me go home today?"

"I'll ask him," he said, sitting up straighter. "Nell's getting a room ready for you. While Marge and the girls are away, you'll stay with Nell and me."

"I wish Marge was here," she said involuntarily.

He sighed. Marge was improving, too, but she was worried about Tellie. Dawn had let it slip that she'd been in a wreck, but J.B. had assured her that Tellie was going to be fine. There was this little problem with her memory, of course, and she'd have to stay at the house with him until it came back.

Marge was reassured, but still concerned. He knew that she'd sensed something was wrong between her brother and Tellie, but she couldn't put it into words. He wasn't about to enlighten her. He had enough on his plate.

"I'll be in the way there," she protested.

"You won't," he replied. "Nell will be glad of the company."

She studied her hands on the sheet. "There's something that bothers me, J.B.," she said without looking at him.

"What?"

She hesitated. "What was I doing at your house, at night, in the rain?"

He sat very still. He hadn't considered that the question would arise so soon. He wasn't sure how to answer it, to protect her from painful memories.

She looked up and met his turbulent green eyes. "You were mad at me, weren't you?"

His heart seemed to stop, then start again. "We had an argument," he began slowly.

She nodded. "I thought so. But I can't remember what it was about."

"Time enough for that when you're back on your feet," he said, rising up from the chair. "Don't borrow trouble. Just get well."

So there was something! She wished she could grasp what it was. J.B. was acting very oddly.

She looked up at him. "You leaving?" she asked.

He nodded. "I've got to get the boys started moving the bulls to summer pasture."

"Not on roundup?"

"Roundup's in March," he said easily.

"Oh." She frowned. It wasn't March. She knew it wasn't. "Is it March?"

He ignored that. "I'll talk to Coltrain on my way out," he said.

"But it's not time for rounds…"

"I met him coming in. He had an emergency surgery. I expect he's through by now," he replied.

"J.B., who is that man Grange?" she asked abruptly. "And why did you let me go out with him? He said he's twenty-seven, and I'm just seventeen. You had a hissy fit when I tried to go hiking with Billy Johns."

He looked indignant. "I don't have hissy fits," he said shortly.

"Well, you raged at me, anyway," she corrected. "Why are you letting me see Grange?"

His teeth set. "You're full of questions this morning."

"Answer a few of them," she invited.

"Later," he said, deliberately checking his watch. "I have to get to work. Want me to bring you anything?"

"A nail file and a ladder," she said with resignation. "Just get me out of here."

"The minute you're fit to leave," he promised. He smiled faintly. "Stay put until I get back."

"If I must," she sighed.

He was gone and she was left to eat breakfast and while away the next few hours until Dr. Coltrain showed up.

He examined Tellie and pronounced her fit to leave the hospital.

"But you still need to take it easy for a week or two," he told her. "Stay out of crowds, stick to J.B.'s house. No parties, no job, nothing."

She frowned. "I thought it was just a mild concussion," she argued.

"It is." He didn't quite meet her eyes. "We're just not taking chances. You need lots of rest."

She sighed. "Okay, if you say so. Can I go horseback riding, can I swim…?"

"Sure. Just don't leave J.B.'s ranch to do them."

She smiled. "What's going on, Dr. Coltrain?"

He leaned forward. "It's a secret," he told her. "Bear with me. Okay?"

She laughed. "Okay. When do I get to know the secret?"

"All in good time," he added, as inspiration struck him. "Keep an eye on J.B. for me."

Her eyebrows arched. "Is something wrong with him...?" she asked worriedly.

"Nothing specific. Just watch him."

She shook her head. "Okay. If you say so."

"Good girl." He patted her shoulder and left, congratulating himself on the inspiration. While she was focused on J.B., she wouldn't be preoccupied with her own health. Far better if she licked the amnesia all by herself. He didn't want her shocked with the truth of her condition.

J.B.'s house was bigger than Tellie remembered. Nell met them at the door, all smiles and welcome.

"It's so good to have you back," Nell said, hugging the younger woman. "I've got a nice room all ready for you."

"Don't think you're going to get to wait on me," Tellie informed her with a grin. "I'm not an invalid."

"You have a concussion," Nell corrected, and the smile faded. "It can be very dangerous. I remember a cowboy who worked here..."

"Remember us something to eat, instead," J.B. interrupted her, with a meaningful look.

"Oh. Of course." She glared at J.B. "You had a call while you were out. I wrote the information on the pad on your desk."

He read through the lines and assumed it was from Bella. "I'll take care of it."

"Who's bringing Tellie's suitcase?" Nell asked.

J.B. stood still. "What suitcase?"

"I'll have to go over to Marge's and get my things," Tellie began.

"I'll go—!"

"I can do that," J.B. interrupted Nell. "You look after Tellie."

"When haven't I?" Nell wanted to know belligerently.

"You two need to stop arguing, or I'm going to go sit on the front porch," Tellie told both of them.

They glared at each other. J.B. shrugged and went into his den. Tellie's eyes followed him past the big sofa. The sofa… She frowned. Something about that sofa made her uneasy.

"What's wrong?" Nell prompted.

Tellie put a hand to her forehead and laughed faintly. "I don't know. I looked at the sofa and felt funny."

"Let's go right up and get you settled," Nell said abruptly, taking Tellie by the arm. "Then I'll see about some lunch."

It was almost as if Nell knew something about the sofa, too, but that would be ridiculous, Tellie told herself. She was getting mental.

She'd wanted to watch television, but there wasn't one in the bedroom. Nell told her that there was a problem with the satellite dish and it wasn't working. Odd, Tellie thought, it was almost as if they were trying to keep her from watching the news.

She had to stay in bed, because Nell insisted. Just after she had supper on a tray, J.B. walked in, worn and dusty, still in his working clothes.

Tellie was propped up in bed in pink-striped pajamas that made her look oddly vulnerable.

"How's it going?" he asked.

"I'm okay. Why is the satellite not working?" she added. "I can't watch the Weather Channel."

His eyebrows arched. "Why do you want to?"

"You said it was March, but Nell says it's May," she said. "That's tornado season."

"So it is."

She glowered at him. "Grange said it was March and Marge and the girls were away on Spring Break."

He pursed his lips.

"I know better, so don't bother trying to lie," she told him firmly. "If it's May, where are they?"

He leaned against the doorjamb. "They're around, but you can't see them just yet. Nothing's wrong."

"That's not true, J.B.," she said flatly.

He laughed mirthlessly and twirled his hat through his fingers. "No use trying to fool you, is it? Okay, the concussion did something to your head. You're a little fuzzy about things. We're supposed to let your mind clear without any help."

She frowned. "What's fuzzy about it?"

He jerked away from the door. "Not tonight. I'm going to clean up, then I've got…someplace to go," he amended.

"A date," she translated, grinning.

There was faint jealousy in her expression, but she was hiding it very well. He felt uncomfortable. He was taking Bella out, and here was Tellie, badly injured on his account and hurting.

"I could postpone it," he began guiltily.

"Whatever for?" she exclaimed.

His eyebrows arched. "Excuse me?"

"I'm seventeen," she pointed out. "Even if I were crazy about you, it's obvious that you're far too old for me."

He felt odd inside. He studied her curiously. "Am I?"

"I still don't understand why you're letting Grange date me," she mused. "He's twenty-seven."

"Is he?" He considered that. Grange was seven years his junior, closer to Tellie's own age than he was. That stung.

"You're hedging, J.B.," she accused.

He checked his watch. "Maybe so. I've got to go. Nell will be here if you need anything."

"I won't."

He turned to go, hesitated, and looked back at her, brooding. If she tried the television sets, she'd discover that they all worked. "Don't wander around the house."

She gaped at him. "Why would I want to?"

"Just don't. I'll see you tomorrow."

She watched him go, curious about his odd behavior.

Later, she tried to pump Nell for information, but it was like talking to a wall. "You and J.B. are stonewalling me," she accused.

Nell smiled. "For a good cause. Just relax and enjoy being here, for the time that's left." She picked up the empty iced-tea glass on the bedside table, looking around the room. "Odd that J.B. would put you in here," she said, thinking aloud.

"Is it? Why?"

"It was his grandmother's room," she said with a smile. "She was a wonderful old lady. J.B. adored her. She'd been an actress in Hollywood in her youth. She could tell some stories!"

"Does he talk about her?" Tellie wondered.

"Almost never. She died in a tornado." She nodded, at Tellie's astonished look. "That's right, one of the worst in south Texas history hit here back in the eighties," she recalled. "It lifted the barn off its foundations and twisted it. His grandmother's favorite horse was trapped there, and old Mrs. Hammock put on a raincoat and rushed out to try to save it. Nobody saw her go. The tornado picked her up and put her in the top of an oak tree, dead. They had to get a truck with a cherry picker to get her down, afterward," Nell said softly. "J.B. was watching. He hates tornadoes to this day. It's why we have elaborate storm shelters here and in the bunkhouse, and even under the barn."

"That's why he looked funny, when I mentioned liking to watch the Weather Channel," she said slowly.

"He watches it religiously in the spring and summer," Nell confided. "And he has weather alert systems in the same places he has the shelters. All his men have cell phones with alert capability. He's something of a fanatic about safety."

"Have I ever been in a tornado?" she asked Nell.

Nell looked surprised. "Why do you ask?"

"J.B. said I'm fuzzy about the past," she replied. "I gather that I've lost some memories, is that it?"

Nell came and sat down in the chair beside the bed. "Yes. You have."

"And the doctor doesn't want me remembering too soon?"

"He thinks it's better if you remember all on your own," Nell said. "So we're conspiring to keep you in the dark, so to speak," she added with a gentle smile.

Tellie frowned. "I wish I could remember what I've forgotten."

Nell burst out laughing. "Don't rush it. When you remember, we'll leave together."

Tellie gaped at her. "You're quitting? But you've been here forever!"

"I've been here too long," Nell said curtly, rising. "There are other bosses who don't yell and threaten people."

"You yell and threaten back," Tellie reminded her.

"Remembered that, did you?" she teased.

"Yes. So why are you leaving him?"

"Let's just say that I don't like his methods," she replied. "And that's all you're getting out of me. I'll be in the kitchen. Just use the intercom if you need me, okay?"

"Okay. Thanks, Nell."

Nell smiled at her. "I like having you here."

"Who's he dating this week?" Tellie called after her.

"Another stacked blonde, of course," came the dry reply. "She has the IQ of a lettuce leaf."

Tellie chuckled. "Obviously he doesn't like competition from mere women."

"Someday he'll come a cropper," she said. "I hope I live to see the day."

Tellie watched her close the door with faint misgivings. J.B. did like variety, she seemed to know that. But there was something about the reference, about a blond woman, that unsettled her. Why had she and J.B. argued? She wished she could remember.

Her light was still on when he came home. She was reading a particularly interesting book that she'd found in the bookcase, an autobiography by Libbie Custer, the woman who'd married General George Custer of Civil War and Little Bighorn fame. It was a tale of courage in the face of danger, unexpectedly riveting. Mrs. Custer, it seemed, had actually gone with her husband to the battlefield during the Civil War. Tellie had never read of women doing that. Mrs. Custer was something of a renegade for her oppressed generation, a daring and intelligent woman with a keen wit. She liked her.

J.B. opened the door to find her propped up in bed on her pillows with the book resting against her upraised knees under the covers.

"What are you doing up at this hour?" he asked sternly.

She glanced at him, still halfway in the book she was reading. He looked elegant in a dinner jacket and black tie, she thought, although the tie was in his hand and the shirt was open at the throat, over a pelt of dark hair. She frowned. Why did the sight of his bare chest make her heart race?

"I found this book on the shelf and couldn't put it down," she said.

He moved to the bed, stuck the tie in his pocket and sat down beside her. He took the book in a big, lean hand and checked the title. He gave it back, smiling. "Libbie Custer was one of my grandmother's heroines. She actually met her once, when she gave a speech in New York while my grandmother was visiting relatives there as a child. She said that Mrs. Custer was a wonderful speaker. She lived into her nineties."

"She wrote a very interesting book," Tellie said.

"There are three of them altogether," he told her. "I believe you'll find the other two on the shelf as well, along with several biographies of the Colonel and the one book that he wrote."

"General Custer," she corrected.

He grinned. "That was a brevet promotion, given during the Civil War for outstanding courage under fire. His actual military rank was Colonel, at the time he died."

"You read about him, too?" she asked.

He nodded. "These were some of the first books I was exposed to as a child. My mother was big on reading skills," he said coolly. "Her picks were nonfiction, mostly chemistry and physics. Grandmother's were more palatable."

She noted the play of emotions on his lean, hard face. "Your mother was a scientist," she said suddenly, and wondered where the memory came from.

"Yes." He stared at her intently. "A research chemist. She died when we were young."

"You didn't like her very much, did you?"

"I hated her," he said flatly. "She made my grandmother miserable, making fun of her reading tastes, the way she dressed, her skills as a homemaker. She demeaned her."

"Was your grandmother your mother's mother?"

He shook his head. "My father's mother. In her day, she was an elegant horsewoman. She won trophies. And she was an actress before she married. But that, to my mother's mind, was fluff. She only admired women with Mensa-level IQs and science degrees."

"What about your father, couldn't he stop her from torment-ing the old lady?"

He scoffed. "He was never here. He was too involved with making money to pay much attention to what went on around the house."

Her eyes narrowed. "You must have had an interesting childhood."

He cocked an eyebrow. "There's a Chinese curse—'may you live in interesting times.' That would have been appropriate for it."

She didn't quite know what to say. He looked so alone. "Nell said she died in a tornado. Your grandmother, I mean."

He nodded. "She was trying to save her horse. She'd had him for twenty-five years, ridden him in competition. She loved him more than any other thing here, except maybe me." He grimaced. "I'll never forget watching them bring her down from the treetop. She looked like a broken doll." His eyes closed briefly. "I don't have much luck with women, when it comes to love."

That was a curious thing to say. She felt odd as he said it, as if she knew something more about that, but couldn't quite call it up.

"I guess life is a connected series of hard knocks," she mused.

He glanced at her. "Your own life hasn't been any bed of roses," he commented. "You lost your father when you were born, and your grandfather and your mother only six months apart."

"Did I?" she wondered.

He cursed under his breath. "I shouldn't have said that."

"It didn't trigger any memories," she assured him, managing a smile. "I'm pretty blank about recent events. Well, I remember I'm graduating," she amended, "and that I borrowed Marge's car to drive to your house…" She hesitated. "Marge's car…"

"Stop trying to force it," he said, tapping her knee with a hard finger. "Your memory will come back when it's ready to."

"Nell said she was quitting. Did you have a row with her?"

"Did she say that I had?" he asked warily.

"She didn't say much of anything, J.B.," she muttered. "I can't get a straight answer out of anybody, even that nice man who was in the emergency room with me." She hesitated. "Has he come by to see me?"

He shifted restlessly. "Why ask me?" he wondered, but he wouldn't meet her eyes.

"He did come to see me!" she exclaimed, seeing the truth in the ruddy color that ran along his high cheekbones. "He came, and you wouldn't let him in!"

Eight

J.B. not only looked angry, he looked frustrated. "Coltrain said you didn't need visitors for two or three days, at least," he said firmly.

She was still staring at him, with wide pale green eyes. "But why not? Grange won't tell me anything. Every time I asked a question, he pretended to be deaf." Her eyes narrowed. "Just like you, J.B.," she added.

He patted her knee. "We're all trying to spare you any unnecessary pain," he said.

"So you're admitting that it would be painful if I remembered why you and I argued," she said.

He glared. "Life is mostly painful," he pointed out. "You and I have had disagreements before."

"Have we? And you seem like a man with such a sunny, even disposition," she said innocently.

"Ha!" came an unexpected comment from the hall.

They both turned to the doorway, and there stood Nell, in a housecoat with her hair in curlers, glaring at both of them.

"I have an even disposition," he argued.

"Evenly bad," Nell agreed. "She should be asleep," she said, nodding at Tellie.

He got to his feet. "So she should." He took the book away from Tellie and put it on the bedside table. "Go to sleep."

"Can I get you anything before I go to bed, Tellie?" Nell asked.

"No, but thanks."

J.B. pulled the pillows out from under her back and eased her down on the bed. He pulled up the covers, studied her amusedly and suddenly bent and brushed his hard mouth over her forehead. "Sleep tight, little bit." He turned off the lamp.

"I don't need tucking in," she said.

"It never hurts," he mused. He passed Nell. "You going to stand there all night? She needs her sleep."

"You're the one who was keeping her awake!" Nell muttered.

"I was not…!"

Their voices, harsh and curt, came through the closed door after he'd pulled it shut. Tellie sighed and closed her eyes. What an odd pair.

The next morning, there was heavy rain and lightning. Thunder shook the house. Alarmed, Tellie turned on the weather alert console next to her bed and listened to the forecast. There was a tornado watch for Jacobs County, among others in south Texas.

She grimaced, remembering tornadoes in the past. She'd seen one go through when she was a little girl. It hadn't touched down near their house, but she could never forget the color of the clouds that contained it. They were a neon-green, like slimy pond algae, enclosed in thick gray swirls. She got to her feet, a little shakily, and went to the window to look out.

The clouds were dark and thick and lightning struck down out of them so unexpectedly, and violently, that she jumped.

"Get away from that window!" J.B. snapped from the doorway.

She turned, her heart racing from the double impact of the storm and his temper. "I was just looking," she protested.

He closed the door behind him, striding toward her with single-minded determination. He swung her up in his powerful arms and carried her back to bed.

"Lightning strikes the highest point. There are no trees taller than the house. Get the point?" he asked.

She clung to his strong neck, savoring his strength. "I get it."

He eased her down on the pillow, his green eyes staring straight into hers as he rested his hands beside her head on the bed. "How's your head?"

"Still there," she mused. "It does throb a bit."

"No wonder," he said. He searched her eyes for so long that her heart raced. He looked down at her pajama jacket and his teeth clenched. She looked down, too, but she didn't see anything that would make him frown.

"What's wrong?" she asked.

He drew in a long breath. "You're still a child, Tellie," he said, more for his own benefit than for hers. He stood up. "Ready for breakfast?"

She frowned. "Why did you say that?"

He stuck his hands in his pockets and went to the window to look out.

"You'll get struck by lightning," she chided, throwing his own accusation back at him.

"I won't."

His back was arrow straight. She stared at it longingly. It had been sweet to lie in his arms while he carried her. She felt an odd stirring deep in her belly.

"You really hate storms, don't you?" she said.

"Most people do, if they've ever lived through one."

She remembered what he'd told her about the grandmother he loved so much, and how she'd died in a tornado. "I've only seen one up close."

He turned toward her, his eyes watchful and quiet.

"What are you thinking?" she asked.

"I don't remember you going out on more than two dates the whole time you were in high school."

The reference to the past, luckily, went right over her head. She blinked. "I was always shy around boys," she confessed. "And none of them really appealed to me. Especially not the jocks. I hate sports."

He laughed softly. "Was that why?"

She twisted the hem of the sheet between her fingers and stared at them. "You must have noticed at some point that I'm not overly brainy or especially beautiful."

He frowned. "What does that have to do with dating?"

"Everything, in high school," she reminded him curtly. "Besides all that, most boys these days want girls who don't mind giving out. I did. It got around after I poured a cup of hot chocolate all over Barry Cramer when he slid his hand under my skirt at a party."

"He did what?" he exclaimed, eyes flaming.

The rush to anger surprised her. He'd never shown any particular emotion about her infrequent dates.

"I told him that a hamburger and a movie didn't entitle him to that sort of perk."

"You should have told me," he said curtly. "I'd have decked him!"

Her cheeks colored faintly. "That would have got around, too, and I'd never have had another date."

He moved close to the bed and studied her like an insect on a pin. "I don't suppose you'd have encouraged a boy to touch you like that."

"Whatever for?" she asked curiously.

His jaw clenched, hard. "Tellie, don't you…feel anything… with boys?"

She cocked her head. "Like what?"

"Like an urge to kiss them, to let them touch you."

The color in her cheeks mushroomed. She could barely meet his eyes. "I don't…I don't feel that way."

"Ever?"

She shifted, frowning. "What's gotten into you, J.B.? I'm only seventeen. There's plenty of time for that kind of thing when I'm old enough to think about marriage."

His fist clenched in his pocket. Even at her real age, he'd never seen her get flustered around anything male, not even himself. The one time he'd kissed her with intent, on his own sofa, she'd given in at once, but she'd been reticent and shocked more than aroused. He was beginning to think that she'd never been aroused in her life; not even with him. It stung his pride, in one way, and made him hungry in another. It disturbed him that he couldn't make Tellie want him. God knew, most other women did.

"Is that what you meant, when you called me a kid earlier?" she asked seriously.

He moved to the foot of the bed, with his hands still shoved deep in his pockets, and stared at her. "Yes. That's what I meant. You're completely unawakened. In this modern day and age, it's almost unthinkable for a woman your age to know so little about men."

"Well, gee whiz, I guess I'd better rush right out there and get myself a prescription for the pill and get busy, huh?" she asked rakishly. "Heaven forbid that I should be a throwback to a more conservative age, especially in this house! Didn't you write the book on sexual liberation?"

He felt uncomfortable. "Running with the crowd is the coward's way out. You have to have the courage of your convictions."

"You've just told me to forget them and follow the example of the Romans."

He glowered. "I did not!"

She threw up her hands. "Then why are you complaining?"

"I wasn't complaining!"

"You don't have to yell at me," she muttered. "I'm sick."

"I think I'm going to be," he said under his breath.

"You sure have changed since I was in the wreck," she murmured, staring at him curiously. "I never thought I'd see the day when you'd advise me to go out and get experienced with men. I don't even know any men." She frowned. "Well, that's not completely true. I know Grange." Her eyes brightened. "Maybe I can ask him to give me some pointers. He looks like he's been around!"

J.B. looked more and more like the storm outside. He moved toward the bed and sat down beside her, leaning down with his hands on either side of her face on the pillow. "You don't need lessons from Grange," he said through his teeth. "When you're ready to learn," he added on a deep, husky breath, "I'll teach you."

Ripples of pleasure ran up and down her nerves, leaving chill bumps of excitement all over her arms. Her breath caught at the thought of J.B.'s hard, beautiful mouth on her lips.

His eyes went down to her pajama jacket, and this time they lingered. For an instant, he looked shocked. Then his eyes began to glitter and he smiled, very slowly.

She looked down again, too, but she couldn't see anything unusual. Well, her nipples were tight and hard, and a little uncomfortable. That was because of her sudden chill. Wasn't it?

Her eyes met his again, with a faint question in them.

"You don't even understand this, do you?" he asked, and suddenly, without warning, he drew the tip of his forefinger right over one distended nipple with the faintest soft brushing motion.

She gasped out loud and her body arched. She looked, and was, shocked out of her mind.

J.B.'s green eyes darkened with sudden hunger. His gaze fell to her parted, full lips, to the pulse throbbing in the hollow of her throat. He ached to open her pajama top and put his mouth right on her breast. Unthinkable pleasures were burning in the back of his mind.

Tellie was frightened, both of what was happening to her body, and of letting him know how vulnerable she was. There was something vaguely unsettling about the way he was looking at her. It brought back a twinge of memory, of J.B. mocking her because she was weak toward him…

She brought up her arms and crossed them over her breasts.

"Spoilsport," he murmured, meeting her shocked eyes.

She fought to breathe normally. "J. B. Hammock, I'm seventeen years old!" she burst out.

He started to contradict her and realized at once that he didn't dare. He scowled and got to his feet abruptly. What the hell was he thinking?

He ran a hand over his hair and turned away. "I've got to go to town and see a Realtor about a parcel of land that's just come up for sale," he said in a strangely thick tone. "It adjoins my north pasture. I'll send Nell up with breakfast."

"Yes, that would be…that would be nice."

He glanced back at her from the door. He felt frustrated and guilty. But behind all that, he was elated. Tellie was vulnerable to him, and not just in the girlish way she had been for the past few years. She was vulnerable as a woman. It was the first time her body had reacted to his touch in that particular way.

He should have been ashamed of himself. He wasn't. His eyes slid over her body in the pajamas as if she belonged to him already. He couldn't hide the pride of possession that he felt.

It made Tellie shake inside. Surely he wasn't thinking…?

"Don't beat yourself to death over it," he said. "We're all human, Tellie. Even me. See you later."

He went out quickly and closed the door behind him, before

his aching body could provoke him into even worse indiscretions than he'd already committed.

Nell brought breakfast and stared worriedly at Tellie's high color. "You're not having a relapse, are you?" she asked, worried.

Tellie wished she could confide in the housekeeper, or in someone. But she had no close friends, and she couldn't even have told Marge. She couldn't talk to Marge about her brother!

"Nothing's wrong, honest," Tellie said. "I went to look out the window, and a big flash of lightning almost made me jump out of my skin. I'm still reeling."

Nell's face relaxed. "Is that all?" She smiled. "I don't mind storms, but J.B. is always uneasy. Don't forget his grandmother died in a tornado outbreak."

"He told me," she said.

"Did he, now?" Nell exclaimed. "He doesn't talk about the old lady much."

Tellie nodded. "He doesn't talk about much of anything personal," she agreed. She frowned. "I wonder if he confides in his fashion dolls?"

Nell didn't get the point at first, but when she did, she burst out laughing. "That was mean, Tellie."

Tellie just grinned. She was going to forget what J.B. had done in those few tempestuous seconds. She was certain that he'd regretted it.

Sure enough, he didn't come in to see her at all the rest of the day. Next morning, he went out without a word.

About lunchtime, Grange showed up. Since J.B. wasn't there to keep him out, Nell escorted him up to Tellie's room with a conspiratorial grin.

"Company," Nell announced. "He can stay for lunch. I'll bring up a double tray." She went out, but left the door open.

Grange moved toward the bed with his wide-brimmed hat in his hand. He'd had a haircut and a close shave. He smelled nice, very masculine. His dark eyes twinkled as he studied Tellie in her pink pajamas.

She felt self-conscious and pulled the sheet up higher.

He laughed. "Sorry."

She shrugged. "I'm not used to men seeing me in my nightclothes," she told him. It wasn't totally true. He didn't know, and J.B. seemed to constantly forget, that she'd been almost assaulted by a boy in her early teens. It hadn't left immense scars, but she still felt uneasy about her body. She wasn't comfortable with men. She wondered if she should admit that to J.B. It might soften his provocative attitude toward her.

"I'll try not to stare," Grange promised, smiling as he sat down in the chair beside her bed. "How are you feeling?"

"Much better," she said. "I wanted to get up, but Nell won't let me."

"Concussion is tricky," he replied, and he didn't smile. "The first few days are chancy. Better you stay put in bed, just for the time being."

She smiled at him. "I'll bet you've seen your share of injuries, being in the military."

He nodded. "Concussion isn't all that uncommon in war. I've seen some nasty head injuries that looked pretty innocent at first. Better safe than sorry."

"I hate being confined," she confessed. "I want to get out and do things, but Dr. Coltrain said I couldn't. Nell and J.B. are worse than jailers," she added.

He chuckled. "Nell's a character." He hesitated. "Did you know there's a chef in the kitchen, complete with tall white hat and French accent?"

She nodded. "That's Albert," she replied. "He's been here for the past ten years. J.B. likes continental cuisine."

"He seems to be intimidated by Nell," he observed.

"He probably is. Gossip is that when Albert came here, Nell was in possession of the kitchen and unwilling to turn it over to a foreigner. They say," she added in a soft, conspiratorial tone, "that she chased him into the living room with a rolling pin when he refused to make dumplings her way. It took a pay raise and a color television for his room to keep him here. J.B. and Nell had a real falling out about that, and she threatened to quit. She got a raise, too." She laughed shortly. She'd remembered something from the past! Surely the rest couldn't be far behind now.

Grange chuckled at what she'd told him about Nell. "She seems formidable enough."

"She is. She and J.B. argue most of the time, but it's usually in a good-natured way."

He put his hat on the floor beside his chair and raked a hand through his neatly trimmed straight dark hair. "When they let you out of here, we'll go take in a new science-fiction movie. How about that?"

She smiled. "Sounds like fun." She was curious about him. He didn't seem the sort of man to be vulnerable to women, but it was apparent that he liked Tellie. "Do you have family here in Jacobsville?" she asked in all innocence.

His face hardened. His dark eyes narrowed. "No."

She frowned. She'd struck a nerve. "I'm sorry, is there something else I don't remember—?"

"There's a lot," he cut her off, but gently. "You're bound to wander into a few thickets before you find the right path. Don't worry about it."

She drew in a long breath. "I feel like I'm walking around in a fog. Everybody's hiding things from me."

"It's necessary. Just for a week or so," he promised.

"You know about me, don't you? Can't you tell me?"

He held up a hand and laughed. "I'd just as soon not get on the wrong side of Hammock while you're living under his roof. I'd lose visiting privileges. I may lose them anyway, if Nell spills the beans that I've been here while he was out."

"Doesn't he like you?"

"He doesn't like most people," he agreed. "Especially me, at the moment."

"What did you do to him?"

"It's a long story, and it doesn't concern you right now," he said quietly.

She flushed. His voice had been very curt.

"Don't look like that," he said, feeling guilty "I don't want to hurt you. J.B. and I have an unfortunate history, that's all."

She blinked. "It sounds unpleasant."

"It was," he confessed. "But it happened a long time ago. Right now, our only concern is to get you well again."

Footsteps sounded on the staircase and a minute later, Nell walked in with a tray holding two plates, two glasses of iced tea and a vase full of yellow roses.

"Never thought I'd get up the stairs with everything intact," she laughed as Grange got up and took the tray from her, setting it down gently on the mahogany side table by the bed.

"The roses," Tellie exclaimed. "They're beautiful!"

"Glad you like them," Grange said easily, and with a smile. "We do live in Texas, after all."

"'The Yellow Rose of Texas,'" she recalled the song. She reached over and plucked one of the stems out of the vase to smell it. There was a delicate, sweet scent. "I don't think I've ever had a bouquet of flowers in my life," she added, confused.

"You haven't," Nell replied for her. She sounded irritated. "Nice of Grange to remember that sick people usually like flowers."

She smiled at him. "Wasn't it?" she laughed. "I'll enjoy them. Thank you."

"My pleasure," he replied, and his voice was soft.

Nell stuck a plate in his hands and then put Tellie's on her lap. "Eat, before the bread molds," she told them. "That's homemade chicken salad, and I put up those dill pickles myself last summer."

"Looks delicious," Grange said. "You didn't have to do this, Nell."

"I enjoy making a few things on my own," she said. She grimaced. "I had to lock Albert in the closet, of course. His idea of a sandwich involves shrimp and sauce and a lettuce leaf on a single piece of toasted rye bread." She looked disgusted.

"That's not my idea of one," Grange had to admit.

"This is really good," Tellie exclaimed after she bit into her sandwich.

"Yes, it is," Grange seconded. "I didn't have time for breakfast this morning."

"Enjoy," Nell said, smiling. "I'll be back up for the tray later."

They both nodded, too involved with chewing to answer.

Grange entertained her with stories from his childhood. She loved the one about the cowboy, notorious for his incredible nicotine habit, who drove his employer's Land Rover out into the desert on a drunken joyride, forgetting to take along a shovel or bottled water or even a flashlight. He ran out of gas halfway back and when they found him the next morning, almost dead of dehydration, the first thing he asked for was a cigarette.

"What happened to him?" she asked, laughing.

"After he got over the experience, the boss put him on permanent barn duty, cleaning out the horse stalls. The cowboy couldn't get a job anywhere else locally because of that smoking habit, so he was pretty much stuck."

"He couldn't quit?"

"He wouldn't quit," he elaborated. "Then he met this waitress and fell head over heels for her. He quit smoking, stopped drinking and married her. He owns a ranch of his own now and they've got two kids." His dark eyes twinkled. "Just goes to show that the love of a good woman can save a bad man."

She pursed her lips. "I'll keep that in mind."

He laughed. "I'm not a bad man," he pointed out. "I just have a few rough edges and a problem with authority figures."

"Is that why you don't get along with J.B.?"

He shook his head. "That's because we're too much alike in temperament," he said. He checked his watch. "I've got to run," he said, swooping up his hat as he got to his feet. "Can't afford to tick off my boss!"

"Will you come again?" she asked.

"The minute the coast is clear," he promised, laughing. "If Nell doesn't sell us out."

"She won't. She's furious at J.B. I don't know why, nobody tells me anything, but I overheard her say that she'd quit and had to come back to take care of me. Apparently she and J.B. had a major blowup before I got hurt. I wish I knew why."

"One of these days, I'm sure you'll find out. Keep getting better."

"I'll do my best. Thanks again. For the roses, and for coming to see me."

"I enjoyed it. Thanks for lunch."

She grinned. "I'll cook next time."

"Something to look forward to," he teased, winking at her.

J.B. came in late. Apparently he'd been out with whichever girlfriend he was dating, because he was dressed up and a faint hint of perfume clung to his shirt as he sat down in the chair beside Tellie's bed. But he looked more worried than weary, and he wasn't smiling.

She eyed him warily. "Is something wrong?" she asked.

He leaned back in the chair, one long leg crossed over the other. She noted how shiny his hand-tooled black boots were, how well his slacks fit those powerful legs. She shook herself mentally. She didn't need to notice such things about him.

"Nothing much," he said. Actually he was worried about Marge. She was in the early stages of treatment for high blood pressure, and she'd had a bad dizzy spell this afternoon. The girls had called him at work, and he'd gone right over. He'd phoned Coltrain, only to be reassured that some dizziness was most likely a side effect of the drug. She was having a hard time coping, and she missed Tellie, as well as being worried about her health. J.B. had assured Marge that Tellie was going to be fine, but his sister wanted to see Tellie. He couldn't manage that. Not yet.

He drew in a long breath, wondering how to avoid the subject. That was when he looked at her bedside table carelessly and saw the huge bouquet of yellow roses. His green eyes began to glitter as he stared at her.

"And just where," he asked with soft fury, "did you get a bouquet of roses?"

Nine

"They were a present," Tellie said quickly.

"Were they?" he asked curtly. "From whom?"

She didn't want to say it. There was going to be a terrible explosion when she admitted that she'd had a visitor. It didn't take mind-reading skills to realize that J.B. didn't like Grange.

She swallowed. "Grange brought them to me."

The green eyes were really glittering now. "When?"

"He stopped by on his lunch hour," she said. She glared up at him. "Listen, there's nothing wrong with having company when you're sick!"

"You're in your damned pajamas!" he shot back.

"So?" she asked belligerently. "You're looking at me in them, aren't you?"

"I don't count."

"Oh. I see." She didn't, but it was best not to argue with a madman, which is how he looked at the moment.

His lips made a thin line. "I'm family."

She might have believed that before yesterday, she thought, when he'd touched her so intimately.

The memory colored her cheeks. He saw it, and a slow, possessive smile tugged up his firm, chiseled lips. That made the blush worse.

"You don't think of me as family?" he asked softly.

She wanted to dive under the covers. It wasn't fair that he could reduce her to this sort of mindless hunger.

He leaned over her, the anger gone, replaced by open curiosity and something else, less definable.

His fingers speared through her dark hair, holding her head inches from the pillow behind her. His chest rose and fell quickly, like her own. His free hand went to her soft mouth and traced lazily around the upper lip, and then the lower one, with a sensuality that made her feel extremely odd.

"I'm…seventeen," she choked, grasping for a way to save herself.

His dark green gaze fell to her parted lips. "You're not," he said huskily, and the hand in her hair contracted. "It can't hurt for you to know your real age. You're almost twenty-two. Fair game," he added under his breath, and all at once his hard, sensuous mouth came down on her lips with firm purpose.

She gasped in surprise, and her hand went to his chest. That was a mistake, because it was unbuttoned in front and her fingers were enmeshed in thick, curling dark hair that covered the powerful muscles.

His head lifted, as if the contact affected him. His eyes narrowed. His heart, under her fingertips, beat strongly and a little fast.

"You shouldn't…" she began, frightened of what was happening to her.

"I've waited a long time for this," he said enigmatically. He bent to her mouth again. "There's nothing to be afraid of, Tellie," he whispered into her lips. "Nothing at all…"

The pressure increased little by little. Her fingers dug into his chest as odd sensations worked themselves down her body, and she shivered.

He smiled against her parted lips. "It's about time," he murmured, and his mouth grew insistent.

She felt his body slowly move closer, so that they were lying breast to breast on the soft mattress. One lean hand slid under the pajama top, against her rib cage, warm and teasing. She should grab his wrist and stop him, her mind was saying, because this wasn't right. He was a notorious womanizer and she was like his ward. She was far too young to be exposed to such experienced ardor. She was...but he'd said she was almost twenty-two years old. Why hadn't she remembered her age?

His hand contracted in her soft hair. "Stop thinking," he bit off against her mouth. "Kiss me, Tellie," he breathed, and his hand suddenly moved up and cupped her soft, firm breast. His head lifted, to watch her stunned, delighted reaction.

For an instant, she stiffened. But then his thumb rubbed tenderly over the swollen nipple, and a ripple of ardent desire raged in her veins. She drew in a shivery, shaking breath. The pressure increased, just enough to be arousing. She arched involuntarily, and moaned.

"Yes," he said, as though she'd spoken.

His hand swallowed her whole, and his mouth moved gently onto her parted lips, teasing, exploring, demanding. All her defenses were down. There was no tomorrow. She had J.B. in her arms, wanting her. Whether it was wrong or not, she couldn't resist him. She'd never known that her body could experience anything so passionately satisfying. She felt swollen. She wanted to pull him closer. She wanted to touch him, as he was touching her. She wanted...everything!

Her arms slid up around his neck and she arched into the warm pressure of his hand on her body.

His mouth increased its pressure, until he broke open her mouth and his tongue moved inside, in slow, insistent thrusts that made her moan loudly. She'd never been kissed in such an intimate way. She'd never wanted to be. But this was delicious. It was the most delicious taste of a man she'd ever had. She wanted more.

He hadn't meant to let things get so far out of control, but he went under just as quickly as she did. His hand left her breast to flick open the buttons of her pajama jacket. She whispered something, but he didn't hear it. He was blind, deaf, dumb to anything except the taste and feel of her innocence.

He kissed her again, ardently, and while she followed his mouth, he stripped her out of the pajama top and opened the rest of the buttons over his broad chest. He gathered her hungrily to him, dragging his chest against hers so that the rasp of hair only accentuated the pleasure she was feeling.

When his lean, hard body moved over hers, she was beyond any sort of protest. Her long legs parted eagerly to admit the intimacy of his body. She shivered when she felt him against her. She hadn't realized how it would feel, when a man was aroused, although she'd read enough about it in her life. Other women were vocal about their own affairs, and Tellie had learned from listening to them talk. She'd been sure that she would never be vulnerable to a man like this, that she'd never be tempted to give in with no thought beyond satisfaction. What she was feeling now put the lie to her overconfidence. She was as helpless as any woman in love.

Even knowing that J.B. was involved more with his body than his mind didn't help her resist him. Whatever he wanted, he could have. She just didn't want him to stop. She was drowning in sensation, pulsating with the sweetest, sharpest hunger she'd ever known.

"I've waited so long, Tellie," he groaned into her mouth. His hand went under her hips and lifted her closer into a much more intimate position that made her shudder all over. "God, baby, I'm on fire!"

So was she, but she couldn't manage words. She arched up toward him, barely aware that he was looking down at her bare breasts. He bent and put his mouth on them, savoring their firm softness, their eager response to his ardor.

Her nails bit into his shoulders. She rocked with him, feeling the slow spiral of satisfaction that was just beginning, like a flash of light that obliterated reason, thought, hope. She only wanted him never to stop.

His lean hand went to the snap that held her pajama bottoms in place, just as loud footsteps sounded on the staircase, accompanied by muttering that was all too familiar.

J.B. lifted his head. He looked as shocked as Tellie felt. He looked down at her breasts and ruddy color flamed over his high cheekbones. Then he looked toward the hall and realized belatedly that the door was standing wide open.

With a furious curse, he moved away from her and got to his feet, slinging the cover over her only a minute before Nell walked in with a tray. Luckily for both of them, she was too concerned over not dumping milk and cookies all over the floor to notice how flushed they were.

J.B. had time to fasten his shirt. Tellie had the sheet up to her neck, covering the open pajama jacket she'd pulled on.

"Thought you might like a snack," Nell said, smiling as she put the tray down next to the vase of roses.

"I would. Thanks, Nell," Tellie said in an oddly husky tone.

J.B. kept his back to Nell as he went toward the door. "I've got a phone call to make. Sleep tight, Tellie."

"You, too, J.B.," she said, amazed at her acting ability, and his.

When he was gone, Nell moved the roses a little farther onto the table. "Aren't they beautiful, though?" she asked Tellie as she sniffed them. "Grange has good taste."

"Yes, he does," Tellie said, forcing a smile.

Nell glanced at her curiously. "You look very flushed. You're not running a fever, are you?" she asked worriedly.

Tellie bit her lower lip and tasted J.B. there. She looked at Nell innocently. "J.B. and I had words," she lied.

Nell frowned. "Over what?"

"The roses," Tellie replied. "He didn't like the idea that Grange was here."

Nell sighed, falling for the ruse. "I was afraid he wouldn't."

"Do you know why he dislikes him so much?" Tellie asked. "I mean, he agreed that I could go out with Grange, apparently. It seems odd that he wouldn't have stopped me."

"He couldn't," Nell said. "After all, you're of age…" She stopped and put her hand over her mouth, looking guilty.

"I'm almost twenty-two," Tellie said, avoiding Nell's gaze. "I…remembered."

"Well, that's progress!"

It wasn't, but Tellie wasn't about to admit to Nell that she'd had a heavy petting session with J.B. in her own bed and learned about her age that way. She could still hardly believe what had happened. If Nell hadn't walked up the staircase just at that moment… It didn't bear thinking about. What had she done? She knew J.B. was a womanizer. He didn't love women; she knew that even though she couldn't remember why. She'd given him liberties that he wasn't entitled to. Why?

"You look tired," Nell said. "Drink up that milk and eat those cookies. Leave the tray. I'll get it in the morning. Can I bring you anything else?"

A good psychiatrist, Tellie thought, but didn't dare say. She smiled. "No. Thanks a lot, Nell."

"You're very welcome. Sleep well."

She'd never sleep again, she imagined. "You, too."

The door closed behind her. Tellie sat up and started to rebutton her jacket. Her breasts had faint marks on them from J.B.'s insistent mouth. She looked at them and got aroused all over again. What was happening? She knew, she just knew, that J.B. had never touched her like that before. Why had he done it?

She lay awake long into the night, worrying the question.

* * *

The next morning, Nell told her that J.B. had suddenly had to fly to a meeting in Las Vegas, a cattlemen's seminar of some sort.

Tellie wasn't really surprised. Perhaps J.B. was a little embarrassed, as she was, about what they'd done together.

"He didn't take his girlfriend with him, either," Nell said. "That's so strange. He takes her everywhere else."

Tellie felt her heart stop beating. "His girlfriend?" she prompted.

"Sorry. I keep forgetting that your memory's limping. Bella," she added. "She's a beauty contestant. J.B.'s been dating her for several weeks."

Tellie stared at her hands. "Is he serious about her?"

"He's never serious about women," Nell replied. "But that doesn't mean he won't have them around. Bella travels with him, mostly, and she spends the occasional weekend in the guest room."

"This room?" Tellie asked, horrified, looking around her.

"No, of course not," Nell said, not noticing Tellie's look of horror. "She stays in that frilly pink room that we usually put women guests in. Looks like a fashion-doll box inside," she added with a chuckle. "You'd be as out of place there as I would."

The implication made her uneasy. J.B. was intimate with the beauty contestant, if she was spending weekends with him. The pain rippled down her spine as she considered how easily she'd given in to him the night before. He was used to women falling all over him, wasn't he? And Tellie wasn't immune. She wasn't even respected, or he'd never have touched her when she was a guest in his house. The more she thought about it, the angrier she got. He was involved with another woman, and making passes at Tellie. What was wrong with him?

On the other hand, what was wrong with her? She only wished she knew.

* * *

She got out of bed and started helping Nell around the house, despite her protests.

"I can't stay in bed my whole life, Nell," Tellie argued. "I'll never get better that way."

"I suppose not," the older woman admitted. "But you do have to take it easy."

"I will." She pushed the lightweight electric broom into the living room. The sofa caught her attention again, as it had when she'd come home from the hospital. She moved to its back and ran her hand over the smooth cloth fabric, frowning. Why did this sofa make her uneasy? What had happened in this room in the past that upset her?

She turned to Nell. "What did J.B. and I argue about?" she asked.

Nell stopped dead and stared. She was obviously hesitating while she tried to find an answer that would be safe.

"Was it over a woman?" Tellie persisted.

Nell didn't reply, but she flushed.

So that was it, Tellie thought. She must have been jealous of the mysterious Bella and said something to J.B. that hit him wrong. But, why would she have been jealous? She was almost certain that J.B. had never touched her intimately in their past.

"Honey, don't try so hard to remember," Nell cautioned. "Enjoy these few days and don't try to think about the past."

"Was it bad?" she wondered aloud.

Nell grimaced. "In a way, yes, it was," she replied. "But I can't tell you any more. I'll get in trouble. It might damage you, to know too much too soon. Dr. Coltrain was very specific."

Tellie gnawed her lower lip. "I've already graduated from high school, haven't I?" she asked.

Nell nodded, reluctantly.

"Do I have a job?"

"You had a summer job, at the Ballenger Brothers feedlot. That's where you met Grange."

She felt a twinge of memory trying to come back. There was something between J.B. and Grange, something about a woman. Not the beauty contestant, but some other woman. There was a painful secret…

She caught her head and held it, feeling it throb.

Nell moved forward and took her by the shoulders. "Stop trying to force the memories," she cautioned. "Take it one day at a time. Right now, let's do some vacuuming. Then we'll make a cake. You can invite Grange over to supper, if you like," she added, inspired. "J.B. won't be around to protest."

Tellie smiled. "I'd enjoy that."

"So would I. We'll call him at the feedlot, when we're through cleaning."

"Okay."

They did the necessary housekeeping and then made a huge chocolate pound cake. Grange was enthusiastic about coming for a meal, and Tellie was surprised at the warm feeling he evoked in her. It was friendly, though, not the tempestuous surging of her heart that she felt when she remembered the touch of J.B.'s hard lips on her mouth.

She had a suitcase that she didn't remember packing. Inside was a pretty pink striped dress. She wore that, and light makeup, for the meal. Grange showed up on time, wearing a sports jacket with dress slacks, a white shirt and a tie. He paid for dressing. He was very good-looking.

"You look nice," Tellie told him warmly as he followed her into the dining room, where the table was already set.

"So do you," he replied, producing another bouquet of flowers from behind his back, and presenting them with a grin.

"Thanks!" she exclaimed. "You shouldn't have!"

"You love flowers," he said. "I didn't think you had enough."

She gave him a wary look. "Is that the whole truth?" she

asked suspiciously and with a mischievous grin, "or did you think you'd irritate J.B. if I had more flowers in my room?"

He chuckled. "Can't put anything past you, can I?" he asked.

"Thanks anyway," she told him. "I'll just put them in water. Sit down! Nell and I chased Albert out of the kitchen and did everything ourselves. I understand he's down at the goldfish pond slitting his wrists…"

"He is not!" Nell exclaimed. "You stop that!"

Tellie grinned. "Sorry. Couldn't resist it. He seems to think he owns the kitchen."

"Well, he doesn't," Nell said. "Not until I leave for good."

Leave. Leave. Tellie frowned, staring into space. Nell had quit. Tellie had been crying. Nell was shouting. J.B. was shouting back. It was raining…

Grange caught her as she fell and carried her into the living room. He put her down on the sofa. Nell ran for a wet cloth.

Tellie groaned as she opened her eyes. "I remembered an argument," she said huskily. "You and J.B. were yelling at each other…"

Nell frowned. "You couldn't have heard us," she said. "You'd already run out the door, into the rain."

Tellie could see the road, blinded by rain, feel the tires giving way, feel the car going into the ditch…!

She gasped. "I wrecked the car. I saw it!"

Nell sat down beside her and put an arm around her. "Grange saved you," she told the younger woman. "He came along in time to stop you from drowning. The ditch the car went into was full of water."

Tellie held the cloth to her forehead. She swallowed, and then swallowed again. There were odd, disturbing flashes. J.B.'s furious face. A blond woman, staring at her. There were harsh words, but she couldn't remember what they were. She didn't want to remember!

"Did I thank you for saving me?" she asked Grange, trying to ward off the memories.

He smiled worriedly. "Of course you did. How do you feel now?"

"Silly," she said sheepishly as she sat up. "I'm sorry. There were some really odd flashbacks. I don't understand them at all."

"Don't try to," Nell said firmly. "Come on in here and eat. Let time take care of the rest."

She got up, holding on to Grange's arm for support. She drew in a long, slow breath. "One way and another, it's been a rough few days," she said.

"You don't know the half," Nell said under her breath, but she didn't let Tellie hear her.

The next day was Saturday. Tellie went out to the barn to see the sick calf that was being kept there while it was being treated. In another stall was a huge, black stallion. He didn't like company. He pawed and snorted as Tellie walked past him. He was J.B.'s. She knew, without remembering or being told. She moved to another stall, where a beautiful Palomino mare was eating from a feed trough. The horse perked up when she saw Tellie, and left her food to come to the front of the stall and nose Tellie's outstretched hand.

"Sand," Tellie murmured. She laughed. "That's your name. Sand! J.B. lets me ride you!"

The horse nudged her hand again. She smoothed the white blaze between the mare's eyes lazily. She was beginning to recover some memories. The rest, she was sure, would come in time.

She wandered past the goldfish pond on the patio and stared down at the pretty red and gold and white fish swimming around water lilies and lotus plants. The facade was stacked yellow bricks, and there were huge flat limestone slabs all around it, making an endless seat for people to watch the fish. There were small trees nearby and a white wrought-iron furniture set with a patio umbrella. In fair weather, it must be heavenly to sit there. She heard a car drive up and wondered who it was. Not J.B., she was sure. It was too soon for him to be back. Monday, Nell said, was the earliest they could expect him. Perhaps it was one of the cowboys.

It was a dreary day, not good exploring weather. She wondered how Marge and the girls were, and wanted to see them. She dreaded seeing J.B. again. Things had changed between them. She was uneasy when she considered that J.B. had left town so quickly afterward, as if his conscience bothered him. Or was it that he was afraid Tellie would start thinking about something serious? She knew so little about relationships...

She walked back through the side door into the living room and stopped suddenly. There was a beautiful blond woman standing in the doorway. She was wearing a yellow dress that fit her like a second skin. She had long, wavy, beautiful hair and a perfectly made-up face. She was svelte and sophisticated, and she was giving Tellie a look that could have boiled water.

"So you're the reason I've had to be kept away from the house," the woman said haughtily.

That blonde was familiar, Tellie thought suddenly, and she wanted to run. She didn't want to talk to this person, to be around her. She was a threat.

The woman sensed Tellie's discomfort and smiled coldly. "Don't tell me you've forgotten me?" she drawled. "Not after you walked right in and interrupted me and J.B. on that very sofa?"

Sofa. J.B. Two people in the sofa, both half-naked. J.B. furious and yelling. Nell rushing to see why Tellie was crying.

Tellie put her hands to her mouth as the memories began to rush at her, like daggers. It was all coming back. J.B. had called her ugly. A stray. He could never love her. He didn't want her. He'd said that!

There was more. He'd missed her graduation from college

and lied about it. He'd had his secretary buy Tellie a graduation present—he hadn't even cared enough to do it himself.
He'd accused Tellie of panting after him like a pet dog. He'd
said he was sick of her…pawing him…trying to touch him.

She felt the rise of nausea in her throat like a living thing.
She brushed past the blonde and ran for the hall bathroom,
slamming the door behind her. She barely made it to the sink
before she lost her breakfast.

"Tellie?"

The door opened. Nell came in, worried. "Are you all right?
Oh, for goodness sake…!"

She grabbed a washcloth from the linen closet and wet it,
bathing Tellie's white face. "Come on. Let's get you back to bed."

"That woman…" Tellie choked.

"I showed her the door," Nell said coldly. "She won't come
back in a hurry, I guarantee!"

"But I recognized her," Tellie said unsteadily. "She and
J.B. were on the sofa together, half-naked. He yelled at me.
He accused me of trying to paw him. He said he was sick of
the way I followed him around. He said…" She swallowed the
pain. "He said I was nothing but an ugly stray that he'd taken
in, and that he could never want me." Tears rolled down her
cheek. "He said he never…wanted to see me again!"

"Tellie," Nell began miserably, not knowing what to say.

"Why did he bring me here, after that?" she asked tearfully.

"He felt guilty," Nell said gently. "It was his fault that
you wrecked the car. You would have died, if Grange hadn't
found you."

Tellie wiped her eyes with the wet washcloth. "I knew there
was something," she choked. "Some reason that he wasn't
giving me. Guilt. Just guilt." Was that why he'd kissed her so
hungrily, too? Was he trying to make amends for what he'd
said? But it was only the truth. He didn't want her. He found
her repulsive…

The tears poured down her face. She wanted to climb into a hole. That beautiful blonde was J.B.'s woman. She'd come to Marge's house with J.B., and she'd insulted Tellie. They'd argued, and J.B. had shown Tellie what a hold he had over her, using her weakness for him as a punishment. She closed her eyes. How could he have treated her so horribly?

"I want to go back to Marge's house," Tellie said shakily. "Before he comes home." She looked into Nell's eyes. "And then I never want to see him again, as long as I live!"

Ten

Nell couldn't talk Tellie into staying at the house, not even when she assured her that J.B. wouldn't be back until Monday. Tellie had remembered that Marge had a heart attack, and she was frantic until Nell assured her that Marge was going to be all right. It was even lucky that they'd found the high blood pressure before it killed her.

Now that Tellie remembered everything, there were no more barriers to her going to Marge. She remembered her job at the feedlot, as well, and hoped she still had it. But she phoned Justin at home and he assured her that her job would be waiting when she was recovered. That was a load off her mind.

She didn't dare think about J.B. It was too terrible, remembering the hurtful things he'd said to her. She knew she'd never forgive him for the way he'd reacted when she'd tried to tell him about Marge, much less for his ardor when he knew there was no future in it. He'd taunted her with her feelings one time too many. She wondered what sort of cruel game he'd been playing in her bedroom at his house.

Marge and the girls met her at the door, hugging her warmly. Nell had driven her there, and she was carrying two suitcases.

"Are you sure about this?" Nell asked worriedly.

Marge nodded, smiling warmly. "You know you're welcome here. None of us will yell at you, and we'll all be grateful that we don't have to depend on Dawn's cooking for…"

"Mother!" Dawn exclaimed.

"Sorry," Marge said, hugging her daughter. "I love you, baby, but you know you're terrible in the kitchen, even if you can sing like an angel. Nobody's perfect."

"J.B. thinks he is," Nell muttered.

Marge laughed. "Not anymore, I'll bet. I hope you left him a note, at least."

"I did," Nell confessed. "Brief, and to the point. I hope that blond fashion doll of his can cook and clean."

"That isn't likely," Tellie said coolly. "But they can always get takeout."

"Are you sure you're okay?" Marge asked Tellie, moving to hug her, too. "Your color's bad."

"So is yours, worrywart," Tellie said with warm affection, returning the hug. "But I reckon the two of us will manage somehow, with a little help."

"Between us," Marge sighed, "we barely make one well person."

"I'll fatten you both up with healthy, nonsalty fare," Nell promised. "Dawn and Brandi can see me to my room and help me unpack. Right?"

The girls grinned. "You bet!" they chorused, delighted to see the end of meal preparation and housework. Nell was the best in town at housekeeping.

They marched up the staircase together, the girls helping with the luggage.

Marge studied Tellie closely, her sharp eyes missing nothing. "You wouldn't be here unless something major had happened. What was it?"

"My memory came back," Tellie said, perching on the arm of the sofa.

"Did it have any help?" the older woman asked shrewdly.

Tellie grimaced, her eyes lowering to the sea-blue carpet. "Bella kindly filled me in on a few things."

Marge cursed under her breath as forcefully as J.B. ever had. "That woman is a menace!" she raged. "Copper Coltrain said it would be dangerous for us to force-feed you facts about the past until you remembered them naturally!"

"I'm sure she only wanted J.B. to herself again, and thought she was helping him get me out of the way. I don't mind," Tellie added at once. "J.B. raised hell when Grange came and brought me roses. At least you're not likely to mind that."

Marge smiled. "No, I'm not. I like your friend Grange."

Tellie's eyes were sad and wise. "He's been a wonderful friend. Who'd have thought he'd turn out to be pleasant company, with his background?"

"Not anyone locally, that's for sure." Marge sat down on the sofa, too. She was still pale. "Nothing wrong," she assured Tellie, who was watching her closely. "The medicine still makes me a little dizzy, but it's perfectly natural. Otherwise, I'm seeing an improvement all around. I think it's going to work."

"Goodness, I hope so," Tellie said gently. She smiled. "We can't lose you."

"You aren't going to. Nice of you to bring Nell with you," she added wryly. "Housework and cooking was really getting to us, without you here. Did she come willingly?"

"She met me at the front door with her suitcase," she replied. "She was furious at what Bella had done. She thinks maybe J.B. put her up to it."

Marge scowled. "That isn't likely. Whatever his faults, J.B. has a big heart. He was really concerned about you."

"He felt guilty," Tellie translated, "because he felt responsible for the wreck. He yelled at me and said some terrible things," she added, without elaborating. Her sad eyes were evidence enough of the pain he'd caused Tellie. "I couldn't stay under his roof, when I remembered them."

Marge picked at a fingernail. "That bad?"

Tellie nodded, averting her eyes.

"Then I suppose it's just as well for you to stay here."

"I don't want to see him," she told Marge. "Not ever again. He's had one too many free shots at me. I'll finish out the week at Ballenger's when I get back on my feet, and then I'm going to ask my alma mater for an adjunct position teaching history for night students. I can teach at night and go to classes during the day. The semester starts very soon."

"Is it wise, to run away from a problem?" the other woman queried.

"In this case, it's the better part of valor," she replied grimly. "J.B. didn't just say unpleasant things to me, Marge, he actually taunted me with the way I felt about him. That's hitting below the belt, even for J.B."

"He did that?" Marge exclaimed.

"Yes. And that's why I'm leaving." She got up. She smiled at Marge. "Not to worry, you'll have Nell to take over here for me, and pamper all three of you. I won't have to be nervous about leaving you. Nell will make sure you do what the doctor says, and she'll cook healthy meals for you."

"J.B. is going to be furious when he gets home and finds you both gone," Marge predicted. She was glad she wasn't going to have to be the one to tell him.

It was dark and raining when J.B. climbed out of the limo he'd hired to take him to and from the airport. He signed the charge slip, tipped the driver with two big bills and carried his flight bag and attaché case up the driveway to the house.

It was oddly quiet when he used his key to open the front

door. Usually there was a television going in Nell's room, which could be heard faintly coming down the staircase. There were no lights on upstairs, and no smells of cooking.

He frowned. Odd, that. He put down his suitcase and attaché case, and opened the living room door.

Bella was stretched out on the sofa wearing a pink gown and negligee and a come-hither smile.

"Welcome home, darling," she purred. "I knew you wouldn't mind if I moved into my old room."

He was worn-out and half out of humor. Bella's mood didn't help. What in the world must Tellie be thinking of this new development, despite her lack of memory.

"What did you tell Tellie?" he asked.

Her eyebrows arched. "I only reminded her of how she found us together the night your sister had to go to the hospital," she drawled. "She remembered everything else just fine, after that, and she went to your sister's." She smiled seductively. "We've got the whole night to ourselves! I'm cooking TV dinners. They'll be ready in about ten minutes. Then we can have champagne and go to bed…"

"You told her that?" he burst out, horrified.

She glowered, moving to sit up. "Now, J.B., you know she was getting on your nerves. You never go to those stupid seminars, you just wanted to get away from her."

"That isn't true," he shot back. And it wasn't. He'd gone to give Tellie, and himself, breathing space. Her ardent response had left his head spinning. For the first time in their relationship, Tellie had responded to him as a woman would, with passion and hunger. He hadn't slept an entire night since, reliving the delicious interlude time after time. He'd had to leave, to make sure he didn't press Tellie too hard when she was fragile, make sure he didn't force memories she wasn't ready for. He'd hoped to have time to show her how tender he could be, before she remembered how cruel he'd been. Now the chance was gone forever, and the source of his failure was sprawled on his sofa in a negligee planning to replace Tellie. He felt a surge of pure revulsion as he looked at Bella.

"Nell!" he called loudly.

"Oh, she went with the girl to your sister's," Bella said, yawning. "She left a note on your desk."

He went to his study to retrieve it, feeling cold and dead inside. The note was scribbled on a memo pad. It just said that Nell was going to work for Marge, and that she hoped Bella was domesticated.

He threw it down on the desk, overwhelmed with frustration. Bella came up behind him and slid her arms around him.

"I'll check on the TV dinners," she whispered. "Then we can have some fun…"

He jerked away from her, his green eyes blazing. "Get dressed and go home," he said shortly. He took out his wallet and stuffed some bills into her hand.

"Where are you going?" she exclaimed when he walked toward the front door.

"To get Nell and Tellie back," he said shortly, and kept walking.

Bella actually screamed. But it didn't do any good. He didn't even turn his head.

Marge met him at the door. She didn't invite him in.

"I'm sorry," she said, stepping onto the porch with him. "But Tellie's been through enough today. She doesn't want to see you."

He shoved his hands into his pockets, staring at her. "I leave town for two days and the world caves in on me," he bit off.

"You can thank yourself for that," his sister replied. Her dark eyes narrowed. "Was it necessary to use Tellie's weakness for you against her like a weapon?"

He paled a little. "She told you?" he asked slowly.

"The bare bones, nothing more. It was low, J.B., even for you. Just lately, you're someone I don't know."

His broad shoulders lifted and fell. "Grange brought back some painful memories."

"Tellie wasn't responsible for them," she reminded him bluntly.

He drew in a sharp breath. "She won't give up Grange. It's disloyal."

"They're friends. Not that you'd recognize the reference. You don't have friends, J.B., you have hot dates," she pointed out. "Albert phoned and said your current heartthrob was preparing dinner for you. Frozen dinners, I believe...?"

"I didn't ask Bella to move in while I was away!" he shot back. "And I sure as hell didn't authorize her to fill Tellie in on the past!"

"I'm sure she thought she was doing you a favor, and removing the opposition at the same time," Marge said, folding her arms across her chest. "I love you, J.B., but I'm your sister and I can afford to. You're hard on women, especially on Tellie. Lately it's like you're punishing her for having feelings for you."

His high cheekbones went ruddy. He looked away from Marge. "I didn't want anything permanent, at first."

"Then you should never have encouraged Tellie, in any way."

He sighed roughly. He couldn't explain. It flattered him, softened him, that Tellie thought the world revolved around him. She made him feel special, just by caring for him. But she hadn't been able to give him passion, and he was afraid to take a chance on her without it. For years, he'd given up passionate love, he was afraid of it. When Tellie left for college he didn't want her to be hurt, but he didn't want to be hurt himself. He loved too deeply, too intensely. He couldn't live with losing another woman, the way he'd lost his late fiancée. But now Tellie was a woman, and he felt differently. How was he going to explain that to Tellie if he couldn't get near her?

"Tellie's changed in the past few weeks. So have I." He shifted. "It's hard to put it into words."

Marge knew that he had a difficult time talking about feelings. She and J.B. weren't twins, but they'd always been close. She moved toward him and put a gentle hand on his arm. "Tellie's going back to Houston in a week," she said quietly. "Do her a favor, and leave her alone while she finishes out her notice at the feedlot. Let her get used to being herself. Then maybe you can talk to her, and she'll listen. She's just hurt, J.B."

"She wasn't going back to school until fall semester," he said shortly. "She's been through a lot. She shouldn't start putting pressure on herself this soon."

"She doesn't see it that way. She's going to teach adult education at her college at night and attend classes during the day during summer semester." She lowered her eyes to his chest. "I want her to be happy. She's never going to be able to cope with the future until you're out of her life. I know you're fond of her, J.B., but it would be kinder to let her go."

He knew that. But he couldn't let her go, now that he knew what he wanted. He couldn't! His face reflected his inner struggle.

Her hand closed hard on his forearm. "Listen to me," she said firmly, "you of all people should know how painful it is to love someone you can't have. Everyone knows you don't want marriage or children, you just want a good time. Bella's your sort of woman. You couldn't hurt her if you hit her in the head with a brickbat, she's so thick. Just enjoy what you've got, J.B., and let Tellie heal."

He met her eyes. His were turbulent with frustrated need and worry. "I wanted to try to make it up to her," he bit off.

"Make what up to her?"

He looked away. "So much," he said absently. "I've never given her anything except pain, but I want to make her happy."

"You can't do that," his sister said quietly. "Not unless you want her for keeps."

His eyes narrowed in pain. He *did* want her for keeps. But he was afraid.

"Don't try to make her into a casual lover," Marge cautioned. "You'd destroy her."

"Don't you think I know?" he asked curtly. He turned away. "Maybe you're right, Marge," he said finally, defeated. "It would be kinder to let go for the time being. It's just that she cared for me, and I gave her nothing but mockery and indifference."

"You can't help that. You can't love people just because they want you to," Marge said wisely. "Tellie's going to make some lucky man a wonderful wife," she added gently. "She'll be the best mother a child could want. Don't rob her of that potential by giving her false hope."

Tellie, with a child. The anguish he felt was shocking. Tellie, married to another man, having children with another man, growing old with another man. He'd never considered the possibility that Tellie could turn her affections to someone else. He'd assumed that she'd always worship him. He'd given her the best reason on earth to hate him, by mocking her love for him.

"I've been taking a long look at myself," he said quietly. "I didn't like what I saw. I've been so busy protecting myself from pain that I've inflicted it on Tellie continuously. I didn't mean to. It was self-defense."

"It was cruel," Marge agreed. "Throwing Bella up to her, parading the woman here in Tellie's home, taunting her for wanting to take care of you." She shook her head. "I'm amazed that she was strong enough to take it all these years. I couldn't have."

"What about Grange?" he asked bitterly.

"What about him?" she replied. "She's very fond of him, and vice versa. But he isn't really in the running right now. He's a man with a past, a rebel who isn't comfortable in domestic surroundings. He likes having someone to take to the movies, but he's years away from being comfortable with even the idea of marriage."

That made J.B. feel somewhat better. Not a lot. He was thinking how miserable Tellie must be, having been force-fed the most horrible memories of her recent life. Coltrain said that her mind had been hiding from the trauma of the past. He didn't know that J.B. was responsible for it. He kept seeing Tellie on the gurney as she came into the emergency room, bruised and bleeding, and unconscious. If Grange hadn't shown up, Tellie would have drowned. He'd have had two dead women on his conscience, when one had always been too many.

The thought of Tellie, dead, was nauseating. She'd looked up to him since her early teens, followed him around, ached to just have him look at her. He'd denigrated those tender feelings and made her look like a lovesick fool. That, too, had been frustration, because he wanted a woman's passion from Tellie and she hadn't been able to give it to him. Not until now. He was sorry he'd been cruel to her in his anguish. But he couldn't go back and do it over again. He had to find some way back to Tellie. Some way to make up for what he'd done to her. Some way to convince her that he wanted a future with her.

"Tell her that I'm sorry," he said through his teeth. "She won't believe it, I know, but tell her anyway."

"Sorry for what?"

He met her eyes. "For everything."

"She'll be all right," Marge told him. "Really she will. She's stronger than I ever imagined."

"She's had so little love in her life," he recalled bitterly. "Her mother didn't really care much for her. She lost her grandfather at the time she needed him most. I shoved her off onto you and took it for granted that she'd spend her life looking up to me like some sort of hero." He drew in a long breath. "She was assaulted, you know, when she was fourteen. I've pushed that to the back of my mind and neither of us insisted that she go on with therapy after a few short sessions. Maybe those memories had her on the rack, and she couldn't even talk about them."

Marge chuckled. "Think so? Tellie beat the stuffing out of the little creep and testified against him, as well. He never even got to touch her inappropriately. No, she's over that, honestly."

"Even if she is, I made her suffer for having the gall to develop a crush on me."

He sounded disgusted with himself. Marge could have told him that it was no crush that lasted for years and years and took all sorts of punishment for the privilege of idolizing him. But he probably knew already.

He looked up at the darkening sky. "I know how it must look, that I've had Bella staying at the house, and taken her on trips with me. But I've never slept with her," he added with brutal honesty.

Marge's eyebrows arched. That was an odd admission, from a rounder like her brother. "It can't be from lack of encouragement," she pointed out.

"No," he agreed. "It couldn't."

She felt inadequate to the task at hand. She wondered if she was doing the right thing by asking him not to approach Tellie. But she didn't really know what else there was to do. She felt sorry for both of them, especially for her brother who'd apparently discovered feelings for Tellie too late.

"I don't want a wife right now," he said, but without the old conviction. "She knows that, anyway."

"Sure she does," his sister agreed.

He turned and looked down at her with soft affection. "You doing okay?"

She nodded, smiling. "Nell's going to be a treasure. I can't do a lot of the stuff I used to, and the girls hate cooking and housework. With Tellie gone, it's up to us to manage. Nell will make my life so much easier. I can probably even go back to work when the medicine takes hold."

"Do you want to?" he asked curiously.

"Yes," she said. "I'm not the sort of person who enjoys staying at home with nothing intellectually challenging to do. I'd at least like to work on committees or help with community projects. Money isn't enough. Happiness takes more than a padded bank account."

"I'm finding that out," J.B. agreed, smiling. "You take care of yourself. If you need me, I'm just at the other end of the phone."

"I know that. I love you," she said, hugging him warmly.

He cleared his throat. "Yeah. Me, too." Expressing emotion was hard for him. She knew it.

She pulled away. "Go home and eat your frozen dinner."

He grimaced. "I sent Bella home in a cab. It's probably carbon by now."

"Albert will fix you something."

"When he finds out why Tellie's gone, I wouldn't bet on having anything edible in the near future."

"There are good restaurants all over Jacobsville," she pointed out.

He laughed good-naturedly. "I suppose I'll find one. Take care."

"You, too. Good night."

She closed the door and went back inside. Tellie's light was off when she went upstairs. The younger woman was probably worn completely out from the day's turmoil. She wished Tellie had never spent any time with J.B. at all. Maybe then she'd have been spared so much heartache.

Tellie was hard at work on her last day at the feedlot. It was a sweltering hot Friday, and storm clouds were gathering on the horizon. The wind was moving at a clip fast enough to stand the state flag out from its flagpole. When she went to lunch, sand blew right into her face as she climbed into Marge's car to drive home and eat.

The wind pushed the little car all over the road. It wasn't raining yet, but it looked as if it might rain buckets full.

She turned on the radio. There was a weather bulletin, noting that a tornado watch was in effect for Jacobsville and surrounding counties until late that afternoon. Tellie was afraid of tornadoes. She hoped she never had to contend with one as long as she lived.

She ate a quick lunch, surrounded by Marge and Nell and the girls, since it was a teacher workday and they weren't in school. But when she was ready to leave, the skies were suddenly jet-black and the wind was roaring like a lion outside.

"Don't you dare get in that car," Marge threatened.

"Look at the color of those clouds," Nell added, looking past them out the door.

The clouds were a neon-green, and there was a strange shape growing in them, emphasized by the increasing volume and force of the wind.

While they stood on the porch with the doors open, the sound of a siren broke into the dull rumble of thunder.

"Is that an ambulance?" Dawn asked curiously.

"No," Nell said at once. "It's the tornado alert, it's the siren on top of the courthouse." She ran for the weather radio, and found it ringing its batteries off. There was a steady red light on the console. Even before it blared out the words *tornado warning,* Nell knew what was coming.

"We have to get into the basement, right now!" Nell said, rushing to the hall staircase. "Come on!"

They piled after her, down the carpeted stairs and into the basement, into the room that had been especially built in case of tornadoes. It was steel-reinforced, with battery-powered lights and radio, water, provisions and spare batteries. The wind was audible even down there, now.

They closed themselves into the sheltered room and sat down on the carpeted floor to wait it out. Nell turned on the battery-powered scanner and instead of the weather, she turned to the fire and police frequencies.

Sharp orders in deep voices heralded the first of the

damage. One fire and rescue unit was already on its way out Caldwell Road from a report of a trailer being demolished. There came other reports, one after another. A roof was off this building, a barn collapsed, there were trees down in the road, trees down on power lines, trees falling on cars. It was the worst damage Tellie had heard about in her young life.

She thought about J.B., alone in his house with memories of his grandmother dying in such a storm. She wished she could stop caring about what happened to him. She couldn't. He was too much a part of her life, regardless of the treatment he'd handed out to her.

"I hope J.B.'s all right," Tellie murmured as the overhead light flickered and went out on the heels of a violent burst of thunder.

"So do I," Marge replied. "But he's got a shelter of his own. I'm sure he's in it."

The violence outside escalated. Tellie hid her head in her crossed arms and prayed that nobody would be killed.

Several minutes later, Nell eased the door open and listened for a minute before she went up the staircase. She was back shortly.

"It's over," she called to the others. "There's a little thunder, but it's far away, and you can see some blue sky. There are two big oak trees down in the front yard, though."

"I hope nobody got hurt," Marge mumbled as they went up the staircase.

"Call the house," Tellie pleaded with Nell. "Make sure J.B.'s all right."

Nell grimaced, but she did it. Argue they might, but she was fond of her old boss. The others stared at Nell while she listened. She winced and put down the receiver with a sad face.

"The lines are down," she said worriedly.

"We could drive over there and see," Dawn suggested.

Tellie recalled painfully the last time she'd driven over to

J.B.'s place to tell him about a disaster. She couldn't bear to do it again.

"We can't get out of the driveway," Marge said uneasily. "One of the oaks is blocking the whole driveway."

"Give me your cell phone," Nell told Marge. "I'll call my cousin at the police department and get him to have someone check."

The joy of small-town life, Tellie was thinking. Surely the police could find out for them if J.B. was safe. Tellie prayed silently while Nell waited for her cousin to come to the phone.

She listened, spoke into the phone, and then listened again, grimacing. She thanked her cousin and put down the phone, facing the others with obvious reluctance.

"The tornado hit J.B.'s house and took off the corner where his office was. He's been taken to the hospital. My cousin doesn't know how bad he's hurt. There were some fatalities," she added, wincing when she saw their faces go white. Arguments and disagreements aside, J.B. was precious to everyone in the room.

Tellie spoke for all of them. "I'm going to the hospital," she said, "if I have to walk the whole five miles!"

Eleven

As it happened, they managed to get around the tree in their rain-coats and walk out to the main highway. It was still raining, but the storm was over. Marge got on her cell phone and called her friend Barbara, who phoned one of the local firemen, an off-duty officer who agreed to pick them up and take them to the hospital.

When they got there, J.B. was in the emergency room sitting on an examination table, grinning. He had a cut across his forehead and a bruise on his bare shoulder, but his spirit seemed perfectly unstoppable.

Tellie almost ran to him. Almost. But just as she tensed to do it, a blond head came into view under J.B.'s other arm. Bella, in tears, sobbing, as she clung to J.B.'s bare chest mumbling how happy she was that he wasn't badly hurt.

She drew back and Marge and Nell and the girls joined her, out of sight of J.B. and Bella.

"You go ahead," she told them. "But...don't tell him I was here. Okay?"

Marge nodded, the others agreed. They understood without a word of explanation. "Go on out front, honey," Marge said gently. "We'll find you there when we're through."

"Okay. Thanks," Tellie said huskily, with a forced smile. Her heart was breaking all over again.

As Marge and the girls moved into the cubicle, Tellie walked back to the front entrance where there were chairs and a sofa around the information desk. She couldn't bring herself to walk into that room. J.B. hadn't looked as if he disliked Bella, despite what Marge had told her about his anger that Bella had spilled the beans about Tellie's past. He looked amazingly content, and his arm had been firm and close around Bella's shoulders.

Why, Tellie asked herself, did she continually bash her stupid head against brick walls? Love was such a painful emotion. Someday, she promised herself, she was going to learn how to turn it off. At least, as far as J. B. Hammock was concerned!

She didn't see Bella walk past the waiting room. She hardly looked up until Marge and the girls came back.

"He's going to be all right," Marge told her, hugging her gently. "Just a few cuts and bruises, nothing else. Let's go home."

Tellie smiled back, but only with her eyes.

J.B. buttoned his shirt while Bella stood waiting with his tie. He felt empty. Tellie hadn't even bothered to come and see about him. Nothing in recent years had hurt so much. She'd finally given up on him for good.

"We can get Albert to fix you something nice for breakfast," Bella said brightly.

"I'm not hungry." He took the tie and put it in place. "At least Marge and the girls cared enough to brave the storm to see me. Tellie couldn't be bothered, I guess," he said bitterly.

"She was in the waiting room," Bella said blankly.

He scowled. "Doing what?"

Bella shrugged one thin shoulder. "Crying."

Crying. She'd come to see about him after all, but she hadn't come into the room? Then he remembered that when Marge and the girls came in, he had Bella in his arms. He winced mentally. No wonder Tellie had taken off like that. She thought…

He looked down at Bella shrewdly. "I'm going to have to let Albert go," he said with calculated sadness. "With all the damage the storm did to the house and barn, I'm going to go in the hole for sure. It's been a bad year for cattle ranchers anyway."

Bella was very still. "You mean, you might lose everything?"

He nodded. "Well, I don't mind hard work. It's a challenge to start from scratch. You can move in with me, Bella, and take over the housekeeping and cooking…"

"I, uh, I have an invitation from my aunt in the Bahamas to come stay the summer with her," Bella said at once. "I'm really sorry, J.B., but I'm not the pioneering type, and I hate housework." She smiled. "It was fun while it lasted."

"Yes," he said, hiding a smile. "It was."

The next day was taken up finding insurance adjusters and contractors to repair the damage at the ranch. He'd lost several head of livestock to injuries from falling trees and flying debris. The barn would have to be rebuilt, and the front part of the house would need some repair, as well. He wasn't worried, though. He could well afford what needed doing. He smiled at his subterfuge with Bella. As he'd suspected, she'd only wanted him for as long as she thought he was rich and could take her to five-star restaurants and buy her expensive presents.

When he had the repairs in hand, he put on a gray vested business suit, polished boots and his best creamy Stetson, and went over to Marge's to have a showdown with Tellie.

Nell opened the door, her eyes guilty and welcoming all at once. "Glad you're okay, boss," she said stiffly.

"Me, too," he agreed. "Where is everybody?"

"In the kitchen. We're just having lunch. There's plenty," she added.

He slipped an arm around her shoulders and kissed her wrinkled forehead with genuine affection. "I've missed you," he said simply, and walked her into the kitchen.

Marge and the girls looked up, smiling happily. They all rushed to hug him and fuss over him.

"Nell made minestrone," Marge said. "Sit down and have a bowl with us."

"It smells delicious," he remarked, putting his hat on the counter. He sat down, looking around curiously. "Where's Tellie?"

There was a long silence. Marge put down her spoon. "She's gone."

"Gone?" he exclaimed. "Where?"

"To Houston," Marge replied sadly. "She phoned some classmates and found an apartment she could share, then she phoned the dean at home and arranged to teach as an adjunct for night classes. Orientation was today, so she was able to sign up for her master's classes."

J.B. looked at his bowl with blind eyes. Tellie had gone away. She'd seen him with Bella, decided that he didn't want her, cut her losses and run for the border. Added to what she'd remembered, the painful things he'd said to her the day of the wreck, he couldn't blame her for that. She didn't know how drastically he'd changed toward her. Now he'd have to find a way back into her life. It wasn't going to be easy. She'd never fully trust him again.

But he wasn't giving up before he'd started, he told himself firmly. He'd never really tried to court Tellie. If she still cared at all, she wouldn't be able to resist him—any more than he could resist her.

* * *

Tellie was finding her new routine wearing. She taught a night class in history for four hours, two nights a week, and she went to classes three other days during the week. She was young and strong, and she knew she could cope. But she didn't sleep well, remembering Bella curled close in J.B.'s arm the night of the tornado. He wouldn't marry the beautiful woman, she knew that. He wouldn't marry anyone. But he had nothing to offer Tellie, and she knew, and suffered for it.

One of her classmates, John, who'd helped her find a room the night before she came back to Houston, paused by her table in the college coffeehouse.

"Tellie, can you cover for me in anthropology?" he asked. "I've got to work tomorrow morning."

She grinned up at him. John, like her, was doing master's work, although his was in anthropology. Tellie was taking the course as an elective. "I'll make sure I take good notes. How about covering for me in literature? I'll have a test to grade in my night school course."

"No problem," he said. He grinned down at her, with a hand on the back of her chair. "Sure you don't want to go out to dinner with me Friday night?"

He was good-looking, and sweet, but he liked to drink and Tellie didn't. She was searching for a reply when she turned her gaze to the door.

Her heart jumped up into her throat. J.B. was standing just inside the door of the crowded café, searching. He spotted her and came right on, his eyes never leaving her as he wound through the crowd.

He stopped at her table. He spared John a brief glance that made veiled threats.

"I'd better run," John said abruptly. "See you later, Tellie."

"Sure thing."

J.B. pulled out a chair and sat down, tossing his hat idly

onto the chair beside hers. He didn't smile. His eyes were intent, curiously warm.

"You ran, Tellie."

She couldn't pretend not to know what he was talking about. She pushed back her wavy hair and picked up her coffee cup. "It seemed sensible."

"Did it?"

She sipped coffee. "Did the tornado do much damage at the ranch?"

He shrugged. "Enough to keep me busy for several days, or I'd have been here sooner," he told her. He paused as the waitress came by, to order himself a cup of cappuccino. He glanced at Tellie and grinned. "Make that two cups," he told the waitress. She smiled and went to fill the order, while J.B. watched Tellie's face. "You can't afford it on your budget," he said knowingly. "My treat."

"Thanks," she murmured.

He leaned back in his chair and looked at her, intently, unsmiling. "Heard from Grange?"

She shook her head. "He phoned before I left Jacobsville to say he was going back to Washington, D.C. Apparently he was subpoenaed to testify against his former commanding officer, who's being court-martialed."

He nodded. "Cag Hart told me. He and Blake Kemp and Grange served in the same division in Iraq. He said Grange's commanding officer had him thrown out of the army and took credit for a successful incursion that was Grange's idea."

"He told me," she replied.

The waitress came back with steaming cappuccino for both of them. J.B. picked his up and sipped it. Tellie sniffed hers with her eyes closed, smiling. She loved the rich brew.

After a minute J.B. met eyes again. "Tellie, is this what you really want?" he asked, indicating the coffeehouse and the college campus.

The question startled her. She toyed with the handle of her

cup. "Of course it is," she lied. "When I get my doctorate, I can teach at college level."

"And that's all you want from life?" he asked. "A career?"

She couldn't look at him. "We both know I'll never get very far any other way. I have plenty of friends who cry on my shoulder about their girlfriends or ask me to take notes for them in class, or keep their cats when they go on holiday." She shrugged. "I'm not the sort of woman that men want for keeps."

He closed his eyes on a wave of guilt. He'd said such horrible things to her. She already had a low self-image. He'd lowered it more, in a fit of bad temper.

"Beauty alone isn't worth much," he said after a minute. "Neither is wealth. After I got out of the emergency room, I went home to an empty house, Tellie," he said sadly. "I stood there in the vestibule, with crystal chandeliers and Italian marble all around me, mahogany staircases, Persian rugs…and suddenly it felt like being alone in a tomb. You know what, Tellie? Wealth isn't enough. In fact, it's nothing, unless you have someone to share it with."

"You've got Bella," she said with more bitterness than she knew.

He laughed. "I told her I was in the hole and likely to lose everything," he commented amusedly. "She suddenly remembered an invitation to spend the summer in the sun with her aunt."

Tellie's eyes lifted to his. She was afraid to hope.

He reached across the table and curled her fingers into his. "Finish your cappuccino," he said gently. "I want to talk to you."

She was hardly aware of what she was doing. This must be a dream, J.B. sitting here with her, holding her hand. She was going to wake up any minute. Meanwhile, she might as well enjoy the fantasy. She smiled at him and sipped her cappuccino.

He took her out to his car and put her in the passenger side. When he was seated behind the wheel, he reached back and brought out a shopping bag with colored paper tastefully arranged in it. "Open it," he said.

She reached in and pulled out a beautiful lacy black mantilla with red roses embroidered across it. She caught her breath. She collected the beautiful things. This was the prettiest one she'd ever seen. She looked at him with a question in her eyes.

"I picked it out myself," he told her quietly. "I didn't send Jarrett shopping this time. Don't stop. There's more, in the bottom of the bag."

Puzzled, she reached down and her fingers closed around a velvety box with a bow on it. She pulled it out and stared at it curiously. Another watch? she wondered.

"Go on. Open it."

She took off the bow and opened the box. Inside was... another box. Frowning, she opened that one, too, and found a very small square box. She opened that one, too, and caught her breath. It was a diamond. Not too big, not too small, but of perfect quality in what looked like expensive yellow gold. Next to it was an equally elegant band studded with diamonds that matched the solitaire.

J.B. was holding his breath, although it didn't show.

She met his searching gaze. "I...don't understand."

He took the box from her, lifted out the solitaire and slid it gently onto her ring finger. "Now, do you understand?"

She was afraid to try. Surely it was still part of the dream. If not, it was a cruel joke.

"You don't want me," she said bitterly. "I'm ugly, and you can't bear me to touch you...!"

He pulled her across into his arms and kissed her with unabashed passion, cradling her against his broad chest while his mouth proceeded to wear down all her protests. When she was clinging to him, breathless, he folded her in his arms and rocked her hungrily.

"I was ashamed that you found me like that with Bella," he said through his teeth. "It was like getting caught red-handed in an adulterous relationship. For God's sake, don't you have any idea how I feel about you, Tellie?" he groaned. "I was frustrated and impatient, and Bella was handy. But I've never slept with her," he added firmly. "And I never would have. You have to believe that."

She was reeling mentally. She let her head slide back on his shoulder so that she could see his face. "But…why were you so cruel…?"

His lean hand pressed against her cheek caressingly. "Do you remember when you were eighteen?" he asked huskily. "And I made love to you on the couch in the living room?"

She flushed. "Yes."

"You loved being kissed. But when I started touching you, I felt you draw back. You liked kissing me, but you weren't comfortable with anything more intimate than that. You didn't feel anything approaching passion, Tellie. You were like a child." He sucked in a harsh breath. "And I was burning, aching, to have you. I knew you were too young. It was unfair of me to push you into a relationship you weren't nearly ready for." He studied her shocked face. "So I drew back and waited. And waited. I grew bitter from the waiting. It made me cruel."

Her eyes were wide, shocked, delighted, as she realized what had been going on. She hadn't dreamed that he might feel something this powerful for her, and for so long.

"Yes, now you see it, don't you?" he breathed, lowering his mouth to hers again, savoring its shy response. "I was at the end of my rope, and you seemed just the same. Desperation made me cruel. Then," he whispered, "you lost your memory and I had you in my house. I touched you…and you wanted me." He kissed her hungrily, roughly. "I was over the moon, Tellie. You'd forgotten, temporarily, all the terrible things I said to you when you caught me with Bella. But it ended, all too soon. Your memory came back." He buried his face in her neck, rocking her. "You hated me. I didn't know what to do. So I waited some more. And hoped. I might still be waiting, except that Bella told me she saw you crying in the emergency room when I thought you hadn't even come to see about me after the tornado hit." He kissed her again, hungrily, and felt with a sense of wonder her arms clinging to him, her mouth answering the passion of his own.

"You brought that awful woman to Marge's house and let her insult me," she complained hotly.

He kissed her, laughing. "You were jealous," he replied, un-ashamedly happy. "It gave me hope. I dangled Bella to make you jealous. It worked almost too well."

"You vicious man," she accused, but she was smiling.

"Look who's talking," he chided. "Grange gave me some bad moments."

"I like him very much, but I didn't love him," she replied quietly.

"No. You love me," he whispered. His eyes ate her face. "And I love you, Tellie," he whispered as he bent again to her mouth. "I love you with all my heart!"

She closed her eyes and gave in to his ardor, blind to the fact that they were sitting in a parked car on a college campus.

She felt some disturbance around her and looked up. In front of the car were three students with quickly printed squares of poster paper. One said "9," and two said "10." They were grading J.B. on his technique. He followed her amused gaze and burst out laughing.

He drew her up closer. "Don't protest," he murmured as his head bent. "I'm going for a perfect score…"

He took her back to his hotel. His intentions were honorable, of course, but it was inevitable that once they were alone, he'd kiss her. He did, and all at once the raging fever he'd contained for so many years broke its bonds with glorious abandon.

"J.B.," she protested weakly as he picked her up and carried her into one of the bedrooms in his suite, closing the door firmly behind them.

"You can't stop an avalanche, honey," he ground out against her mouth. "I'm sorry. I love you. I can't wait any longer…!"

She was flat on her back, her jeans on the floor, swiftly joined by her blouse and everything underneath. He looked down at her with a harsh, heartfelt groan. "I knew you'd be perfect, Tellie," he whispered as he bent to touch his mouth reverently to her breasts.

There was hardly any sane answer to that sort of rapt delight. She felt faintly apprehensive, but she was wearing an engagement ring and it was apparent that it wasn't a sham, or a dream. She came straight up off the bed as his mouth increased its warm pressure on her breast and began to taste it with his tongue.

"Like that, do you?" he whispered huskily. "It's only the beginning."

As he spoke, he sat up and quickly removed every bit of fabric that would have separated them.

Shyly she looked at his hard, muscular body with eyes that showed equal parts of awe and apprehension.

"People have been doing this for millennia," he whispered as he lowered his body against hers. "If it didn't feel good, nobody would indulge."

"Well, yes, but…" she began.

His lean hand smoothed over her belly. "You have to trust me," he said softly. "I won't hurt you. I swear it."

Her body relaxed a little. "I've heard stories," she began.

"I'm not in them," he replied easily, smiling. "If I were less modest, I'd tell you that women used to write my telephone number on bathroom walls."

That tickled her and she laughed. "Don't you dare brag about your conquests," she muttered.

He laughed. "Practice," he said against her mouth. "I was practicing, while I waited for you. And this is what I learned, Tellie," he added as his body slid against hers.

She felt his hands and his mouth all over her. The lights were on and she couldn't have cared less. Sensation upon sensation rippled through her untried body. She saw J.B.'s face harden, his dark green eyes glitter as he increased the pressure of his powerful legs to part hers, as his mouth swallowed one small, firm breast and drew his tongue against it in a sweet, harsh rhythm.

He was touching her in ways she'd only read about. She gasped and moaned and, finally, begged. She hadn't dreamed that her body could feel such things, could react in this headlong, demanding, insistent way to a man's slow, insistent ardor.

The slow thrust of his body widened her eyes alarmingly and she tensed, but he whispered to her, kissed her eyes closed, and never stopped for an instant. He found the place, and the pressure, that made her begin to sob and dig her nails into his hips. Then he smiled as he increased the rhythm and heard her cry out again and again with helpless delight.

It seemed hours before he finally gave in to his own need and shuddered against her in a culmination that exceeded his wildest dreams of fulfillment. He held her close, intimately joined to him, and fought to get enough air to breathe.

"Cataclysmic," he whispered into her throat. "That's what it was."

She was shivering, too, having experienced what the self-help articles referred to as "multiple culminations of pleasure."

"I never dreamed…!" she exclaimed breathlessly.

"Neither did I, sweetheart," he said heavily. "Neither did I."

He moved and rolled over, drawing her close against his side. They were both damp with sweat and pulsating in the aftermath of explosive satisfaction.

"Marge would kill us both," she began.

He chuckled. "Not likely. She's been busy on our behalf."

"Doing what?" she asked.

He ruffled her dark hair. "Sending out e-mailed invitations, calling caterers, ordering stuff. Which reminds me, I hope you're free Saturday. We're getting married at the ranch."

She sat up, gasping. "We're what?"

"Getting married," he replied slowly. "Why do you think I bought two rings?"

"But you've been swearing for years that you'd never get married!" Then she remembered why and her eyes went sad. "Because of that woman, the one you were going to marry," she said worriedly.

He drew her down beside him and looked at her solemnly. "When I was twenty-one, I fell in love. She was my exact opposite, and because my father opposed the marriage, I rebelled and ran headlong into it. She took the easy way out, rather than fighting him. You were right about that, although it hurt me to acknowledge it," he said quietly. "You'd have marched right up to my father and told him to do his worst." He smiled. "It's one of the things I love about you, that stubborn determination. She wasn't strong enough to stand up to him. So she killed herself. It would have been a disaster, if she hadn't," he added. "I'd have walked all over her, and she'd have been miserable. As things worked out, she saved her brother from prison and both of us from a bitter life together. I'm sorry it happened that way. I think she was mentally unstable. She was unhappy and she couldn't see a future without me. If she'd been able to talk to anyone about it, I don't think she'd have done it. I'll always regret what my father did, but he paid for it, in his way. So did I, unfortunately. Until you came along, and shook up my life, I didn't have much interest in living."

She felt happier, knowing that. She was sad for his fiancée, but she couldn't be sad that she'd ended up with J.B.

He traced her eyebrows, exploring her face, her soft body, with slow, tender tracings. "I never knew what love was, until you were eighteen. It was too soon, but I'd have married you then, if you'd been able to return what I felt for you."

Her arms closed around him. "It was too soon. I have a degree and I've had independence."

"And now?" he asked. "What about college?"

She drew in a slow, lazy breath. "You can always go back to college," she murmured. "I'd like to be with you for a few years. We might have a baby together and I'll be needed at home for a while. I can teach adult education at our community college if I get the urge. I only need a B.A. for that, and I've got it."

"We might have a baby together?" he teased, smiling. "How would that happen?"

She drew up one long leg and slid it gently over one of his. "We could do a lot more of what we've just done," she suggested, moving closer to him. "If we do it enough, who knows what might happen?"

He pursed his lips and moved between her legs. "More of this, you mean?" he drawled, easing down.

"Definitely…more of this," she whispered unsteadily. She closed her eyes and tugged his mouth down over hers. Then she didn't speak again for a long, long time.

Twelve

Nell was overcome with delight when Tellie walked into Marge's house with J.B.'s arm around her. "You're back," she exclaimed to Tellie. "But what…how…why?"

J.B. lifted Tellie's left hand and extended it, with the diamond solitaire winking on her ring finger.

"Oh, my goodness!" Nell exclaimed, and hugged both of them with tearful enthusiasm. "Have you told Marge and the girls?" she asked.

"Marge is making all the arrangements for us," J.B. said with an ear-to-ear grin. "I'm sure she's told the girls. But it looks as if she was saving it as a surprise for you!"

"I can't believe it," Nell repeated, dabbing at her wet eyes. "I've never been so happy for anyone in my life! Have you had lunch?"

"Not yet," J.B. replied. "I thought we might have it with you, if that's all right?" he added with unexpected courtesy.

Nell's eyebrows went up. "Well! That's the first time you've ever treated me with any sort of courtesy."

"She's been working on me," he said, nodding toward Tellie.

"To good effect, apparently, too," Nell agreed. "I'm just floored!"

"Cook while you're getting adjusted," J.B. suggested. "I'm going to get Tellie's bag from her room and put it in the car. Marge packed it for her."

"Thanks," she said shyly, and not without a smile.

"How did you do it?" Nell asked when he was out of sight.

Tellie shook her head. "I have no idea. He showed up at the café where I was having coffee, and the next thing I knew, I was engaged. I thought he was involved with Bella."

"So did I," Nell agreed.

"But he wasn't," she replied, with a happy smile. "I went away thinking my life was over. Now look at me."

"I couldn't be happier for you," Nell said. "For both of you."

"So am I," Tellie told her. "In fact, I'm over the moon!"

Later, Marge and the girls came home, and all of them spent the evening going over wedding plans, because there wasn't much time.

J.B. drove Tellie to his house and installed her in the same guest bedroom he'd given her when she stayed with him during her bout of amnesia. They'd already decided that they'd abstain from any more sensual adventures until after the wedding, however old-fashioned it sounded.

The next day, J.B. bounced Tellie out of bed early. "Get up, get up," he teased, lifting her free of the covers to kiss her with pure delight. "We're going shopping."

"You and me?" she asked, breathless.

He nodded, smiling. "You look pretty first thing in the morning."

"But I'm all rumpled and my hair isn't brushed."

He kissed her again, tenderly. "You're the most beautiful

thing in my house, and in my heart," he whispered against her lips.

She kissed him back, sighing contentedly. She had the world in her arms, she thought. The whole world!

Albert fixed them croissants and strong coffee for breakfast, and J.B. privately lamented the lack of bacon and eggs and biscuits that Nell had always provided. Albert considered such a breakfast too heavy for normal people.

After breakfast, J.B. drove Tellie to a boutique in San Antonio to shop for a wedding gown.

"But you can't see it!" she insisted.

He glowered at her. "That's an old superstition!"

"Whether it is or not, you aren't looking," she said firmly. "Go get a cup of coffee and come back in an hour. Okay?"

He sighed irritably. "All right."

She reached up and kissed him sweetly. "I love you. Humor me."

He stopped glowering and smiled. "Headache," he accused.

"I'll make it all up to you. I promise."

He bent and brushed his mouth over her closed eyelids. "You already have. Everything!"

She hugged him close. "Go away."

He laughed, winking as he left her to go down the street toward a nearby Starbucks shop.

The owner of the boutique gave her a wicked grin. "You manage him very well."

"I do, don't I? But he doesn't know I'm doing it, and we're not going to tell him. Deal?"

"Deal! Now let me show you what I've got in your size…"

Tellie ended up with a gloriously embroidered gown with cape sleeves, a tight waist, a vee neckline and an exquisite long train, also embroidered. The veil was held in place by jeweled combs and fell to the waist in front. It was the most beautiful gown she'd ever seen, and it suited her nice tan.

"I love it," Tellie told the owner. "It's a dream of a wedding gown."

"It looks lovely on you," came the satisfied reply. "Now for the accessories!"

By the time J.B. came back, the gown and accessories were all neatly boxed and ready to carry out.

"Did you get something pretty?" he asked.

"Something beautiful," Tellie told him, smiling.

"I wish you'd let me pay for it," he said as they drove home. "I'd have taken you to Neiman Marcus."

"What I got is lovely," she said, "and one of a kind. The owner of the boutique is a designer in her own right. You'll see. It's going to make a stir."

He clasped her hand tight in his own. "You'll make the stir, sweetheart. You're lovely."

She gave him an odd look, and his jaw tautened.

"I didn't mean it, Tellie," he said quietly. "I was ashamed and frustrated and I took it all out on you. I wanted you so much. I thought you'd never be able to feel desire for me. It made me cruel."

"Maybe if you'd tried a little harder," she pointed out, "it wouldn't have taken me so long."

He sighed. "Leave it to you to put your finger on a nerve and push," he said philosophically. "Yes, I should have. But I was still living in the past, afraid of being devastated again by love. It wasn't until Grange came along, and cauterized the wound, that I realized I was using the past as an excuse. Maybe I sensed that it was going to be different with you."

"I can see why you were reluctant," she said. Her hand tightened in his. "But I'd never hurt you, J.B. I love you too much."

"Thank God for that," he said, sighing contentedly. He smiled. "You'll never get away from me, Tellie."

"I'll never want to." She meant it, too.

The wedding was a small, private one, but two reporters with cameramen showed up, and so did Grange, resplendent in a blue vested suit. He looked very different from the cowboy Tellie had dated. The Ballengers were there, also, with their wives, and of course Marge and Dawn and Brandi and Nell. Even Albert put on a suit and gave Tellie away.

Tellie couldn't see much of J.B. as she walked down the aisle with her veil neatly in place. But when she got to the altar, she was shocked, delighted and amused to see what he was wearing with his suit. It was one of the ties—the gaudy, green-and-gold dragon tie that she'd given him for every single birthday and Christmas for years. She had to force herself not to laugh. But she didn't miss his wink.

When the minister pronounced them man and wife, he turned and lifted her veil, and the look on his face was the most profound she'd ever seen. He smiled, tenderly, and bent and kissed her with soft, sweet reverence.

Nell and Marge cried. The girls sighed. Tellie pressed close into J.B.'s arms and just hugged him, feeling radiant and happier than she'd ever been in her life. He hugged her back, sighing contentedly.

"I suppose the best man won," Grange mused at the reception Albert and the caterers had prepared in the ballroom at the ranch.

"I guess he did," J.B. replied, with a forced smile.

"She's very special," the other man said quietly. "But it was always you, and I always knew it. I'm a bad marriage risk."

"I thought I was, too," J.B. replied. He looked toward Tellie with his heart in his eyes. "But maybe I'm not."

Grange just laughed, and lifted his champagne glass in a toast.

"How'd you come out at the court-martial?" J.B. asked.

Grange grinned. "He got five years. I got a commendation and the offer of reinstatement."

"Are you going to take them up on it?"

Grange shrugged. "I don't know yet. I'll have to think about it. I've had another offer. I'm thinking it over."

"One that involves staying here?" J.B. asked shrewdly.

"Yes." He met the other man's gaze. "Is that going to be a problem."

J.B. smiled wryly. "Not now that Tellie's married to me," he drawled.

Grange laughed. "Just checking."

J.B. sipped champagne. "The past is over," he said. "We can't change it. All we can do is live with it. I loved your sister. I'm sorry things worked out the way they did."

"She was a sad person," the other man replied solemnly. "It wasn't the first time she'd thought about taking her own life. There were two other times, both connected with men she thought didn't want her."

J.B. looked shocked.

Grange grimaced. "Sorry. Maybe I shouldn't have said anything. But in the long run, you're better off with the truth. She was emotionally shattered, since childhood. She went to a psychiatrist when she was in high school for counseling, because she slashed her wrists."

"I didn't know," J.B. ground out.

"Neither did I until my father was dying, and told me everything. He said my mother had always worried that suicide would end my sister's life. She couldn't handle stress at all. It's nothing against her. Some people are born not being able to cope with life."

"I suppose they are," J.B. said, and he was remembering

Tellie, and how she would have handled the same opposition from his father.

Grange clapped J.B. on the shoulder. "Go dance with your wife. Let the past bury itself. Life goes on. I hope both of you will be very happy. And I mean that."

J.B. shook his hand. "Thanks. You can come to dinner sometimes. As long as you don't bring roses," he added dryly.

Grange burst out laughing.

That night, Albert went to see his brother for the weekend, and Tellie and J.B. spent lazy, delicious hours trying out new ways to express their love for each other in his big king-size bed.

She was shivering and pouring sweat and gasping when they finally stopped long enough to sip cold champagne.

"I just didn't read enough books," she said breathlessly.

He grinned. "Good thing I did."

She laughed, curling close to his hairy chest. "Don't brag."

"I don't need to. Will you be able to walk tomorrow?"

"Hobble, maybe," she murmured sleepily. "I'm so tired…!"

He bent and kissed her eyelids shut. "You're magnificent."

"So are you," she said, kissing his chest.

He took the champagne glass away, put it on the table along with his own and stroked her hair. "Tellie?"

"Hmm?"

"I hope you want kids right away."

"Hmm."

He drew in a lazy breath and closed his eyes. "That had better be a yes, because we forgot to think about precautions."

She didn't answer. He didn't worry. She'd already made her stand on children very clear. He figured he'd get used to fatherhood. It would be as natural as making love to Tellie. And *that* he seemed to do to perfection, he thought, as he glanced down at her satisfied, dreamy expression.

"It's just indecent, that's what it is," Marge groaned as she and Tellie went shopping at the mall outside Jacobsville. She glowered at the younger woman. "I mean, honestly, J.B. didn't have to be so impatient!"

"It was a mutual impatience," Tellie pointed out with a grin, "and I'm happier than I ever dreamed I could be."

"Yes, but Tellie, you've just been married two weeks!"

"I noticed."

Marge shook her head. "J.B.'s strutting already. You shouldn't let him send you on errands like this. I mean, things do go wrong, sometimes…"

"They won't this time," Tellie said dreamily. "I'm as sure of it as I've ever been of anything. Besides," she added with a grin, "tell me you aren't excited."

Marge grimaced. "Well, I am, but…"

"No buts," Tellie said firmly. "We just take one day at a time and enjoy it. Hi, Chief!" she broke off to greet their police chief. "How's it going?"

"Life is beautiful," Cash Grier said with a grin.

"We heard that Tippy laid a frying pan across the skull of her would-be assassin," Marge said, digging gently.

"She did. And have you seen the tabloid story about it, by any chance?" he asked them, and his dark eyes twinkled.

"The one that says you're getting married soon?" Tellie teased.

"That's the one. In fact, we're getting married tomorrow." He chuckled. "I'm not going to let her get away now!"

"Congratulations," Tellie told him. "I hope you'll both be as happy as J.B. and I are."

"We're going to be," he said with assurance. "I expect to grow old fighting what little crime I can dig up here in Jacobsville. In between, Tippy may make a movie or two before we start our family."

Tellie put a hand on her belly. "J.B. and I already have started," she said, smiling from ear to ear. "The blood test came back positive just yesterday."

He whistled. "You two don't waste time, do you? You've only been married two weeks!"

"We were sort of in a hurry," Tellie chuckled.

"A flaming rush," Marge added. "And now we're out prematurely buying maternity clothes, do you believe it?"

"That's the spirit," Cash said. "If you've got it, flaunt it, I always say."

He went on toward his squad car, and Tellie dragged Marge into the maternity shop.

Three months later, J.B. came in looking like two miles of rough road. He was wet and muddy and his chaps were as caked as his shirt. But when he saw Tellie in her maternity pants and blouse, all the weariness went out of his face.

He chuckled, catching her by the waist. "I love the way that looks," he said, and bent to kiss her. "I'm all muddy," he murmured when she tried to move closer. "We don't want to mess up that pretty outfit. Tell you what, I'll clean up and we'll call Marge and the girls and go out for a nice supper. How about that?"

She hesitated, looking guilty. "Well…"

His eyebrows arched. "Is something wrong?" he asked, suddenly worried.

"It's not that."

"Then, what?"

"So you're finally home!" came a stringent voice from the direction of the kitchen. Nell came out, wearing a dirty apron and carrying a big spoon. "I made you chicken and dumplings, homemade rolls and a congealed fruit salad," she announced with a smile.

J.B. drew in a sharp breath. "You're back? For good?" he asked hopefully.

"For good," she said. "I have to take care of Tellie and make sure she eats right. Marge is getting some help of her own, so it isn't as if I'm leaving her in the lurch. And I gave her Albert. Is that okay?" she added worriedly.

"Thank God!" he exclaimed. "I didn't have the heart to let him go, but I'm damned tired of French cooking! All I want is meat and potatoes. And apple pie," he added.

"I made one," Nell said. "Albert likes Marge, and the girls love his cooking. They're of an age to like parties. So, all our problems are solved. Right?"

He grinned. "Most of them, anyway. I'll get cleaned up and we'll have a romantic dinner for…"

"Six," Nell informed him.

"Six?" he exclaimed.

Tellie moved close to him and reached up to kiss his dirt-smudged cheek. "I invited Marge and the girls over for chicken and dumplings. It will be romantic, though, I promise. We'll have lots of candles."

He laughed, shaking his head. "Okay. An intimate little romantic dinner for six." He kissed her back. "I love you," he said.

She smiled. "I love you back."

He went upstairs and Nell sighed. "I never thought I'd see the boss look like that," she told Tellie. "What a change!"

"I inspire him," Tellie mused. "And while I'm inspiring, I'd really like to remodel that frilly pink bedroom and make a nursery out of it."

Nell wriggled her eyebrows. "Count on me as a coconspirator. I'll be in the kitchen."

Tellie watched her go. She looked toward the staircase, where J.B. had disappeared. So much pain, she thought, had led to so much pleasure. Perhaps life did balance the two after all. She knew that she'd been so happy. J.B. and a baby, too. Only a few months before, she'd been agonizing over a lonely, cold future. Now she was married, and pregnant, and her husband loved her obsessively. It was a dream come true.

She turned and followed Nell into the kitchen. Life, she thought dreamily, was sweet.

Later, she spared a thought for that poor young woman

who'd died so tragically years ago, and for Grange, who'd paid a high price for his illegal activities. She hoped Grange would find his own happiness one day. He'd gone to D.C., but was planning to come back and do something a little more adventurous than working for the Ballengers, but he didn't mention what it was. He'd sent her a post-card telling her that, with his new address. J.B. had seen the card, and murmured that he hoped Tellie wasn't planning any future contact with Grange. She assured him that she hadn't any such plans, and kissed him so enthusiastically that very soon he forgot Grange altogether.

Marge and the girls were happy about the baby, and Marge was finally in the best of health on her new medicines. Tellie was relieved that she continued to improve.

That night, while J.B. slept, Tellie sat and watched his lean, hard face, wiped clean of expression, and thought how very lucky she was. He wasn't perfect, but he was certainly Tellie's dream of perfection. She bent and very softly kissed his chiseled mouth.

His dark eyes slid open and twinkled. "Don't waste kisses, sweetheart," he whispered, and reached up to draw her down into his warm, strong arms. "They're precious."

"Yours certainly are," she whispered back, and she smiled contentedly against his mouth.

"Yours, too," he murmured.

She closed her eyes and thought of a happy future, where they'd be surrounded by children and, later, grandchildren. They'd grow old together, safe in the cocoon of their love for each other, with a lifetime of memories to share. And this, Tellie thought with delight, was only the beginning of it all! Her arms tightened around J.B. Life was sweeter than her dreams had ever been. Sweeter than them all.

BRANDED
Annette Broadrick

Annette Broadrick believes in romance and the magic of life. Since 1984, Annette has shared her view of life and love with readers. In addition to being nominated by *Romantic Times Magazine* as one of the Best New Authors of that year, she has also won the *Romantic Times* Reviewers' Choice Award for Best in its Series; The *Romantic Times* WISH award; and the *Romantic Times Magazine* Lifetime Achievement Awards for Series Romance and Series Romantic Fantasy. Annette Broadrick has written over fifty books.

Prologue

The Crenshaws were having a barbecue and everyone for miles around had been invited. Strings of lights decorated the large live oaks surrounding the hacienda-style homestead and dozens of tiki lamps discouraged mosquitoes. The patio had been cleared for dancing to the music of a local country-western band. Joe finished serving the last of the line of guests barbecued ribs, beef and sausage he'd prepared, pleased to see everyone having fun. He and Gail always enjoyed giving parties.

"Fill you a plate and c'mon over here and sit down, Joe," Randy, one of his friends, called. "We've been talking about the Crenshaw family and my grandson's asking all kinds of questions I can't answer."

Joe laughed, filled his plate and ambled over to the long picnic table where he sat down with some of the guests. After polishing off some ribs, Joe asked, "What's your questions, Teddy?"

The twelve-year-old blushed. "I was wondering how long the Crenshaws have lived here."

"Since 1845."

Teddy's eyes rounded. "Wow!"

"Yep, it's been a long time since Jeremiah Crenshaw rode in to Texas. Back then, it was still a republic. So we've been here longer than Texas has been a state."

"What made him come to the Hill Country?"

"He'd heard about the area from people he'd met after he arrived in Texas. When he checked out the place, he knew this was where he wanted to settle. Luckily for him, the Republic was struggling financially and he bought the land at a good price."

"How much land?"

Before Joe could answer Teddy's question, Randy said, "It's not polite to ask how much land a person has, son. It's like asking how much money a man's got in the bank."

Joe grinned. "Oh, I don't think Jeremiah would have been offended by the question. He was proud of his holdings. I don't have the exact figures in front of me, but I know it was several thousand acres. He tended to keep track of it in miles rather than acres."

"I betcha he had to hire a bunch of people to work for him, didn't he?"

"That's true and once again J.C. lucked out. Once Texas joined the United States the following year, people from back East headed to Texas, where land was plentiful and cheap. Jeremiah sold off small parcels of land to those who wanted to work for him. He built homes and bachelor quarters for those who didn't want to buy."

"How did he feed so many people?" Teddy asked.

Joe grinned. "He was a wheeler-dealer, that's for sure. He convinced the railroad owners to run tracks out here. That way he could ship his cattle, wool and leather products out and have needed supplies shipped back."

"Was New Eden already a town?"

"More like a settlement at first. Some people didn't want to ranch, so mercantile stores and livery stables and—"

"—And saloons!"

"And saloons, as well as feed stores and a hotel, were built around the end of the railroad line. Back then, the town was called Trail's End."

Randy said, "Well, I'll be. I never knew that. You sure know your history, Joe."

"It helped that as the years passed, some of the wives of the Crenshaw men decided to keep a sort of diary of events that eventually formed a history of the family and the area. My dad had it published several years back. You could find a copy in the library, if you want to know more."

The table discussion turned to other things but Joe kept thinking about Crenshaw history. Once the others decided to listen to the live band and maybe dance some, Joe wandered over to the edge of the crowd and sat in one of the lawn chairs ranged beneath one of the large live oak trees.

The party was just one of many traditions handed down in the family. As time passed, schools and churches had been built, bringing in more people. The family helped newcomers settle and adjust to the western frontier. The common threat of Indian raids, rustlers and drought, as well as the loneliness that was part of living in Texas at the time, drew people together and forged the character of those who fought to keep their property. The Crenshaw heirs had always considered themselves guardians of their land. Each one inherited Jeremiah's strength, determination, toughness and a rowdiness that was a part of life in Texas, Joe thought, smiling.

Eventually the ranch and other holdings were incorporated, making each member of the family a shareholder as well as apportioning land to each family. Even now there was more than enough land to provide every Crenshaw with a large lot on which to build a home. Not all of them chose to work the land, but there was no question that they belonged to the Hill Country.

His second-in-command on the ranch, Kenneth Sullivan, walked over to where Joe sat, carrying a couple of long-necked bottles of beer.

"Hope you don't mind if I join you, Joe," he said.

"Not at all. Glad to have the company. I like getting away for a while to watch everyone enjoying themselves."

Ken settled into the chair next to Joe and handed him one of the beers. "They're doing that, all right, especially Ashley. I can't thank you enough for throwing this birthday party for her. Sixteen is a pretty important milestone in a girl's life."

"My four guys counted the days, remember? They could hardly wait to get their driver's license so they could drive somewhere besides on the ranch."

Ken nodded to a group gathered beneath a cluster of trees on the other side of the clearing where the party was taking place. "It's hard enough for me to get used to the idea that my Ashley's growing up so fast, but I swear those boys of yours are adding inches to their height every day!"

Joe smiled. "Not to mention the increased food bill. When Jake returned home from college a couple of years ago, there was a noticeable increase in the amount of food hauled into the house."

Ken laughed and said, "You got to admit he's putting in some long hours now that he's officially in charge of the livestock on the ranch."

"He always has, Ken. I told Gail the other night I figure he must be old Jeremiah come back in the flesh. He loves this place. I couldn't be more pleased that he's taking over for me."

He watched his tall, broad-shouldered, narrow-hipped and deeply tanned sons, their bodies honed by nature into mean, lean, fighting machines—each one too handsome for his own good.

The oldest—Jake—was twenty-four.

Jared, recently graduated from college at twenty-two, was already showing his skill at finding oil. He loved the land as well and was making plans to look for oil on the Crenshaw property.

At twenty, Jude was living up to the Crenshaw men's reputation as rowdy and reckless.

The youngest, Jason, was eighteen and still in high school. Unfortunately, he considered Jude to be the perfect role model and was well on his way to building his own reputation as a hell-raiser.

"Hi there, you two," Gail said, walking up to Joe and Ken. "The party's a success, don't you think?" she said, sounding a little breathless. She had been dancing the two-step and Joe had watched her graceful moves, thinking she looked barely old enough to vote. The band now played a slow, romantic song.

"Looks like," he agreed amiably. "You having fun?"

She laughed. "I always have fun throwing a party, as you well know. Will you come dance with me?"

"Have you ever heard me turn down the opportunity to get my arms around you?" he asked, winking at Ken. He stood and dropped his arm around her shoulder. "C'mon, Ken. It's time for you to find a dance partner."

The Crenshaw sons watched the revelry from a safe distance. None of them cared all that much for dancing and they'd made themselves scarce by standing in the shadows.

Jake had been keeping a protective eye on Ashley for most of the evening, amused and pleased to see her enjoying her party.

Ashley had been a tomboy all her life, preferring jeans and western-style shirts to frills and dresses. Seeing her tonight all dressed up had been a shock to him. The short skirt revealed shapely legs, and the combination of a special hairdo—instead of the braid she generally wore—and her carefully made-up face caused a strange and uncomfortable stirring inside him.

She was born on the ranch and had been a large part of his life since she was old enough to follow him around. She'd ridden with him on his horse by the time she was three or four years old and continued to do so until she was old enough to ride alone. He'd kept an eye on her while she tagged along with him to watch ranch hands rewire fences and haul feed when the area hadn't received enough rain to provide enough vegetation for the cattle, sheep and goats.

She'd generally had two or three dogs following her around the place, strays that had quickly found a home once they discovered her soft heart.

There was no sign of that child now. Tonight, she looked like a young woman, provocative and alluring, which bothered him for some reason.

"Looks like your little shadow has grown up, Jake."

Jake glanced at Jude with a half smile. "That she has," he replied thoughtfully.

"It's hard to believe she's sixteen," Jared said, watching Ashley dance the two-step with her dad. "I can still remember how she used to dog your footsteps when we were kids. I never understood where you got your patience."

Jake smiled. "I never minded."

"Not even when she kept telling everybody that she planned to marry you when she grew up?"

"Aw, c'mon. She was—what, six or seven years old? Kid stuff, Jared. She outgrew it."

Jason, who was two years older than Ashley, said, "I wonder if she'd go out with me now? She always laughed before whenever I asked her. Maybe I should try again now that she's older."

Jake frowned. "Considering the reputation you've worked so hard to acquire, I seriously doubt that Ken will let you anywhere near his daughter."

Jason's cheeks turned red. "C'mon, Jake. You know I wouldn't try anything with her. Ken would tear me to bits."

"And when he got through with you, I'd be waiting my turn," Jake replied.

Jude gave Jake a level look. "Why don't *you* date her?"

Jake looked at him, wondering if Jude had lost his mind. "You're kidding, right? I'm much too old for her. Besides, she's always been like a little sister to me." His eyes followed her as she changed partners. "I have to admit, though, that she doesn't look like anybody's little sister in that dress."

"Like I said, she's all grown up. So when are you going to ask her to dance?" Jude teased.

"She prizes her toes too much to want to dance with me," Jake drawled with a slow grin. "She looks to be doing just fine without me. Look at the line of guys waiting to dance with her."

"So, Jake," Jared said. "How do you feel about Dad talking retirement now that you're back home for good?"

"I think he and Mom deserve to take it a little easier," Jake replied. "Mom's already looking at house plans for a smaller place she wants to build down the road a piece. I haven't seen her this excited in a long time. She said she hopes to get Dad to do more traveling. I told 'em to go for it."

He took a drink from his beer before he said to Jared, "I'd be glad to share some of the workload with you, if you'd decide to stay in one place for longer than it takes to drill a well."

"Tending animals 24/7 isn't my idea of fun, bro. I'm happy doing what I do."

"What about you, Jude?" Jake asked. "You want to try your hand at ranching?"

"I don't mind helping out whenever you need me, Jake, you know that, but I sure don't want to make a career of it. Who knows what I'll end up doing. Right now I'm just enjoying life."

Jake's eyebrow raised. "According to Sheriff Boynton, you've been enjoying life a little too much these days. It wouldn't hurt you to work a little harder at staying out of trouble. You could take on more responsibility around here, you know."

"So Dad keeps saying," he replied defensively. "I have to listen to his lectures. I sure don't have to listen to yours."

Someone touched Jake's sleeve and he turned to find Ashley standing at his elbow, smiling at him. She wore her dark hair pulled back from her face, tumbling onto her shoulders in natural waves. Her green eyes sparkled up at him as she said, "May I talk to you, Jake?" she asked.

"Sure." He was surprised when she turned and walked away from his brothers.

She waited until they were several yards from his brothers to speak. "Dance with me," she said wistfully. "I've danced with practically everybody here…except you."

He was already shaking his head before she finished speaking. "Not me, honey. There's a bunch of guys over there mooning over you. Get one of them to dance. You don't want to dance with an old guy like me."

"Old! Twenty-four isn't old."

"It is where you're concerned," he replied without smiling.

She dropped her gaze and looked back at the party. "The party's great, isn't it?" she said, without looking at him. "Your mom and dad have been wonderful, getting this all set up."

"I'm glad you're enjoying it. The folks enjoy throwing parties and Mom had fun planning this one."

"Well, I guess I'll go back and…" Her voice trailed off. She turned back to Jake and said, "If you won't dance, at least give me a birthday kiss."

Jake nodded. He'd kissed her on her nose when she was a kid, causing her to giggle. Now that she was so grown up, he would kiss her cheek, he decided. At least, that was his plan. Only it didn't turn out that way.

She slid her arms around his neck and stood on tip-toe, pressed closely against him. He placed his hands at her waist and when he bent to kiss her, she quickly turned her head and caught his mouth with hers.

He stiffened and attempted to pull away, but she clung to him so tenaciously he didn't want to hurt her. Her soft, moist lips pressed firmly against his, her tongue playfully darting at the seam of his lips. Caught off guard, Jake attempted to say something and when he opened his mouth, her tongue danced lightly across his lips and touched his tongue.

The kiss was erotic and explicit and Jake felt a surge of lust shoot through him that shocked him with its intensity.

This was Ashley! he reminded himself, wondering who had taught her to kiss like that. He grabbed her wrists and shoved her away from him, breathing hard and irritated with himself for not stopping the kiss sooner.

"What the hell do you think you're doing!"

She blinked slowly, as though only now becoming aware of their surroundings. Her mouth was moist from his and her eyes, when she opened them, reflected that she had also been strongly stirred by their kiss.

He was furious with both of them. She had no business kissing any man—especially him—like that. It was indecent, it was—

"Damn it, Ashley. Don't play your teenage games with me. Go find someone your own age to flirt with."

He saw the glint of tears in her eyes as she turned away. How the hell was he supposed to handle this? She'd been practicing her wiles on him, that's all. Maybe she felt safe with him, but if she did she was wrong. She was far from safe when she could turn him on so quickly.

He reached for her wrist and she stopped without turning around.

"I'm sorry, honey, it's just that—"

She tugged her arm loose and continued on her way. He heard her say, "No need to explain further, Jake. You've made yourself quite clear."

Jake turned and slowly walked back to where his brothers stood. It was obvious they had seen and heard what had happened, which didn't help his mood any.

The four of them stood there silently while Jake wrestled with his libido.

"Why are you so shocked, Jake?" Jared finally asked. "You know how she feels about you—you've been her idol all her life. You should have seen that one coming."

"That's bull and you know it. She may have had a childish crush at one time, but—"

"But nothing!" Jude stopped him. "If she had a childish crush, that crush has grown up, Jake. You didn't have to treat her like she was contagious or something."

Jake rubbed his forehead. "All right, all right. You've made your point. I could have been more diplomatic, but she caught me so off-guard that I—" He saw her reach the dance floor and sighed with resignation. "I need to go apologize."

Jake went after her, trying to come up with an explanation for his behavior that wouldn't shock an innocent girl.

He looked for her on the crowded dance floor, but didn't see her. He ran into his mom and asked if she'd seen Ashley.

"She's hard to keep track of, especially tonight." Gail glanced around before saying, "Maybe she went into the house."

He made his way through clusters of guests until he reached the house. Once inside, he frowned at the number of people there, making his search tougher. Because of the hacienda's size, it took him a while to discover that she wasn't in the house.

She was nowhere to be found.

One

Nine years later

"**I**'m in and I raise you twenty-five," Jake said to Tom McCain, the president of the largest bank in town. He glanced at the others—ranchers Kent and Lew, and Curtis, a local lawyer. They were in the back room of the Mustang Bar & Grill, located on the outskirts of New Eden, for their weekly poker game.

Jake sat with his back to the wall, his chair balanced on two legs and his Stetson low on his forehead. He could hear the rowdy noise of the barroom through the thin walls. Cigar smoke eddied and circled around them, and the gathering of beer bottles on the table attested to the fact they had been playing for some time.

By upping the stakes, he would let the others know he was serious about this hand. Since they played dealer's choice, Curtis had chosen seven-card stud.

Jake had learned the small giveaway movements of each player because they had played together for years. Kent absently moved his wedding ring around his finger with his thumb when he had a good hand. Curtis whistled or hummed when he was bluffing. Jake knew that Curtis was unaware of his nervous habit.

Lew had trouble sitting still and had a habit of shifting restlessly in his chair when he couldn't decide if his hand was good enough to win. Jake carefully watched Tom, the banker, looking for possible clues. Tom never fidgeted or changed expression, which made him a tough adversary and a damn good poker player. Probably made him a good banker, as well.

Jake considered any night he bested Tom to be a good night.

Tonight looked to be one of those nights. Tom had two jacks, a ten of spades and a three of diamonds showing. His raises this hand had been strong enough to make Jake wonder if he was holding more than two pair or if he was bluffing.

There was no way to know by his demeanor, but Jake intended to find out.

Kent said, "Too rich for my blood, hombres," and tossed down his cards with a sigh.

Tom was next. He glanced at Jake over his bifocals and said, "I'll meet your twenty-five and raise you fifty."

The other two quickly folded as well.

Curtis dealt them each their last card.

There was a pile of money on the table and the three onlookers watched intently. Jake said, "I'll meet your fifty and call."

Tom studied his cards but, before he could answer, the door from the bar opened, banging against the wall, and a sea of noise swept into the room.

Neither Jake nor Tom acknowledged the intrusion.

Jake kept his eyes on Tom, wondering if he had the cards to beat him.

Jake's concentration was suddenly shattered when his cousin Jordan spoke immediately beside him.

"Sorry to interrupt, Jake, but you're needed at the ranch right away."

Jake shook his head without turning. "Not now, Jordan. Whatever it is, you can handle it."

"Wish I could, but I can't. You need to get out there. Now."

Tom smiled at Jake. "Go on, Crenshaw, I'll guard the pot," causing the other three to laugh.

"I just bet you will. If you're staying in, pay up and let me see what you have."

Tom paid, then placed his cards on the table—three jacks and a pair of tens, a full house. "I hope this teaches you something, Crenshaw," he said and reached for the pot.

"Yeah, Tom, it teaches me that I should have raised you a hundred," Jake replied, and turned the three cards he had down face up. He had a straight flush, three through seven, of clubs. He stood and reached for the money. "I hate to break this up, but as you can see, I'm needed elsewhere."

The rest of them gave him a bad time about winning and leaving immediately afterward, accusing him of planning it that way. Tom leaned back in his chair and said, "Well, hell, Crenshaw, the least you could do is give me a chance to win some of my money back!"

Jake lifted the corners of his mouth in a slight smile. "Next week, Tommy, my boy," he said to the banker. "You'll get your chance."

He finished folding the money and stuck it into his shirt pocket. For the first time since Jordan had barged into the room, Jake turned and actually looked at him.

Twenty-six-year-old Jordan was generally laid-back and low-key. Jake had never seen him this agitated before.

Jake said his goodbyes and walked into the other room, Jordan close on his heels. He continued moving through the crowd, responding to greetings without pausing, until they were outside in the graveled parking lot.

He turned and faced his cousin with considerable irritation.

"All right, Jordan, what the hell is so blasted important that you had to interrupt me at the game tonight? This is my only time to relax, kick back and enjoy myself. If the place were on fire, you would have called the fire department. If you'd spotted rustlers, you would have called the sheriff. So what, in your mind, couldn't wait until I got home?"

"Tiffany."

Jake stiffened. "What are you talking about?" His voice grew louder.

"She's at the ranch."

Jake stared at Jordan, stunned. Why would his ex-wife show up after all this time? He gave his head a quick shake. "Did she say what she wanted?"

Jordan got into his truck and slammed the door. "I'll let her explain that. Told her I'd come get you and I have. Now I'm headed home. If I hadn't been concerned about one of my mares, I wouldn't have been there when she showed up." He gave a brief wave and left.

Jake stood there, his hands on his hips, staring at the taillights until they disappeared from view. Tiffany Rogers had come back to the ranch after she'd vowed never to step foot on the place again. Wasn't that just dandy? He'd never expected to see her again and couldn't imagine what she wanted from him now.

He shook his head in frustration before he climbed

into his truck and headed toward the ranch, thirty miles from town.

What could she want—he glanced his watch—at close to midnight on a Friday night? Hadn't the woman caused him enough trouble?

He remembered the night before she left. She'd been sleeping in a guest bedroom earlier in the week, which wasn't unusual when she didn't get her way about something. By that time in their marriage, he felt he had done everything he could to make her happy and had learned to ignore her sulking. Despite her princess attitude, he'd loved her. He'd hoped that, given time, she would eventually mature into the woman he got glimpses of from time to time.

When he awakened that night and felt her in bed with him, he thought she'd gotten over her latest snit and was ready to make up. He'd sometimes wondered if she picked fights with him because she enjoyed their ritual of reconciling. Whatever her reason, he hadn't put up much resistance, he remembered ruefully.

When he'd left the house at dawn the next morning, as was his habit, he believed that everything was fine between them. When he returned to the house later that day, she was gone, having taken all her possessions as well as some of his.

Within hours, he'd been served with divorce papers. That was when he knew she hadn't been making up with him. She'd been saying goodbye.

They'd been divorced long enough now for him to recover from the shock and devastation he'd felt at the time. They'd been married almost four years when their relationship had blown up in his face.

Of course, he should have known that a Dallas socialite wouldn't be happy living in the country but she'd insisted she didn't care where they lived as long as they were together, and he had been too besotted to realize that their marriage wouldn't work. She'd said what he wanted to hear and he had believed her.

Anyone with half a brain would look at the woman and know that Tiffany Rogers of the Dallas Rogerses would never be content as his wife. He hadn't seen it at the time, probably because his brain hadn't been the part of him making his decisions. Later, during one of her frequent tirades, she'd told him the only reason she'd married him was that he was a Crenshaw—a member of one of the most wealthy and powerful families in the state.

Their divorce had been far from amicable, as the lawyers liked to call a divorce where the husband rolls over and plays dead while the wife walks off with everything. Four years hardly constituted a long-term union and his lawyer—and poker-playing friend, Curtis Boyd—had vigorously fought her when she'd asked for an outrageous amount of money for alimony. He and Curtis knew she didn't need the money. She'd just wanted to get back at him because he refused to let her stomp all over him.

The day he walked out of the courthouse a free man, he made a vow to himself never to get married again. He'd learned his lesson well. Marriage might be great for other people, but he wanted no part of it. He was content to remain a bachelor for the rest of his life.

Now she was back here for God only knew what reason, and once again he was being forced to face her.

The road to the ranch had little traffic at this time of night. He followed its winding path through picturesque hills until he had to slow for the turn into the ranch entrance.

The entrance was framed on either side by curving walls of limestone fashioned years before he was born. He and his brothers used to play king of the mountain on their broad surfaces until the time their dad caught them. Tonight, Jake scarcely noticed the entrance as he continued along the paved private road that eventually led to the main ranch house.

When he reached the house and parked, Jake noticed a black limousine sitting in the shadows beneath the trees. That would be Tiffany, all right, always traveling in style.

With an irritated sigh, Jake got out of the cab of the truck, slammed the door with a satisfying sound and strode toward a side entrance. The sharp sound of his boots on the patio echoed his impatience. He stepped inside the door that opened into the kitchen.

He stopped just inside the doorway. Tiffany sat at the kitchen bar, calmly sipping a glass of iced tea. She'd cut her hair since he'd last seen her and she had on slacks and an open-necked shirt, looking as though she were waiting for a modeling shoot, her hair and makeup impeccable.

As soon as she saw him, Tiffany slipped off the stool and faced him, smiling brilliantly. He recognized—only because he knew her so well—that she was nervous.

Smart woman.

It took a lot of nerve for her to walk into his house when he wasn't there and make herself at home.

He leaned against the doorjamb, folded his arms and waited, his eyes shaded by his hat.

Her smile dimmed.

"Hello, Jake," she said in her sultry voice.

There had been a time when that voice had done all kinds of things to him. He was considerably older and a great deal wiser now.

"What're you doing here?"

A tiny frown appeared between her brows as she fluttered her lashes in simulated surprise. "Is that any way to greet me?" she finally replied, her bottom lip sliding out enough to form a provocative pout. "Ed brought me all the way out here to see you. You could at least be polite."

"I'm not feeling particularly polite at the moment. Who's Ed?"

"Edward James Littlefield Jr."

"Never heard of him."

She made a face. "Of course not. He and his family are quite well known in the Dallas area...banking, you know."

"You haven't answered my question."

She clasped her hands together and attempted another smile, her nervousness more obvious as her bracelets jangled around her wrists.

"I brought you something."

He straightened and started toward her. "Cut out the games, Tiffany. They don't work any more. I don't want anything from you. So if that's why you're here—"

She turned and hurried across the room toward the hallway and said, "But you haven't seen what I brought you, yet," she said over her shoulder.

He strode after her. "Where the hell do you think you're going?" he asked once he reached the front foyer.

"You'll see," she replied lightly as she ran up the wide, curving staircase toward the second floor. She didn't look back.

Damn, but she was irritating! Always playing games, never saying what she actually meant. He shook his head in disgust and followed her. By the time he reached the top of the stairs, she was hurrying toward his wing of the house as if she knew he would stop her if he caught up with her.

He wanted to shake her silly. Once he reached her, he would haul her butt out of his house, but by the time he was close enough, she was already entering one of the bedrooms. Surely she didn't actually think he'd hop in bed with her, did she? He reached the bedroom door and peered inside. She stood beside the bed, her finger to her lips. A night-light that wasn't there earlier gave the room a soft glow.

When she remained silent, he walked over to where she stood and glanced at the bed.

He froze when he saw what was there. Or rather, who was there. A little girl, clutching a faded pink stuffed rabbit with an ear missing, lay there sound asleep, the covers pulled to her shoulders.

He glanced at Tiffany, wondering what she was up to now.

The child had blond curly hair and delicate features. He had no idea how old she was or why she was there.

He shook his head wearily and walked out of the room. He didn't stop until he reached the kitchen. Once there, he went to the refrigerator and reached for a beer. When Tiffany followed him into the room, he turned to face her. "What in the hell is going on, Tiffany?"

"She's your daughter. Her name is Heather and I'm leaving her here with you."

Two

Jake looked at her in silence for several moments before he shook his head in disgust. "Very funny, Tiffany. You'll notice that I'm not laughing, however. Need I remind you that we never had children? As I recall, once we were married, you informed me that you didn't want children because pregnancy would ruin your figure."

He drank a swallow of beer and struggled to hang on to his temper. "What game do you think you're playing here? I haven't seen you in years. Did you suddenly decide that I'm an easier touch than the father of that little girl? Sorry, but that kite won't fly. I'm not paying you child support, Tiffany. You can't hang that one on me. I want you to go upstairs, get your daughter and get the hell out of my home."

It wasn't the child's fault her mother had no integrity, he reminded himself. He couldn't help but feel sorry for the little girl, given her circumstances.

He rolled the bottle he held across his forehead to cool off. What he needed was to stick his head into one of the horse troughs outside. If he stayed in the same room with Tiffany much longer, he might forget that his mama had taught him always to be a gentleman, regardless of the provocation.

Without a word, Jake walked outside and sat down at one of the patio tables.

He stared into the night. The moon was high in the sky, almost full, giving enough light to see the rolling hills beyond his home. The vista usually had a calming effect on him. He hoped it would work this time.

There was no reason to let her get under his skin like that. Getting him to react had probably been her plan all along, wanting to see what he would say and do. Well, she had her answer.

The door opened behind him. He turned his head and watched Tiffany come outside empty-handed. His jaw tightened as she walked in and out of the shadows to the table where he sat. She sat across from him, the light from the kitchen window falling across her face.

He waited for her to speak and when she didn't, he said, "Didn't you forget something? I want you *and* your little girl gone. Now."

Tiffany lifted her chin and stared back at him. He knew that look. She was ready to fight him if she didn't get her own way. Well, too bad. She could throw as many temper tantrums as she wanted to throw, but they wouldn't work. He wasn't going to take her child and pretend it was his.

"Do you remember the night before I moved out of here?"

"Are you talking about the night you crawled into my bed after I was asleep?" he asked grimly.

She smiled at him and nodded. "Yes. I wanted to

show you that you might deny me other things, but you never denied me sex."

"You made your point. Making love to you was the only thing I seemed to do that you approved of. So what?"

"Well, as things turned out, I was a little too eager that night and since you were more than half asleep, we didn't use protection. Imagine my surprise when I discovered I was pregnant." She looked down at her clasped hands, resting on the table. "Mother Nature's little joke on me." Her voice had flattened by the time she'd stopped speaking.

"And I'm supposed to believe that?"

She looked up at him, her gaze meeting his. "I really don't care what you believe. She was born nine months after that night. Do the math."

"I doubt I was the only man who was in your bed around that time."

"I refuse to get into name-calling, Jake. Regardless of what you may want to believe, your name is on Heather's birth certificate. If you have any doubts, have the tests run."

He swallowed, thinking back to that night. He'd made love to her until they were both exhausted. She was right. He hadn't used protection. He supposed the surprise would have been if she *hadn't* gotten pregnant. If he gave the matter any thought after being served with papers, he probably figured she had used protection.

In the silence between them, he could hear the night sounds, the rustle of animals foraging by moonlight, the occasional deep croak of a bullfrog, the distant sound of a dog barking. "If you were pregnant at the final hearing," he said after several minutes, "why didn't the information come out in court?"

She sounded irritated and impatient. "Because I hadn't paid attention to my monthly cycles during that horrible time. I was so distraught that I put any irregularity down to stress. The divorce was final before I discovered the truth."

Which still didn't explain why he didn't know about it. Knowing Tiffany, as soon as she found out, she would've been screaming for his head… or other, more delicate parts of his anatomy…to be removed from his body.

"Why didn't you tell me once you found out?"

"Because I didn't want to have anything more to do with you, that's why! I decided to raise her on my own. There are lots of single mothers who raise their children alone. You'd been so hateful during the divorce proceedings I decided you didn't deserve to know you were going to be a father!"

"So you decided to punish me by not letting me know, is that it?"

"Yes!"

"The only problem with your logic, Tiffany," he said wearily, "is that it isn't punishment if I didn't know about her."

If what she said was true—and it would be easy enough for him to find out—then he really was the father of the little girl upstairs.

His stomach knotted at the thought and he broke into a cold sweat. For more than three years he'd had a child that he never knew existed.

"Why tell me now? Did you figure I'd been punished enough after all this time? You've kept her very existence from me for all these years, Tiffany, including the pregnancy itself. Care to explain to me why, after all this time, you brought her here tonight?"

She shifted and appeared to be trying to decide how to answer him, clasping and unclasping her hands.

Uh-huh. This was going to be good, watching her squirm. If he could find any pleasure in this encounter, which was certainly doubtful, it would be watching Tiffany as she tried to figure a way to justify her actions, which were inexcusable. He knew she was self-absorbed and permanently immature, but he never thought she would stoop so low as to keep a child from her father in order to get revenge.

She looked away from him, chewing her bottom lip. Finally, as though answering his question, she said, "Soon after Heather was born, my schedule became so hectic that my grandmother offered to keep her for me, which worked out great for everyone. Gram had someone to entertain and play with, and I was able to spend time with Heather as often as possible without disrupting her schedule." She paused and rubbed her forehead, as though she had a headache. "The thing is, Gram had a stroke two weeks ago and she's now bedridden. She won't be able to care for Heather."

"So much for raising a child on your own, right, Tiffany? But having your grandmother raise her for you has nothing to do with why you're just now telling me about her." He raised his brow. "Or does it? Without your permanent babysitter you don't know what else to do with her, is that it?"

"No, that is not *it*!" Her calm demeanor fell away and her anger took over. "Certain things have recently changed in my life, for your information. Ed loves and respects me—something *you* never did—and he wants to marry me! We had all our plans made—we wanted to get married in Vegas and honeymoon in Hawaii, and then visit Japan and Australia. Everything would have worked out perfectly if Gram hadn't had her stroke. The timing couldn't have been worse!"

Jake stared at her in amazement. Did this woman care about anyone other than herself? There was no sign that

her grandmother's illness was anything more to her than
an inconvenience.

"Let me get this straight. You planned to go off for
months and leave Heather with your grandmother?"

She lifted a shoulder. "She would have been fine with
Gram. They got along well together. Besides, I've taken
trips before. I doubt she even misses me when I'm gone."

"You must have considered the situation desperate
for you to break your silence to bring her to me."

Tiffany ran her hand through her carefully coiffed
hair, another indication that this meeting wasn't going
the way she'd planned. He wondered what she'd expected he would do when she showed up? Welcome her
and the child with open arms? Be so thrilled to discover
he was a father that he'd ignore the fact she'd kept the
knowledge from him for all this time?

If so, she was even shallower than he'd always
thought.

In a quieter voice, she said, "I thought I'd worked everything out just fine. I told Ed that we'd have to take
Heather with us."

He dropped his head to hide a smile. After a moment
he looked at her and said, "I somehow doubt he was
thrilled with that particular idea. Most men expect to
have their bride all to themselves at that stage of their
marriage."

"I thought he had accepted the idea, although taking
a three-year-old on your honeymoon is certainly not
what either of us planned or wanted!"

"Couldn't your mother have looked after her?"

"That's another problem, entirely. Heather won't behave for Mother."

Another proof that she was probably his. He had to
admire Heather's discrimination. Tiffany's mother was
just an older, even more spoiled, version of her daugh-

ter. Too bad he hadn't recognized the similarity sooner. If he had, none of this would be happening.

On the other hand, if Mrs. Rogers and her grand-daughter—and boy, he would have loved to have seen her face when she found out she was going to be a grandmother!—had gotten along, he would never have known about Heather.

Funny how life worked sometimes.

"We left Dallas this morning," Tiffany continued, intent on her story. "I thought everything had worked out just fine. Ed never said a word to make me believe he hadn't accepted the situation until we were on the road. That's when he told me he wasn't interested in raising someone else's child. He hadn't expected to become a full-time parent when he proposed to me. He assured me that he wouldn't mind if she visited us occasionally, but he didn't want her around all the time."

Tiffany appeared to have run out of steam and just sat there looking at him.

After a moment, he said in a neutral tone, "And you still plan to marry him."

She looked at him with tears in her eyes. "Please understand, Jake. I love him, really love him. He's older, more mature. I've known who he was for years but I never expected him to show any interest in me. When he did, it never occurred to me that accepting Heather would be a problem for him. He knew about her, he'd even met her once, and I thought he would adore her as much as I do." She pulled a handkerchief from her purse and carefully blotted beneath her eyes. "When he told me that, once he realized I wasn't going to leave her in Dallas, he'd arranged for Heather to stay with a professional sitter in Las Vegas while we were overseas, I was horrified. I really was. He made it clear he didn't intend for Heather to go with us and I didn't want her to stay with a stranger. I didn't know what to do."

Jake didn't know what to say. If she still intended to marry this weasel, he figured they deserved each other.

She sighed and said, "That's when I thought about you. I remembered how you were always talking about wanting children. I decided to forgive you for being so mean to me back then. I knew that Heather would be better off with her own flesh and blood for a few months, instead of with some stranger in Vegas."

Maybe the child *was* better off with him, if this was the way she was being treated. He was still having a little trouble absorbing the fact that people could be so callous to their offspring.

He leaned back in his chair, his gaze steady, and said, "You need to understand something before this conversation goes any further, Tiffany. If you intend to leave that little girl with me after not having the decency to tell me she even existed until tonight, I refuse to allow you to bounce her between us in order to suit your convenience."

She frowned at him. "I don't know what you mean, Jake. She's your child, after all. If we can make an arrangement where each of us keeps her part of the time she'll get to know both of us. I realize that I made a mistake keeping her from you. She deserves to know her father."

Damned if she didn't sound pious.

He folded his arms. "You're treating her like a toy you grew tired of playing with. So let me make myself perfectly clear. If you leave here tonight without taking her with you, or if you decide to leave her somewhere in Las Vegas once you get there—and believe me, I'll be keeping tabs on that—I'll make certain you lose all parental rights to her. You will see her only when I think she's capable of handling it."

She looked at him as if he'd slapped her. "You'd take her away from me?" she asked in horror. She started sobbing. "I should have known better than to let you know about her at all. I should have followed my instincts and kept you out of both our lives! I *knew* you were going to be hateful about this. I just knew it!"

He stood. "C'mon, I'll help you get her back to your car."

She jumped up. "No! I can't take her with us. I just can't! I want what's best for her, I really do." Tears continued to run down her cheeks and her nose glowed where she kept wiping it with her handkerchief. She twisted the beleaguered piece of cloth between her hands. "It's just so hard, Jake," she said pathetically, "you know? I don't know the first thing about taking care of her. She won't behave, she ignores what I say, and just the other day she found some cosmetics in my purse and smeared them all over her face. I know she knew better, but she did it just to spite me! I've been doing the best I can, but I just don't know how to deal with her!"

"And you think I do."

Still wringing her handkerchief, she said, "Well, at least I'll know she's with part of her family. I don't think you'll have any trouble getting along with her because you've always been good with children. This is the best thing for Heather. You'll find someone here on the ranch to keep an eye on her when you can't watch her."

Jake held his wrist up to the light. "At one o'clock in the morning? Somehow I doubt that very much."

She seemed to regain control of her emotions, long enough to blow her nose. "I'm sure she'll be okay for a day or two until you find someone to look after her." Tiffany looked around the patio vaguely, no doubt wishing she was anywhere but here. "I, uh, hadn't realized it was so late. Ed and his driver have been so patient, waiting hours for you to come home." She gave him a half smile. "Sorry if I broke up a hot date with one of the local yokels."

Despite her words, she didn't move away. Instead, she continued to stand there, warily watching him.

"I meant what I said, Tiffany. I'm not going to punish this child by moving her back and forth between us at your convenience."

Her shoulders slumped. "I know, Jake. I love her so much, but I'm really not cut out for the whole mother thing, you know? I was horrified when I found out I was pregnant after being extra careful all those years. I didn't know what to do. Gram talked me into having her, promising me to help with her, and I'm not sorry I did. Honestly, I'm not. It's just that…" She paused as though searching for words. "I've always been high-strung, and trying to deal with her has just been too much for me. My nerves can't stand the pressure day in and day out."

She dropped her eyes and slowly turned away.

He made no comment as she left the patio. She'd almost disappeared around the corner of the house when she stopped and said, "I almost forgot, Jake. I brought all the necessary papers you'll need for her—her birth certificate, a record of her shots, that sort of thing. I'd already packed them, thinking she'd need credentials to go overseas with us. I also brought her clothes and other belongings. She's familiar with them and I hope they'll help her to adjust." She looked at him through the shadows. "Goodbye, Jake. Take good care of her."

Jake continued to stand there on the patio without moving. He was numb with all that had happened tonight. In a few moments, he heard the purr of a well-tuned engine and watched as headlights swept across the driveway.

The silence of the country night returned.

Now that she'd gone, he needed to face what had happened. If Tiffany was telling the truth, he had a daughter. A daughter he'd discovered long after he'd finally accepted that he would never have a family of his own.

That was the good news. That was the great news.

The bad news was that he had a daughter who would be waking up in the morning in strange surroundings without a familiar face to reassure her that she was safe. He had a daughter who would probably be afraid of him, at least at first.

Jake rubbed the back of his neck and picked up his empty bottle. He walked into the kitchen, tossed the bottle in one of the recycling bins on hand and looked around, trying to force his mind to wrap around the idea of instant fatherhood.

A large manila envelope he hadn't noticed before lay on the kitchen bar. He sat down on the bar stool Tiffany had used and opened the envelope.

Her birth certificate was on top. Her name was Heather Anne Crenshaw and she'd been born on Sept. 28, which meant she would be four years old in a little over six weeks.

He was listed as her father.

He stared at the document until it grew blurry. He hadn't been there when she was born. He hadn't been there when she learned to sit up, to stand, to take her first step or say her first word. He hadn't been there to watch the infant turn into a little girl.

He'd already missed so much of her life.

Jake removed his hat and hung it on the rack beside the door, turned out the lights downstairs and went up to his room. After he sat on the side of his bed and removed his boots, he returned to Heather's room in his stockinged feet. She had shifted and now lay on her side, still clutching her bedraggled rabbit. He noticed several more stuffed animals sitting at the end of the bed. She looked so innocent lying there, sleeping so soundly. She had no idea how her world had changed yet again. Her great-grandmother's sudden illness must have been devastating to her. And now this.

Eventually he quietly checked the closet and chest of drawers. Yes, Tiffany had amply provided for her, he was thankful to see.

What was he supposed to do now? Come morning, this sweet-looking child was going to wake up and face new people and new surroundings. Of course she would be afraid. She would need to be dressed and fed and...

He froze. Was she housebroken? How would he know? Raised with three brothers, his only experience around little girls was watching Ashley grow up.

Ashley.

She would know what Heather needed, wouldn't she? Would she be willing to help him out for a few days? He hadn't seen much of her in the past several years, not since she'd gone off to Texas A&M, but at one time they'd been the best of friends.

He certainly needed a trusted friend about now.

Would Ashley be able to help him?

She was a doctor, wasn't she?

Sort of. She was a veterinarian. That was close enough, wasn't it?

She was a woman, besides. She'd know what to do with a little girl, since she'd been one herself.

At the moment, he didn't have many options. He was desperate. Surely she would be willing to do whatever needed to be done for his daughter.

Jake returned to his bedroom, looked up her number and called her.

Three

Ashley Sullivan unlocked the door to her small apartment in time to hear her phone ringing. She groaned. It was the middle of the night and she was exhausted. Because this was her weekend on call, she'd already been out on two emergencies tonight, once for a mare having trouble with a breech birth and the other to check out a steer whose owner thought had been bitten by a snake. And this was only Friday night.

A call in the middle of the night was always ominous. She dropped her medical bag and grabbed the phone.

"This is Dr. Sullivan," she said, her voice weary.

"Uh, hi, Ashley."

She sank to the side of her bed, shaken by the realization of who was calling her.

When she didn't immediately respond, he added, "This is Jake Crenshaw. I hope I didn't wake you."

As if she wouldn't know the sound of his voice. Adrenaline shot through her as she thought of possible reasons he would be calling her at this time of night.

"What's happened?" she said with dread. "Is it Dad?"

"No, no. Nothing like that." He paused and she wondered what was going on. She hadn't spoken to Jake in years. "I, uh, I've got an emergency on my hands out here. I hate to ask this of you, but would you mind coming out to the ranch?"

She checked the time and winced. *"Now?"*

He cleared his throat. "I know it's late but I really need you."

"What's wrong?" She had never heard those words from Jake before and they shook her.

When he didn't answer right away, she wondered if he'd hung up. When he did answer, he was frustratingly vague. "I'd rather show you once you get here, all right?"

It was her turn to pause and think about his request. She was exhausted and therefore vulnerable. Let's face it, she would be vulnerable around him no matter when she saw him.

"I'd like to help you out, Jake, but I've been working nonstop since seven this morning. Can this wait until tomorrow?"

"No, it can't." He sounded impatient and irritable, which meant he was being his normal and oh-so-charming adult self, not the boy she'd grown up with. When she didn't reply, he said, "This is something personal. You were the first one I thought of when I knew I needed help."

Ashley put her hand over her heart and tried to breathe. She wasn't prepared for this. Someday, maybe, when she was…oh, sixty-something…she'd be able to deal with her reactions where Jake was concerned.

"I'm sorry—" she began when he interrupted her.

"I know we haven't been as close these past few years as we once were, Ashley," he said.

Ashley pulled the phone away from her ear and frowned at it in disbelief. Talk about understatement!

He continued to speak and she forced herself to listen. "I hoped that you would be willing to help me out based on the friendship we once shared."

Wasn't that just like a man? Oh, yeah, I carelessly trampled on your heart with my size thirteen boots, but, hey, you've patched it up just fine, so how about giving me another go at it.

"Jake," she began, "I really don't think—"

"Ashley," he said, suddenly sounding panicked. "I just received the shock of my life tonight. Tiffany was here earlier and told me that we have a daughter who will soon be four years old. She left her here and I haven't a clue what to do for her or about her or with her."

Ashley was glad she was sitting down. Jake had a daughter? She struggled to breathe around the sudden constriction in her throat.

"The thing is," he continued, "she's going to wake up in a few hours in a strange place to see a man she doesn't recognize." His voice deepened. "I'm hoping you'll come out and be here when she wakes up."

Oh, dear. She was definitely in trouble here. That low, intimate tone of his had always melted her heart. This conversation was not going well at all. "You mean stay at Dad's?" she finally asked.

"I mean stay here with me and Heather. That's her name, by the way. Heather Anne Crenshaw."

Ashley closed her eyes. What should she do? She was too exhausted to think straight. Being anywhere around Jake—and in his home, no less—would be so painful for her.

But this wasn't about Jake.

He has a daughter. The daughter she'd dreamed someday they would have together. Sure, she'd been a

naïve kid at the time who'd thought his casual acceptance of her in his life meant more than it had. Harsh
reality had set in years ago, but his having a daughter
seemed to trigger a whole bunch of memories she'd
hoped she'd buried.

"All right," she finally said, resigned to the coming or-
deal. "I wouldn't want to be the one responsible for scar-
ring her for life because she had to face you first thing in
the morning." A hint of a smile hovered on her lips.

She heard the relief in his voice. "Thank you, Ashley. I promise you won't regret this."

Oh yeah? She was already regretting it, but he'd hit
a weak spot she'd always had for children. "I'll be there
as soon as I can," she said and hung up.

She glanced down at her clothes and wearily shook
her head. After a day in the office and an evening around
large animals, she had to clean up before going anywhere. Although she'd scrubbed up at each place, her
clothes were far from clean.

Ashley walked into the bathroom and stared at herself in the mirror. She was glad she'd had her hair cut
last year, saving her precious time and worry with her
busy schedule. The short style was definitely a wash-
and-wear hairdo.

Deep shadows beneath her eyes reflected her weariness. She closed them briefly. You can do this. Dredge
up some energy somewhere and do it.

She stripped out of her clothes and stepped into the
shower, letting the water flow over her while she did her
best to make her mind blank.

Instead, more memories flooded her.

Jake at twelve, following their dads everywhere they
went, with her four-year-old self trailing along behind.
Riding in front of him in the saddle, asking jillions of
questions, making him laugh. He'd been tall for his age,

with a shock of thick blond hair that invariably looked untidy, the most gorgeous eyes that changed from a smoky blue to a silvery gray, depending on his mood, and a smile that could stop a female's heart at twenty paces.

Not that any of that registered with her at four years old. All she knew then was that she didn't want to let him out of her sight.

By the ripe old age of seven, she'd known that this was the person she would marry someday and told everyone who would listen. Now she wondered how fifteen-year-old Jake had dealt with the teasing he must have gotten back then. If he'd been embarrassed by her remarks, he'd never let on to her.

Jake had made her childhood magical. He'd taught her how to ride a horse, rope a calf and how to safely handle and shoot a rifle. He'd cautioned her never to leave the settlement alone without protection from the wild animals that lived in the hills. They'd spent many hours following various animal tracks until she could recognize what had made them and how to avoid the dangerous ones.

He'd been in college when Ashley was twelve and her mother left. As soon as he heard about it, Jake had come home to check on her and make sure she was able to cope. With his help and the ongoing concern of his family and her dad she'd eventually adjusted to being left behind.

Her childhood ended when her mother left. She wondered what she would have done during that time without her dad and the Crenshaw family.

Her love for Jake grew steadily stronger as the years went by.

She'd looked forward to her sixteenth birthday for years, having decided that sixteen was the time when she would be truly grown up, the time when Jake would see her as a woman, when he might declare his feelings for her and promise to wait for her until she was finished with school and they could be married.

A stupid dream had come crashing down the night of her birthday. Oh, he'd declared his feelings, all right, but his declaration had been nothing like she'd imagined it would be, and she'd been forced to recognize that she had been a complete fool where he was concerned.

Any lingering doubts about his feelings for her were put to rest two years later, when he married Tiffany a few weeks before Ashley graduated from high school.

She'd cried for days, trying to come to grips with her shattered dreams. Many a night she had dreamed about Jake—a penitent Jake, begging her to forgive him for the way he had treated her, promising to make up for his behavior by offering his undying love to her and begging her to marry him.

She'd gone to the wedding with her dad, despite the fact they had to drive to Dallas and stay the weekend. Her dad told her that Jake had paid all the expenses for the families living on the ranch who wanted to attend his wedding.

She would never forget the look on his face the day Tiffany walked down the aisle toward him. He'd never looked at *her* like that. That was when she knew with absolute certainty that he had never thought of her as anything more than a kid, a nuisance that he'd accepted as part of his life.

A few weeks later, she'd convinced her dad to let her begin college that summer and she had left soon after Jake and Tiffany returned from their honeymoon. There was no way she could hang around the ranch watching them together. Except for brief visits to see her dad over the years, she'd stayed away from the ranch, concentrated on her schooling and put him firmly out of her mind…or so she'd convinced herself.

Now she had agreed to help Jake care for the child of that marriage.

She was an idiot.

After drying off, Ashley pulled on a fresh pair of faded jeans and a cotton sweater, grabbed a pair of running shoes, packed an overnight bag and headed out once again, promising herself that she absolutely would not succumb to any lingering feelings she might have for the man.

It was two-thirty by the time Ashley reached Jake's home. She stopped in front of the house, parked her truck and walked toward the solid wood double doors in front.

Jake must have been watching for her because he opened one of the doors as soon as she got out of her truck and waited in the doorway as she walked toward him.

She slowed as soon as she saw him silhouetted against the light before she forced herself to continue to where he waited.

"Thank you for coming," he said, closing the door behind her. He looked as tired as she felt. He turned and led the way to the staircase. She closed her eyes briefly, glad he couldn't see her reaction to him. The deep timbre of his voice caused chills to race up and down her spine.

When she'd walked past him, he'd been close enough for her to feel the warmth of his body, to hear the sound of his breathing and to catch a faint whiff of the combination of scents that were Jake. He still used the same aftershave.

"No problem," she replied, lying through her teeth. "Where is she?"

"Up here." He started up the stairway.

This house had been her second home as a child. Jake's parents had surrounded her with their love, treating her as though she were one of their own. She hadn't expected the barrage of memories that swept over her as she followed Jake up the stairs.

You can do this, you know you can. Just because you haven't been here or this close to him in…nine years or more…is no reason to react to him now. You're not the same person. Of course, neither is he, a thought she didn't find particularly reassuring.

Once they were upstairs, Jake led the way down one of the hallways before he paused in front of a slightly open door.

She waited for him to enter. Instead, he waved her into the room without speaking.

The first thing Ashley saw when she drew closer to the bed was a mop of golden curls. Not surprising, since both he and Tiffany had blond hair. Of course, there was a good chance that Tiffany's came from a bottle.

Meow.

Heather lay on her side facing Ashley and as soon as she saw her, Ashley knew she was a goner. Her delicate features were a feminine version of Jake's.

Later, Ashley would look back on this moment and realize that she had fallen in love with Heather at first glimpse.

Heather wore bright yellow pajamas with Disney characters dancing on them and she had her arm around a rather beat-up-looking stuffed animal that might have been pink at one time.

Ashley leaned closer and replaced the light covers that Heather had kicked off, tucking them around the child's shoulders. She muttered something in her sleep and rolled onto her back, one arm flung out.

She was adorable. Of course, she was. What had she expected, with parents who looked like Jake and Tiffany?

Heather's chubby cheeks and heart-shaped face were so innocent. How could a mother abandon such a sweet child? She certainly knew how it felt to be abandoned by a mother.

Ashley stood there for several minutes, coming to terms with the fact that her life had shifted in a significant way. Regardless of what happened where Heather was concerned, Ashley's life would never be the same.

She found Jake waiting in the hallway when she walked out of the room. They retraced their steps until they reached the foyer. He motioned for her to go into a sitting area made comfortable by soft pillows on the sofas and chairs.

"She's beautiful, Jake," she said, walking to one of the chairs and sitting down. Her voice broke slightly.

"Yeah," he said gruffly. "She's that, all right." He sat down across from her.

"Tell me what happened tonight. I need to understand what I'm dealing with here. Will Tiffany be back in a few days?"

Although he sounded calm enough, the knuckles of his folded hands were white and she knew he was struggling with his own emotions.

"I arrived home tonight to find Tiffany here. She'd already put Heather to bed and had unpacked her belongings, making sure she had the advantage when I walked into the house. In a nutshell, she's getting married to some jerk who doesn't want to deal with a child. He didn't mention until after they left Dallas today that he planned to leave Heather with someone in Vegas, where they're getting married. They'd made plans for an extended honeymoon and as far as the fiancé was concerned Heather wasn't a part of those plans."

"That's terrible! How could she choose to marry a man who would abandon her child like that?"

"I gave up trying to understand Tiffany a long time

ago. I'm still coming to grips with the idea that I have a daughter and was never told about her until tonight."

Ashley stood and walked over to the large fireplace that was the focal point of the room. If she was feeling overwhelmed, she could only guess what Jake must be feeling.

He watched her in silence until she knew she had to say something. But what? "I don't see where my being here is going to help you, Jake. I'm as much a stranger to her as you are."

"I know. However, she's been with women—her great-grandmother and to some extent Tiffany—and I hope she'll feel less threatened by a woman during those first few minutes. At least, that's my hope."

"Then what, Jake? Even if I knew how to take care of a child—which I don't—I don't have time to help you with her, except for maybe a few hours in the morning. What about April? Is she still managing the house for you? Maybe she can help out."

Jake stood as well. "April has enough to do supervising the cleaning and cooking around here. And Craig would never go for the idea of his wife spending her evenings here, as well. Meanwhile, I have a daughter and not a clue about how to care for her. She's going to wake up in a few hours and I have no idea how she'll react when she finds out her mother isn't here. I admit I'm grasping at straws. I guess I hoped you would have some suggestions about what I can do."

"Why me, Jake? There are several women here on the ranch you could have called."

"The truth?" he asked, kneading the back of his neck. "Because I remember you at that age and how happy you were. I thought you might know what little girls like to do. What's important to them and all the mysterious things that I don't have a clue about where she's concerned. I have no idea what she likes to eat and drink, or if she can even dress herself. Hell, for all I know she could still be in diapers."

Ashley's heart sank at the implications. Committing to helping Jake for any length of time would be emotional suicide. And yet... she couldn't get that sweet face out of her mind.

"Jake, let's take this one step at a time, okay. I can't think clearly right now. I'm exhausted. I need sleep. My brain has rolled over and is playing dead." She stared at him, wishing she were anywhere but here. "I know this is horrendously difficult for you. However, the upside is that you've been given a precious gift. I never knew Tiffany, but the fact that she chose to have Heather is admirable."

"Yeah," he muttered. "I was surprised she went through with the pregnancy. She made it clear soon after we married that she didn't want to have children." He sounded as tired as he looked. "Perhaps if I'd known she felt that way before we married..." His voice trailed off.

"You would have married her anyway," she said, finishing his sentence. "You were so obviously in love with her," and probably still are. Hearing that Tiffany was getting married again must have been another harsh blow for him.

She was so engrossed in her thoughts that she didn't realize Jake had stepped toward her until he wrapped his arms around her and held her tightly against him, her toes barely touching the floor. "Thank you for doing this."

Oh, help. This was not good, not good at all. He was too close, too big, too male, too...Jake.

She could already feel the cracks in her heart widening. No matter what she decided, her damaged heart was already at risk.

Four

Jake placed his hand on the back of her head and held her to his chest without speaking.

She relaxed against him, closed her eyes and wanted to cry. It wasn't Jake's fault. It was just that she was too tired to fight...him or herself.

When he released her, he cupped her face with his hands. "I had no idea how much I've missed you until I saw you tonight. It's been a long time, hasn't it?"

"Yes," she replied, not meeting his eyes. "I'm no longer the little girl who used to live here on the ranch."

He smiled his endearing, lopsided smile and gently brushed her lips with his. "Don't I know it," he said, straightening. "You've grown into a beautiful woman, Ashley."

"Thank you. We haven't spent time together in years, Jake. Don't make assumptions about who I am based on our shared past."

He stepped away. "You're right. I guess I still see you as the girl you used to be. It's past time we got reacquainted, isn't it?" When she didn't answer him, he rubbed her shoulders with his large, strong hands and said, "But not tonight." He took her hand and led her out of the room. "I'll give you your choice of bedrooms. There's one on either side of her room and one across the hallway. You can decide which one suits you." He snagged the bag she'd left at the bottom of the steps without breaking stride and continued up the stairs, still holding her hand.

It was just as well. She was almost too tired to walk.

They paused in the hallway near Heather's door while Ashley glanced into the three rooms he'd mentioned and said, "I'll take the one across from her."

"Okay. Each bedroom has its own bath. I think you'll find everything you need. If not, let me know and I'll get it for you." He handed the bag to her.

She walked inside the room and placed her bag on one of the chairs. "Your mother is going to be so thrilled to hear that she has a granddaughter," she absently commented, turning back the covers on the bed. "She once said to me that she sometimes wondered if any of you would ever settle down and produce offspring." When he didn't respond, she thought he'd left, so Ashley was surprised when she straightened to find him standing in the doorway with a startled look on his face.

"What's wrong?"

"My folks. I need to tell my folks."

"I thought they were out of town."

"They are, somewhere in the Northwest, but they check in regularly. Mom will want to rush back home as soon as I tell her."

"Nothing wrong with that. She'll be able to watch Heather for you until you can make other arrangements."

He shook his head. "I can't use her like that, Ashley. It wouldn't be fair. She deserves to travel with Dad after all these years without worrying about what's going on here. I'll figure out some other way to muddle through this." He turned away and she closed the door behind him.

Once Jake left, Ashley took a closer look at the room. The furniture looked to be lovingly cared-for heirlooms, while the furnishings were elegantly contemporary.

She slipped off her clothes and crawled into bed, barely getting the lamp off before she was sound asleep.

Jake walked into his bathroom and closed the door behind him, leaning against it. Tonight had certainly been a night of shocks for him…a definite emotional overload. Discovering that he was a father of a little girl had been a jolt; having her be his sole responsibility was another. But seeing Ashley again after so many years of casually waving when she was visiting her dad hadn't prepared him for the woman she'd become.

He turned on the shower and undressed, thinking about Ashley.

The woman who arrived tonight was a heart-stopping, alluring woman. He'd seen glimpses of the woman she would become in the teenage tomboy he'd known so well. But he'd never expected her to affect him this strongly.

He stepped into the shower and let the water beat against his tense muscles.

She was still small, but her body had filled out into breath-stealing shapeliness. The single braid she'd always worn as a kid was gone, replaced with a short boyish cut that looked anything but boyish on her. Her hair curled around her cheeks and ears, drawing attention to her exotically shaped green eyes, her high cheekbones and her long, graceful neck.

Even as a child, those eyes of hers had made it difficult for him to resist doing anything she asked.

Tonight they had been shadowed with fatigue and he'd felt like a louse for insisting she come out here at this hour. His hug and kiss had been spontaneous, expressing his relief at her willingness to help him out. He hadn't been prepared for the strong reaction that had hit him like a sledgehammer when he'd barely brushed her lips.

He was suddenly reminded of the night years ago when she'd kissed him until his head swam and his heart pumped blood to places it had no business going…at least not with Ashley! His strong reaction to her back then had horrified him as he recalled, and he hadn't handled the situation well.

She'd been a kid, experimenting with her new-found sensuality and wouldn't have understood the reaction she'd stirred in him.

He doubted she even remembered the incident now, but it had been a strong wake-up call for him to stay away from her until she was old enough to understand what was happening between them.

She was an adult now and the attraction certainly hadn't cooled off where he was concerned. With all the sudden turmoil going on in his life—had it been only four hours ago that his only concern in life was to beat Tom McCain at poker?—the last thing he needed was the added stress of dealing with his feelings for Ashley on top of everything else.

Once she prepared Heather to meet a father she didn't know and eased their first meeting, Ashley would leave and he'd be able to deal with the situation on his own.

He hoped.

He'd have to wait until Monday to call employment agencies in Dallas, Austin and San Antonio and alert them to his immediate need for someone qualified to care for his daughter.

Jake turned off the water and briskly toweled off before he returned to his bedroom. When he crawled into bed, he suddenly realized that it wasn't a good idea to continue sleeping in the nude now that his daughter was here. It occurred to him that dressing differently for bed was only the beginning of the changes he needed to make in his life now that Heather lived here.

He smiled as he closed his eyes. He was the father of a precious little girl. Any changes needed would be worth it.

Ashley had barely fallen asleep when someone shook her shoulder. She groaned and muttered, "Go away," without opening her eyes.

However, Jake's voice close to her ear was all that was needed to yank her from a sound sleep and remind her where she was.

"Ashley," he whispered. "I'm sorry to wake you but Heather's stirring. She's still in bed, but she's called for 'Gram' a couple of times. Now's she's calling for 'Mommy.'"

His voice shook as though there were a bomb ready to detonate in the next room.

Ashley rubbed her eyes and through sheer willpower forced them to stay open. "What time is it?"

"A little after six. I'll make coffee while you go talk to her."

Ashley looked at him. He was freshly shaved and wore crisp, clean clothes. How could anyone look so good this early in the morning?

As soon as he left, she threw back the covers and found her clothes.

Once dressed, Ashley opened her door and was surprised to see Jake hovering in the hallway. "C'mon, Jake," she whispered. "She's just a little girl. You're acting as though the house is about to explode or something!"

"Sorry. It's just that," he ran his fingers through his hair, "I don't want her frightened. She's so little. What if she starts crying!"

His eyes looked wild.

She shook her head. One of the roughest, toughest guys in Texas brought to a trembling halt by the fear of a child crying. Who would believe it?

"All children cry from time to time, Jake," she said patiently. "It isn't the end of the world. Go make the coffee you promised me and I'll see what I can do."

They'd been talking in low voices and she wondered if Heather could hear them. Once Jake left, she peered around the doorway and saw the little girl kneeling in the middle of the bed, her arms overflowing with stuffed animals.

Ashley took a deep breath and pasted a smile on her face. *Here goes.* "Good morning, Heather," she said cheerfully, walking slowly into the room. "How are *you* this morning?"

Heather started and turned to face her, clutching her toys closer.

"I don't know you," she said, her blue eyes round and her voice trembling. "Where's my mommy?"

To give Heather time to adjust to her presence, Ashley walked over to the window and opened the blinds, allowing the sun to flood the room. She turned and moved slowly toward the bed, sitting at the foot of it.

"My name is Ashley. Your mommy left you here last night so you could spend time with your daddy." How much of all this would a three-year-old understand? Ashley prayed for guidance to say the right things to Heather without making her more upset than she already was.

Heather looked at her for a long moment, frowning. "I don't have a daddy."

The stark words wrenched her heart. The poor baby. This was going to make the meeting with Jake more difficult than either of them had guessed.

"Sure you do," Ashley replied softly. "He's very happy that you've come here to see him and he can hardly wait to see you. You want to meet him?"

Heather looked down at her rabbit. When she raised her eyes, they glistened with tears. "I have to go to the bafroom."

"Oh, of course you do." Why hadn't she thought of that? "See that door over there? You have your very own bathroom. Do you need help?"

Heather quickly shook her head, slid off the bed on the side opposite Ashley and ran into the bathroom, firmly closing the door behind her.

Ashley's shoulders slumped. Well, that had gone well. Yeah, right. What did she know about little girls? Having been one certainly wasn't a qualification for helping a frightened little girl deal with a whole new environment.

She heard the toilet flush and water running. Someone had trained her well. When she finally opened the door, Heather was trying to pull up the bottoms of her pajamas that were in a twist with her panties.

"Need some help, sunshine?"

Heather stopped and looked up. "I'm Heather. Not sunshine."

"I think you look like a ray of sunshine in your bright yellow pajamas, your pretty blond curls and bright blue eyes. Sunshine is like a nickname, a playful name."

"Oh."

Heather solved her problem by pulling off the uncooperative apparel.

Ashley quickly got up and walked over to the

dresser. "Let's look in here and find you some clothes to wear, okay?"

Heather followed her, tugging at her pajama top. "You got clothes at your house that fit me?"

Ashley didn't believe this would be a good time to discuss ownership of the house. "Your mommy brought us yours," she replied, opening one of the drawers. Ashley pulled out a pair of navy blue pants and a pretty pink T-shirt. She could smell the enticing scent of freshly brewed coffee drifting from downstairs and mentally blessed Jake.

"How about these?" she asked, holding the shirt and pants up for inspection."

Heather shook her head. "That's not right," she said, and peeked into the drawer. When she couldn't find what she was looking for, she pulled out each of the drawers, then she reached into one of them and held up a pair of pink pants that did, indeed, match the shirt.

Heather retrieved panties and pink socks to wear with the sneakers sitting on top of the dresser.

Ashley knelt in front of the little girl, unbuttoned her shirt and slipped it off Heather's shoulders. When Heather didn't protest, Ashley held out the panties and Heather stepped into them, holding on to Ashley's arm for balance.

"Where's my daddy?" Heather whispered, looking around the room nervously.

"He's downstairs in the kitchen. We'll go see him as soon as you're dressed."

Ashley was relieved that Heather seemed to have relaxed a little by the time she had her clothes on, her shoes tied and her hair brushed. When Ashley held out her hand, Heather took it without hesitation, causing Ashley to feel as though she had achieved a giant victory.

What a darling. And certainly independent. She was

very particular about her clothes and her hair, which
Ashley found amusing. She would enjoy watching Jake
with her, being shown the right way to do things. Jake's
daughter might well be as strong-willed as he was.

Ashley smiled at the thought. Couldn't happen to a
more deserving guy.

They reached the bottom of the stairs and were
headed toward the kitchen when Heather spoke. "This
house is old, isn't it?" she said, looking around curiously
at the Spanish wrought-iron sconces and western paint-
ings decorating the walls of the foyer. "Is my daddy
old, too?"

Ashley's lips twitched and she firmly bit down on her
lower one until she could say, "Well, that depends on
what you think is old," in a sober voice. Before Heather
could ask another question, they entered the kitchen.

Heather stopped abruptly and stared at Jake, who
was leaning against the counter across the room, sipping
a cup of coffee and warily watching her. She stared at
him, the silence stretching until it seemed to fill the
room, her eyes enormous as she slowly took in his size.

He carefully placed his cup behind him and went
down on his haunches so that he was on her level.

The first words Jake heard his newfound daughter
utter were, "You got boots on." She pointed to his feet.

He blinked and glanced quickly at Ashley before focusing on Heather once again. "Uh, yes, I do," he replied, softly. "You certainly look pretty in pink. Are
those cartoon characters on your shirt?"

"Uh-huh." Heather continued to grip Ashley's hand,
leaning against her leg while she studied Jake with a great
deal of interest, which was a good sign, in Ashley's es-
timation. At least she didn't appear to be afraid of him.

"I don't have a daddy." As though to clarify her statement, Heather added, "Mommy said so."

Ashley saw a muscle flex in Jake's jaw and his eyes narrow, but when he spoke his voice remained soft. "Maybe your mom forgot, honey, because I'm really your dad." His voice broke on the last word.

Heather looked around the large kitchen. "Do you live in this old house?"

Jake slowly smiled. "That's right. I've lived here all my life."

"I bet you're really old, aren't you?"

"To you, maybe, although this house is older than I am."

Heather was quiet, then, until she looked up at Ashley and whispered, "I'm hungry."

Ashley had been watching Jake and when he glanced at her once again, she gave him a discreet thumbs-up gesture.

Jake sucked in some air and slowly exhaled. "Okay." He looked around as though expecting to find food on the table. "I bet I have something here you'd like to eat." He didn't sound all that sure but he walked to the pantry and looked inside. "Let's see. I have cereal and oatmeal—"

Heather wrinkled her nose in disgust. "Yuck. I hate oatmeal."

"Okay. Then I have—"

"Can I have pancakes?" she asked hopefully, looking at Ashley. She smiled winningly.

Ashley laughed. "Does that work on your mother, sunshine?"

Heather grinned. "Mommy don't feed me. Gram does. But mommy says I can't stay at Gram's anymore 'cause she's sick."

"What does Gram feed you for breakfast?"

Heather gave a quick shrug. "You know, cereal and eggs and stuff, but sometimes she makes pancakes."

"I tell you what," Ashley said, hoping to move things

along. "I'll make us some eggs, toast and bacon and we'll leave the pancakes for another morning. How's that?"

"I won't be here another morning. Mommy will come get me 'fore then."

Ashley and Jake exchanged gazes. When he didn't say anything, she turned her attention to Heather and said, "Why don't you sit at the table and I'll get breakfast going."

Easier said than done, she thought. She had no idea where to find anything and wondered if April worked on Saturdays, or if she made breakfast for Jake at all.

Ashley went to the refrigerator and was relieved to find it well-stocked.

By the time food was on the table, Jake had constructed a makeshift booster seat for Heather from a couple of thick phone books. Heather waited in the middle of the kitchen until Ashley was ready to sit down and then held her arms up to her. She had kept a careful distance from Jake since she'd first seen him. This was going to take time, Ashley knew, and she could only imagine how Jake must feel about his daughter's wariness around him.

He watched without expression while she lifted Heather onto the pile of books, which was across from Jake's place. "There you go," she said, pulling the chair closer to the table before she sat down next to her.

"You don't talk," Heather said conversationally to Jake after he'd sat down and Ashley had placed some food on Heather's plate.

"Sometimes I do," Jake said slowly. "When I have something to say."

"I always have sum'ping to say," she replied with a wise nod.

"I'm beginning to understand that." He took a bite of food, looking a little harried.

They were almost through eating when Jake said, "Da—darn it! I just remembered that I'm supposed to meet Jordan at the bank at ten o'clock. I promised him I'd be there for a meeting he's scheduled with Tom McCain." He rubbed his forehead as though getting a headache.

Oh, dear, what now? This was the time she'd planned to wave goodbye to the Crenshaw duo and let them sort out their situation on their own. Since he didn't intend to ask April to help him out with Heather, Ashley had a sinking sensation that her services were going to be needed today, as well. She couldn't imagine Heather being content to sit still for a business meeting. For that matter, neither would she.

She glanced at Heather, who really had been hungry. She'd eaten her scrambled eggs, two pieces of bacon and was presently munching on toast in between humming some kind of tune.

Now that Jake mentioned it, she recalled Jordan telling her earlier in the week that he had applied for a loan in order to build a second horse barn at his place, rather than to continue to use Jake's facilities. All of Jordan's cash was tied up in keeping his stud farm and boarding operation running.

Making up her mind—and what real choice did she have, anyway?—Ashley smiled at Heather and said, "How would you like to come with me this morning?"

"Where?"

"To where I work. I'm an animal doctor. Do you like kittens and puppies?"

"Gram says they're too messy."

"Well, they can be. If you want to come with me I could show you some."

Heather looked at her uncertainly before she glanced at Jake. "What's he going to do?" she asked as though he couldn't speak for himself.

"Well, he'll be going to a meeting and afterwards," she paused to look at Jake in a silent question, "he'll come pick you up and bring you home."

"This isn't home," Heather reminded her. "When's my mommy coming back?"

Jake tensed. "That's a good question, honey. We can talk about that once I pick you up, okay?"

Heather nodded thoughtfully. "Okay," she finally said.

"Good," Ashley said, rising. She helped Heather down and took her to the sink where she washed her hands for her. While Heather wandered around the room exploring, Ashley walked over to where Jake stood pouring himself another cup of coffee. "Are you going to be okay with her?" she asked quietly.

"I'll do the best I can under these circumstances. I appreciate your taking her with you today. I never gave the meeting a thought last night."

"You had a few other things on your mind, as I recall. It's okay, Jake. Wendy can help me with her."

"Wendy Modean? She's working for you and Woody Morris now?"

"She was the first one to show up when we advertised for office help. Now that her kids are grown, she said she's bored sitting at home."

"Well, I'll be darned. You lucked out. You couldn't have found anyone as competent as she is. I understand she worked at the bank years ago and was one of the best employees there, according to Tom. You got yourself a business professional."

"I know. She's been a lifesaver as we take on more and more clients." She glanced at her watch. "I need to go. So we'll see you around eleven or so?"

"No later than twelve, for sure." He touched her arm. "Thank you." His expression held gratitude and…something more. Ashley remembered the hug and brief kiss they'd shared last night and clamped down on her emotions. She could do this. A few more hours and she'd be done with the Crenshaws. Thank goodness. Another look from Jake like that one and she'd be throwing herself at him and begging him to love her!

She'd already learned that lesson the hard way, and she'd learned it well.

Five

Most people considered Jake to be a strong, courageous man who met life head-on without hesitation. No one would dare call him a coward, either to his face or behind his back. He could face down man or beast without flinching.

So how could a pint-size little girl reduce him to quivering jelly?

He stood in the driveway, his hands in his back pockets, and watched Ashley drive away with Heather strapped into the backseat of the truck, both of them seemingly content with today's hasty arrangement. Before they left, Ashley suggested he get a car seat first thing, a booster seat for the table and whatever else a child that age needed.

Well, how in the world would he know?

He shook his head at the feeling of inadequacy that engulfed him and, once they were out of sight, returned to the house to wait for April. She needed to know about the sudden change in the size of his family.

April's shock when he told her about Heather was the reaction he knew he'd get from everyone. By the time he'd explained as much as he could to her, the two women who came to clean and do laundry had arrived and April told them his news.

The delay caused him to be running late.

On the way to town, Jake made a mental list of what he needed to accomplish today. He didn't think he could handle Heather on his own just yet. She was still too wary of him. For good reason, of course. He hoped that Ashley would consider helping him with Heather for a day or two, just until he felt easier about looking after her.

A sudden picture of Ashley asleep this morning interrupted his train of thought. He'd opened the door and quietly called to her, careful not to let Heather hear him. Unfortunately Ashley hadn't heard him, either.

He'd walked into the bedroom and paused, shaken by her beauty. He'd seen her asleep many times as a child but if he'd needed a reminder that she was no longer a child, the glimpse of her lying there had given it to him.

A slight scent of perfume had lingered in the room. He had taken a deep breath. Ashley. The perfume smelled of flowers and summer days. He still remembered the tomboy who once would have scoffed at the girlie stuff women wore.

He'd reached for her shoulder, feeling the delicate bones beneath his fingers.

"Go away," she had mumbled.

"Ashley," he'd said a little louder. "You need to wake up. Heather's awake."

Those thick eyelashes of hers had fluttered and her eyes had slowly opened. She'd stared at him sleepily.

He found her tousled hair and rumpled look sexy as hell. The thought of waking up each morning beside her suddenly flashed through his mind and scared him.

After his retreat to the kitchen, he'd spilled some of the coffee grounds putting them into the filter and splashed water on the counter.

He didn't know who was affecting him more at the moment—Heather or Ashley. Right now, he needed to keep his mind on Heather and off Ashley.

Jake drove around the courthouse square of downtown New Eden and parked in front of the bank. Jordan got out of his truck when Jake pulled up beside him.

"I'm sorry to be late," he said, striding toward the front door of the bank. Jordan grinned as he matched his steps to Jake's. "We're okay on time, I think." He gave Jake a speculative look. "So, big daddy, how's life treatin' you?"

Six

"Where are we?" Heather asked from the back seat when they parked behind the animal hospital.

"We're in New Eden and this is where I work," Ashley replied, getting out of the truck. She opened the back door and unstrapped Heather. Heather held out her arms in such a trusting gesture that Ashley had to swallow the lump that suddenly formed in her throat.

She reached for Heather and swung her to the ground.

Heather looked around. The office was on the edge of town, with only a few businesses around it.

"Is it a town?"

"Yes."

"It don't look like a town."

"Probably not, considering what you're used to." She took Heather's hand and guided her to the side door.

"You won't have to stay here very long, you know. Before you know it, your daddy will be here to pick you up."

"Why?"

Ashley paused in mid-stride. "Why, what, sunshine?"

"Why is he coming to pick me up?"

"So you can go back home with him."

"But I want to stay with you," Heather explained in a patient voice.

Oops. "We'll talk about that a little later."

Ashley walked into the reception area, grateful to see that Wendy was already there.

Here was the woman who ran the office and helped Ashley and Woody Morris hang on to their sanity.

Wendy glanced up absently from some paperwork on her desk and was already looking back down when her head snapped up again in surprise.

"Is there something you've been hiding from us, Ashley?" she asked with a grin, coming around the counter to get a closer look at Ashley's companion.

Heather clutched Ashley's hand and leaned against her leg in the same bashful way she had when she met Jake.

"Heather, this is my very good friend, Mrs. Modean. She has a granddaughter just about your age named Mary Ann." Ashley turned to Wendy. "Mrs. Modean, may I introduce you to Ms. Heather Crenshaw?"

Wendy's brows drew together. "Crenshaw? From which family?"

Ashley could picture the wheels churning in Wendy's head. To save time, she answered without comment, "Jake's daughter."

"Oh! Well. What a surprise." Wendy gave Ashley an assessing look before she held out her hand to Heather and said, "How do you do, Ms. Crenshaw."

Heather, still leaning against Ashley, timidly held out her hand. "Fine," she said shyly. Wendy straightened and gave Ashley a big grin. "This is so interesting, whichever way you want to look at it. Jake with a daughter…and you looking after her."

"Just helping out a friend," Ashley replied blandly. She turned to Heather and said, "Are you ready to go look at some of our visitors in the back room?"

Heather nodded, looking around the front office. The walls were covered with drawings made by a preschool class in New Eden. They had drawn pictures of their pets. Ashley and Woody had a local artist carefully reproduce the pictures large enough to be seen and admired by all.

Wendy noticed Heather's interest and asked, "Do you like to draw, Heather?"

"Uh-huh."

"Well, when you get through looking at the animals in the back, you can come up here with me and I'll have some pencils and paper for you to use."

Ashley mouthed a grateful thank you and led Heather into the back.

The various dogs and cats that vocally greeted them in a cacophony of sound immediately enthralled Heather. Roy, one of the high school boys who helped out on Saturdays, joined them in the back area. After the necessary introductions, she told Heather she had to go out front for a moment. Heather was too engrossed in a litter of motherless puppies to care, so Ashley left Roy to keep an eye on her.

When she returned to the front, Wendy said, "If I'd known she was coming, I could have brought some of the coloring books I keep around the house for my grandkids." She eyed Ashley thoughtfully. "So. How come I never heard anything about Jake Crenshaw having a daughter?"

Ashley chuckled. "Gee, Wendy. I don't know. You must be slipping."

"Must be. She's a cute little thing, isn't she?"

"Yes. Now that she's a little more comfortable around me, I've discovered she's quite a talker."

"How long have you known her?"

"Not long."

"Sure looks like a Crenshaw, I'll give you that."

"That she does."

"Is it possible she's Tiffany's daughter?"

"Absolutely."

"Wonder why Jake never mentioned having a daughter?"

"Well, Jake's a man of few words."

Wendy leaned back in her chair, smiling. "I can remember when he used to haul you to town with him when you weren't much older than Heather, the two of you hitching a ride from the ranch with one of the hands to pick up supplies. You were always so cute, tagging along with him. I recall how patient he was with you, despite the incessant questions you were generally asking. None of the rest of us could keep up with you."

"Yep, that's me. As faithful as a hound and twice as vocal." She scanned the appointment book for today to see how busy she was likely to be.

"You know, it's funny how things work out," Wendy mused. "Somehow I always figured that once you grew up, Jake would end up married to you. Instead, he upped and married some socialite from Dallas. I never could figure that one out."

"I'm not his type, Wendy. I couldn't be more opposite in looks and temperament from Tiffany. She's big city and I'm pure country."

"You notice they're no longer married, though," Wendy pointed out with raised eyebrows.

"Not because Jake wanted out of the marriage, I'm sure. Remember, she was the one who left."

"Well, she never made much of an effort to fit in around here, as I recall. Always flitting back and forth to Dallas in that flashy fire-engine red convertible Jake bought her."

Ashley glanced at the clock. "I've got to get to work. If you know of anyone who could stay out at Jake's and take care of Heather until he can hire someone permanently, be sure to mention it when he comes in to pick her up, okay? In the meantime, you might give him some pointers on how to care for a three year old."

"You still haven't explained why you're the one who's helping him."

"Good question, Wendy. I'm not really sure about that myself."

It was close to noon when Wendy buzzed Ashley on the intercom and said, "Jake's holding on line two."

Ashley had just finished giving two Australian shepherd puppies their checkups and first shots for one of the ranchers in the area. She was washing up when Wendy called her. Woody had called earlier to say he wouldn't be in today because he'd pulled a muscle in his back. As a result, she'd been busier than she'd expected to be and hadn't had a chance to check on Heather to see how she and Wendy were getting along out front. At least she hadn't heard screaming or crying from either one of them.

Since Wendy had raised several kids of her own, Ashley had counted on her expertise to keep Heather entertained.

Other than asking a gajillion questions on their ride into town this morning, Heather had been well behaved—for a curious three-year-old—and Ashley knew things could have been much worse. What if Heather hadn't wanted to stay at the animal hospital? What if she'd demanded her mother? The possibilities didn't bear thinking about.

She reached for the phone. "Sorry to keep you holding, Jake. It's been a little hectic this morning. Are you about ready to pick her up? I'm going out in the field this afternoon to a few places, including stopping by your place to check on one of Jordan's pregnant mares."

"Actually, I'm at the hospital."

"Oh, no! What's happened? Were you in an accident?"

"Red Malone fell into one of the canyons and was banged up some. A few of the hands got him back to the house and Ken called me on my cell phone to tell me he was bringing him in. I haven't been able to talk to a doctor yet, so I don't know how serious it is. I'm not going to be able to leave until I know something."

"Of course not." She thought for a moment. "I suppose Heather can come with me on my rounds. Since I'll be at your place, anyway, I'll make the ranch my last stop and stay with her until you get there."

She heard his sigh of relief. "Thanks, Ashley. That's one less responsibility to worry about."

"Give Red my love. I hope his injuries aren't too serious."

"I second that," he replied and hung up.

When Ashley walked out front, she found Heather asleep on a pile of blankets beside Wendy's desk.

"Whose blankets?" Ashley asked in a quiet voice.

"Oh, I had Lurline run some things over that belong to Mary Ann. Since Ed and Lurline are looking to have more family, I figured she might have saved some things." She pointed to a box. "Lurline also brought one of her extra car seats for Heather until Jake can pick one up on his own. Mary Ann's already grown out of it, so Lurline's in no hurry to get it back."

Ashley could have hugged her. "What a relief. Tell

Lurline how much I appreciate it. Jake's at the hospital with Dad. Red Malone got hurt this morning and they're waiting to hear how he's doing, so I'll have Heather with me this afternoon. By the way, I didn't hear any loud voices out here this morning. How'd she do?"

"Just fine. Lurline brought a coloring book with crayons and a couple of dolls for her to play with. Heather seemed to be content with them. I also read to her whenever I had time." She held up a children's book. "She seemed to enjoy watching your patients come in and out. She really wasn't much trouble. Didn't even resist my suggestion that she take a nap, once I convinced her you wouldn't go off and leave her."

"I'd appreciate it if you would help me install the car seat before I wake her."

Wendy chuckled. "Good as done."

While they were outside, Ashley said, "She must be starving by now. I wonder what I should feed her?"

"Lurline brought over some snacks and juice when she came by. If you can wait, I'll make a list of things she'd probably like to eat."

Ashley had lucked out. "Wendy, once again, you're a lifesaver. As long as you're at it, let me know what else you think a three-year-old might need and we'll go shopping before we leave town."

After getting Heather into the seat without fully waking her, Wendy said, "She told me some very interesting things this morning." Her eyes were twinkling. "I'd love to know if even half of 'em are true."

"There's no telling." She started the motor. "I'll see you Monday."

"Hope you get some rest before you start in again next week."

"I fully intend to. Once I get home this afternoon, I'm

going to sleep until I get an emergency call. Keep your fingers crossed there won't be many of them this weekend."

After their shopping trip, she and Heather headed out of town on her first call. She should be at Jake's place by three and home asleep by four.

She could definitely use the down time after the emotional turmoil she'd been through during the past several hours. She would not have thought that anything could make her agree to spend time around Jake Crenshaw.

Except for a bright-eyed angel child who belonged to him.

Seven

Jake glanced at his watch as he strode out of the hospital and swore beneath his breath. It was already past seven o'clock. Ashley—who had been reluctant to do more than ease his first meeting with Heather—had been responsible for Heather the entire day.

He called his house as he got into his truck. When his answering machine came on, he said, "Ashley, if you're there, please pick up."

She came on the line. "I'm here."

"I'm leaving the hospital now and will be there as soon as I can."

"Okay. I've been wondering whether I should go ahead and feed Heather, but I think she can wait another half hour."

"Damn. I forgot that she'd need to eat something! How did you feed her today?"

"Wendy was a big help. She gave me a list of kid-friendly meals and other items she might like. I picked them up before we left town."

"Remind me to fall on my knees and thank you as soon as I get there."

"Well, if you insist."

He laughed, the first time he'd felt like laughing all day.

"How's Red?" she asked.

"He's out of surgery. Besides a broken leg, he had a ruptured spleen and plenty of scrapes and bruises. Doc says he'll have no permanent damage once his leg heals. I stayed with Amy until we found out."

"I know. Dad told me when he stopped in earlier, so I'm not all that surprised that you're just now getting home."

"I'll see you soon."

"Oh, Jake?"

"Yeah?"

"Jordan was over the moon this afternoon. Said you were a big help in his getting his loan."

"All I did was lend moral support. He'll have no trouble paying a loan back, not with the business he's already built up."

"I think it was a nice thing for you to do. I'll see you."

He hung up smiling and headed out of town. It occurred to him on the way that he hadn't asked how Ashley had managed today with Heather. He'd been too wrapped up in his own day. Probably why he was divorced. There were times he struggled to juggle his responsibilities and sometimes, despite his best intentions, he still dropped the ball. This was one of those times.

Making his daughter his first priority was another one of the things he had to concentrate on. He had to remember that he had a family now.

Speaking of family, his call to Ashley had been so domestic, he cringed at the memory. "Sorry I'm late, hon, how was your day?" kind of thing. Shades of married life!

The best thing about today was that it was almost over. He could relieve Ashley and let her get back to her own routine. For all he knew, she could have a date tonight.

He frowned. He wasn't sure why the thought bothered him. She was a single, attractive—make that very attractive—woman. It would be strange if she weren't dating, especially on a Saturday night.

When Jake entered the kitchen, he caught a savory scent of something cooking. He paused in the doorway and looked around. Heather sat at the table in a new booster seat busily coloring in a coloring book. Ashley had her back to him while she leaned over and took something out of the oven.

The absolute last thing he needed to see at the moment was the enticing view of Ashley's shapely backside in those tight jeans. No matter how tired he was, he certainly wasn't immune to the fact that she was a fine-looking woman.

"That man's here," Heather announced, when she looked up from her coloring and spotted Jake.

Ashley set a steaming casserole on top of the stove and turned. "Ah. There you are. Perfect timing. We're just about ready to eat."

He nodded, strangled by the lust that had grabbed him when he first saw her.

She looked at Heather. "That wasn't a very nice way to greet your daddy, you know."

Heather tucked her chin to her chest and didn't say anything.

"I'll go wash up," Jake finally managed to say before leaving the room.

By the time he returned, he'd given himself a stern talking to about inappropriate thoughts and keeping better control of his reactions to her.

Once they were seated, Jake said, "This is wonderful, Ashley. I really appreciate your feeding us tonight."

"Actually, April had the casserole prepared when we got here. All I had to do was pop it in the oven. She said she made enough for the two of you to eat tomorrow since she's off on Sundays. I'll put what's left in the fridge before I head on home."

Heather looked at her with dismay. "Don't leave, Ashley."

Ashley smiled at her. "I have to, sweetie. This isn't my house. I live in an apartment in town. Maybe you and your daddy can come visit me there sometime. Would you like that?"

Heather stared at her with a horrified look, her lip quivering. Ashley smiled gently at her. "After you eat, I'll give you a bath and get you ready for bed before I go, if you'd like. Okay?"

Heather shook her head no and tears rolled down her cheeks. "Please don't go, Ashley," she whispered, her voice shaking. "I'll be good, I promise. Please don't leave me."

Jake's throat closed with sudden emotion. Those two had certainly bonded today while he was racing around putting out fires. Ashley glanced at him before taking Heather's hand. "You'll like staying here with your daddy, you know. When I was a little girl your age, he used to take me riding on his horse. There's all kinds of fun things to see on a ranch—horses and cows and sheep and goats."

Heather leaned her cheek on Ashley's hand and whispered, "I want to stay with you." She began to sob.

Ashley gave him a pleading look. He knew he had to say something, but what?

"Heather? Honey, listen to me, okay?" Jake said.

Ashley patted Heather's cheeks with a tissue and

Heather slowly raised her head, those blue eyes of hers looking desolate. He felt like some kind of monster.

"I want my mommy," Heather said, hiccupping.

If he could have gotten his hands on Tiffany right about now, he would have cheerfully wrung her neck. Poor baby. How could he explain what had happened without causing her to feel more abandoned than she already felt?

"I hope you aren't afraid to stay here with me, Heather," he finally said. "I'll take good care of you."

She gave a hitching sob and her tears fell faster than Ashley could dry them. "I want my Gram," she whispered.

Jake's heart sank. "Honey, your Gram is really sick, remember?"

"When's mommy coming to get me?"

"Well, the thing is, your mommy has gone on a long vacation," he began, racking his brain for a way to explain to a three-year-old why her dad had taken over parenting her.

"I could go on a bacation, too," Heather whispered to her plate.

She was breaking his heart and he had no idea how to console her.

Ashley spoke up without looking at him. "I have an idea," she said cheerfully. "Maybe we could have a sleepover tonight. I don't have to go to work tomorrow so I could stay here tonight. After your bath, we could read books until you get sleepy. Would you like that?"

Jake held his breath. Ashley was offering him an eleventh-hour reprieve and he prayed Heather would be willing to accept it.

They both watched Heather. Her cheeks were red from crying and Ashley continued to wipe her nose and face. Her tears undid him. How could he look after her when a tear could effectively bring him to his knees?

Heather finally nodded. "Uh-huh."

Ashley looked at Jake, her brows raised in a silent question. He silently mouthed "thank you" to her.

"But first, we have to clean our plates." She passed the casserole to Jake with a smile. He automatically took it, but his appetite was gone. He took a ragged breath, wondering how he could be expected to know how to comfort his daughter when he had no parenting skills.

Thinking out loud, he said, "As far as I'm concerned, Ashley can stay here every night." Could she understand how helpless he felt and how much he needed her support?

Her face suddenly bloomed bright red and he realized how his remark must have sounded to her. Man-oh-man. He was way over his head here, with both of them and sinking fast. He tried to think of some way to correct the impression he must have given her when Ashley spoke.

She reached for her glass of tea and said, "Let's deal with this night, okay? We can discuss the matter later," she said to no one in particular. She took a long drink and applied herself to the meal.

He hadn't meant to put her in a corner. She was right. They needed to talk once Heather was in bed and decide what he could do to help Heather adjust to all the changes taking place in her life.

Once they finished eating, Jake helped Ashley clean the kitchen. He couldn't help but notice that he and Ashley fell into a rhythm of doing chores together as if they'd been doing them for years.

Some time later, Jake watched Ashley bathe Heather, another routine parenting task he hadn't a clue about how to handle. Once she had put Heather to bed, he sat down and listened while Ashley attempted to read to

Heather amid a barrage of questions from the little girl about the pictures on each page.

He was lost in deep thought when he realized that Heather was talking about him. "Does he read?" she asked, and Jake tuned in on the conversation going on across the room.

"Does who read, sunshine?" Ashley asked, looking at Jake.

Heather nodded toward Jake. "Him."

"You mean your daddy?"

"Uh-huh."

"Maybe you could ask him."

Heather looked at him for what seemed to Jake like an hour before she asked with skepticism, "You aren't *really* my daddy, are you?"

"Yes, ma'am, I really am."

"Mommy tol' me Mr. L'lefield was going to be my daddy."

He kept his gaze steady. "Well, when he marries your mother, he'll be your stepfather, so that's probably why she told you that."

"Mama said we're going on a long trip with Mr. L'lefield and for me to be good while we was on our trip. I was good but I fell asleep. When I woke up I was here."

He cleared his throat, praying that he would say the right thing. "Here's the thing, sweetheart. Your mom was afraid to take you on such a long trip so she decided to let you stay with me. That way we can get to know each other. Wouldn't you like to do that?"

She gave him another one of her level stares and he realized he'd seen that same expression in every photograph ever taken of him. He found the stare a little daunting when aimed at him and had a sudden flash of sympathy for his parents.

"Can I ride a horse? And play with your dogs? And

go swimming at the creek like Ashley did when she was little?"

Jake felt an overwhelming sense of relief. She sounded more like the Ashley he'd known as a child.

"I think we can arrange that. As for a dog, one of the workers has a bit—a mama dog who had some puppies last week. We can visit his place and maybe he'll let you pick out one."

Her eyes grew wide. "Really? For my very own?"

"Yep."

Heather turned to Ashley and said, "Did you hear? I can get a puppy like the ones you have at your work."

"Sounds like fun," she said, grinning at Jake. "Nothing more entertaining than housebreaking a dog and discovering that they like to chew on everything they see."

Heather frowned. "Would they chew on my fingers?"

"A little, maybe. Mostly they chew on boots and shoes, socks and anything else left on the floor. You and your dad are going to have sooo much fun training a little puppy." She winked at Jake.

Jake rubbed his neck. The pups wouldn't be weaned for another month. Maybe that would give him some time to adjust to the idea.

"Would you like to have a birthday party?" he asked.

"With balloon animals and magic and clowns and—"

"I'm not sure we can have all of that. What I've been thinking," he paused and looked at Ashley, wondering what *she* was thinking, before saying, "we could have a big party on your birthday and have some barbecue and maybe some hot dogs and hamburgers and we could invite my mom and dad and your uncles and cousins. We'd put lights in the trees and…" He stopped and looked beseechingly at Ashley.

"Once upon a time," she said to Heather, "we had a big party here for *my* birthday. There was music and games and dancing. It was so much fun. I bet you'd have fun, too."

Jake stared at her. "I remember that party well."

She looked at him without expression. "I remember everything about that party, too." She returned her attention to Heather and said, "Guess what, Heather?"

"What?"

"It's your bedtime."

"Uh-uh."

"In fact, you were supposed to go to sleep while I read to you, instead of asking all those questions." She hugged her close and said, "Let's make a final stop in the bathroom and get a drink of water so you can go to sleep."

Heather thought about the suggestion and finally nodded. "Awright. You're going to be here when I wake up, aren't you?"

Ashley thought about this morning when Heather had awakened in new surroundings. "Of course I am."

Heather slid off the bed, took Ashley's hand and they made their rounds. When they returned, Jake was no longer there. Heather picked up her pink rabbit and crawled into bed. Ashley gave her a hug and a kiss, tucked her into bed and said, "I'll be across the hall if you need me during the night."

She turned out the light, leaving the night-light to soften the darkness.

Ashley found Jake in the living room, standing at the picture window and looking out into the evening. He'd slipped his hands in his back pockets, a habitual stance for him, and stood as though braced for the next unexpected wave to hit him.

She couldn't say she blamed him.

He had no idea how his familiar stance caused a rush of awareness to sweep over her.

"I know I should have checked with you first before telling Heather I'd stay the night," she said quietly. "It was an impulsive suggestion that I hope hasn't made things more difficult for you."

He turned at the sound of her voice. A small lamp near the sofa was on, leaving his face in shadows. He slipped his hands out of his pockets and came toward her.

"And I shouldn't have blurted out that you could stay forever. I'm sorry if I put you in an awkward position. It's definitely time for us to discuss the present situation." He motioned to the sofa. Once she sat down, he sat at the opposite end.

She waited for him to speak.

He leaned forward, his hands clasped between his knees. Without looking directly at her, he said, "I appreciate your help more than I can possibly say. I understood why you offered to stay tonight. Heather needs something or someone here who she feels she can trust and she's made it clear that person isn't me. I have to face reality. Her life has been turned upside down as much as mine has. It's a blessing she's taken to you so quickly."

Ashley couldn't remember ever seeing Jake this upset. Her heart went out to him. "You've done everything you can, which she'll understand once she's older. She did a lot of talking today while I made my rounds. I gathered that she seldom saw her mother for more than a brief visit once in a while. Most of her conversation was about the things she and her Gram did together."

Jake shook his head, his mouth grim.

"She quotes her Gram on everything from brushing her teeth, eating with her mouth closed, being polite and the reasons she's supposed to take a bath every day. I'm impressed that at her age she remembers them so clearly. It's obvious her great-grandmother has been a very good influence in her life. She's a very well-mannered child." She smiled, recalling their afternoon together. "Of course when Heather's tired, she's not quite so manageable."

When he didn't respond, she decided to remain silent. There was nothing more she could say to comfort him.

When he spoke, his voice shook. "What am I going to do, Ashley? When I went to town Friday night I had no responsibilities other than running this ranch. My life had mellowed out and I was content. I had no idea what was in store for me when I got home. I'm not equipped with the knowledge to care for her. I've never felt quite so helpless before. My world is spinning out of control. Where do I start in order for her to feel that this is her home?"

She moved closer to him and touched his clasped hands. "Love her, Jake. That's what she needs from you; that's what you can do for her."

He straightened and turned to her, his expression reflecting his pain. "And how do I do that when she won't have anything to do with me?"

When she started to move her hand away, he clasped it in his. His touch was so familiar to her. How many times had he been there to comfort her when she'd needed someone? Now it was her turn to help him.

"I know that this situation isn't going to be worked out in a day or two," she said quietly, "but you could plan things the two of you could do together. For instance, set up a routine where you read to her every night. I stopped by the bookstore before we left town today and bought several books for children her age. That should get you started."

"She's afraid of me," he muttered, looking away from her. "She's made that obvious."

Ashley tightened her grip on his hand in silent sympathy. "That's not fear, really. She's shy around you, that's all. A father is something new in her life. Give her some time to get to know you, Jake. She's a well-adjusted child and isn't afraid to meet new people, which is a good indication she's been well-treated and loved. She'll come around."

He sighed. "I appreciate your optimism. I just wish I could share it."

"I've enjoyed getting to know her. She's a character. Shy one moment, chatty the next. I know you're going to enjoy her once the two of you spend time together."

"It's the meantime that concerns me at the moment." He took both her hands in his, stroking the back of her hands with his thumbs. He looked up, his eyes silver in the muted light around them. "Since she's comfortable with you, I was wondering if you'd be willing to spend the next few nights here…just until I can figure things out. I'll find someone to live here permanently as soon as possible. In the meantime, I think she and I might be able to muddle through during the day if she knew you'd be here at bedtime and breakfast."

"It's worth considering, I suppose," she said slowly.

"I know it's not what either of us planned when I called you last night. I'm sorry for that."

"I know, Jake."

Sitting this close to him, she felt the magnetic pull he'd always had for her.

"Thank you for being so understanding, Ashley." The gentle look he gave her mesmerized her. This was Jake and he needed her. How could she say no?

And then he kissed her.

He was just expressing his gratitude, she nervously reminded herself, but the kiss slowly escalated into something more. Much more.

A part of her was thinking, "This shouldn't be happening," while a louder part was saying, "Oh, shut up and enjoy the moment, for Pete's sake!"

Jake was kissing her, really kissing her, for the first time in her life.

She placed her hands on his shoulders and leaned closer. He wrapped his arms around her and pulled her onto his lap, his mouth hot and passionate. Yes-oh-yes-oh-yes. She wanted him so much and this time he wasn't shoving her away. She slid her fingers into his thick hair, wanting him to make love to her, to satisfy the onrush of desire building in her.

Ashley opened her mouth in silent invitation and he groaned as if in pain even as he accepted her offering. His marauding tongue teased her…exploring her lips, dueling with her tongue, igniting flames inside her.

She felt his arousal near her hip and knew he wanted her. Encouraged, Ashley slipped her hand down his chest, his stomach and abs, moving slowly until she reached the evidence of his desire. She sighed and laid her hand along the ridge behind his zipper.

With no warning, Jake jerked away from her, scooping her off his lap and back onto the sofa. He strode across the room and into the shadows near the window, his back to her. She could hear his harsh breathing and watched as he dropped his head to his chest, rubbing the back of his neck.

She covered her face, feeling as though he'd just dumped a bucket of ice over her. Like an idiot she'd let a kiss of gratitude go to her head, thinking he actually wanted her. Furiously, she dashed the unexpected tears away. She never cried. That wasn't who she was at all. Only Jake had the ability to reduce her to tears…and she hated her vulnerability where he was concerned.

She needed to go upstairs, to get away from him, to

exorcise from her brain what had just happened, but she was shaking too hard to risk standing right now.

Tremors coursed through her body, whether from the sudden onrush of desire the kiss had provoked or because of the humiliation she felt at the realization that once again she'd allowed herself to be captivated by Jake. She supposed it didn't matter why. All she knew was that she hurt.

She wrapped her arms around her waist and rocked, her eyes closed.

Ashley had no idea how long the room remained silent before Jake spoke. "I am so sorry, Ashley," he said gruffly. He cleared his throat. "I didn't mean that to happen. I, uh, I wouldn't blame you in the least if you left right now. My behavior was inexcusable."

She opened her eyes and saw that he'd walked back over to where she was. She took a couple of long, deep breaths and once she felt she was steady enough to speak, she replied, "There's no need for an apology, Jake. I'm the one who keeps offering my heart on a platter. Why blame yourself? This is a tough time for you…an emotional time." Forget about your flayed emotions, she told herself. They aren't his problem. Feeling calmer, she added, "I can understand what happened without reading anything into it."

When he remained silent, she said wryly, "You needn't worry about my reading something into an impulsive kiss. I learned and accepted a long time ago that you'll never be interested in me."

He sat on the edge of the chair across from her. His ferocious frown might have alarmed her if she'd had any energy left. "What are you talking about?"

"C'mon, Jake," she said, weariness settling deep within her. "The last time we kissed like that you treated me as though I had some kind of contagious disease."

He stared at her for a moment before speaking. "Are you talking about your birthday party?" He sounded puzzled.

"I'm sure you don't remember, but you completely humiliated me in front of your brothers that night." She took another deep breath. "Of course, I got over it eventually." A bolt of lightning should strike her for lying.

"I, uh, went looking for you that night to apologize, but I couldn't find you. After that, you never seemed to be around." He scrubbed his face with his hand. "I never, ever, meant to hurt you."

She nodded. "Probably not. However, I got your message loud and clear."

"I had no idea that you took my behavior that night to be a rejection of you." He shook his head in remorse. "Believe me, honey, it was anything but. You'd suddenly blossomed into a beautiful young woman and I was embarrassed that I reacted so strongly to you. You jolted me into seeing you as very desirable, which is why I had no business allowing this kiss to escalate tonight. I know how I react when you're around. I just wasn't thinking."

Puzzled by his explanation, she asked, "Are you saying you weren't repulsed by me that night?"

He raised his brow. "That's exactly what I'm saying. I'd never been turned on so fast in my life and it shocked me. I knew I had to stay away from you."

Ashley looked at him, trying to come to grips with this new revelation. If what he was saying was true, she'd completely misinterpreted his behavior that night. She'd caught him off guard and he hadn't known how to handle the situation.

A weight lifted from her, one she'd carried for much too long a time.

She wistfully smiled at him. "Thank you for telling

me that. It means more than I can possibly express." His expression eased a little. She wanted badly to throw her arms around him, but that would only make matters worse at the moment. "About tonight. I'm no longer a teenager, Jake."

His frown returned. "I'm well aware of that, Ashley. I've been fighting the attraction I've had for you for years. Tonight was a mistake. We both know that. I just want you to know that you have my word that I won't take advantage of you if you should decide to stay here with Heather and me."

"I don't need your assurances, Jake." She paused, gathering her thoughts. The subject was too important to ignore now that she was in possession of knowledge about his feelings toward her. Her heart raced at the possibilities that were opening up for her. "The thing is, Jake, I see no reason for us to ignore the feelings we have for each other at this point in our lives. I've never made an attempt to hide how I feel about you and now you're saying that you're attracted to me, as well, that you've been attracted to me since I was sixteen…oh…except for the small matter of your having married someone else a couple of years later." Oh, boy. Now comes the hard part. I've come this far, I can't stop now. After another deep breath, she said, " But you're no longer married, Jake. And I'm no longer a child."

He flinched. She couldn't believe it. What was wrong with him? Couldn't he see the possibilities for their future? Or was he more interested in an intimate relationship only, with no strings attached.

"I agree, Ashley. You're no longer a child. But you're still young. You've got your whole life ahead of you. I don't want to…" He stopped speaking as though at a loss for words.

Why was he denying them the opportunity to explore the possibilities they might have? She couldn't believe this man!

"What are you, old and broken? Come on, Jake. The last I heard, thirty-three doesn't put you in the senior citizen group."

"The gap between us is important, though," he went on doggedly. "I'm more experienced, more—"

"So what if I told you I slept with every college guy I dated for seven years? Would that make a difference in your thinking?"

He stared at her in shock. "You did *what?*"

She was having trouble keeping a straight face, but she gave it her best shot. "Well," she said in her most reasonable voice, "if it's just a matter of who has more experience...." She shrugged her shoulders slightly and left the comment unfinished.

He blanched beneath his tan and it was only then that she realized he'd actually thought she was serious. "Oh for Pete's sake, Jake! I'm kidding. You know me better than that." Feeling stronger now that they were actually discussing their relationship, she stood. At least she'd given him food for thought. "As for my staying here to be with Heather for a while longer, let me sleep on it and I'll let you know my decision tomorrow."

He stood as well while she finished her remarks by saying, "As far as the relationship you and I have...you have the right to feel anyway you want where I'm concerned. It might help you come to terms with the idea of our spending time together if you dismiss the age difference between us that no longer matters, forget about the little girl you watched grow up and take a look at who I am today."

Jake rubbed a hand over his face and she saw how exhausted he was. "The thing is," he said wearily, "I'm not cut out to be a husband. I learned that the hard way.

If I were to attempt to have a relationship with you, I know I'd lose control and end up making love to you. I don't want to use you that way. You deserve a man without so much baggage. Right now, I feel considerably older than thirty-three, believe me." He raised his hand as though to touch her cheek, then dropped it. "I never ever want to hurt you, Ashley. I'm sorry that my clumsiness when you were a teenager gave you grief. That was the last thing I wanted."

"So what you're saying is that I need to forget about my feelings for you."

His ears turned red. Doggedly, he said, "I'm just saying that a relationship between us would be wrong for you."

She eyed him thoughtfully for a moment. "Tell you what. You let me worry about what's right or wrong for me, okay? You've made it clear I have no place in your life and I accept that. For now."

She turned and walked away from him.

"Ashley," Jake said, following her from the room. "I'm sorry. I know I'm not good with words and I don't explain myself well. I apologize if I offended you."

She paused at the bottom of the staircase and turned to him. "Oh, you haven't offended me, Jake. You've just made me question my sanity and my lack of intelligence for still being in love with you after all these years."

Eight

Ashley absently closed the door to her bedroom, going over what had been said just now.

She'd misinterpreted his actions all those years ago. He'd admitted that he was attracted to her.

That said, she knew he still carried a torch for Tiffany. How could he not? Jake loved her when he married her and he was very loyal to those he loved. Hearing that she was on her way to get married again must have been painful. Added to that pain was his discovery that he had a daughter and Tiffany hadn't told him.

No wonder he was still reeling.

She understood that he was vulnerable; otherwise he wouldn't have admitted that he was attracted to her. She also knew that Jake had no intention of acting on that attraction, but his reasons puzzled her.

Why did he consider himself poor husband material? Why did he blame himself for Tiffany deciding to leave?

How could he believe that marriage wasn't for him? Maybe nothing would work out for the two of them in the long run, but couldn't he at least give their relationship a chance?

He was being as honest with her as he could be, she knew. He'd always been an honorable man. She was one of the few people who saw beneath his strong, taciturn surface to his kind and gentle heart.

Of course he didn't want to hurt her.

However, she knew that if she decided to stay here to be with Heather until he found someone permanently, there was a strong chance that despite his best intentions she and Jake would end up in bed together—considering the sparks that flew whenever they were around each other. The electricity created could light up New Eden.

Ashley had to be honest with herself. She could very easily end up with her heart broken—again—unless she accepted the reality of her situation.

Whether the decision was reasonable or not, Jake had no intention of getting married again. They might become sexually involved, but an affair was the most she could expect from him. Her childhood dreams about him were just that—from her childhood—and had no bearing on any choices she made now.

Her problem was that she'd wanted Jake Crenshaw from the time she understood what all those hormonal changes meant. Unfortunately, the past twenty-four hours had taught her that those feelings hadn't died away. Her life had turned into something magical and exciting since he'd come back into it, and that was without including Heather in the equation. She had definitely lost her heart to that little girl.

Before going to bed, Ashley checked on Heather. She smiled to find her sound asleep, covers in disarray.

Who wouldn't love this little chatterbox with the insatiable curiosity and outrageous remarks guaranteed to cause an adult to cringe with embarrassment?

Once in bed, Ashley was almost asleep when she remembered that she didn't have clean clothes to wear for tomorrow. She'd need to go to her dad's first thing in the morning and see what she might have left to wear at his place.

When Ashley opened her eyes the next morning, she found a pink rabbit in her face. She lifted her head and saw Heather lying on the other side of the rabbit, quietly humming to herself.

"Good morning, sunshine," Ashley said, feeling as if she'd been up most of the night. She felt more tired this morning than she had when she went to bed.

She pushed herself into a sitting position. "I didn't hear you come in. Why didn't you wake me up?"

Heather replied, "Mommy gets mad when I wake her up."

Ashley hugged her. "Well, I don't mind." She brushed blond curls away from Heather's face. "I bet you're starving, aren't you?"

She nodded vigorously. "Where's my daddy?"

"I don't know. Did you look in his bedroom?"

Heather nodded vigorously. "His covers were hanging off his bed, but he wasn't there."

"Maybe he's in the kitchen."

"Uh-uh. I looked. Maybe he's gone outside somewhere. After breakfast can I go outside?"

Ashley smiled and stroked Heather's cheek. "Do you want to look for your daddy?"

Heather dropped her gaze and nodded her head. "'Cause he might take me for a ride on a pony."

"Well, I guess you'll have to ask him the next time you see him. Why don't you wait while I get showered and dressed, then we'll get you dressed and make some breakfast? How does that sound?"

"Pancakes?" Heather asked hopefully.

"Sounds like a plan." Ashley bent and kissed Heather on the forehead. Before she could straighten, Heather hugged her around the neck and kissed her cheek. "I like you, Ashley. I hope you stay with me all the time."

"Well, we don't have to decide all of that now." She picked up her clothes from the day before and went in to take her shower. She wondered what kind of mood Jake was in this morning

There was no telling.

Once dressed, Ashley returned to find Heather on her own bed, playing with her plush animal friends. They settled on what Heather would wear, with Heather giving Ashley pointers on coordinating colors.

When they went downstairs they found the kitchen empty and most of a pot of coffee gone. She knew Jake got up early and tried not to read anything into the fact that he wasn't there. After all, he had no reason to see how Heather reacted this morning. However, there was a niggling thought at the back of her mind that suggested he might not be too eager to see her.

Since she'd finally decided to accept his offer of staying there nights, she guessed he'd have to live with her presence.

For Heather's sake, of course.

By the time Ashley had pancakes ready and a second pot of coffee waiting, she heard Jake's footsteps on the patio. He seemed to have built-in radar where food was concerned.

He walked into the kitchen and his eyes immediately sought out Ashley. The tension in him was palpable and the look in his eyes seared her with its intensity. She couldn't control the heat that immediately spread through her in response. Oh, boy, what a way to get your motor running first thing in the morning!

"Mornin'," he said with a brief nod. He went immediately to the coffeepot and filled his cup. Glancing at her out of the corner of his eye, he asked, "Did you sleep okay?"

"Yes. And you?"

"I slept just fine," he said through clenched teeth.

"I slept fine, too," Heather said, already at the table eating. "And look!" she said to Jake with a grin. "Pancakes!"

Ashley had made silver-dollar-size pancakes for her and she'd been eating them like they were ambrosia. Heather glanced at Jake hopefully. "Once I eat my brea'fast, could we go for a ride on a pony?"

Jake looked at his daughter and chuckled, his expression lightening somewhat. "I'm glad to hear you slept fine, too, and I think we might be able to work in a horse ride for you this morning."

Ashley placed three glasses of orange juice on the table and added coffee to Jake's cup. He sat down and sniffed appreciatively. "They sure smell good," he said. "Hope you didn't eat them all up before I got here."

Heather giggled. "Ashley made a whole bunch, see?" She pointed to the platter that Ashley set before them. Heather's mouth was dappled with syrup. She took a drink of milk before saying, "She's a good cooker, isn't she?"

Each of them looked at her in surprise. This was the first time she'd shown so much pleasure since she'd been there.

Ashley could see the emotion Jake fought to cover. "Yes, she is," he finally replied.

She sat next to Heather again and across from Jake. She admired how yummy he looked in the morning, freshly shaved. The cotton shirt he wore, its sleeves rolled above his elbows, emphasized his muscular arms and shoulders.

She made herself focus on her meal and the two of them ate in silence while Heather entertained them. She gave Jake a highly imaginative description of everything she'd seen yesterday while she'd been with Ashley, waving her fork in the air to punctuate some of her remarks.

Once they were finished, Ashley cleared the table while Heather watched Jake expectantly. "Is it time to go riding now?"

He stood and held out his hand. "Let's get some of that syrup off your face and hands and we'll go outside and look for a horse."

She slid out of her chair and hesitantly walked to him. Ashley watched Heather shyly slip her tiny hand into his. Heather looked up at him, her head bent back. "You're really big up close."

Jake went down on his haunches. "Would you like me to carry you so you can see everything from up here?"

She nodded and allowed him to wash her face and hands before she wrapped her arms around his neck and said, "Let's go."

Jake looked at Ashley and gave her a slow smile. Relieved that Heather was being a little friendlier to her father this morning, Ashley walked over to them and kissed each one on the cheek.

The look he gave her weakened her knees. Darn it, why did she have to blush right then, causing his mouth to tilt into a slight smile.

"Thank you for breakfast, Ashley. I enjoyed it."

"Me, too," Heather parroted. "I enjoyed it, too."

"It was my pleasure." She looked into his eyes. "By the way, I believe I'll take you up on the offer you made last night."

He eyed her warily. "What offer?"

"Why, to spend my nights here for now." She batted her lashes. "What did you think I meant?"

"Oh. Good. I think."

She laughed. "You cowboys go out and ride the range or something and I'll see you later."

"I'm not a boy!" Heather said indignantly.

"Of course you aren't. I should have said cowgirl."

Heather grinned at her, pleased with the correction.

Once again electricity seemed to bounce back and forth between Ashley and Jake. This was certainly going to be an interesting visit.

After they had gone outside, Ashley stood by the sink, her hands clasped beneath her chin, and watched as Jake pointed out to Heather all the different buildings and equipment around the ranch.

They were so beautiful together. She blinked furiously, not willing to give in to the emotions threatening to engulf her. She would enjoy spending time with them, she knew. It was getting used to being without them in her life that would be the hardest adjustment.

Nine

"This is a big place," Heather announced from above Jake's head. They stood in the ranch yard while he tried to decide where to take her first.

The idea of placing her on his shoulders wasn't one of his better ones. He felt naked outdoors without his hat on but there was no way he could wear it while she had a death grip on his hair. He had one hand holding her steady and the other holding his hat.

"You know what we forgot?"

"What?" she asked.

"We forgot to get you a hat. If you're going to ride a horse, you need one."

"Like yours?"

"If I can find one. We'll go look in the barn."

She swung her legs again his chest.

"Ow," he said. "That hurts."

"Oh. Sorry."

As soon as they reached the barn, he swung her over his head and placed her on her feet, making her giggle. "You're strong."

"Sometimes, maybe. I've gotta admit you're heavy." She grinned. "'Cause I eat so much, right?"

"And because you're getting to be a big girl." He headed to the tack room to see if there was anything he could place on her head to shade her fair skin.

"Ooooh," she said and he realized that she'd stopped. He turned around. Heather had discovered Jordan's horses. "Look at the ponies," she whispered. "They're really big, aren't they?"

"I doubt that Jordan would appreciate your referring to his thoroughbreds as ponies, but you're right, they're big."

"Can I ride one of them?"

He held out his hand and she took it as naturally as if she were used to doing so. "Well, we'll find one to ride, but not from this group." He let her walk into the tack room ahead of him. She was fascinated by the saddles, bridles, curry combs and other items needed around horses.

He spotted a small hat on one of the hooks. Probably belonged to one of the kids on the ranch. He sat it on her head, then knelt to see if it fit. It was a little big but better than nothing. He'd have to take her into town and get her some clothes that could stand up to ranch life.

The hat slipped over one of her eyes and she giggled. "I can't see."

He grinned and straightened it. "There. You'll have to hang on to it, though, or it's going to fall off."

"Howdy, you two," Jordan said, walking toward them. "How's everything going?"

Heather grabbed Jake's hand and leaned against his leg. "Who's that?" she whispered.

"This is my cousin, Jordan Crenshaw. Jordan, please

meet Heather Anne Crenshaw, who has taken up permanent residence with us."

Jordan raised his brows. "Well. How about that? I'm pleased to meet you, Miss Heather." He held out his hand.

She eyed it uncertainly, looked at Jake and then seemed to remember something. "These are your ponies, aren't they!" She took his hand briefly, then leaned against Jake again.

Jake cleared his throat, trying not to laugh at the expression on Jordan's face.

"Oh, well, yeah, I guess so."

"Do you get to ride all of them?"

He walked over to a bale of hay and sat down, which Jake thought was a good idea. He led Heather to another one nearby where they could be more at Heather's level.

"Not all of them, no. But I ride some of them."

She edged closer to Jordan. "He's going to take me riding on a pony."

"He? Don't you call him Daddy?"

She dropped her head and shook it slowly.

"We haven't gotten around to that, quite yet," Jake said easily. "It'll come."

"Well, you can call me Uncle Jordan, if you like. How about it?"

"Unca Jordan. Okay." She looked at Jake and he saw the flash of mischief in her face before she added, "And I'll call *him* Papa Jake!"

Jordan laughed and Jake joined in, shaking his head ruefully. "She's a character," Jake said, "I've already discovered that."

"Mommie calls me a pest sometimes," she nonchalantly shared with them. "Is that like a char—a chara—" She stopped, obviously frustrated. "I can't say it," she said, disgustedly.

Jordan picked her up, hugged her and set her back on

her feet. "You're a darling, is what you are. How come your daddy got so lucky, getting a little girl like you?"

Jake swallowed a couple of times in an effort to get the lump out of his throat. He needed to change the subject fast or his daughter was going to wonder what was wrong with him.

"Jordan, tell Heather about the time one of your horses jumped the fence and took off, why don't you?"

While Jordan described the incident, Heather came to Jake and held up her arms for him to pick her up. She settled onto his lap, rested her head on his chest and listened to the story about trying to catch a horse that didn't want to be caught.

Jake leaned down and softly kissed the top of her head.

Since April didn't work on Sundays, Ashley cleaned the kitchen and made up the beds. Afterwards, she went outside, wondering where her favorite Crenshaws might be.

She spotted them as soon as she stepped inside the barn. They were looking at a few of Jordan's horses. Jordan, who looked enough like Jake to be his brother rather than cousin, was talking to Heather, who appeared completely relaxed with the two men, which was an excellent sign that she was adjusting to her new situation.

Ashley stood there watching them. Chemistry was a strange thing, she thought, studying the two men. Jordan had the same Crenshaw stamp on him as Jake, so why was it only Jake Crenshaw who started her body humming?

Giving her head a quick shake, she called out to them. "I'm going to Dad's. Do you want to come with me, Heather?"

Both men turned at the sound of her voice, their brief smiles of greeting another similarity between them, their gleaming white teeth flashing in their darkly tanned faces.

Heather scrunched her face up—obviously in deep thought—and then shook her head. "I wanna stay with Papa Jake and Unca Jordan."

Papa Jake. So she'd found a name she was comfortable calling her father and uncle was as good a title for Jordan as any. Better than Cousin Jordan.

She waved and said, "See you later, then. Have fun."

Ashley took her time on the drive to her dad's place. She spotted deer grazing in one of the meadows and a red-tailed hawk watching for prey from the top of a utility pole. She loved this place and she didn't come out nearly often enough. Other than looking at Jordan's stock whenever he needed her, or checking on sheep or cattle that her dad called her about, she was rarely there.

She pulled up at Ken's house and parked beneath one of the cottonwood trees. Several large trees shaded the house, keeping the sun off the metal roof for most of the day. His truck was in the carport, so she knew he was home. She was looking forward to spending some time with him.

Her dad sat in his favorite easy chair, reading the Sunday paper and sipping on a cup of coffee.

"Hi, Dad," she said and smiled broadly.

He lowered the paper and looked at her with pleased surprise. "Well, hello, there, young-un," he said, getting up and giving her a bear hug that lifted her off her feet. "What brings you out here this fine summer morning? Not that I'm complaining, you understand."

"Jake probably told you about my keeping his daughter yesterday."

He nodded and motioned for her to precede him into the kitchen. "Yes, he did. Between worrying about Red, comforting his wife and feeling guilty that he hadn't gotten his daughter from you as planned, he was a bundle of nerves the entire day."

She poured herself a cup of coffee, filled his cup and sat at the kitchen table. Ken followed her, prepared to sit and chat. They'd spent many hours around this table over the years. Her dad had been a wonderful father and she counted herself very lucky. She had a parent who loved her unconditionally. She'd discovered while she was away at college how rare that was and how much she had to be grateful for.

She forced her mind back to the subject at hand.

"Well, as it turned out, Heather didn't want me to leave her once Jake got home, so I ended up staying over again. Rather than drive into town this morning for more clothes I thought I'd check my closet to see if I can find something I've left here."

He studied her, concern wrinkling his brow. "So you've spent two nights at Jake's," he finally said.

"That's right, Dad. Jake asked me last night if I would be willing to stay out here with Heather nights until he hires someone to look after her. I really don't mind the drive for a week or so. I fully expect him to find someone suitable by then."

Ken leaned on his crossed arms. "Do you think that's wise, honey?"

They both knew what he was concerned about.

"You mean because of that crush I used to have on him?" She chuckled. "Oh, I'm well over that by now." Of course you are, the voice in her head said with a sneer. You're crazy in love with him and you know it.

She cleared her throat. "Jake and I have been friends my entire life. I see no reason why I shouldn't help out a friend when he needs it."

"Maybe I'm behind the times, but two unmarried people of the opposite sex living together can cause a lot of grief for everyone concerned, friends or no friends."

"It's a big house, Dad. My time will be spent with Heather, not Jake. She trusts me and I don't want to let her down."

"Could this newly formed attachment you have with Heather have anything to do with her being Jake's daughter?" Ken asked with a lopsided smile.

She squeezed his forearm and smiled. "Probably," she admitted, "but she's really adorable. Once you meet her, you'll see what a little darling she is."

He covered her hand with his. "I just don't want to see you hurt, sweetheart. You've gone through enough grief in your young life."

"I know, Dad," she said softly.

"You're old enough to make your own decisions. I know that. And I think the world of Jake. Always have. I watched those boys grow up and I know the values they were taught.

"Jake is an honorable man, but his world has changed drastically and he's still reeling. He's vulnerable right now. As far as that goes, he's always been vulnerable where you're concerned. He's a man with strong emotions. The combination of his state of mind and your living there with him could be more than he can handle right now."

Ashley valued her dad's opinion because he knew Jake almost as well as he knew her. "Are you saying my being there will only make things worse for him? I want to make things a little easier for him."

Her dad had pointed out all the thoughts that had run through her head last night. Yes, Jake was vulnerable. Well, so was she.

"You have to do what you think best, sweetheart. I guess I'm concerned about the possible fallout. He's always had a soft spot for you."

She cocked her head. "I can't tell who you're most protective of, Dad, me or Jake."

"Both!" he immediately replied and they both laughed.

"Guess I'll go see what I can find to wear," she said after draining her cup. "While I'm here on the ranch, you'll be seeing more of me, you know."

"I'll hold you to that, young-un," he replied, patting her shoulder.

"I love you, Dad."

"Right back at you, sweetheart."

It was almost noon by the time she returned to Jake's place. She saw him on one of his horses with a tow-headed little girl in front of him, wearing a hat that she could barely peer out from under. She smiled at the picture they made. He must find it natural to have a little girl once again clamoring for a ride with him.

When Ashley got out of her truck, Heather waved at her and yelled, "Look at me, look at me, Ashley! I'm riding!"

Ashley waved back. "Good for you, sunshine." She drew closer and looked up at Jake. "You two get washed up and I'll see what's on hand to feed us."

"Good idea," Jake replied, looking relieved. "This gal has plumb worn me out."

"I can relate, believe me. I'll have something prepared by the time you finish your ride." She hurried into the house, not wanting to betray to him how touched she was by the sight of his big hand gently holding Heather close to his chest, keeping her safe.

When the riders walked into the kitchen, Ashley had soup and sandwiches waiting. By the time Heather finished her meal, she was almost asleep, her head nodding and her lashes drooping.

Jake came around the table and quietly picked her up. Ashley followed as he carried Heather upstairs to her room. After stopping in her room, she waited in the hallway, smiling. After a couple of minutes, he rushed out of the room, looking panicked. "Have you seen her—" He stopped when he saw Ashley holding the pink rabbit out to him.

"She left it in my room this morning."

"Thanks," he said, his relief obvious. He disappeared into Heather's room again and Ashley heard Heather's sleepy murmur and his deeper voice, barely audible.

When he came out, she joined him companionably as they walked downstairs.

Ashley stopped in the hallway and said, "You know, I think that while she's asleep, I'll go into town and pack some things. I won't need much, since I'll be stopping by my apartment each day to check my mail. That is, if you don't mind being here alone with her."

"I really hate to ask you to do this. I know you've got better things to do with your time than to hang around here."

"I wouldn't be doing it if I didn't want to. I had a choice, you know. Nobody forced me." She smiled. "Don't worry so much, Jake," she said. "Let's take this one day at a time."

"It's not the days I'm worried about," he replied darkly.

"Really? Well, maybe you should be," she said, and went up on tiptoe to kiss him.

Jake froze when her lips touched his and she thought he was going to push her away. Instead, he took over the kiss.

How quickly she'd become addicted to his touch. She loved the feel of his hands on her back, the muscled hardness of his chest. Oh, yes, this was what she needed.

When he finally released her, they were both breathing hard.

"You're not helping, you know," he said, his voice raspy.

She widened her eyes. "I'm not? I thought I took part in that kiss, but if I didn't, here, let me try again."

He stepped back, shaking his head and chuckling. "That's not what I meant and you know that very well."

"Jakc? I see no reason why we can't enjoy being together and enjoying each other's company. Why are you fighting this?"

They hadn't moved away from the bottom of the stairs. She leaned against the newel post and looked at him.

"You're not that naïve, Ashley. This isn't about stealing a couple of kisses now and then. I told you how I felt about you last night. Now you're using my remarks against me."

"I'm not asking for anything from you that you aren't willing to give. If our making love will ease the tension between us—and we both acknowledge that it's what we want—what harm can it be?"

"Maybe you're used to casual affairs, but I'm not. I will not allow myself to get involved with you when there's no future in it."

She looked at him in silence before she finally said, "You're really angry at me, aren't you?"

He let out a gust of air and dropped his head. "Not really. I just don't want you to tease me when you know I have no intention of following up. We need some boundaries if you're going to stay here."

She folded her arms across her chest. "I see. So I'm making matters worse by showing my affection for you."

He turned away. "It's bad enough as it is, Ashley. I can't sleep at night, knowing you're down the hall from me, and if I do manage to sleep, I dream of you," he said, pacing.

"That pretty well describes my nights, too," she said softly.

He flinched. "I could have gone all day without knowing that, but at least you're being honest."

"I've always been honest, Jake. That's never been the issue. You seem to have some knight-like attitude toward me, treating me as your lady fair who can't be sullied by your base desires."

He glanced at her from beneath his brows and smiled sheepishly. "That bad, huh?"

"I'm not going to beg you, Jake. If you feel that your conscience won't allow physical intimacy between us, I can accept that. However, I'd appreciate your hiring someone as quickly as possible so that I can get back to my life without you in it. I'm counting on the old adage, 'Out of sight, out of mind.'"

Ten

Ashley closed her apartment door behind her, dropping yesterday's mail on the table, and went to the refrigerator for a soft drink. Popping the top on the soda, she walked to the picture window in her living room and looked out at the traffic going by.

She tried to convince herself that she was relieved to be back in her own home without a chattering little girl and a man who drove her crazy, but by the time she finished her drink she gave up the pretense.

How ironic that for the next week or so, she would be living the life she'd always wanted—living with Jake and caring for his child. Perhaps she should have been more specific in her dreams.

At least he was no longer patting her on the head—metaphorically speaking—and treating her as a child. In a way, his present attitude was worse. Because he was physically attracted to her, he didn't want to be tempted by being affectionate toward her.

She went into the bedroom. In addition to gathering some clothes to wear, she also needed to adopt a new attitude toward the Crenshaw father and daughter. Despite her dad's concern, she wasn't using Heather as an excuse to be there. She wanted to ease the transition for Heather and she knew she could do that.

What she'd do from now on would be to ignore Jake as much as possible. And take sleeping pills at bedtime.

Heather was up from her nap when Ashley returned to the ranch. She could hear her in the kitchen. When she heard Jake laugh, she smiled at the sound and walked into the room.

Jake had found the Popsicles she'd bought yesterday and had given one to Heather, who seemed to be enjoying it immensely—if the strawberry-red color around her mouth and chin were any indication.

"Ashley! You're here. I missed you. I couldn't find you when I waked up."

"I promised you she would be back soon," Jake said, glancing in Ashley's general direction without meeting her eyes. He returned his gaze to Heather. "And here she is."

"I don't want you to leave me, Ashley," Heather scolded. "Not ever again."

Ashley poured herself a glass of water to give herself some time before she said, "Here's the deal, sunshine. I have to go to work every day and I can't take you with me most of the time. Sometimes, maybe, but not often. So you'll be with your daddy during the day and when I finish taking care of the animals who come see me, I'll come home and spend the evening with you."

"And the night," Heather added, sounding insistent.

"For a while, I'll stay the night, too."

"But I want you to always stay here."

Jake was conspicuously silent. Darn him, anyway.

"Won't happen, little girl. You'll have to take what you can get." She picked up her small duffel bag and said, "I'll put this upstairs and see what we can have for supper."

Matching her actions to her words, Ashley went upstairs. When she entered her bedroom, she closed the door and sank into a chair. Her suspicions about herself were confirmed.

She was a masochist.

The following Friday, Ashley ushered out the day's last patient and his owner and stood beside Wendy's desk until they were gone.

"I think that's it for my day. What does tomorrow look like?"

"Busy, as usual. At least you won't be on call this weekend."

"Thankfully. I'm counting the days until the newly graduated doctor of veterinary medicine joins us. Even with Woody and I working full-time, the practice has grown too much for the two of us to handle."

"It hasn't hurt that the two of you have lived here all your life. People trust you."

Ashley wriggled her shoulders and stretched. "That's good to know. At the moment, all I want to do is sink into a steaming bath for an hour and afterwards fall on the bed until morning."

"Sounds like a plan."

Ashley grinned. "With a three-year-old around? Not a chance."

"You haven't mentioned how things are going out there."

"Progress all around. Jake flew to Austin and San Antonio this week and interviewed applicants. He doesn't appear particularly thrilled with any of them, but they're qualified and interested to see the area. Two are scheduled to visit next week sometime. As for Heather...on the one hand, she and Jake are more relaxed around each other. I think she's beginning to develop a certain pleasure from living on the ranch."

"What's on the other hand?"

Ashley sighed. "She still insists she doesn't want me to move back to town. Since Jake hopes to have someone hired by the end of next week, Heather will have to accept that she can't have everything her own way."

"The community has taken quite an interest in the goings-on out at the ranch these days. The buzz that Jake has a child no one knew about has kept the phones hot. With you in the mix, the phones at my place are suddenly quite active as well."

"Too bad there's so little entertainment in town. I can't imagine why anyone cares."

Wendy grinned. "Aw, c'mon, Ashley. Here's the very sexy, very eligible bachelor and his little girl and the very sexy, very eligible veterinarian spending her leisure time with the two of them. That's fodder for any gossip mill and you know it."

"As my grandmother was fond of saying—if they're talking about me, they're leaving someone else alone. It won't be long before something new and scandalous will draw their attention away from us."

"Well, I keep telling those who call that there's absolutely nothing clandestine about this whole setup, but I'm not sure anyone's buying that."

"Too bad."

"If you don't mind my saying so, you're looking pretty tired these days. Maybe you need to schedule a day off."

"I'm okay. Just not sleeping too well."

"I see."

"And the raised eyebrows mean...what?"

"Oh, nothing."

"C'mon, Wendy. You have something to say. Say it."

Wendy straightened in her chair and with a hint of amusement in her eyes, said, "Just wondering if Jake has anything to do with your sleeplessness?"

"If you're suggesting that I'm sleeping with him, you're wrong."

"Ah."

"What does *that* mean?"

"It's possible that the reason you aren't sleeping well is because you're *not* sleeping with him."

Ashley laughed ruefully since she knew her comment was right on the mark, but she'd never tell Wendy that.

"You're incorrigible and I'm out of here. I may have you schedule a day off for me some time next week. We'll keep it in mind and hope that an epidemic doesn't strike any of our clients."

With a final wave, Ashley stepped out of the clinic and decided to go downtown for a few items she needed at the drugstore.

After she parked, Ashley paused a moment to look at the square. From the activity around the business area, every citizen of the community was out shopping today.

Several people spoke or waved to her as she walked to the corner drugstore. She passed one of her former classmates, who asked, "How's Jake?" with such arch meaning Ashley almost laughed out loud.

"Terrific," she replied, continuing into the store. Let her take that any way she pleases.

Once she was on her way to the ranch, Ashley seriously wondered if she could sneak into the house without Heather or Jake spotting her. If so, she might be able to have that long, soaking bath after all.

She and Jake had settled into a routine of sorts. Mostly he stayed out of her way, which was a relief. She spent her evenings with Heather until she went to sleep somewhere around eight o'clock…too early for Ashley to go to bed.

If it weren't for the tension between them, she'd have no problem going downstairs to see how Jake's day went. After the first evening, though, she learned to go to her room and read. He continued to watch her as though expecting her to pounce on him the minute he relaxed.

She sighed. Not that she could blame him, she supposed. She'd initiated the kiss last Sunday and his reaction taught her never to let her impulses get the better of her again.

One night this week, she'd gone to the kitchen for something to drink and saw the light on in his office. The door was closed. I get it, I get it, I'm intruding on your space and I'm sorry.

At least he'd not wasted any time looking for someone to care for Heather. She would be just as glad to return to her normal routine as he was so that she could once again sleep at night.

Jake and his men rode slowly back to the ranch settlement, men and animals exhausted.

The sheriff had called this morning to say that his investigations into the recent rash of car thefts in the area led him to believe that the perpetrators were hiding somewhere on Jake's property. Because of the size of the ranch, there were areas his crew seldom visited, especially the sections that were rough and hard to reach. He flew over these on a regular basis, but no one had actually ridden in for a thorough inspection in a while. If the thieves *were* hiding on the ranch, they must have chosen the most inaccessible places, which didn't make much sense. If that were true, how were they getting in there?

He had gotten the call after Ashley had already left for the clinic. When he explained the situation to Jordan and told him that he and some of his men needed to search the property by horseback, Jordan offered to keep Heather with him. Jordan told him he had to run to town anyway and then go to his place to see how the construction of his horse barn was going, so she wouldn't be a bother.

Jake knew that his daughter could talk the ear off a deaf person, but he needed help. He was reluctant to ask Ashley to do more than she was already doing.

He and his men spent the day looking for tracks and checking the canyons and ravines. Jake brought his map of the ranch and had the men spread out to cover as much ground as possible.

When he got home, Jake wearily unsaddled his horse, rubbed him down and gave him extra rations.

Jake wished he could have a rubdown, as well. His body was signaling that it was no longer used to long trail rides and that he was going to pay for it.

This was the time of day he dreaded the most, when he had to be around Ashley. He made it a point to leave the house before the others were awake, but there was no way to avoid evenings with her until after Heather went to bed. After that, he took the coward's way out and stayed in his office, catching up on his accounts and watching television until he was convinced he could sleep.

Hah! It didn't matter whether he spent time with Ashley or not, his subconscious reminded him of her every time he closed his eyes. As tired as he was, he'd probably pass out as soon as he hit the bed tonight.

Then he remembered that today was Friday and he'd promised his poker-playing pals a chance to win some of their money back.

Damn.

Well, there was no help for it. He had to go. A hot shower and something for his sore muscles would have to do him. At least he didn't have anything planned for the weekend. Maybe he'd take Heather somewhere and get her used to not having Ashley around.

Yeah. He could do that.

Since he hadn't seen Heather all day, he knew she'd be full of stories to tell him. That should get them through the evening until her bedtime. Then he'd head into town.

At least he had a plan of sorts.

Two of the applicants he'd decided were what he might be looking for—after screening at least a dozen or more—were willing to live here in the Hill Country and he'd arranged to fly them to the ranch next week. They were comfortably middle-aged and he hoped whoever he chose would remind Heather of her Gram and ease her away from wanting Ashley there every day.

He wasn't too sure that his thoughts and dreams of her would stop once she'd moved back to town, though.

A small voice in his head had been whispering repeatedly for the last few days, "Marry her."

He'd tried to ignore the thought, but the idea lodged in his brain and he couldn't get rid of it. The little voice refused to shut up. In fact, it built its case by pointing out the differences between his relationship with Tiffany and the kind he already had and could have with Ashley in the future.

He'd already faced the fact that he was in love with her. If he'd had any doubts, the past week had dispelled them. He knew every time he heard her voice and her laughter, every time he saw her, every time he wanted so badly to reach out to her and hold her as tightly as he could.

It wasn't that he doubted his love for her. It was the thought of being married again that gave him nightmares. Tiffany had put him through a great deal during their marriage, which was why he never doubted that she was capable of hiding the existence of his daughter from him.

That's when the voice would start in again.

Tiffany had never liked ranch life. Ashley had known no other. Tiffany spent thousands of dollars on clothes, makeup and keeping her hair and nails looking just right.

He'd rarely seen Ashley in anything but jeans and shirts and if Ashley used makeup at all, it was probably lipstick. She definitely had an easy-to-keep haircut that made her look adorable.

If he'd had any sense, he would have married Ashley in the first place—if she hadn't been so blasted young. "That was then. She's no longer a teenager," the voice slyly pointed out.

When he left the barn, Jake wondered where Jordan and Heather were. His errands should be finished by now. There was Ashley's truck. Maybe Jordan had already dropped Heather off and had gone home.

Once inside the house, he didn't hear a sound, which was pretty much a guarantee that Heather wasn't here, or if she were, she was asleep.

The answering machine was blinking and he punched the play button. The message was from Jordan. He could hear Heather chattering in the background as well as other voices.

"Hey, Jake," Jordan said, sounding amused. "Didn't want you to worry about us. I stopped by the folks' place to show our baby girl off and Mom invited us to stay and have dinner with them tonight. They want to get to know Heather and I didn't think you'd mind. I'll have her home by dark."

Since it was already seven, Jake figured they would be back no later than eight, which would be close to Heather's bedtime and time for him to go to town.

He wondered where Ashley was. She was usually in the kitchen when he came inside. Jake took the stairs two at a time and paused in front of her door. He knocked gently. If she was asleep, he didn't want to disturb her. When there was no answer, he quietly opened the door to make certain she was there, but her bed was untouched.

As he turned to leave he noticed the light on in her bathroom and the door open. "Ashley?" he said and waited for an answer. When none came, he became more alarmed. Was she ill?

He stopped in the doorway of the bathroom and saw her reflected in the mirrored wall. She was in the tub sound asleep. His brain immediately shut down. He stood there frozen as though in suspended animation. He knew he had to leave...he really had to. Seeing her like this was the absolute last thing either one of them needed.

But what if she drowns? It was dangerous for her to sleep in the tub like that.

Jake slowly stepped into the room, trying to figure out a way to wake her without startling her.

She must have been covered by frothy bubbles at one time but now the water was clear except for a few clumps of foam that formed little islands on the surface. The pink tips of her breasts rose slightly above the water.

No longer capable of rational thought, he knelt beside the tub.

She had an air pillow at her neck, cushioning her

ANNETTE BROADRICK 121

head from the porcelain surface. Soft music played from a nearby radio. She looked so relaxed that he suddenly realized how strained she'd looked all week, pretty much the way he looked in the mirror each time he shaved.

Now her face was softened by sleep, her body floating in full view.

There was no doubt in his mind that he'd just lost the struggle to leave her alone. He knelt beside the tub, drinking in her beauty. Her breasts were in proportion to her small build; her waist dipped in and her hips flared in perfect symmetry; her flat stomach and legs were muscled and firm without losing the delicate look that was Ashley.

He closed his eyes, but it didn't help. She was now imprinted on his brain permanently. When he opened them, he said her name like a prayer.

"Ashley," he whispered, hurting inside.

Her thick lashes fluttered and she opened her eyes.

Eleven

Ashley was dreaming of Jake. She wasn't surprised to hear him softly call her name. She opened her eyes and knew that this was no dream. She must have fallen asleep and Jake now knelt beside the tub.

He looked hot, tired and dusty. There was a line across his forehead where his hat had rested. The rest of his face looked like he'd been in the sun most of the day.

Despite his obvious weariness, he wanted her and he made no effort to hide it. Belatedly, she became more fully awake and realized that there must be something wrong for him to be in her bathroom.

"Are you all right?" she asked, sitting up in the tub. When she realized the bubbles no longer covered her, she automatically covered her breasts with her hands.

"Don't," he whispered, as though pleading. He gently lifted her hands away. "You are so beautiful and I want you so badly I ache with it." His voice died away as he trailed his fingers through the water and cupped her breast. His soft touch made her intensely aware of her overwhelming need for him.

She reached for him and he pulled away. "I'm filthy," Jake said. "I have no business in here. It's just…"

She nodded to the glass shower next to the tub. "There's plenty of soap and water right here." She flushed as she added lightly, "I'll be glad to help you bathe."

If that didn't make her feelings for him clear, then nothing would.

As though in a trance, Jake sat on the commode and pulled off his boots and the rest of his clothes. He stood and turned on the shower.

Oh, my, not even her wildest imaginings had done justice to his beautiful, unclothed body. His wide shoulders and muscled back tapered to his waist and down to his firm butt.

He could have posed for Michelangelo with his pure, clean lines and strong, healthy body. She wanted to touch him so badly, needed to love him so much, that she quivered with yearning.

She watched him step into the shower, pick up the soap and begin to lather himself. As though caught in his force field and unable to escape, she slowly stood and silently stepped over the side of the tub. He had his back to her and when the door opened behind him he looked around, startled.

"Here," she said, taking the soap from his hand, "let me."

Without a word, he gave her the soap and turned back to the wall, leaning with his palms against the tile in surrender.

Ashley indulged herself in all the ways she'd dreamed about. She stroked and caressed his shoulders and back with soapy hands, her fingers trailing over him. She took special care to massage his hard backside and noticed his legs had a tremor in them.

When she tugged on his arm he slowly straightened and turned, revealing his arousal, his arms at his sides. He'd closed his eyes and stood before her without moving. She realized that he'd finally surrendered to the inevitable passion between them.

She soaped his shoulders, arms and chest, luxuriating in the freedom to touch him to her heart's content.

He remained still and silent until she carefully washed his groin area, running her fingers down his aroused length and cupping him. He groaned as though in agony and opened his eyes.

"I can't resist you," he whispered brokenly. "No matter how hard I try. I want you so damned much!" He lifted her breasts in the palms of his hands and bent over to kiss them, the spray of water sluicing the soap she'd applied off him.

When his mouth surrounded the tip of her breast, she went up on her tiptoes in encouragement while she restlessly stroked him, wanting him, eager to have him deep inside her.

He slipped his arms around her and lifted. She clung to him, wrapping her legs around his waist. He kissed her, turning so that her back was against the tile. As though a dam had broken inside of him, all his pent-up emotions swept over them and he devoured her, stroking her mouth with his tongue, nibbling on her bottom lip, his hand kneading her breast.

She could feel his arousal pushing lightly against her, ready to enter. Oh yes please oh please yes oh yessss. They were panting for breath as he shifted slightly and—

"Hey, Jake! Ashley? Anybody home?"

They froze and stared at each other in shock. Jake dropped his head back with a groan. "How could I have forgotten?" he muttered. He carefully lowered her to her feet. "It's Jordan, bringing Heather home." They were both shaking and Ashley wasn't certain she could stand without his help.

He braced her and said, "His timing couldn't have been worse."

She focused on the heated expression in his eyes. "Either that, or you were saved from breaking your rules by a metaphorical bell," she shakily replied.

"The rules never entered my mind, but we've got to get out of here before he comes upstairs looking for us."

Her brain must have been scrambled by lust. She quickly left the shower while he turned off the water. She threw him a towel while she quickly dried off. "I can't believe I totally forgot about her!" she whispered in panic.

"What about me? I knew they would be here soon and I still forgot!"

"Stay here. I'll get you some fresh clothes in a few minutes," she said in a low voice, pulling on underwear. She raised her voice and called out. "Just a minute, Jordan, I'll be right there."

Jake finished drying off and wrapped the towel around his waist. He quickly gathered up his dirty clothes. "I think they're on their way up here. If so, take them downstairs and I'll be able to get to my room."

Ashley slipped into a pullover shirt and jeans and left the bedroom barefooted. She found Jordan at the top of the staircase holding Heather. "Hi, Jordan!" she said brightly, hoping he couldn't read anything in her expression. "And Heather, you look like you're more than half asleep! Sorry I didn't hear you when you first got here." She motioned to her wet hair. "I was in the shower." She knew she looked flushed and hoped Jordan thought it was due to the hot water and not because she'd been with Jake.

Ashley led the way downstairs as she talked. "I thought Heather was with Jake. How come you have her?"

Jordan put her down and said, "Oh, he'll explain once he gets home. We had a great day, didn't we, sprout? Took her over to show her off to my folks. I think Heather has pretty well talked herself into silence—at least for today."

"Can you stay? I'll get something together to eat and—"

"We ate at Mom's and I need to be going."

"Ah."

"Tell Jake to call me when he gets in."

"I'll do that."

Without a word, Ashley scooped Heather up in her arms and they went upstairs. Heather was almost half-asleep as Ashley took a washcloth and bathed her face and hands, put her in her pajamas and slipped her into bed. She placed the pink rabbit in the curve of her arm, kissed her on the cheek and left.

She heard the radio softly playing in her bathroom. When she went in to turn it off, she saw the water still in the tub. She drained and cleaned the tub, then went in search of Jake.

When she tapped on his door, he gave a muffled answer.

Standing outside his closed door, she said, "Jordan said to call him when you get in."

"I will."

After a moment of indecision, she finally spoke again. "I'm going to make us something to eat."

"Don't bother. I need to go into town and I'll eat while I'm there."

Stunned that he could leave right now, she managed to say, "Oh. Okay."

Ashley turned and retraced her steps until she reached

the kitchen. Maybe he had enough experience in this kind of situation to ignore the body's screaming need for relief, but she didn't. She could scarcely stand still, so she paced and rubbed her arms, attempting to talk herself down from this new place she'd just discovered.

Sometime later, while she stood at the kitchen bar half-heartedly eating a sandwich, she heard him come down the stairs, cross the foyer without pausing and go out the door.

She had never been this sexually aroused before and had no idea what to do about her discomfort. She wasn't in pain, exactly, but her skin was sensitive and she was aware of the clothes she wore touching and rubbing against her. Her whole body felt hot and prickly.

Would a cold shower really help? Somehow—given the circumstances just before Jordan arrived—she didn't think so. After what had almost happened, she'd probably become aroused every time she walked into her bathroom.

She tried to watch television, but nothing appealed to her. She picked up and put down a couple of magazines and searched the shelves for a book to read, but nothing caught her eye.

Finally, she gave up and went to bed, lying awake for hours wondering where Jake had gone and why. Had he already planned a meeting in town when he found her in the tub? She still didn't know why Jordan had kept Heather. She and Jake hadn't done much talking.

She buried her head in her pillow and groaned.

Had he gone to another woman to take care of his needs? The thought really depressed her.

Ashley eventually fell asleep, her dreams filled with images of Jake.

Jake drove into town as though all of the demons in hell were after him. He knew he was a coward for not talking to Ashley before he left about what had happened. What could he have said? All his high-minded resolve to leave her alone went up in flames when he saw her asleep in the tub.

Should he admit how much he loved her and, because of those feelings, how little control he seemed to have where she was concerned?

Should he admit how painful it was to love her while knowing she deserved someone better than him? Explain why he didn't ask her to marry him?

When he arrived at the Mustang Bar & Grill, Jake still had no answers, only more questions.

When he went inside, most of his poker-playing buddies were already there, eating hamburgers. He motioned to the waitress to bring him the same and sat down with them.

"Hi," he said to the group.

Kent and Lew, the other ranchers, looked at each other before Kent asked, "Who died?"

The waitress brought his beer and he drank almost a third of it with his first swallow. Once she left, Jake said, "Nobody died that I know of. Why do you ask?"

Banker Tom laughed and said, "Well, you look like you at least lost your last friend, which can't be the case since we're all here." The other three laughed.

"Just tired. I've been on horseback all day and I'm here to tell you I much prefer a pickup. It's a hell of a lot more comfortable."

Lew nodded. "I hear you. That's why I hire men to do that sort of thing for me."

Jake told them why he'd been out searching the ranch and by the time he'd finished eating, the conversation had turned to more general matters.

They went into the back room and gathered around the table. Tom eyed him from over his glasses. "Hope you brought some of my money with you 'cause I intend to win it back tonight."

Jake forced a smile. "You can try."

He kept thinking about Ashley and what had almost happened today. He knew he wouldn't get the image of her in the shower with him out of his head.

"Your turn, Crenshaw," someone said, and Jake obligingly played.

As the night wore on, he knew his concentration was shot. He just couldn't get interested in the hand he had or the growing pot in the middle of the table.

Lew said, "I've been thinking about what the sheriff told you. Guess it could be worse. Instead of stealing cars, they could be rustling cattle."

Kent, who ran a large herd of longhorn cattle, said, "Mine are a little more difficult to crate and haul out of here, but you two running sheep and goats might have a problem."

"Well, gentlemen," Tom said genially, "while you've been discussing the perils of ranching, I just won the pot, or did anyone notice?"

The lawyer, Curtis, said, "Hell's bells, McCain, I've been paying attention. Didn't save me from losing my money any."

Jake yawned and tossed down his cards. "I think I'll head back home, guys. I'm exhausted and you've managed to wipe me out. I'll see you next week."

Once home, Jake paused in Ashley's doorway and watched her for a long time before he finally went to bed.

Jake kept himself as busy as possible during the next week. He and Heather had fallen into a routine of sorts since she'd arrived. She stayed with him mornings while he checked with Ken about what needed to be done that day and sometimes helped to supervise the work.

Around noon, he returned to the house where April had
lunch waiting for them.

April had suggested during their first day on their
own that she'd keep an eye on Heather while she
napped, which would give him time to handle details
without having to watch out for Heather. April would
call him on his cell phone when Heather woke up and
he'd swing by and pick her up, and then he would keep
her with him until Ashley got home.

He asked Jordan's mother if she would watch
Heather two afternoons that week while he flew to pick
up each of the two applicants he considered qualified
to be Heather's nanny. He didn't want his daughter to
meet the applicants until he'd had a chance to evaluate
them in his surroundings.

The first candidate gushed over everything she saw—
the hacienda, the ranch buildings, the horses. She was
so bubbly that he knew she would drive him crazy
within a week…or sooner.

The second one, Charlotte James, seemed all right.
She was calm with a gentle manner that reassured him
she would be good with Heather. When he flew her
back to the city, they discussed salary and when she
might be able to come to work. They agreed that a
thirty-day trial period would give them a chance to see
if Heather took to her and if Mrs. James liked living
so far from San Antonio. She told him she'd be able to
start at the beginning of next week, which was fine
with him.

Now that he'd found someone, he could rest easier.
However, Jake knew that Heather wouldn't be happy
about Charlotte's arrival if it meant that Ashley wouldn't
be coming out to see her every day. She'd made that
clear in a dozen different ways.

Heather was perfectly content to spend her days with

him, whether he was checking on things around the ranch, working on the books at home or running errands.

However, come evening, it was a whole new story. Ashley had worked late two nights this week and Heather had begun chanting "Where's Ashley?" as soon as the sun disappeared from the sky.

There were times when he felt like joining the coyotes baying at the moon. How had his life become so complicated in such a short time?

If Jordan hadn't shown up last week when he did, he would have been inside Ashley within seconds. Since then, he'd spent most of his evenings away from the ranch, leaving Heather to enjoy Ashley's company without his presence.

Ashley made no reference to what had happened. He'd wanted to apologize, but she seemed to be avoiding him as well and he could never catch her at a time when Heather wasn't there.

He'd had no business walking in on her like that and they both knew it. But it had happened. He'd long since forgotten about the little girl he used to know. His memories of seeing her in the tub and shower had shoved earlier memories of her out of his mind. The thought of attempting another marriage made him break out in a cold sweat. He didn't think he could survive another failure. However, he was beginning to think he didn't have a choice if he planned to protect her.

When Friday came, he was glad he had somewhere specific to go, rather than to continue driving the back roads listening to music on the radio until he felt safe in returning home.

He played a little better tonight and by the time they broke up, he was a little ahead.

It was midnight when he arrived at the house. He peeked in on Heather, who was blissfully asleep, straightened her covers and took a shower. He wasn't tired enough to guarantee that he'd immediately go to sleep, so rather than toss and turn, Jake decided to see what he could find in the refrigerator to eat. Maybe he'd watch a little television until he thought he could fall asleep. He'd spent way too many restless nights in bed to look forward to more of the same.

Ashley came awake, thinking she heard a noise. Her ear was attuned to Heather now and she wondered if Heather was having a bad dream. She didn't bother turning on a light before she went into Heather's room.

The little girl lay quietly sleeping. Ashley smiled. This child had two speeds—nonstop and sound asleep. Ashley was really going to miss her when she returned to her apartment.

Jake had mentioned, during one of his two-minute conversations with her this week, that he'd found someone suitable to stay with Heather. She would be coming to work on Monday.

She knew the announcement was his not-so-subtle way of letting her know she'd be leaving soon.

Thank goodness.

The tension in the house had grown worse this past week. They were like two magnets that immediately veered away from the other if they accidentally came too close.

The damage had already been done as far as she was concerned. Now she no longer had to imagine what Jake looked like nude and her dreams were much more erotic and explicit. Consequently, her sleep had suffered.

Once back in her room, she realized she was now wide awake. She decided to go downstairs for a glass of milk in hopes it would help her go back to sleep.

When she walked into the dark kitchen, she realized

that she *had* heard something. Jake, who stood in front of the open refrigerator gazing inside, must have made the noise.

His only apparel appeared to be jeans riding low on his hips.

As though sensing he was no longer alone, Jake turned and saw her. Silently he shut the refrigerator door, leaving the room lit only by the rays of the halogen light outside.

"I—uh—thought I'd get a glass of milk," she said, barely above a whisper.

He stood there in silence without moving.

How much more awkward could this be? He'd made it abundantly clear this past week that he had no intention of finishing what they had started in the shower. In fact, he'd acted as though it had never happened, which showed her how much he'd been affected by it.

She told herself to leave. She no longer wanted the milk. What she wanted to do was to disappear in a puff of smoke and be magically transported back to her bed. By morning, she would think of this as only a dream. A bad one, at that.

Ashley forced herself to take a step backwards but froze when he slowly moved toward her. He crossed the room in silence and stopped in front of her, then pulled her to him and held her, his face buried in her hair.

Her head rested on his chest and she could feel his heart racing. She hesitantly slipped her arms around his waist and stroked his bare back. He shivered and pulled her closer and she could feel his rigid length pressing against her.

"Ashley," he murmured as though in pain.

She tightened her hold and when he raised his head she looked up at him. "Yes."

They both knew what she meant and her softly spoken word seemed to release him from hidden restraints. He picked her up and strode to the living room directly across the foyer. He gently placed her on the sofa, unfastened his jeans so that they fell to his ankles, stepped out of them and knelt between her thighs.

Her short sleep shirt was no barrier as he eased it up to her waist. Then he waited, looking at her, although there wasn't enough light to see his face. She raised her arms and pulled him down where she could kiss him.

He caressed her, running his hands along her body until he reached her nest of curls. He teased her nipple with his tongue at the same time his fingers found the dampness between her legs.

Ashley exploded in a mind-blowing climax, bucking against him as she continued to keep her arms and legs around him.

His breath was ragged as he placed nipping kisses on her cheeks, along her jaw and her ears before blindly searching for her mouth. He pushed into her and paused.

"You're so small," he managed to get out. "I don't want to hurt you."

"If you stop now, *you'll* be in a world of hurts!" she whispered fiercely.

He made a sound of pained amusement. "I couldn't stop now if a train was bearing down on me." Matching actions to words, he pushed deeper inside her.

She tried not to flinch but she had to adjust to his size. He was huge. Of course, she had no experience in these matters but—

He eased up and began to pull away, but she tightened her hold around him with her arms and legs and forced his full length inside. This sensation was what she'd missed in the shower. If she'd only known, she might not have let him out of the shower, Jordan or no Jordan.

She knew when he discovered she was a virgin because he cursed beneath his breath, but he didn't stop. He kissed her, his tongue moving in rhythm to his movements. Her body clenched tightly around him and once again she went up in flames as she pulsated around him. He cried out and moved frantically inside her until he made one final lunge, holding still for a moment before he slumped against her, his weight absorbed by the cushions beneath them. His skin was damp everywhere they touched. She weakly ran her hands along his back, luxuriating in her ability to explore him at her own pace.

Her system continued in overload while her legs languidly slid along his hips and thighs and down to the sofa. They lay quietly for a few minutes before he began to withdraw from her.

"Don't!" she whispered, her arms reaching for him. He stood and yanked his jeans up, fastening them, and then picked her up and carried her to his room. After he closed the door behind him with his foot, he placed her on the bed and disappeared into his bathroom. When he returned, he placed a warm, wet washcloth between her legs, carefully touching her.

She should be embarrassed, she supposed, her mind lazily following what he was doing. But nothing Jake could do to her would make her shy.

When he crawled into bed with her, he pulled her over to him. She placed her palm on his chest, feeling the strong beat of his heart. When she leisurely slid her hand down his body she was surprised to discover that he was once again as hard as a rock.

"Jake?" she whispered.

"Go to sleep, love. I don't want you more sore than you already are."

She leaned over him and kissed him as seductively as she knew how. She slid her leg across him, straddling him, a position that placed him snugly against her. She pulled her sleep shirt over her head and tossed it aside.

"Ashley—" he said warningly but she had no intention of listening to him. Clumsily she reached down and guided him inside her, sighing with pleasure when he automatically lifted his hips against her.

She felt in control—gently rocking over him, kissing him, flicking her tongue against his coin-shaped nipples, and listening to his gasps of pleasure when she changed the angle or rhythm.

Although she wanted to keep her pace slow, her breathing quickened, the new and wonderful sensations building and building until she lost herself in them. Only then did Jake place his hands on her hips, picking up her rhythm and increasing it until they both exploded in a burst of heat and light, her sigh of satisfaction mingling with his.

When she could get her breath, she managed to say, "Wow."

He traced her spine with his fingers. "Yeah."

"I had no idea…" She didn't have the words to describe how she felt.

"Neither did I," he replied in a deep rumble.

She wanted to talk to him about what had happened and how it changed their relationship, but she was so relaxed that her mind wouldn't work.

She fell asleep on top of him and knew nothing more until she woke up in her own bed the next morning. She wondered at first if her dreams were getting more realistic until she moved and discovered that she *was* sore, just as Jake had predicted.

Ashley stretched and smiled. She had no intention of complaining. She was almost asleep again—neither one of them had gotten much sleep last night—when she heard a soft tap at the door. Could it be Jake? She hoped so.

"Come in," she said.

Heather peeked around the door.

"Good morning, sunshine. I guess you're ready for breakfast, aren't you?"

Heather shook her head. "Daddy feeded me and told me he had some important errands to run and for me to stay with you today."

Ashley sat up and quickly held the sheet against her bare body. "Did he say how long he'd be gone?"

"Uh-uh, but he wrote something down and left it in the kitchen."

Her heart sank. Was he going to continue to avoid her despite what had happened last night?

Not if she could help it.

"Why don't you play in your room while I get my shower and dress, okay?"

"'Kay."

Fifteen minutes later Ashley walked into the kitchen. As Heather had told her, she saw a handwritten note lying on the breakfast bar. Oh, this was going to be good. She began to read.

Sorry to leave Heather with you, but I have some errands to run and Heather wouldn't be happy trying to keep up with me. If you don't want to take her to your office this morning, Jordan said he'd watch her until you get home. I'll see you tonight and we'll sit down and discuss our relationship. Jake.

"Why, Jake, honey," she said in a syrupy southern voice, "I swear, you do write the most romantic notes of anyone I know." In her natural voice, she added, "You rat."

"Who ya talking to, Ashley?" Heather said behind her.

"To myself," she replied. She turned and said,

"Would you like to stay with Uncle Jordan today while I go to work?"

"Why?"

"Why do I have to go to work?"

"Why can't I go to work with you?"

I'm going to kill that man as soon as I see him.

"Well, I'm going to be really busy today and I don't want you to get bored."

"Oh."

"But I'll be home in time to have lunch with you and we'll have the afternoon together. Won't that be fun?"

Heather smiled. "Uh-huh."

After she ate, Ashley took Heather outside to search for Jordan. He was never hard to find because he was generally with the horses. Sure enough, they found him in the barn.

As soon as she saw him, Ashley called, "Hey, Jordan, are you ready for a young visitor this morning?"

He'd been cleaning one of the horse's hooves when she called. He straightened and flashed his trademark Crenshaw smile. "You bet! Hi ya, Heather, I've got all kinds of fun things planned for us today." He winked at Ashley and said, "Try not to work too hard. We'll be here when you get back."

Ashley drove to town, still angry at Jake. Last night had been the most magical night of her life and she thought he'd felt the magic, as well.

So Jake wanted to talk about their relationship, did he? Well, she had a few things to discuss as well, such as his annoying habit of disappearing after making love to her.

What was his problem, anyway? Did he think she was going to insist that he make an honest woman of her? If so, she'd set his mind at ease. Chivalry certainly wasn't dead as far as Jake was concerned. No doubt he was somewhere rehearsing his speech about how he had taken advantage of her, and that what happened last night would not—could not—happen again.

Fine with her. Thank goodness Mrs. James would be here Monday and she could get on with her life without the stubborn man.

Jake could test the patience of a saint and she was certainly no saint!

Twelve

Twelve

Ashley and Heather were coloring in one of Heather's coloring books when Jake walked in around four o'clock.

"Hi, Daddy. Look what I'm coloring," Heather said by way of greeting. She held up her artwork.

Ashley had done her best to deal with the pain she felt at his disappearance today, but all it took was one look at him and the churning emotions she'd held in all day flooded over her.

He nodded at her without meeting her gaze and said to Heather, "What a pretty picture. I've never seen a green coyote before. I bet they're rare."

"Uh-huh, and guess what? Me and Unca Jordan went to this place where they have all kinds of games. You can throw balls and try to hit somep'n and then we went to this really noisy place and had hamburgers and—"

"Sweetheart, slow down and take a deep breath," Jake said, laughing and hugging her. "I'm glad you had a good time. I bet you were ready for your nap by the time you got home."

She nodded vigorously. "Ashley laid down with me and we both took a nap. She said she was really, really sleepy."

Jake flicked a glance at Ashley who sat at the table, her arms crossed. "So now you're awake and I bet more rested."

"Uh-huh, and you know what? I won a big dog at the game place!"

Jake started. "A dog? What kind of dog?"

"Wait here and I'll show you," Heather replied, racing out of the kitchen.

Jake went to the refrigerator and poured himself a large glass of iced tea. "Want some?" he asked, holding up the pitcher.

"No thanks."

He sat down across from her. "What kind of dog did she bring home?"

She looked at him and almost laughed at the apprehension in his face. "Don't worry. It's only a stuffed one."

"Whew! That's a relief." He drank some of his tea before speaking. "Did you sleep okay?" he asked, finally meeting her eyes.

"I must have, since I don't remember returning to my own bed last night."

He flushed and looked down at his tea. "I didn't think it would be a good idea for Heather to find us together."

"I agree."

Silence fell between them. Ashley could think of nothing to say that wouldn't include a comment about his leaving this morning.

The tension between them was so thick Ashley could almost see it.

Finally, he said, "I thought we'd wait until after her bedtime to talk about things."

"All right." She'd known this time would be coming soon. After all, Charlotte would be here in the next day or two. She needed to pack and go home, but not before she had to listen as Jake apologized profusely for what happened the night before.

She really didn't want to hear it.

Heather came skipping back in the room carrying a large stuffed dachshund by its middle, its body dangling on either side. "Here he is. Isn't he cute? I named him Ralph."

"Ralph?" Jake echoed. "Why Ralph?"

"'Cause I like that name."

"Then Ralph it is." He studied the stuffed animal a moment and added, "Ralph's certainly big."

Ashley watched him chat with his daughter, laughing at her stories, enjoying her presence. There were so many things that she loved about Jake, which was the reason she ached so. Why did she have to fall for this one particular man? There were a couple of men in town she had gone out with from time to time. They were better-looking than Jake, they were younger than Jake, but the problem for her was, they weren't Jake.

Well, she'd known when she agreed to stay out here that being around him would cause her more pain. Being fair, though, she knew that making love to him had been a healing of sorts for her. When she left, she'd have her memories of him as he'd been while making love to her, gentle and oh, so loving. Those memories would replace the unhappy ones she'd carried since her teens.

While she waited, she prepared herself for rejection yet another time.

Once Heather was in bed, Jake suggested they sit out on the patio. Ashley didn't mind because it was darker out there. She appreciated the fact that he didn't suggest the living room.

They took the pitcher of iced tea and ice-filled glasses with them and sat at the glass-topped table.

Once seated, Ashley waited to hear what he had to say…as if she didn't know. His first words surprised her.

"You're upset, aren't you?"

She frowned. "Why do you ask?"

"I've known you too long not to recognize most of your moods. Do you want to talk about it?"

She drew a deep breath. "All right," she said after a long pause. This was as good a place to start their conversation as any. "After both occasions when we made love, you disappeared. I more or less understood that you'd gone to your weekly poker game on Friday, so I waited for the chance to talk with you. You avoided me all week. Until last night. I woke up this morning and you were gone.

"I guess what's upset me is how you can be so warm and loving one moment and then pull your disappearing act the next. Last night was the most beautiful experience for me and I thought we'd reached a new understanding in our relationship. Apparently, I was wrong."

"I left before you woke up because I wanted to get back as soon as possible." He reached into his shirt pocket and pulled out something, placing it on his palm. "I flew to Dallas to get this for you."

Ashley stared at the ring in astonishment that he would purchase something so obviously expensive. Was this how he intended to repay her for helping with Heather? Surely he wasn't crude enough to offer it because they'd gone to bed together.

Was he?

"The ring's beautiful, Jake, but it really isn't necessary. I've enjoyed looking after Heather and there's no reason for you to—"

"I guess I'm not making myself very clear, here," he said, sounding nervous. "The ring is my rather awkward way of asking you to marry me."

"I don't understand. You've made it clear to everyone who knows you that you never intend to remarry." The shock of the ring and his proposal had her thoughts scattering. What was going on here? Jake Crenshaw proposing? Hadn't she dreamed of this very moment for years?

She looked at him for a long moment trying to read his expression, but he wasn't giving anything away. This must be his poker face.

"Why?"

He blinked, obviously startled by her unexpected question.

"Why do I want to marry you?" he carefully repeated, as though not sure he understood her question.

"Yes."

"Why does anyone propose marriage, Ashley? I thought this was what you wanted."

"Generally, a proposal is offered when there's love involved."

He looked offended. "Well, of course I love you and you've said you love me. I just thought that—"

"Is this about last night?"

He dropped his gaze. "Well, sure, that's part of it. But then there's Heather. She needs a positive mother figure in her life and since you've got to know her, I figured this will work out well for all of us."

"I see." She truly did. If he couldn't have Tiffany, he'd settle for convenience and she was already here. His feelings weren't so deeply involved that she could hurt him, even if she turned him down.

Was she going to turn him down?

At the moment, she was too confused to make a decision. There was a battle going on between her heart and her head. Her head pointed out what it would do to her, being in a marriage of convenience and the only one in love. Sure, he loved her. He'd loved her as a kid. This was more of the same, a symbolic pat on the head that said, "You've been a good girl, so I'll offer you your heart's desire and marry you."

Her heart kept saying, "At least you'd be with him and with Heather. You could have the family you always wanted, the one with little Jakes running everywhere…and a few little Ashleys as well."

Was it worth the price she'd have to pay?

"Ashley? Did you fall asleep?" He sounded half joking and half concerned.

"Oh, I'm awake, Jake. Finally." She leaned her forearms on the table and said, "What this proposal and its timing is all about is that we made love last night. Isn't that true?"

"Last night maybe rushed things along a little." His lips turned up in the corners. "Let's just say that I'm sorry our wedding night came before the proposal." He shrugged. "I guess it's obvious by now that I have no control where you're concerned."

"Tell me something, Jake."

"What?"

"Do you propose marriage to every woman you have sex with?"

He stared at her as if she'd slapped him.

"What kind of question is that?"

"One you might want to take a look at. You say you can't control your reactions to me and this is your way of having sex without guilt. Well, thank you for the offer," she said, her heart crumbling into aching pieces. "But I believe I'll pass."

He looked shocked. Guess he'd never been turned down before. She fought the tears that threatened. The last thing she wanted was for him to know how devastated she was by his reasons for proposing. The irony didn't escape her. Her youth had been filled with dreams of the time when he'd propose to her and now that he had, she'd refused him.

Finally, he said, "So what was last night all about, Ashley? You wanted a little fun in the sack and thought I'd be the one to experiment with? Is that all it was to you?"

"No! Of course not. It's just that I don't believe last night created a reason for us to get married." She handed him back the ring.

He stood. "I'm sorry that you find my proposal—and my ring—so offensive." He turned and went inside, quietly closing the door behind him.

She had to get away. Otherwise, she was going to make a blubbering fool of herself. As was the practice on the ranch, she'd left her keys in the truck. She hurried to her truck and drove to her dad's house.

He took one look at her face when she walked in, closed the door and held her. "Oh, Daddy, you were so right," she said, between sobs.

"I usually am," he said with exaggerated humility. "Exactly what have I been right about now?"

"I should never have moved in with Jake and Heather."

"Ah."

They stood there in the living room until she managed some semblance of control. He handed her his handkerchief in silence.

"I've been such a fool."

"Why do you say that?" He led her into the kitchen and poured her a glass of her favorite wine.

"Because it's true." She took a sip of wine, paused, and took another, larger drink. "This tastes so good. Thanks."

"Let's go sit in the living room and you can tell me what's happened."

They each sat in one of the overstuffed chairs facing each other. Ashley tried to gather her thoughts while she sipped the wine. The last thing she could tell her father was that she and Jake had made love. He'd call her all kinds of fool and she'd have to agree with him. How could something so beautiful turn out to be so painful?

She sighed. "He asked me to marry him," she said quietly.

"No kidding! Well, no wonder you're upset! Do you want me to give him a good talking-to for insulting you that way?"

She looked at him in disgust. "Not funny, Dad."

"Well, I think you could lighten up a little, don't you? I can't see why him asking you to marry him would upset you."

She swallowed. "Because it would be convenient for him to marry me. I'd be there for Heather, and for him." She stumbled over the last words.

Ken frowned and leaned forward, elbows on his knees. "What is it, sweetheart? Are you afraid of marital intimacy? I know I wasn't very good at explaining all that, and I'm sorry."

She rolled her eyes. "Oh, Dad, please. Every child living on a ranch knows all about the mating process and no, I'm not afraid of marital intimacy. I just don't want to have three people in the bed, that's all."

"Three!" He stiffened. "Are you telling me that Jake actually—"

"I'm talking about the ghost of Tiffany, the woman

he loves but no longer can have. I guess I thought that I loved him enough to be the one he settled for...until he actually asked me. At least he was honest and didn't try to wrap the proposal in romantic phrases."

"Are you sure he's still in love with her? He's been pretty upset that she kept Heather a secret from him."

"Oh, Dad, it's so obvious when you think about it. He was so upset the night she came here. Part of it was because of Heather, I know that. But I also think he was hurt when he heard she was getting married. He wouldn't admit that to me, of course. But I saw the pain in his eyes."

"Could be, I suppose. He doesn't talk about his feelings much."

"Tell me about it." She sat back in the chair and did her best to detach herself from the emotional turmoil she felt. "It's kind of interesting when you think about it. Every time I'm convinced that I've fully recovered from my passion for Jake, I end up being around him again. That's when I know that I'm not. Probably never will be. But that doesn't mean I have to make a decision that will end up making both of us miserable. A one-sided love would be miserable and I'm not willing to place myself in that position." She straightened and glanced at her watch. "I need to get a good night's sleep and deal with all of this tomorrow."

"You can stay here tonight, if you want."

She shook her head and stood up. He stood as well. "Thanks for the offer but all my things are at the house. Heather's nanny is supposed to be here tomorrow or Monday. I can hold out that long. Then I'll go home, lick my wounds and work to overcome my relapse."

Ken walked her to the door. He pulled her to him and

kissed her on the forehead. "You know, you could do a lot worse than to marry Jake. He'd be good to you, we both know that."

"I know. It's just that I can't marry someone who offers because he can't have the one he loves. I have more self-respect than that."

Thirteen

Ashley woke up the next morning relieved to discover that Jake had left and taken Heather with him. He'd left her a note in the kitchen, short and to the point.

Heather and I will be gone most of the day.

Which suited her just fine. The two of them had bonded and no longer needed her presence. She packed up her things, left her own brief note—"I've moved back home. Tell Heather I'll stay in touch."—and drove back to her apartment.

She'd done what she could for him and for his daughter. He'd found help, just what he'd told her he would do, and she was no longer needed. It wasn't his fault that she'd left her heart behind.

Now was the time to get over him and to get on with her life. She knew that would be a little tough since she intended to stay in touch with Heather. At least she wouldn't be seeing him. She'd make sure not to visit when he was there. That could be arranged easily enough. Because there was no way she'd step out of Heather's life. She'd already been abandoned once. Twice, if Ashley counted the loss of her great-grandmother. Ashley didn't want Heather to experience the pain she had gone through when her mother had abandoned her.

No. She would always be there for Heather.

Jake rented a car at the San Antonio airport and he and Heather went to meet Charlotte James.

"Why is she coming to live with us?"

"Because you need someone with you when you're not with me or Ashley."

"Oh."

Blessed silence...for almost ten seconds.

"Does she have kids like me?"

"Her name is Mrs. James. I'd appreciate it if you'd call her by her name."

"Mrs. James," she immediately parroted.

"That's right."

"Does Mrs. James have kids like me?"

"I don't think so. If she does, her children are probably grown."

"Is she old?"

"Uh," he stopped speaking because he needed to concentrate on the traffic. There was the exit sign for the street he was looking for. "Well," he said once they were off the freeway and stopped at a light, "I guess it depends on what you consider to be old."

"As old as you?"

Since he figured Mrs. James to be in her mid-fifties,

he wasn't certain how to answer that. Finally, he said, "Maybe she's little older than me. Why?"

"Will she get sick and will an am'blance come get her and take her away and I won't see her ever again?"

He glanced in the rearview mirror, where Heather sat in the car seat he'd brought with them. "You don't have to worry about that."

He hoped. Because if Mrs. James decided not to stay after the trial period, he would have to deal with Heather's fears.

Once they arrived at Charlotte's home and she met her, Heather seemed to relax. She was shy at first, as she usually was when she first met someone. Jake told Charlotte to enjoy the quiet while she could.

The three of them stopped at a kid-friendly restaurant for lunch and then took Heather to the zoo.

Jake had never seen Heather quite this excited before. After following Heather for more than an hour and listening to her running commentary, Charlotte smiled at Jake and said, "I see what you mean," and they both laughed.

Heather fell asleep in the plane. Once at the ranch, he held her while Charlotte installed the car seat, then put her down without her once stirring.

The zoo had worn her out. She wasn't the only one.

Heather woke up when they stopped in front of the house. "We're home!" she said gleefully.

She couldn't have said anything to make him feel happier. She'd adjusted to being left here with strangers remarkably well.

Heather said, "I gotta go tell Ashley what we did today!" at the same time that Jake realized her truck wasn't there.

"You may have to wait a little while because she's not here. Maybe she went to see her dad."

He moved Charlotte's luggage to the room where she'd be staying, which was close to Heather, so it was a while before he went downstairs for something to drink.

His note was still there, but something had been added. He read the note, then dropped it. So she was gone. Why did it hurt so much that she'd turned him down? She's just a kid, after all. She doesn't know what she wants.

Oh, really. And was that a kid in the shower and in bed with you?

His chest hurt. How could wanting to marry her because they'd slept together be insulting? Didn't he hear complaints from women he knew that most men were love 'em and leave 'em kind of guys?

Since he'd gotten to know Ashley as an adult, he'd been irritated with himself for marrying Tiffany. Why hadn't he waited until Ashley was an adult to marry a woman he was compatible with?

Too late to do that now. His past mistakes kept rearing their heads to haunt him. He'd have to learn to live with them. It wasn't the first time he'd been kicked in the face by a woman he loved. Or in Tiffany's case, thought he loved. Ashley's rejection hurt a thousand times more because he finally understood what love was all about and how deeply he'd been in love with Ashley as far back as her teenage years, if he'd just recognized it.

No wonder he'd reacted so violently to her sixteen-year-old kiss. Too bad he hadn't understood at the time what he was feeling. Somehow, he'd managed to screw up his life royally. At least he had Heather to love and care for. Having her would have to be enough.

"Hey, Jake, got a second?"

Jake had just come in from supervising the move of

a herd of sheep to a better feeding ground. There was nothing more stupid than sheep. If there was a wrong way to go, they would find it every time.

"Sure, Ken, what do you need?"

"Well, this is kind of personal, so I was wondering if you'd like to come over and have a cool one with me."

Jake glanced at his watch. "Sure. Heather won't be expecting me home for a while."

Ken slapped his back. "Good. See you at the house."

While Jake followed Ken's truck, he wondered what was wrong with Ken. Did he get some bad news about his health? Was something wrong with Ashley?

Don't go there. His breath became restricted every time he thought of her, just as though his lungs had stopped working.

When he walked into Ken's place, Ken was already standing there with a couple of bottles of cold beer. They drank in unison, wiped their mouths and grinned at each other before sprawling in Ken's comfortable chairs.

"Since Heather's been with me, I've switched to drinking iced tea at home, but I gotta tell ya, there's nothing like a cold beer on a hot Texas day!"

Ken smiled. "She's seemed settled in. How long has she been here?"

"Almost three weeks. She's got a birthday coming up soon. The folks promised to get back in time to plan one of their barbecue bashes for her."

"That's good. Really good. It'll be good to see Joe and Gail. They've been gone a while."

"They're the smart ones, you know. They like to spend summers in Washington and Oregon to get away from the heat. It will still be hot on the 28th of September, but they're willing to give up their comfort to meet their grandbaby."

"By the way," Ken said, "I meant to tell you that the sheriff called today. They found the car thieves on Mc-Grady's ranch, north of town. He thought you'd want to know."

"That's good to know."

They finished their beer and Ken went to get more. When he returned, Jake said, "You said there was something personal you wanted to talk to me about."

"Uh, yeah, that's right. It's probably none of my business but that's never stopped me before. Usually a dad asks a man if his intentions toward his daughter are honorable. In this case, I know yours are. I guess what I've been wondering is why you asked Ashley to marry you?"

Jake stared at him like the man had lost his mind. "Why the hell do you think, Ken?"

"Oh, I figure there could be several reasons. You need help with your daughter. You enjoy Ashley's company. You're tired of living alone."

"You seem to have as good an opinion of my character as Ashley. I thought you knew me better than that." He took another drink. "Just for the record, I asked her to marry me because I can't imagine my life without her in the center of it and because I'm crazy about her. Probably always have been, if you want to know the truth. I was just too dumb to understand what it was I was feeling all this time. Not that any of that matters. She turned me down."

"So I understand. Ashley's under the impression that you're still in love with Tiffany."

Jake shook his head in disbelief. "That's a bunch of crap and you know it as well as I do. I fell out of love with Tiffany years ago, if I ever loved her in the first place. I fell in love with who I thought she was. Once I got to know her, I learned my mistake. Ashley knows that."

"Does she? If you really love her, then you'd better

find a way to convince her of that. She's always worshipped you and, to be frank, I was hoping she'd outgrow it. For a while I thought she had…until your daughter showed up. That's when I knew Ashley had only been kidding me as well as herself that she'd gotten over her feelings for you."

Jake squeezed his eyes closed. "Tiffany is part of the past I can't change. The only good thing that happened from the marriage was Heather. I want to look forward to the future instead of spending energy dwelling on past mistakes that can't be undone."

"I know you were pretty torn up when she left you."

"I don't deny that, but it wasn't because I loved her. I was shocked at her leaving so unexpectedly. I didn't have a clue that she was making plans to divorce me. I really thought I'd done everything possible to make the marriage work."

"From what I could see, you did."

"It was the sense of failure that continued to eat at me long after I accepted that she was gone."

Ken smiled ruefully. "You know, Jake, you couldn't have chosen to marry two women more opposite from each other."

Jake nodded. "I know. I'd like to think I'm older and wiser now, Ken. But Ashley's made it clear she doesn't want to marry me and I have to respect her decisions. She deserves to be loved and cherished. I hope she finds the man who will do that."

"Ever thought about explaining your feelings to her?"

"You mean, tell her she's out of her mind if she thinks I have any feelings for Tiffany?"

"Well, maybe you might want to do it without calling her crazy. Just a suggestion, of course. I'm a little curious. Did you happen to mention that you're in love with her and have been for years?"

"Of course I did! It didn't seem to matter to her, though." Jake rubbed the cold bottle across his forehead. "I don't know, Ken. I think she mentioned Tiffany to you as an excuse. I used to believe that she truly loved me, but hell, I don't know anything anymore. All I know is she turned me down and moved out. Pretty strong evidence that she meant what she said."

Fourteen

A week after she left the ranch, Ashley arrived home in time to hear her phone ringing. Good grief. Couldn't she at least get inside before her phone started to ring off the wall? Obviously not.

"All right!" she said after the fourth ring. "I'm coming, I'm coming." She grabbed the phone and took a deep breath. "H'lo?"

"Hi, sweetheart. Haven't heard from you in a while. How's life treatin' you?"

"Hi, Dad. How've you been?"

"Good. And you?"

"Very well, actually. Our new vet started with us last week and he's already carrying his load. Woody and I are finally getting out earlier because of the extra help."

"Ah, that explains it. When I called the office, Wendy said you'd already left."

"So what's up?" She was tired and at the moment just wanted to take a cool shower and relax.

"The reason I'm calling," Ken said, "is to invite my favorite girl to go out to dinner with me tonight. Are you up for it?"

She glanced at her watch. "What a nice idea. I'd love to have dinner with you. Dress or casual?"

"You have to ask?"

She laughed. "Okay. Jeans it is."

"I'm leaving now."

"I'll be here."

She was in the shower when she realized that Heather's birthday was coming up in a couple of weeks. She needed to talk to Jake to see what he wanted to do about the party he'd mentioned having for Heather. Her heart did a double beat at the thought of seeing him again…as a friend only.

She spoke to Heather on the phone almost every day. A couple of times, Charlotte had brought her in to the clinic to say hi when they were in town. Charlotte was a jewel and Heather adored her. She was glad to see that the feeling was mutual.

She hadn't seen Jake since she'd moved back in town. That wasn't really surprising, since she'd seen next to nothing of him before he called her that one memorable night.

She shook her head as she toweled off and started dressing. Was she sorry for answering his distress call that night?

She didn't have an answer. She understood the adult Jake much better now that she was an adult. Unfortunately for her, her newfound knowledge had only made her love him more.

Heather had brought out mothering instincts Ashley would never have believed she was capable of feeling.

After all, she was her mother's child and her mother had made it clear when she left that she wasn't cut out for raising a kid and taking care of a husband. So maybe Ashley wasn't like her mother, after all.

How could she be sorry for learning more about herself and Jake?

The knowledge, however, didn't take the pain of loss away.

Ken took her to one of the steak houses on the outskirts of town. She liked the rustic atmosphere and friendly waitresses. After they ordered and their drinks arrived, Ken said, "You're looking good, kiddo."

"Thank you, Dad. You, on the other hand, are pushing yourself too hard."

He shrugged. "I'm no spring chicken, but I do a full day's work without complaining."

"To what do I owe this honor—you driving into town after a long day? Anything special?"

He took a drink from his large glass of iced tea. "Well, I guess there is, although I know I should come in more often to see you. Time just slips by so quick, you know?"

She reached over and patted his hand. "I know, Dad."

He cleared his throat. "The thing is, I, uh, spoke to Jake this afternoon."

Since she knew that Jake and her dad spoke every day, his nervousness must mean that they'd discussed her.

"Oh?"

"He's hurtin', Ashley. He's hurtin' real bad."

Fear shot through her. Jake had been hurt? When? How? "Oh, no! What happened? Was he in an accident? Why didn't somebody tell me? I talked to Heather yesterday and she never—"

"He's been having some trouble gettin' around ever since you ripped his heart right out of his chest."

She leaned back in her chair. "What are you talking about, Dad? I haven't done anything to Jake."

"You refused to marry him."

"I never knew you had such a flare for drama. Ripped his heart out, indeed. What nonsense. He was probably relieved, actually. You know Jake. Always doing the right thing."

"Why would him proposing be doing the right thing? Or do I want to know?"

"You don't want to know."

"Damn." He sat there silently drinking his tea. Neither one of them spoke until after their steaks were delivered.

As far as Ashley concerned, the subject was over.

Halfway through their meal, Ken said, "Is there a possibility that just maybe he had others reasons to want to marry you?"

"Are we still talking about Jake?" she asked whimsically, picking up her glass.

"You mean you've got other men proposing to you?"

"I was teasing, Dad. Do you think you know those reasons?"

"You know what your problem is, missy," he said, pointing his fork at her. "You think too much like a woman!"

She laughed. "Imagine that."

"Jake doesn't wear his feelings on his sleeve. Never has. Doesn't mean he doesn't have 'em. He's so blamed in love with you, he's plain pitiful."

"Did he tell you that?"

"As a matter of fact, he did. He also told me that not only did he not love Tiffany, he didn't even like her. Once he got a good look at the woman he married and how little they had in common, he realized that marrying her was the biggest mistake he ever made." He paused. "You know good and well that that man dotes on you. Always has."

"When I was a child, Dad."

"Well, for your information, his feelings have gotten even worse…I mean, even stronger, ever since you stayed out there with him and Heather. You 'bout broke his heart when you refused to marry him."

She stared at her dad in dismay. Could she have made the biggest mistake of her life when she told Jake she wouldn't marry him?

He was in love with her? Well, he'd said so, but in such a casual way she figured he loved her like he loved Blue Bell ice cream.

"Men!" she finally muttered. "It wouldn't have hurt for him to tell me the reason he wanted to marry me was that he was in love with me, instead of all that stuff about Heather needing a mother figure and because I loved *him*!"

"Have you ever known Jake to be real open about how he felt about things?"

The only time he'd opened up to her was the night after Heather arrived. He'd shared his vulnerability with her. Would he have done that with someone he didn't trust and love?

Knowing Jake as well as she did, she had to admit that, no, he generally kept his feelings to himself.

She looked at Ken, feeling awful that she hadn't understood all of this before now. "What do you think I should do?"

"How should I know? I just wanted you to look at things from his viewpoint. I don't know how to get you to fix things with him."

After Ashley went to bed that night, she couldn't stop herself from going over and over her conversation with her dad.

Jake loved her. Why was that so hard to believe? She'd allowed her fear that he would never love her in the way he'd loved Tiffany to blind her to what was happening between them.

He loved her too much to take advantage of their situation.

He loved her enough to propose to her after making it clear to everyone in the county that he never intended to marry again.

He loved her.

She groaned.

She had to talk to him.

She had to apologize to him.

She had to get down on her knees and beg his forgiveness—the sooner the better.

She would go out to the ranch tomorrow after work. She needed to see Heather anyway and she'd enjoy visiting with Charlotte again. Somehow she had to make him understand how much she loved him and how much she wanted to marry him.

And pray that it wasn't too late to make amends.

Fifteen

Heather was the first person to greet Ashley when she arrived at the ranch the next afternoon.

"You came, you came! Yea! Guess what? Me and Miss Charlotte are making gingerbread men! Wanna help?"

"Sounds like fun." Heather grabbed her hand and pulled her along to the kitchen. "Miss Charlotte. Look who's here. Ashley!"

"Hi, Charlotte," Ashley said, sounding breathless.

Charlotte James was comfortably middle-aged, with a calm demeanor and a sweet smile. No wonder Heather liked her. Charlotte looked and acted like a loving grandmother.

"I want you to know that you've won top marks with Heather," Ashley said. "She told me on the phone yesterday that your allowing her to splash in the tub makes you wonderful."

Charlotte laughed. Her laugh was contagious and Ashley joined her. Jake had found a gem in Charlotte.

"How do you like living in the Hill Country?" Ashley asked.

"Oh, I was raised in this area, not far from Fredericksburg. Hal's job took us to San Antonio years ago. After he died, I wanted to come back to this area to live. This job seemed the answer to my prayers."

"Do you have children?"

"Yes. Two boys and a girl…all grown…and none of them interested in making me a grandmother. I consider Heather to be a true blessing in my life. She makes me feel young again."

"I'm glad. She's really special."

"I am?" Heather asked.

"That you are."

"Oh. What does special mean?"

The women laughed. "That I love you very much," Ashley replied.

"That's good." She went back to working on her gingerbread man. Ashley could spot the ones Heather had made because they each struck a different pose. One thing that could be said about Heather—she was certainly creative.

Later, after being an eyewitness to the amount of water Heather could splash on the floor, Ashley said, "I expected that Jake would be home by now."

"He said he goes to town on Fridays and for us not to wait up for him."

Ashley hit her forehead with the palm of her hand. "Of course he does! I can't believe I forgot what day it is. Since I really need to talk to him, I think I'll wait up for him. It would be fun to spend the rest of the evening with Heather." She didn't want to put off her meeting with Jake one more day.

* * *

Jake pulled up beside Ashley's truck sometime after midnight. He wasn't happy to see it sitting there. If she followed Tiffany's example, she was probably waiting inside to offer him his child. Of course, that wouldn't work too well, considering the fact that they'd been together one night and—

Oh, sh—! That could be *exactly* why she was here…to tell him that she was pregnant. Could she tell this soon? He wasn't up on all that stuff. Had she decided to marry him after all?

He sighed.

Heather would be over the moon if she agreed to marry him.

As for him, he'd discovered what his life was like without Ashley.

Lonely.

Sad.

Make that heartbroken.

He opened the door of his truck.

Jake walked into the house with measured steps, pausing only long enough to figure out where she was.

Ah, there she was, asleep on the sofa in the living room.

He sat across from her, looking for any changes since he'd last seen her. She still looked too fragile for comfort. She'd lost weight. Maybe. If he were to strip off her clothing, he would know for sure.

Still wanting her in your bed, Crenshaw? Of course he was. He wanted her next to him for the next fifty years or so, the first person he saw each and every morning of his life.

Ashley stirred and looked at her wristwatch. She sat up and only then did she see him.

She blinked in surprise. "I didn't hear you come in."

"Mm."

"Have you been here long?"

"Ashley, you aren't here at this time of night in order to make polite conversation. Just say what you came to say."

"Oh." She frowned. "Well, I was hoping you'd be in a better mood."

"I'm not."

"You know, I kind of figured that out for myself." She looked at him as though waiting for him to say something.

He looked at his watch meaningfully. He hoped she'd get the message. The last thing he wanted was to see her when he felt so vulnerable.

She let out a whoosh of air. "All right, then." She gave him a timid smile. "You're probably wondering why I called this meeting." When he didn't change expression, she gave a tiny shrug. "Trying for a little humor here." She glanced down at her clasped hands and then brought her gaze to meet his. "First of all, I owe you a big apology. Once I realized that, I didn't want to wait another day to tell you."

He continued to wait for the purpose of this visit.

"I misunderstood the purpose of your proposal."

He raised his brows. "Really. Seemed clear enough to me at the time."

She rubbed her eyes. "I'm not saying this well." The silence that followed gave Jake the opportunity to feast his eyes on her—damn, but he loved this woman! He was already as hard as a rock and there wasn't a thing he could do about it. Did she have any idea how much her rejection hurt him? Did she think an apology would make it better?

She cleared her throat. "I had dinner with Dad last night. He said I had hurt your feel—actually, he put it more dramatically, but the gist of his conversation was that I'd hurt you."

He shrugged. "I'll get over it."

He told me that you were in love with me."

"I told you the same thing."

"I didn't hear it in the same way, then. You also talked about your guilt for making love to me—before the wedding. You talked about my relationship with Heather and I thought you wanted to marry me because it would be convenient."

"Convenient!" Jake jumped up and glowered at her, his hands on his hips. "You are the least convenient woman I've ever known in my life! You drive me crazy and have for years. Convenience had nothing to do with my asking you to marry me!"

He reminded himself not to call her an idiot, but he came very close at that moment. He took a deep breath. "I've loved you all your life. I thought I made that clear to you a long time ago. I've been in love with you since you were sixteen, when I was ashamed to have such lustful thoughts about a teenager. I thought you were too young for me. After the divorce, I knew I'd blown my chance with you, but not ever during that time have I not been in love with you. So yeah, I guess you could say that my feelings were hurt when you turned me down. But that's life and I'm dealing with it."

He spun around and went over to the window in an effort to cool off before he said too much. What would that be, anyway? He'd just poured out his soul to her. What more did she want. Blood?

When she spoke she was directly behind him, causing his muscles to contract.

"Is there any way you can forgive me for being a complete idiot?"

Guess it was okay if she called herself that, as long as he didn't. He slowly turned and looked at her. "Ashley, just tell me what it is you want from me, okay? I guess I'm too dense to understand why you're here."

She folded her arms. "Because I want to marry you," she said quietly.

He never knew what to expect from her. Tonight was no different.

"Don't tease me, Ashley. You've already got me at the end of my rope."

She dropped her arms and walked closer. She placed her hands on his chest and said, "I do well and truly love you, Jake Crenshaw. I loved you as a child, as a teenager and as an adult. I can't imagine marrying anyone but you, if you still want me."

"That's never been the question." The truth began to seep into his brain. She loved him and she wanted to marry him. He prayed he wasn't dreaming. He pulled her against him and held her, his heart beating wildly. This was really happening. "I want to marry you, too," he mumbled hoarsely, not certain she could tell what he'd said around the lump in his throat.

She held on to him with a tight grip, her arms encircling his waist. He felt her trembling as he leaned his head on top of hers.

"I love you so much that I ache inside," he whispered. "I don't know how else to tell you so that you'll believe me."

"I believe you. I want to marry you as soon as possible, especially if you don't intend to make love to me until after the wedding."

He laughed out loud, swinging her around in a circle. "I believe we can work something out about that. I suggest we go upstairs and discuss the matter."

He looked down at her and saw tears in her eyes. "I'd like that," she whispered.

Jake picked her up and carried her to his room.

As soon as he closed the bedroom door behind them, Jake carried her into the bathroom and placed her on her feet. He reached into the shower and turned on the water.

"I think we need to start our shower over, don't you? As I recall, we were forced to end it a little prematurely." He was teasing her again, like he always used to do. Ashley felt like laughing and crying at the same time. What if her dad hadn't talked to her? She would never have known how wrong she'd been about him.

It didn't bear thinking about.

He took his time undressing first her, then him. After adjusting the spray, he stepped under the water and tugged her in as well.

This really was like that afternoon, only this time she knew darned well she wasn't dreaming.

He took the soap and, filling his hands with lather, caressed her body, leaving trails of bubbles to mark his path. Her knees were trembling so much she wasn't sure they were going to hold.

She leaned against the tile, much as he had done that first time, and let him explore every inch of her body. Until now, she'd not known she had so many erogenous zones—the backs of her knees, the arch of her foot, her ears, her neck, her—

She stopped thinking.

By the time they were out of the shower and he was drying her off, she wanted him so badly that she was shaking. He quickly ran the towel over himself, took her hand and led her to the bed.

Once they were lying side by side, he raised up on his elbow, resting his head on his hand. "Now let's see," he drawled, "I believe we were going to discuss dates for our wedding—" She stopped him with a kiss.

He already had her teetering on the edge and if she couldn't see the evidence with her own eyes, she would think that the only thing on his mind at the moment was to have a lazy discussion.

"Yes, I believe that was the subject we were discussing downstairs," she finally replied, inches from his mouth. She slid her hand from his chest down to his groin, wrapping her fingers around that very evidence. He jolted up like a jackknife, pushing her hand away.

"No fair. You're going to have this over with before we've started."

"Really? And what was that you were doing to me in the shower?"

He grinned. "My, you really do have a memory problem. Here. Let me show you."

He leaned over her and wrapped his moist tongue around the tip of her breast while his hands moved over her. He began to kiss her, starting with the arch of her foot and not stopping until he was stretched out over her, his mouth locked with hers.

Once again, his magic fingers touched her wetness and he slowly stroked her until she lifted her hips toward him, mutely pleading for him to take her.

As though he could no longer ignore her invitation, he slid deeply inside her, rocking gently against her.

"I love you so much," she whispered into his ear and he turned his head to catch her lips with his, never slowing down. His pace quickened until they were both panting. She wrapped her legs and arms around him, pushing to be as close to him as she could get until each of them was straining to envelop the other.

Ashley cried out when her body seemed to explode into a million pieces of joy. His groan immediately followed as he continued to move rapidly within her, eventually collapsing on top of her.

His harsh breathing caused the wisps of hair around

her ear to flutter and she realized that she was breathing just as rapidly.

Ashley felt lazily content and was drifting toward sleep when he began to kiss her once again. She felt him hard against her thigh and reached for him, guiding him inside.

She felt that they were making love in slow motion, each movement choreographed to excite the other. She nipped the lobe of his ear and then licked it, causing him to shudder. He palmed her breast and massaged it until she knew she couldn't take much more.

She grabbed his butt and pushed him into a faster rhythm, meeting him thrust after thrust, and making him laugh.

She loved to hear Jake laugh. It made her want to laugh with joy, as well.

This time when they broke through the pleasure barrier, he rolled to her side. He lay there, face down, without moving.

"Jake?" she whispered. "Are you all right?"

"Mmph."

"Oh. Well, I feel much better now. Thanks for the reassurance."

He turned his head to see her. "You know, I don't remember your having such a smart mouth."

"I learn from my elders," she replied primly.

He chuckled without moving.

Eventually Jake went into the bathroom. When he returned to bed, he drew her head onto his shoulder. "You know, when I saw your truck parked in front of the house, I thought you might be here to tell me you're pregnant."

She didn't say anything.

He gave her a little shake. "So. Are you pregnant?"

She smiled at him and said, "Not yet, cowboy, but at the rate we're going, it's only a matter of time."

Epilogue

The Crenshaws were having a barbecue and everyone for miles around had been invited.

Joe and Gail Crenshaw were back from their latest trip.

Jared had flown in from Saudi Arabia.

Jude drove in from his undercover assignment in San Antonio.

Only Jason wasn't there. He had made the Army a career and worked in special ops, so there were several hot spots in the world where he might be. No one really knew where he was or how to contact him. Gail sent regular e-mails to him and he responded when he could without telling her where he was.

However, there were enough cousins, aunts and uncles there to make up for his absence.

Strings of lights were in all the trees. There were live musicians, lots to eat, plenty to drink, a great deal of talk and a great deal of laughter.

Everyone had gathered in order to officially meet Jake's four-year-old daughter on her birthday. The large group must have intimidated her because she'd been clinging to Jake, who was carrying her, since people had begun to appear.

"Honey, don't you want to get down and go play with Mary Ann?" he asked her. "See?" he pointed. "She's over there with her mother."

"Uh-uh." She tightened the deathlike grip she had on his neck.

"Uh, then could you ease your hold on me a little so I can breathe?"

There might have been a slight lessening of her hold. Very slight.

"I thought you'd enjoy having a birthday party, sweetheart. You're finally four years old today. You were so excited while we were planning this party. You helped blow up balloons and decorate your pretty cake. We're supposed to be celebrating, you know. Don't be scared."

She buried her head in his shoulder.

"You have to admit, Jake," Ashley said at his side, "seeing so many Crenshaws gathered in one place can be a little daunting. She'll get used to them soon enough. Just give her some time and she'll adjust."

"Well, I need to go help Dad—"

"You're doing exactly what you're supposed to be doing, you know...being Heather's safe place. Your dad's been doing this for years. I doubt he needs any assistance."

He kissed the top of Heather's curls. "So," he said, peering down at her, "you're going to spend the evening in my arms, is that it?"

She nodded her head and Jake laughed.

"What's so funny?" Jared asked, sauntering up to them, holding a drink in his hand.

"I'm just enjoying my daughter. How are things with you?"

"Let's just say I'm glad to be home after the past fourteen months overseas."

"It was pretty bad over there, huh?"

"Worse than bad but I managed to survive. I don't have to go back until the first of the year." He turned to Ashley. "It's good seeing you here with Jake, Ashley. The three of you look like a family."

Jake cocked his head. "You know, that's an idea." He turned to Ashley. "What do you think, honey? Jared may have a good idea there." Ashley punched his free arm, then held out her left hand to show Jared her engagement ring.

"Wow! When did *this* happen?"

Ashley thought a moment before she said, "Oh, somewhere around my seventh birthday. It just took Jake a while to give me the ring."

Jared laughed. "Good point, Ashley. I'm glad everything has worked out for y'all. I'm serious; Jake, I've never seen you so happy."

"That's not surprising since I've never been this happy before."

Heather raised her head. "Daddy?"

"What, sweetheart."

"'Member when you said I could have a puppy?"

Jake's eyes widened in dismay. He looked at Ashley, silently pleading for help. She returned his gaze with a smile, her raised eyebrow signaling he was on his own with this one.

He cleared his throat. "Well, yes. Yes, I do. It's just that—"

"Can I get my puppy tonight?"

"May I?" Ashley asked.

He lowered his brow in a mock frown. "Not you, too."

Heather knew what she meant. "*May* I have my puppy tonight?" She grinned at him. "It's for my birthday."

If she but knew it, he'd walk barefoot over hot coals for this little girl. However, that didn't mean she could have everything she wanted. Besides, after the night he'd first mentioned the idea, she'd never said another word about wanting a puppy until now.

"Don't you want to wait a while to get a puppy?" he asked hopefully. "Puppies take lots of care and training."

She shook her head, her eyes sad.

Jake looked at Jared and Ashley and sighed. "If you'll excuse us. It looks like we have to go see a man about a dog."

Jared watched him walk away before he turned to Ashley. "I don't know what you did, Ashley, but you somehow made a new man out of Jake. None of us ever expected him to get married again. How did you do it?"

"I just loved him, Jared, like I always have. I guess he finally got around to noticing."

Jared laughed. "Don't kid yourself. I remember one of your birthday parties when he couldn't keep his eyes off you. Do you remember that?"

"One of my fondest memories. Why?"

"I knew then that he was in conflict with himself over you. I'm glad he finally resolved it satisfactorily."

"Me, too."

Jared looked around them before quietly asking, "Has Tiffany contacted him since the night she brought Heather to him?"

Ashley shook her head no. "He had his attorney draw up papers for her to sign giving up all her rights to Heather. I believe they're waiting for her to return from some long trip to sign them."

"Hard to imagine not wanting your own kid."

"How about you? When are you planning to get married and settle down?"

"Me?" He laughed. "You got the wrong guy for that one. I love the ladies but I never met one I wanted to face over the breakfast table every morning for the rest of my life. No, marriage is fine for y'all. I enjoy my freedom too much."

Gail came over to join them. "I think everyone's enjoying themselves tonight, don't you?" she asked.

Jared draped his arm across his mother's shoulders. "What's not to enjoy, Mom? You know how people look forward to your parties. Always have, always will."

"That's good to know," she said. Looking at Ashley, she added, "While I've got you here, I want to talk to you about planning an engagement party for you and Jake soon."

Jared groaned. "Hey, planning engagement parties creeps me out. I'll see y'all later." He waved and walked away.

Gail watched him saunter away and said, "You know what's going to happen to that young man one of these days, don't you? He going to meet a woman who'll have him so tied up in knots he won't know which way to turn. He'll be begging her to marry him, mark my words."

"Couldn't happen to a more deserving guy, if you ask me."

They both laughed.

"Isn't Heather adorable?" Gail asked Ashley a few minutes later, nodding toward Jake, who now held his daughter in one arm and a wriggling black-and-white puppy in the other.

"Absolutely," Ashley replied, watching Heather try to pet the puppy without letting go of Jake's neck.

"You don't suppose we're prejudiced, do you? Because she's ours?"

"Absolutely not. Anyone can see that we're merely stating facts."

Gail grinned at her response. "It's so much fun to watch Jake with her, isn't it? He's adapted to fatherhood rather quickly, considering the circumstances."

Ashley smiled. "Yes, but I'm not surprised, really. Remember how he was with me when I was a child?"

"Yes, of course. He was always so proud of you, just as if you belonged to him."

"I do, Gail. I belong to Jake. Always have…always will."

* * * * *

*We hope you enjoyed BRANDED,
the first book in Annette Broadrick's
new Desire series, THE CRENSHAWS of Texas.*

*Please look for the story of Jake's brother,
Jared—back from the oil fields of Saudi Arabia—
and Lindsay—elegant and off-limits—
who found themselves
CAUGHT IN THE CROSSFIRE
of a manipulative and ruthless power broker,
in the second book of the Crenshaw series
(Desire 1610) next month.*

*For a sneak preview of
CAUGHT IN THE CROSSFIRE, turn the page...*

One

Jared abruptly came awake at the sound of a crashing door. At that moment, he was aware of only two things—he had the mother of all hangovers and the door to his bedroom had flown open hard enough to bounce off the wall.

Since he lived alone, there was no reason for anyone to come charging into the room.

He painfully squinted his eyes open and discovered that the pounding in his head was the least of his problems.

This wasn't his bedroom. So where the hell was he? He stared at the lace-edged canopy above him before slowly moving his gaze to the rest of the room. His bedroom sure as hell didn't smell like flowers or contain this delicate furniture.

He stared at a wall of shelves filled with fancy-dressed dolls before he closed his eyes again.

Maybe the hangover was affecting his vision. He softly massaged his eyes. When he opened them again, he stared in shock.

Two men stood just inside the doorway.

He was having a nightmare, that's what it was. Either that or he'd died and gone straight to hell. He could think of no other reason why his father would be standing in the room with Senator Russell.

Lindsey Russell's father.

What the—?

Jared turned his head and then grabbed it before it tumbled off his shoulders. Lindsey Russell lay on the pillow beside him, facing him, her hand tucked beneath her cheek. How she could still be asleep after the racket the men had made was beyond him.

In fact, everything was beyond him at the moment.

What was he doing in bed with her?

He knew what their visitors thought…hell, he'd be thinking the same thing given their circumstances. What he couldn't figure out was what he was doing here. Even more important, why had she allowed him into her bed?

They'd been seeing each other, sure, but he'd known from the very beginning of their relationship that she wouldn't sleep with him.

He liked her. He liked her a lot. If she'd given him any sign that she would take the next step, he would have been all for it. Is that what happened last night?

If so, why couldn't he remember?

How had he gotten here? He forced himself to think back to the night before.

He hadn't done anything in particular, as he re-called. After hard physical labor all day working for Jake on the ranch, he'd cleaned up at his place and driven into town for something to eat. He'd run into a couple of guys he knew at the Mustang Bar & Grill, so after he ate, he'd stayed a while and shot some pool with them.

He hadn't been drinking. Well, maybe a couple of beers, but nothing that would cause him to wake up with a pounding headache and no idea how he ended up in Lindsay's bed.

He stared at the men who stood in silence looking at him as though he were pond scum.

He really couldn't blame them. If there was one thing that Jared knew on this particular morning, it was that he had no business being in Lindsey Russell's bed.

What had he been thinking?

Jared pushed himself up, rested his elbows on his bent knees and held his head. "I can explain—" he said slowly, his voice the sound of a croaking bullfrog. He cleared his throat. "You see," he said and then paused. He looked at his dad, who now leaned against the door-jamb with his arms crossed and one booted foot across the other. Next, he glanced at Lindsey who had stirred at the sound of his voice. "Actually," he continued, "I have no idea how I got here or why I'm here."

His gaze kept going back to Lindsey, who looked amazingly pretty first thing in the morning, her face slightly flushed with sleep, and her dark hair tumbled around her shoulders and draped across her pillow.

He forced his gaze back to the men.

Joe lifted an eyebrow. "Oh, I think R.W. and I can figure out that last one without any explanation on your part," Joe drawled softly.

LONETREE RANCHERS: MORGAN

Kathie DeNosky

Kathie DeNosky lives in deep Southern Illinois with her husband and three children. After reading and enjoying romances for many years, she is ecstatic about being able to share her stories with others as a Desire™ author. Highly sensual stories with a generous amount of humour, Kathie's books have appeared on the Waldenbooks bestseller list. She enjoys going to rodeos, travelling through the southern and south-western states and listening to country music. She often starts her day at 2:00am, so she can write without interruption, before the rest of the family is up and about. You may write to Kathie at: PO Box 2064, Herrin, Illinois 62948-5264, USA.

*To Charlie, who puts up with my odd hours
and loves me anyway.
And a very special thank-you to the
Professional Bull Riders*

One

"What the hell do you think you're doing in here?"

In the process of building a fire in the big stone fireplace, Samantha Peterson jumped and spun around at the sound of the man's angry voice and the old wooden door slamming back against the wall. The biggest cowboy she'd ever seen stood like a tree rooted in the middle of the threshold. Lightning flashed outside behind him and every story she'd ever heard about the bogeyman flooded her mind.

His eyes were hidden by the wide brim of his black cowboy hat pulled down low on his forehead, but if the grim set of his mouth was any indication, he was not only the biggest cowboy she'd ever seen, he was also the angriest. He took a step forward at the same time a gust of wind whipped his long black coat around his legs. That's when Samantha noticed he held a rifle in one big gloved hand.

"I...I'm...ooh—" Samantha bent forward slightly, squeezed her eyes shut and groaned from the sudden tightness gripping her stomach.

"Good God, you're pregnant!" He sounded shocked.

Anger coursed through her. He'd scared the bejeebers out of her and all he had to say was, "You're pregnant?"

"Thank you for informing me...of that fact," she said through clenched teeth. "I doubt that I'd...have noticed otherwise."

"Are you all right?"

His voice sounded too close for comfort, but that was the least of Samantha's concerns. She had a feeling this wasn't one of the Braxton-Hicks contractions that she'd been experiencing for the past couple of weeks. It felt too different to be false labor. This felt like it might be the real thing. But that wasn't possible, was it? She still had three weeks before she reached her due date.

"No, I'm not all right," she said as the tight feeling decreased. Ready to give the man a piece of her mind, she straightened to her full height. "You scared the living daylights..."

Her voice trailed off as she looked up—way up— at the man standing next to her. The sheer size of him sent a shiver of apprehension slithering up her spine and had her stepping away from him. The top of her head barely reached his chin. At five foot six, she wasn't an Amazon by any means, but she wasn't short either. But this man was at least ten inches taller and appeared to be extremely muscular.

"Look, I'm sorry I yelled," he said, his deep baritone sending another tremor through her that had nothing whatsoever to do with fear. "I expected to find one of the local teenage boys getting ready to throw one of his Saturday night beer busts."

"As you can see, I'm not a teenage boy." Samantha moved away a couple of extra steps. She needed to put more distance between them, in case a fast getaway was in order. At least, as fast as her advanced pregnancy would allow. "And I can assure you, I'm not getting ready to throw a drinking party."

His mouth curved up in a smile and he used his thumb to push the wide brim of his cowboy hat up, revealing the most startling blue eyes she'd ever seen. "Let's start over." He extended his big hand. "I'm Morgan Wakefield."

When she cautiously placed her hand in his, his fingers closed around hers and a warm tingle raced through her. As he stared at her expectantly, she had trouble finding her voice. "I'm, uh, Samantha Peterson," she finally managed as she tugged her hand from his.

"Nice to meet you, Mrs. Peterson."

"That's *Ms.* Peterson," Samantha corrected. "I'm not married."

His gaze traveled to her swollen stomach, then back to her face before he gave her a short nod. Had that been a hint of disapproval she'd detected in his expression just before he gave her a bland smile?

If so, that was just too darned bad. It was none of his business whether she was married or not.

As they continued to stare wordlessly at each other, the sound of dripping water drew their attention to the corner of the room. Hurrying into the kitchen, Samantha rummaged through the cabinets until she found a large pot.

When she returned to the living room, she shoved it under the steady stream of water pouring from the ceiling. "That's just great. Not even the roof on this place is in decent repair."

She watched Morgan Wakefield's eyes narrow. "Why do you care if the roof leaks or not?" he asked slowly.

"I was hoping it would at least keep me dry tonight," she said, gazing at the rain water collecting in the pot.

"You're staying? Here? Tonight?"

"Yes. Yes. And yes," she said, smiling at his incredulous look. "I inherited it from my grandfather."

"You're Tug Shackley's granddaughter?"

Samantha nodded and walked over to the wide stone hearth to slowly lower herself to a sitting position. Another contraction was building, and making sure to keep her breathing deep and even, she focused on relaxing every muscle in her body.

When it passed, she looked up to find that Morgan had propped his rifle against the armchair and stood with his hands on his narrow hips. He was watching her as if he didn't quite know what to think. "Are you sure you're all right?"

"Yes. I'll be fine just as soon as I have my baby," she said, reminding herself to stay calm, even though the baby was coming earlier than expected. "Do you happen to know where the nearest hospital is?"

If the widening of his vivid blue eyes was any indication, it had been the last thing he'd expected her to ask. "Oh hell, lady. You're not—"

"Yes, I am." She almost laughed at the horrified expression that crossed his handsome face. "Now, if you'll answer my question concerning the location of the nearest hospital, I'll get in my car and go have my baby."

He removed his hat and ran an agitated hand through his shiny sable-black hair. "You can't drive yourself to the hospital."

"And why not, Mr. Wakefield?" she asked, staring up at him.

Not only was he one of the biggest men she'd ever met, he was one of the best-looking. He had a small white scar above his right eyebrow and his lean cheeks sported a day's growth of beard, but it only added to his rugged appeal.

"The name's Morgan," he said, jamming his hat back on his head. "And it's not safe for you to be driving in your condition. What if the pain caused you to run off the road?''

Samantha awkwardly pushed herself to her feet. ''That's a chance I'll have to take. Now, if you'll excuse me, we'll have to get acquainted some other time. Right now, I have to go deliver my baby.''

He stubbornly shook his head. ''Where's your car parked?''

''In the garage, or shed, or whatever you want to call that dilapidated thing behind the house.'' She collected her shoulder bag from the mantel. ''Why?''

''The nearest hospital is over sixty miles from here, in Laramie.'' He held out his hand. ''Give me your keys and I'll drive you down there.''

''That's not necessary,'' she said, shaking her head. ''I'm perfectly capable of—''

Arguing with Morgan, she was unprepared for the contraction that wrapped around her belly and seemed to squeeze the breath out of her. When she dropped her purse and bent double, he caught her by the shoulders and supported her until the feeling eased.

''You can't even stand up when the pain hits.'' He picked up her purse and held it out to her. ''Now, give me your keys and I'll go get your car.''

As much as she hated to admit it, he was right. Digging in her purse, she handed him the keys to her twenty-year-old Ford. ''You might have trouble starting it. It's kind of tricky sometimes. I think it might need a tune-up.''

''Don't worry. I think I can handle starting a car,''

Morgan said dryly. Taking the keys from her, he turned toward the door, but stopped abruptly when she started to follow. ''There's no sense in both of us getting drenched. Stay inside until I get the car pulled up closer to the porch, then I'll help you down the steps.''

''I think I can navigate a set of steps by myself,'' she argued.

''They aren't in the best repair and I don't think you want to deal with a broken leg, in addition to having a baby.''

He left the house before she could argue the point further and sprinted across the yard. He'd waited for this day for almost eighteen months. Tug's heir had finally been found. Unfortunately, she had the idea that she was going to take up residence in the place. And at the moment, she for damned sure wasn't in any shape to listen to his arguments about why she should sell it to him, instead of carrying out her plan of moving in.

He almost laughed as he folded his tall frame into the driver's seat of the compact car. Women. Where did they get these empty-headed ideas anyway? She'd have to be blind not to see that it would take more money than it was worth to fix up this dump.

Inserting the key into the ignition, he turned it and the dull clicking sound that followed sent a chill racing up his spine. He glanced at the dashboard. There wasn't one of the indicator lights lit. He closed his eyes in frustration and barely resisted the urge to pound on the dash with his fist. The battery was as dead as poor old Tug.

When he climbed out of the bucket seat and raised the hood, he rattled off a string of cuss words that would have done a sailor proud. The battery terminals were so covered with corrosion he wouldn't be surprised to see that it had eaten through the cables. He looked around for something to knock some of the oxidation loose, but abandoned that idea immediately. Even if he got rid of most of the crud without breaking the contacts, there was no way to charge the damned thing. He slammed the hood back down with force.

Desperation clawed at his insides as the gravity of the situation settled over him. The only way to get help would involve him riding his horse back to the Lonetree through a pouring rain to get his truck. That would take at least thirty minutes going across country. Then it would take another forty-five minutes to drive the road between the two ranches.

Morgan shook his head as he stared at the sheet of rain just outside the shed's double doors. Riding through a downpour didn't bother him. Hell, he'd done that more times than he cared to count. But the creek between his ranch and this one always flooded when it rained this hard, and it would be impossible to cross now. He could use the road, but that would take a couple of hours to get back to her, and he didn't like the idea of leaving a pregnant woman—a woman in labor, no less—by herself. And he'd bet his right arm that she wouldn't be any crazier about his leaving her alone than he was.

For the first time since meeting Samantha Peterson, he allowed himself to think about his first impression of her. Her golden-brown hair framed a face that could easily grace the cover of a glamour magazine. But her eyes were what had damned near knocked him to his knees when he'd first seen her standing by the fireplace. Whiskey-brown with flecks of gold, they'd made him think of hot sultry nights and long hours of passionate sex.

Morgan sucked in a sharp breath. Now where the hell had that come from?

He cussed a blue streak. It had been quite a while since he'd enjoyed the warmth of a woman's body and the long dry spell was beginning to take its toll. What he needed was a trip to Buffalo Gals Saloon down in Bear Creek for a night of good old-fashioned hell-raising. He was sure to find a willing little filly down there to help him scratch his itch and forget how lonely the long Wyoming winter had been.

Shaking his head, he turned his attention back to the matters at hand. Now was not the time to lament how sorry his sex life was. What he and Samantha Peterson were facing right now was a lot more important.

A sinking feeling settled over him as he reviewed the options to their present dilemma. He might as well accept the inevitable and start preparing for what had to be done. Within the next few hours, he was going to have to add the delivery of a baby to his arsenal of emergency medical skills. Unless, of course, by some miracle someone else showed up. And the chances of that happening were slim to none.

Sighing heavily, he turned back to her car, opened the trunk and rummaged around until he found what he was looking for. Gathering pillows, sheets, blankets and towels, he ran back to the house.

By the time he walked through the door, Samantha sat on the hearth with her gaze transfixed on the faded picture hanging on the opposite wall. She looked as if she was in some kind of daze and he wondered if she might be going into shock.

But as he mentally reviewed what he knew about treating shock victims, she took a deep breath, slowly blew it out, then looked at him expectantly. "Are we ready to go?" she asked, rising to her feet as if nothing had happened.

Relieved that she seemed to be all right, he shook his head and tried to think of a way to break the news as gently as he could. He sighed heavily. Some things just couldn't be sugar-coated.

"The battery's dead. I'm afraid we're stuck here for a while."

Her pretty amber eyes widened considerably as she looked around the room. "But I have to go to the hospital. There's no doctor here. What if…I mean the baby is early. There might be a need for—"

Walking over to her, Morgan placed his hands on her shoulders. The last thing he needed right now was for her to go into a blind panic. "Take a deep breath and listen to me, Samantha. You're not alone. I'm here."

"Are you a doctor?" Her expressive eyes begged him to say that he was.

At the moment, Morgan would have given everything he owned for a medical degree. "No, I'm not," he answered truthfully. "But we'll get through this. You've got my word on that." He just hoped liked hell he could live up to the promise.

"What about your car, or truck, or whatever you came in?" she asked hopefully. "Can't we use that?"

He ran his hand over the back of his neck in an effort to ease some of the mounting tension and shook his head. "I rode my horse. Getting back to the Lonetree, then driving back here in my truck, would take hours."

"Your horse," she repeated, looking more apprehensive by the second.

"I tied it in the barn when I arrived," he said, hoping she didn't get hysterical.

She brightened suddenly, as if she had the answer to the immediate problem. "What about a cell phone? Everyone has a cell phone these days. You can't go to a movie or out to dinner without hearing one ring."

"I have one, but certain areas of this region are dead zones," he explained. "This is one of them. Even if I'd bothered to bring it with me, it would be useless without a signal."

She opened her mouth to say something, but instead of words she let loose with a low moan. The hair on the back of his neck stood straight up and his gut twisted into a tight knot. When she began to fold, Morgan pulled her to him and supported her weight while the pain held her in its grip.

Sweat popped out on his forehead and upper lip. This was going to be hard as hell to deal with. He didn't like seeing anything in pain, and definitely not a woman. He'd rather climb a barbed wire fence buck naked than to see a female in pain.

How was he going to handle Samantha going through hours of labor and not be able to do a damned thing but watch? And what if things didn't go like they were supposed to?

He swallowed around the lump forming in his throat. He knew all too well what could happen if something went wrong. At the age of seven he'd lost his own mother because of complications during the birth of his youngest brother, Colt. And she'd been in the hospital.

The pain ebbed and the woman he held took a deep breath. "I've got to maintain my focus," she said, sounding determined. "It will make all of this much easier if I can do that."

Morgan wasn't sure if she was trying to convince him or herself. But at the moment, it didn't matter. His biggest concern was to get her off her feet, make sure she was as comfortable as possible, then start gathering some of the supplies he'd need.

"Why don't you sit by the fire while I get the

couch pulled over here for you to lie down?'' he
asked, helping her lower herself to the raised stone
hearth.

''You, um, haven't by any chance done this before,
have you?'' she asked. Her hopeful tone caused the
knot in his gut to tighten.

He refrained from answering as he pulled the drop
cloth from the dingy green couch, threw it onto a
chair and shoved the heavy piece of furniture closer
to the warmth of the fire. He'd delivered hundreds,
maybe thousands, of babies in his lifetime. But none
of them had been human. And somehow, he didn't
think Samantha Peterson would be all that impressed
with his expertise as a bovine obstetrician. With any
luck she wouldn't ask him again, and he wouldn't
have to tell her.

''Well, have you?'' she persisted.

Morgan almost groaned out loud. Why couldn't she
just drop it and accept the inevitable? He was the
best—the only—source of help she was going to get.

''Yes, and no.'' He unfolded one of the sheets he'd
retrieved from her car and arranged it over the sagging piece of furniture, along with a couple of pillows. ''If you count the calves and colts I've delivered, yes, I've done this before.'' He helped her up
from the hearth and over to the couch. ''If not, then
no, I haven't.''

She sat down suddenly and went into that trance-
like state that she'd been in when he'd come in from
trying to start the car. Fascinated, he watched her take

deep, rhythmic breaths and lightly massage her swollen belly as she stared at the brim of his hat. Her porcelain cheeks colored a deep rose, but her determination to ride out the pain was evident in the set of her stubborn little chin and her unwavering concentration.

When she came out of the daze, she looked up at him and continued talking as if nothing had happened. It was the damnedest thing he'd ever witnessed.

"There's a book on pregnancy in my handbag. I think it has emergency delivery instructions and a list of things you'll need." She nervously caught her lower lip between her teeth before she continued, "I hope you're a quick study."

If there was one thing Morgan admired, and a sure-fire way of judging what a person was made of, it was watching how they handled themselves in a tense situation. And he'd have to give credit where it was due. The little lady settling herself back against the pillows on the sagging green couch had her share of grit.

He could tell by the shadows in her pretty whiskey-colored eyes that she was scared witless. But the firm set of her perfectly shaped mouth indicated that she wasn't going to panic. Whatever came their way, she was going to deal with it.

Giving her the most reassuring smile he was capable of under the circumstances, Morgan handed her the oversized purse. "You find that book. I'll take care of the rest."

She pulled the book from the depths of the bag,

then, shoving it into his hands, went back into another one of her trances. While she took deep, even breaths and stared off into space, he quickly scanned the index of the book she'd given him for instructions on an emergency, at-home delivery.

Turning to the page the directory had indicated, he read the first entry. Calling 9-1-1 was out of the question. He skipped down to the second directive—if possible call for help.

Well hell, that was a no-brainer. If he could call someone else to assist, he'd call 9-1-1.

When his gaze dropped to the third instruction, he swallowed hard and glanced at her as she came back from wherever she went in her mind to escape the pain.

"What?" she asked when he continued to stare at her.

He cleared his throat. There was no easy way of breaking news like this to a woman he'd known for— he checked his watch—a little less than an hour.

"It says you need to strip from the waist down," he finally answered, making sure to keep his voice even and his gaze steady.

"Is that necessary right now?" she asked just as calmly. He wasn't sure, but it looked as if her already flushed cheeks turned a deeper shade of crimson.

Shrugging, Morgan handed her the book and walked into the kitchen to find another pot. He needed to get some water boiling in order to sterilize a few things he would have to use during the delivery. And she needed to come to grips with the way things had to be.

When he walked back into the living room on his way to set a couple of pots outside to collect rainwater for boiling, he noticed that she'd used one of the blankets he'd brought in from the car to drape over her lap. Glancing to the end of the couch, he saw that her jeans were neatly folded on the arm, while her tennis shoes and socks sat on the floor beside it. She didn't look his way and he didn't comment on the fact that she'd obviously done as the book had indicated.

"Would you feel better lying down?" he asked when he returned from placing the pots on the porch steps.

She shook her head. "Not yet."

Sweat beaded her forehead as she handed him the book and, once again, focused her energy on riding the current wave of pain. Standing there watching her, Morgan had never felt more useless in his entire life. He wanted to help her, but he didn't have a clue how to go about it.

Needing to do something, anything, he turned to the woodbox by the fireplace, removed several logs, then carefully stacked them on the dying fire in the grate. Even though it was early May, and fairly warm, there was a damp chill to the room, and he figured he would need all the light he could get when the time came for the baby's grand entrance. Besides, he needed something to keep himself busy in order to take his mind off what Samantha was going through.

The dry wood caught immediately and the fire

blazed high, chasing away the approaching shadows of late afternoon. He shrugged out of his duster and tossing it toward the chair where he'd thrown the drop cloth, went in search of some other source of light. Fortunately, he found two kerosene lamps in the pantry with full reservoirs. He returned to the living room, placed them on the mantel and lit the wicks with some stick matches he'd found in the kitchen, then sat on the hearth and picked up the book. Running his finger down the list of preparations, he glanced up. Where the hell was he going to find two pieces of sturdy string to tie off the cord?

He scanned the room, then zeroed in on Samantha's tennis shoes sitting where she'd placed them by the end of the couch. Her shoe laces would have to do. He checked the book again. It didn't say anything about sterilizing what he used to tie the cord, but he figured it couldn't hurt. Just to be on the safe side, he'd toss them in the boiling water along with his pocket knife. Even if the hot water caused them to shrink, they should still be long enough for what he needed.

He laid the book within easy reach, then stood up and unfastened the cuffs of his chambray shirt. Rolling the long sleeves to the middle of his forearms, he waited for Samantha to relax her intense focus.

"The book says we need to start timing your contractions in order to tell how you're progressing. Let me know when you feel another one coming on."

She nodded. "They're coming closer together."

They were getting stronger, too. That much he

could tell from the tiny strain lines bracketing her mouth. On impulse he reached out and took her hand in his. Giving it a gentle squeeze, he tried to reassure her. "You're going to do just fine, Samantha."

She squeezed back. "Remind me of that in a few hours."

"Will do," he said, nodding. He had no idea why the trust she was placing in him caused his chest to swell, but it did. Deciding that he could analyze what it meant later, he released her hand and started for the door. "I'll be right back. I'm going to go get the rainwater I've been collecting so that I can put it on the fire to boil."

"Morgan?"

The sound of his name on her soft voice sent a tingle up his spine. He swallowed hard and turned back to face her. "What, Samantha?"

"Thank you for being so calm. It really helps." The look she gave him clearly stated that she was counting on him to get her through whatever happened.

At a loss for words, he nodded and walked out to the porch to get the pots of water. Samantha had no way of knowing that his insides were churning like a damned cement mixer from thoughts of all the things that could go wrong, as they had with his mother.

Morgan took a deep breath, then slowly released it. And if it was the last thing he ever did, he had no intention of letting her find out.

Two

Four hours later, Morgan sat on the hearth in front of Samantha where she perched on the edge of the couch. For the last hour he'd watched her alternate between sitting forward and leaning back against the pillows in her effort to get comfortable. She had his hand in a death grip as she rode the current wave of pain and it surprised him how strong she was. It felt more like a lumberjack had a hold of his hand than a woman, and her nails digging into his palm felt as if she might draw blood. But if it helped her get through this, he'd gladly let her rip the skin clean off.

As he watched her stare off into space and pant her way through the contraction, his admiration for her grew by leaps and bounds. She was in tremendous pain, but her determination to stay on top of it, to ride it out, was amazing.

He was sure she was in what the book called "active labor" because of the duration of her contractions and the time between them. He glanced at his watch. They still had the "transitional labor" to go through and, if the book was right, they probably had another couple of hours before they got to the actual delivery. He just hoped he could last that long. With every contraction Samantha had, his gut twisted tighter and he felt a little more helpless than he had only moments before.

When she blew out a deep breath, signaling that the contraction had ended, he asked, "Is there anything else I can do? The book says that you might have some back pain? Do you need your back rubbed?"

"Would you mind?" she asked, releasing his hand. She winced. "My back is killing me."

Removing his Resistol, Morgan sailed it like a Frisbee to land on the chair with his duster, took a deep breath and eased over to sit next to her on the ugly green couch. He slipped his hand beneath her pink T-shirt to lightly kneed the muscles of her lower back, and valiantly tried to ignore the fact that her skin felt like satin beneath his callused palm. Now was not the time for him to remember how much he missed the way a woman's softness felt.

"Is it helping?" he asked.

"A little." She suddenly took a deep breath and once again focused on riding out another pain.

Morgan continued to rub her back with his right hand as he glanced at the watch on his left wrist. This contraction had come a lot faster than the last one. He watched the second hand sweep around once, then halfway around again before Samantha blew out a deep breath, signaling it was over.

"Stop touching me," she said sharply. "You're making it worse."

"Okay," he said, removing his hand from beneath her shirt. He knew for certain that he hadn't rubbed her back *that* hard.

Frowning, Morgan moved back to the hearth and picked up the book. Unless he missed his guess, they were moving on to the next step.

Yep. Sure as shootin', Samantha had all the signs of a woman in "transitional labor." She'd suddenly become as irritable as a bear with a sore paw, didn't want to be touched, and the most telling of the symptoms was the duration of the last contraction.

He wiped the sweat from his forehead and watched her struggle to stay focused as the next wave of pain hit her. Her face was flushed, her golden-brown hair hung in damp tendrils from perspiration and the lines of strain around her mouth had deepened.

He'd never felt more useless.

When she blew out a deep breath, he laid the book aside and wiped her face with a cool damp washcloth.

Her gaze met his, and it was damned near his undoing when tears filled her pretty amber eyes.

"I don't think…I can't do this, Morgan."

Making sure the book was within easy reach, Morgan took her hands in his. "You're doing just fine, Samantha." The instructions had indicated that he should encourage her and help her stay focused. He wasn't sure how the hell to go about that, but he'd do it or die trying. "You're in the home stretch, sweetheart. It won't be much longer."

He watched her eyes cloud with pain, felt her hands tighten on his in a death grip. She started to say something, but a moan came out instead.

It tore him apart to see her hurting and not be able to do anything to help. "Look at me, Samantha."

Her breathing ragged, she shook her head. "This is…too hard," she said, her voice cracking.

"Come on, Samantha, look at me," he said more firmly.

When she finally did as he commanded, Morgan nodded. "That's it, sweetheart. Stay focused and squeeze my hands as hard as you can. Concentrate on transferring the pain to me."

He wasn't sure if the book supported his way of taking her mind off the contraction, but he didn't care. All that mattered was that it seemed to be working. Samantha held his gaze and damned near cut off the circulation to his fingers as she tightened her hands on his.

What seemed like an eternity, but couldn't have

been more than a couple of minutes later, she suddenly released his hands to lay back against the couch. "I need to push."

The hair on the back of Morgan's neck shot straight up and his stomach did a back-flip. "Are you sure?" he asked, flexing his fingers in an effort to return the circulation.

Nodding, she scrunched her eyes shut, grabbed her knees with her hands and pushed with all her might.

Morgan wanted to run like hell. Instead, he grabbed the book, quickly read what he needed to do, then prayed like he'd never prayed before.

He could do this. Along with his dad and brothers, he'd played baby doctor to the herds of Lonetree cattle for as long as he could remember. Surely he could deliver one little human baby.

Placing the book within easy reach, he washed his hands in one of the pots of water that he'd boiled earlier, then fished his sterilized pocket knife and Samantha's shoelaces from the other. Fortunately, the water had cooled enough that it wasn't scalding, but it was still damned hot. His mind on what was about to take place, he barely noticed.

To Morgan, the next thirty minutes seemed to pass in a fast-forward blur. Samantha worked hard to push her baby out into the world as he uttered words he hoped were encouraging. Then, just after midnight, a little baby boy with dark brown hair slid out into his waiting hands, opened his mouth and started yowling at the top of his tiny lungs.

A lump the size of his fist formed in Morgan's throat as he stared down at the child he'd helped to enter the world. Awed by the miracle he'd participated in, he couldn't have strung two words together if his life depended on it.

"Is my baby all right?" Samantha asked, sounding stronger than he would have thought possible after what she'd been through.

Relieved that things had turned out the way they should, Morgan tied off the cord in two places, cut it between the ties, then wrapped the baby in fluffy towels. His hands shaking slightly, he placed the infant in her waiting arms.

Clearing his throat, he finally managed, "I'm not a doctor, but he looks normal to me." He grinned. "If his squalling is any indication, I'd say he's mad as hell about this whole birthing business though."

"He's beautiful." He watched tears fill Samantha's eyes as she glanced up at him. "I can't thank you enough for helping us, Morgan."

"You did all the work." Finishing the last of what the instructions indicated should be done, he washed up and rolled his sleeves back down to fasten them at his wrists. "Have you picked out a name for him?"

The smile she gave him made Morgan feel as if the sun had broken through on a gray, cloudy day. "As a matter of fact, I think I have," she said softly. "How does Timothy *Morgan* Peterson sound?"

Two days later, Samantha sat on the side of her hospital bed, staring at the discharge papers the nurse had handed her only moments ago. Now what? Where were she and the baby supposed to go? And how were they supposed to get there?

She didn't have her car. And even if she did, it wouldn't run. The morning after Timmy had been born, Morgan rode his horse back to his ranch, then drove over to her grandfather's place in his truck to take her and the baby to the hospital.

She sighed as she looked at her son sleeping peacefully in the bassinet. She could call a cab. But where would she have it take her and Timmy? She certainly couldn't afford the fare for a sixty mile trip back to her newly inherited ranch. She shook her head. Make that her newly inherited dump.

"Do you need help getting dressed?" the nurse asked, strolling back into the room with a complimentary bag of sample baby products. She picked up Timmy from the tiny bed to wrap him in a soft, baby blue receiving blanket. "By the way, I caught your husband in the hall and told him you two were ready to leave."

Dumbfounded, Samantha blinked. "My husband?" The woman had to have confused her with another new mother. "I'm not—"

"I sent him to bring his truck around to the front entrance," the woman said as if Samantha hadn't spoken. "Once you're dressed, I'll get a wheelchair and you and this little darling can be on your way."

"But I still have to go down to the business office to make arrangements to pay the bill. And I'm not—"

"Don't worry, Samantha. It's taken care of," Morgan said, walking through the doorway as if he owned the place. He handed her a shopping bag. "All you have to do is put these clothes on and we can get out of here."

"I'll get the wheelchair," the nurse said, her shoes making a whispering sound against the tiled floor as she quickly left the room.

Samantha stared at the man who had been her rock throughout the birth of her child. He was without a doubt one of the best-looking men she'd ever seen. And apparently one of the most arrogant.

"What do you mean it's taken care of?" she demanded. She wasn't sure what he'd done, but she had a feeling she wasn't going to like it when she found out.

"We'll talk about it on the drive home."

"I think we'd better discuss this right now," she said flatly. She wasn't going anywhere until he told her what was going on.

Completely ignoring her protest, he took the shopping bag from her stiff fingers, opened it and pulled out a cream-colored T-shirt and denim jumper. "I wasn't sure about the size, so I had a clerk pick out everything. She said these were 'one size fits most'— whatever that means." He looked a little unsure as he shoved them into her hands and turned to leave. "Go ahead and get dressed so we can get out of here. I'll be waiting with the truck when the nurse brings you out the front entrance."

"Morgan, I want to know what—"

"I don't want to argue with you, Samantha," he interrupted. "It's not good for you, and I really don't have time for it. I'd like to get back to the Lonetree by lunchtime. So get dressed and I'll meet you out front."

Before she could demand answers, he grabbed the small overnight case she'd brought with her to the hospital, turned and left the room, leaving her to stare after him. She needed to get back to her grandfather's ranch—make that hers now—to see about her car. And with very little money, she really didn't have any other options of getting there.

She sighed heavily, then removing the tags from the jumper and T-shirt, slipped the pieces of lightweight cardboard into her purse. She wasn't a charity case. As soon as she could, she'd pay Morgan back for the clothes.

Hurriedly changing from the hospital gown, she hardened her resolve to find out what he meant about the hospital bill being taken care of. They had a good sixty mile drive ahead of them, and if he'd done what she suspected, they were going to have a long talk on the way. A *really* long talk.

Fifteen minutes later, when the nurse guided the wheelchair through the double glass doors of the hospital's front entrance, Morgan was leaning against the fender of his shiny silver-gray truck, his arms folded across his chest, boots crossed at the ankles. His denim jacket emphasized the width of his shoulders and his well-worn jeans hugged his muscular thighs like a second skin. She gulped. He looked like every woman's fantasy—rugged, handsome and thoroughly masculine.

When he saw her, he smiled as he straightened to his full height and opened the passenger door of the shiny pickup. A tiny shiver coursed through her when his hand brushed her breast as he reached to take Timmy.

"You three make a nice little family," the nurse said, watching Morgan cradle the baby with one arm, while he helped Samantha up onto the bench seat with the other. "Have a safe trip home."

"Thanks. We'll do that," he said, handing the baby to Samantha. He closed the door of the truck before she could correct the nurse about them being a family.

"Why didn't you tell her we aren't together?" Samantha demanded when he slid into the driver's seat and turned the key in the ignition.

"It just seemed faster and a whole hell of a lot easier than explaining the situation," he answered, shrugging one shoulder.

She fastened the seat belt over the car seat she'd had him get from her car the day before when he'd brought her and the baby to the hospital to be checked over. "You don't approve of my having a child without a husband, do you?"

"I can't say that I do, or don't," he said, putting the truck into gear. He steered it out onto the street, then glancing at her, added, "Samantha, I don't know the circumstances." His expression turned grim. "But the baby's father should have been here to help you through this."

She watched the easy way Morgan handled the big truck as he navigated the traffic. He was a man in complete control, and one who could be counted on in any situation. Unlike Timmy's father.

Her chest tightened at the thought of the man who'd fathered a child he cared nothing about. How could she have been so wrong about Chad?

When they first started living together, they'd both worked at achieving the true give and take of a successful relationship. But six months later, Samantha suddenly realized that things had changed between them. She'd been the one doing all of the giving and he'd been the one doing the taking. Then one day she'd come home from work to find that he'd moved to L.A. to pursue his dream of becoming a musician. That's when she realized how shallow and uncaring Chad really was. He hadn't even bothered to face her to tell her things were over between them. He'd left a rather impersonal note stuck to the front of the refrigerator, saying that he'd had fun, but that it was time for him to move on.

"There's really not that much to tell," she found herself saying. Why Morgan's opinion mattered, she had no idea. But for some reason she wanted him to know that the choice to handle everything on her own, hadn't been hers. "We weren't married, and I didn't find out I was pregnant until after he and I had parted company."

She watched Morgan's hands tighten on the steering wheel, and she knew what he was thinking before he even asked, "He doesn't know about the baby?"

"Oh, I told him," she said, trying to keep her voice even. She would not allow herself to dwell on how hurt she'd been by Chad's decision. "I didn't ask him for any kind of help when I told him. I just thought he should know he'd fathered a baby, and that he might want to be part of Timmy's life. But he wasn't interested in knowing his child now, or in the future. He offered to sign away all legal rights to Timmy, and I accepted. End of story."

"Why would he do a dumb-ass thing like that?" Morgan asked bluntly. He shot her a scowl that stated quite clearly what he thought of Chad, and she knew beyond a shadow of doubt that it would be the last thing he'd do in the same situation.

Gazing down at her sleeping son, Samantha blinked back the threatening tears. "I suspect he thought it would insure that I'd never ask for any kind of financial help from him."

Morgan snorted. "I think a man who shirks his responsibilities and denies his child should be shot."

Samantha swallowed around the lump in her throat. "I think Timmy and I are better off this way."

"How do you figure that?" Morgan asked, clearly unable to comprehend her reasoning.

"Chad turned out to be very selfish and self-centered," she answered, gently touching her son's soft cheek. She took a deep breath to chase away the sadness she always felt when she thought of all that Timmy would miss by not having a father. "Why would I want a man like that helping me raise my son? It's not the kind of example I want set before Timmy. Besides, he deserves a father who loves him unconditionally, not one who simply views him as a monthly support check."

Morgan was silent for several long moments before he nodded. "I couldn't agree more. But when a man gets a woman pregnant, whether he ever sees the child or not, he has an obligation to help her."

Reaching the outskirts of Laramie, he set the cruise control, then stretched his right arm out along the back of the seat. His fingers brushed her hair and she felt warmed all the way to her toes.

Startled by her reaction, Samantha scooted over to lean against the door. "I have a question," she said, determined to regain her equilibrium.

He glanced her way and smiled. "And that would be?"

His easy expression caused her pulse to skip a beat. She took a deep breath to chase away her accompanying breathlessness. "When you walked into my room back at the hospital, you said everything had been taken care of at the business office. What did you mean?"

"Just that," he said, staring at the road ahead. "The bill is paid."

Samantha felt her stomach start to churn. "Would you like to tell me who paid it?"

"I did."

Anger swept through her. "Why?"

"Call it a baby gift," he said, his smile so darned charming that she had to fight the warmth filling her chest.

She shook her head as she tried desperately to hang on to her anger. "A baby gift is a high chair, a blanket, a set of bibs. It's *not* paying a hospital bill."

His smiled faded and a muscle began to work along his lean jaw. "Look, Samantha. I've got the money, and I don't mind helping out."

"I don't need your help," she said stubbornly. "I'm not a charity case."

He shook his head. "I never said you were."

"How much was the bill?" Reaching into her purse, she removed a pad of paper and a pen. "I'll reimburse you as soon as I find a job."

"No, you won't."

"Yes, I will."

"Dammit, woman." He looked exasperated. "I said no."

"You're used to people doing what you tell them to do, aren't you?" she asked, already knowing the answer.

He shrugged, but remained silent.

"Well, let me treat you to a reality check, cowboy.'' She stuffed the paper and pen back into her handbag. ''I've been on my own since I was eighteen. I make my own decisions and I pay my own way.''

As she glared at Morgan, the baby suddenly opened his eyes, waved his little fists in protest and wailed at the top of his lungs. Their raised voices had startled him.

''Why don't we put this argument on hold until we get home?'' Morgan asked, steering the truck off the main road.

Samantha quieted the baby, then looking around at the scenery, she frowned. Nothing looked familiar and she knew for certain they hadn't traveled this road when Morgan had taken her and Timmy to the hospital the day before.

''Where are we going?'' she asked, noticing the neatly fenced pastures on either side of the road.

''I'm taking you to the Lonetree,'' he said, as if that explained everything.

''Do you need to pick up something before you take me to my place?'' she asked cautiously.

''No.''

A knot of suspicion began to form in the pit of her stomach. ''Then why are we—''

''I thought you and the baby should stay at my ranch for a few days,'' he said, turning onto another road.

She shook her head vehemently. ''I most certainly will not be staying at your ranch.''

''Don't be stubborn about this, Samantha. Your

grandfather's house isn't in any shape for you and the baby to stay there." He made it sound so darned reasonable, she wanted to scream.

But as she thought about what he'd just said, some of her anger drained away. She hated to admit it, but Morgan was right. The house only had a fireplace in the living room for heat, there was no running water and no electricity. Besides all that, the roof leaked.

Frustrated beyond words, Samantha had to fight the sudden urge to cry. It just brought home how low her circumstances had become. For all intents and purposes, she was as homeless as the foster child she'd been after her mother passed away.

Slowing the truck to a stop, Morgan turned to face her. "I understand how much you value your independence, sweetheart. And I swear I'm not trying to take that away from you. But you have to be realistic about this." He reached over the car seat between them to cup her chin in his big palm, sending a wave of goose bumps shimmering over her skin. "Right now, you need help. Please, let me do the neighborly thing and lend a hand."

She caught her lower lip between her teeth to keep it from trembling. Where else was she going to go? She had a newborn to take care of, no place to live and she'd exhausted her bank account to make the move from Sacramento to Wyoming. If it was just her, she'd politely refuse Morgan's offer. But she had to think of what was best for Timmy now.

"I don't have any other choice," she finally said,

blinking back tears. "And I really hate not having options."

"I know, sweetheart. I feel the same way." His understanding smile warmed her to the depths of her soul. "But you'll be on your feet and back in charge of things before you know it."

As she stared into his incredibly blue eyes, Samantha wondered if he'd ever been in a situation that he couldn't control. She doubted it. A man like Morgan was always in complete command of everything going on around him.

Resigned, she took a deep breath. "I'll need to get some things from my car."

He released her chin and turned his attention to the road ahead of them. Shifting the truck into drive, he nodded. "After I got back from taking you and the baby to the hospital yesterday, I had a couple of my ranch hands take one of the tractors and tow your car over here. One of them is a pretty fair mechanic and he's got it down at the machine shed, trying to get it running again."

Before Samantha could tell him to keep track of how much the repairs cost, they topped a hill overlooking a beautiful valley. A sprawling log ranch house, along with several neat-looking barns and outbuildings stood majestically at one end, while a large herd of black cattle grazed at the other.

"Is that your ranch?"

He nodded. "That's the main house. My brother,

Brant, and his wife, Annie, have their home about three miles east of here.''

"How big *is* this place?'' Samantha asked incredulously.

"We've been on Lonetree land ever since we turned off the highway,'' he answered without blinking an eye.

"That was some time ago,'' she said, awed by the idea of such a large piece of property.

He nodded. "About six miles.''

"Well, it certainly is beautiful,'' she said, marveling at the contrast between her newly inherited property and this well-kept ranch. She wondered if she'd ever be able to get hers looking as nice. If she could, she knew for certain she'd be able to find backers for the camp she wanted to open for homeless children.

Morgan didn't say anything, but she could tell by the slight curving at the corners of his mouth that her comment had pleased him.

When they drew closer, he turned the truck onto a lane that led to the house. Tall wooden posts stood on either side of the road, supporting a log spanning the width between them. As they passed beneath it, Samantha caught a fleeting glimpse of the words Lonetree Ranch carved into a wooden sign suspended from the middle of the arch.

He stopped the pickup at the side of the house, then got out and came around to help her from the passenger side. "I had Bettylou, the wife of the man working on your car, come by and make up one of the guest rooms,'' he said, unfastening the lap belt from the baby's carrier. He lifted it from the center of the bench seat, then using the handle, carried it in one hand as he cupped her elbow with the other to guide her up the steps of the front porch. ''After I get you two settled in your room, I'll go down to the machine shed and check to see if Frank knows what's wrong with your car. I'll get your things while I'm at it.''

His big hand warmed her arm through the light jacket she wore and sent a tremor up her spine. She quickly stepped away from him.

''I won't need everything from the car,'' she said, waiting for him to open the door. ''Timmy and I won't be staying more than a couple of days.''

Holding the door for her, he smiled. ''We'll see.''

She needed to make it clear to him, she wasn't a charity case, nor did she intend to take advantage of his generosity. Before she could respond to his obvious disbelief, they entered the foyer of the Lonetree ranch house and she forgot anything she'd been about to say. The interior of the log home was every bit as impressive as the exterior.

When Morgan led her into the great room, her breath caught. ''This is absolutely gorgeous.''

A huge stone fireplace with a split log mantel stood against the outside wall of the room, the rounded blue, gray and tan stones the perfect accent to the golden hue of the varnished log walls. The house had a warm, friendly feel to it, but it was the openness that Samantha fell in love with. The ceiling was vaulted and open all the way to the huge log rafters, and the rooms seemed to flow from one into another.

"Make yourself at home," Morgan said, placing the car seat with her sleeping son on the most unusual coffee table she'd ever seen.

A thick, flat piece of dark blue-gray slate rested on a pedestal base made from a section of an entire tree trunk. The bark had been left on and contrasted beautifully with the warm patina of the polished hardwood floor and the burnt sienna colored leather furniture.

"Were you going for durability?" she asked dryly.

Chuckling, Morgan shrugged. "Brant and I ruined the surface of my mom's other table so many times by running our cars and trucks over it, that Mom and Dad came up with the idea of a slate topped table before Colt was born. Then after Mom died, and Dad was faced with raising three rowdy boys by himself, I don't think he had much choice but to keep it."

"You were raised by your father?"

She noticed a fleeting shadow in his intense blue eyes a moment before he nodded. "Mom died while giving birth to our youngest brother, Colt."

Samantha gazed up at him for several long seconds. "I'm sorry, Morgan. I know what it feels like to lose your mother," she said quietly. "I was almost seventeen when mine passed away."

As they stood staring at each other, the baby suddenly let loose with a lusty cry, breaking the somber mood that had come over the two adults.

"It's time for him to nurse," she said, releasing the straps securing Timmy in the baby seat. "Is there somewhere I could—"

"I'll show you to your room," Morgan said, nodding toward the staircase behind her. The stairs, banister and railings of the loft area above were crafted from the same golden wood as the walls, and added to the rustic appeal of the house.

Samantha held the baby close and tried to concentrate on breathing as she climbed the split-log steps beside Morgan. He'd placed his arm around her waist to steady her and his touch was doing some very strange things to her insides. Tingles raced the length of her spine and a warm, protected feeling seemed to course through her.

Needing to put a little distance between them, she waited for him to lead the way across the loft and down a hall where several bedrooms were located. Her uncharacteristic reaction to him had to be due to a major postnatal hormone imbalance. That's all it could be, she decided. After giving birth two days ago, there was no way she could possibly be feeling any kind of physical awareness. Was there?

When he opened the door to a room at the end of the hall, her eyes misted over. A cradle, made up with soft-looking, baby-blue bedding sat by a beautiful four-poster bed. She couldn't remember a time since her mother's passing that anyone had been as thoughtful as Morgan had been in the past few hours. He'd made sure she and the baby had a ride home from the hospital, offered them a place to stay and had gone to the trouble of arranging for Timmy to have a warm, comfortable place to sleep.

She put her son in the cradle, then turned back to Morgan. Reaching up to place her hand at the back of his neck, she drew his head down to kiss his lean cheek. "You're the most thoughtful man I've ever met," she said, her voice shaking slightly from the emotion welling up inside of her.

Before she could draw away, Morgan pulled her into his arms, then staring down at her for no more than a split second, lowered his mouth to hers and kissed her. It wasn't anything more than his lips pressed to hers, but her knees shook and her head swam. Then, just as quickly, he released her with a muttered curse.

Looking as startled as she felt, he started backing from the room. "I...I'll get your things from the car."

Before she could remind him that she wouldn't be needing everything, he turned on his heel and left the room so fast Samantha wouldn't have been surprised to see that his boots had left skid marks on the polished hardwood floor.

She brought her fingers up to touch her tingling lips. Why had he kissed her? But more important, why did she feel like she wanted him to kiss her again?

Turning to pick up Timmy, she decided that it would definitely be in her best interest to find somewhere else to stay as soon as her car was repaired. Although Morgan Wakefield had shown her more concern and kind consideration than anyone had in longer than she cared to remember, he also represented a temptation that she wasn't ready to deal with and wasn't sure she would ever be able to resist.

Three

His jaw clenched so tightly it would probably take an oral surgeon to pry it apart, Morgan descended the stairs and crossed the great room to the front foyer. Once he stood outside on the porch, he took in several deep breaths in hopes of clearing his head. He couldn't believe what he'd just done.

Samantha had only meant that little peck on the cheek as an expression of gratitude. There hadn't been anything sexual about the gesture.

But his body hadn't seen it that way. When she'd drawn his head down to press her soft lips to his jaw, he'd responded with a fierceness that had almost knocked him to his knees. And, like a damned fool, he'd grabbed her and kissed her like a teenager with more hormones than sense.

At least he'd come to his senses before he had the chance to take the kiss to the next level. He uttered a pithy curse. So why was he regretting that he'd kept it simple?

Grinding his back teeth, he stared at the acres of pasture stretching out in front of him. Like the grass in the fields, his body was just awakening from an extended dormant period. That's all there was to it. The winter had been a long, cold one, and it was only natural that a man would be feeling the effects of not having a woman around to help him stay warm.

He ran a frustrated hand across the back of his neck and swore a blue streak. What he needed was a night in the arms of a willing woman. Then maybe he could forget how Samantha's amber eyes reminded him of long sultry nights, of tangled sheets and soft sighs.

Unfortunately, he had a feeling that it was more than the need for sexual release that caused his reaction to her. And that's what bothered him.

Since his fiancée's death, he hadn't allowed himself to look at another woman for anything more than a few hours of harmless, consensual fun. And that only happened once or twice a year when the loneliness got so bad he thought he'd jump out of his own skin.

The all too familiar ache of guilt and regret settled in his chest as he thought of Emily Swensen. They should have been celebrating their sixth wedding anniversary in a couple of months. Instead, he would be making his annual trip to the cemetery down in Denver to place flowers on her grave.

Gazing down the lane, Morgan thought about the woman he'd promised to marry. Emily had been his best friend, as well as his lover. And she'd be alive today if it wasn't for him.

He took a deep shuddering breath. He'd been so sure that he knew what was best for her when he'd insisted she make that trip to Denver to visit her sister the week before they were to be married. She hadn't wanted to go, but he'd convinced her of how lonely it would be for her while he caught up on spring chores. She'd finally agreed to make the trip, but the day she left she'd had tears running down her cheeks, as if she'd known they would never see each other again.

That was the last time he'd seen her alive. Two days later, he'd received the phone call that still haunted his dreams. Emily had been killed, and her sister seriously wounded, in the cross fire between police and a couple of thugs trying to rob a jewelry store in downtown Denver.

Guilt knotted his gut, the feeling so strong it took his breath. His presumption that he knew what was best had gotten an innocent woman killed, and proven that his judgement was faulty. He'd never run the risk of making another mistake like that again.

He'd come to terms with never having a wife and family, and he'd learned to live with the loneliness, the cold, empty spot beside him in his bed. And that's the way it was going to remain.

In a few days, he'd offer Samantha quite a bit more

for her grandfather's ranch than it was worth, insuring that she wouldn't have any money worries for a while. Then she and her son could move on, and he'd settle back down to his routine of running the Lonetree and making it the best privately owned ranch in the state of Wyoming.

"Hey, boss? You got a minute?"

Morgan turned toward the sound of Frank Milford's voice. He'd been so lost in his disturbing thoughts, he hadn't heard the man's approach.

"What do you need, Frank?" he asked, descending the porch steps.

"I think you'd better get Ned and Chico to haul that hunk of junk down at the machine shed to a scrap yard," the man said, wiping grease from his hands with a rag.

"It's that bad?" Morgan asked as he continued walking toward the shed.

"It ain't worth the powder and lead to blow it up with," Frank said, falling into step beside Morgan.

"What's wrong with it?"

"What ain't?" Frank asked disgustedly.

"You want to cut to the chase and give me a run-down so I'll know what it will take to fix it?" Morgan asked patiently. He was used to Frank's tendency to exaggerate.

Frank shook his head. "When I put a new battery in it and fired 'er up, there was a real wicked knock in the engine. Besides needin' spark plugs, new belts and hoses, I'd say it's getting ready to throw a rod."

"How long would it take to rebuild the motor?" Morgan asked, knowing it would take longer than he was comfortable with.

The sooner Samantha's car was fixed, the sooner she and her son could be on their way with a nice fat check in her pocket. Then maybe he wouldn't feel as if he were outgrowing his jeans every time she looked at him with those whiskey-brown eyes of hers.

"It'll probably take a couple of weeks," Frank said. "Maybe longer." He followed Morgan into the building they used to repair and maintain the ranching equipment. "Ford doesn't make that model anymore. Hell, I'm not even sure we can still get parts for it."

A relieved feeling swept through Morgan, quickly followed by a knot twisting at his gut. He had a feeling that Samantha would be staying a lot longer than either of them had anticipated. What bothered him was how much the idea appealed to him.

Shaking his head, he decided that a psychologist would have a field day with that one. "Go ahead and make a few calls to see what you can come up with, Frank."

"You're the boss," the man said, tossing the greasy rag onto a workbench. "But if it was me, I'd cut my losses and find another set of wheels."

As Frank walked over to the phone to start calling auto parts stores down in Laramie, Morgan opened the driver's door of Samantha's car to grab the keys from the ignition. Opening the trunk, he pulled out a couple of battered pieces of luggage, and a sack filled with what looked like baby items.

Tucking the sack under his arm, he picked up a suitcase in each hand and started for the house. Samantha wasn't going to be happy about the turn of events. For one thing, she clearly couldn't afford to have the car repaired. And for another, her stay at the Lonetree had just been extended for an indefinite period of time.

The relief he'd felt earlier increased, causing Morgan to utter a cuss word he reserved for the most serious of situations. The long, cold winter must have been longer and colder than he'd realized. He wanted a woman and baby underfoot—reminding him of the family he'd never have—about as much as he wanted to see the cattle market take a nosedive.

"Are you sure it's that serious?" Samantha asked. "When I left Sacramento, it was fine." She frowned. "Except for a clunking sound when the motor was running."

Morgan swallowed the bite of sandwich he'd been chewing and nodded. "It's not a matter of *if* the engine breaks down, it's more like *when.* It might last for another few hundred miles, or it could blow a rod before you got it backed out of the machine shed."

"I can't afford this right now." She placed her sandwich back on her plate untouched. Only moments ago, the roast beef and cheddar melt had looked delicious. But with Morgan's news about her car, Samantha's appetite deserted her.

"Don't worry about it." He took a drink of his iced tea, then shrugged. "It's taken—"

"Don't you dare," she warned.

"What?"

"You know what." She shook her head. "This is my problem and I'll solve it. You took care of the hospital bill before I could stop you. But you will *not* pay for the repairs on my car."

He gave her an exasperated look. "I've already got Frank calling auto parts stores."

"Then you can tell him to stop," she said stubbornly. "I'll just have to take my chances and hope the engine will make it until I'm able to afford to have it repaired."

"Don't be ridiculous, Samantha." His intense blue gaze caught and held hers. "What if you're out on the road with the baby and it breaks down? You can't walk miles for help with an infant, nor can you wait for someone to come along and find you." He shook his head. "This isn't a highly populated area. Out here, there are times when it's hours before another car comes by."

Her heart sank. Morgan was right. She couldn't run the risk of being out with Timmy in an unreliable car.

She took a deep breath and had to force herself to admit defeat. "All right. Have the car repaired. But only on one condition." When he cocked a dark brow, she added, "You have to let me know every penny you spend on it, so that I can reimburse you."

"I'm not worried about—"

"I am," she interrupted. She had to make him understand. "After my father left us without a backward glance, I watched my mother struggle to keep a roof over our heads and food in our mouths. It wasn't easy for her, but she did it without waiting for a man to come to the rescue. I fully intend to do the same." Rising from the table, she wrapped her sandwich and placed it in the refrigerator. "I don't ever intend to rely on anyone for what I want or need. I'll work for it and earn it, or I'll do without."

He looked as if he were about to protest, but Samantha held up her hand to stop him. "I know you mean well, but this is something I feel very strongly about. It's no secret, I've hit a low spot in my life. But it's only temporary. As soon as the doctor releases me to work, I'll get a job and pay you back." She started to leave the kitchen, but a sudden thought had her turning back. "Do you have a housekeeper or cook?"

In the middle of taking a long swig of his iced tea, he slowly placed the glass on the table and shook his head. "No. I usually take my meals down at the bunkhouse with the rest of the guys. And when I need something done to the house, my sister-in-law, Annie, takes care of it, or I pay Bettylou. Why?"

Samantha nodded. "Until my car is repaired and I find a job to pay you back, you won't be needing their help. I'll be cooking your meals and cleaning your house.''

Morgan's eyes narrowed as he watched her turn and slowly walk from the room, shoulders straight, her head held high. He'd always admired those who had the grit to work and make their own way. But Samantha was taking this pride thing to the extreme. He could tell by the way she moved that she was still sore from giving birth, yet she was telling him that she was going to start cooking and cleaning for him?

"Like hell," he muttered.

Scooting his chair back from the table, he rinsed his plate and glass, then placed them in the dishwasher and headed for his study. He had the perfect solution to resolve the money issue that she seemed to think was so important.

She owned the run-down ranch that he wanted to buy. What could be more simple than him offering to buy it from her? He would end up with the land he wanted, and she'd have the cash to get on her feet and start a new, more secure life for herself and her son.

Morgan ignored the twinge in his gut at the thought of Samantha leaving as he dialed his attorney and made arrangements for the man to draw up a purchase option. Assured that the document would be delivered within the next week or two, he climbed the stairs and walked down the hall to Samantha's door. The sound of the baby crying immediately caught his attention.

"Samantha?" he called, tapping on the door.

Nothing.

Opening it a crack, he tried again. "Samantha, I'd like to talk to you—"

The sound of the shower running explained why she wasn't tending to the baby. He glanced from the closed door of the adjoining bathroom to the cradle where Timmy continued to wail at the top of his little lungs. Now what? Samantha was taking a shower and Timmy sounded as if he was gearing up for a real rip-snorter of a fit.

Morgan walked over to the tiny bed to rock it back and forth, hoping to quiet the baby until Samantha finished her shower. "Shhh, little guy. Your mom will be here in just a minute."

If anything the baby cried harder.

Deciding he didn't have a choice, Morgan held his breath and gingerly picked up the infant. The only other times in his life that he'd held a baby had been when he'd helped Samantha give birth, then just a few hours ago when he'd brought her and Timmy home from the hospital. Now what was he supposed to do?

"They should issue 'how-to' manuals on this stuff," he muttered, feeling like a fish out of water.

He mentally reviewed how he'd seen Samantha hold little Timmy when he'd started crying earlier. The baby seemed to be quiet whenever she held him to her shoulder. Maybe that was his favorite position.

Morgan put the infant to his shoulder and rubbed

the little guy's back like he'd seen Samantha do. Timmy instantly stopped crying and let loose with a burp that Morgan was sure rattled his tiny rib cage.

He couldn't help it, Morgan laughed out loud. "I'll bet you feel better now, don't you?" He felt something wet seep through his shirt, and glancing at his shoulder, cringed. "I guess you had a little too much for lunch, huh?"

"What's wrong?" Samantha asked as she came out of the bathroom and hurried over to him. She took the baby, then gasped. "Oh, my. Your shirt." She placed the now quiet baby back in the cradle and grabbed a box of moist towelettes from the dresser. "I'm so sorry."

Morgan swallowed hard and shifted from one foot to the other as Samantha leaned close to wipe the spot from his shirt. Her nearness was doing a hell of a number on his insides. She smelled like lilacs and sweet woman, and her warm breath whispering over the exposed skin at the open vee of his shirt had his heart pounding so hard, he figured she could feel it beneath her fingers.

As he stared down at her, he took note of several things. Her hair was wrapped in a towel on top of her head, exposing the delicate skin of her slender neck. The long thick lashes framing her pretty eyes looked all dewy from her shower.

But the most noticeable, and most disturbing thing about her, was the way the top of her fluffy yellow robe gapped open. It gave him more than a fair view of the slope of her breasts, and the realization that she probably didn't have a stitch on beneath that robe sent blood rushing through his veins and made his jeans feel like they were way too short in the stride.

Quickly backing away from her before he did something stupid, like grab her and kiss her again, he headed for the door. "When you have time, I'd like to talk to you downstairs," he said as he stepped out into the hall. He quickly reached back to pull the door shut. "I'll be in my office."

Samantha stared at the closed door for several long seconds before she finally released the breath she hadn't been aware of holding. The earthy scents of leather, sunshine and virile male had her pulse racing and goose bumps skipping over her skin.

But it had been the feel of Morgan's pectoral muscles beneath her fingers that made her knees feel rubbery and had her catching her breath. The man was built as solid as a rock and she wondered how it would feel to be held against all that sinew, to be wrapped in arms so strong they could easily crush her, yet were gentle enough to hold a baby.

"Stop it," she chided herself.

She plopped the box of baby wipes back on the dresser, then reached up to jerk the towel from her wet hair. Her crazy postnatal hormones had to be the reason for her uncharacteristic behavior. That's all it could be. She wasn't interested in Morgan Wakefield or any other man.

Satisfied that she'd discovered the reason for her strong reaction to him, she dried her hair and traded her robe for a pink cotton, dropped-waist dress that buttoned up the front. Checking on Timmy, sleeping peacefully in the cradle, she turned on one of the baby monitors Morgan had brought in from the trunk of her car, then picking up the listening unit, walked out into the hall.

As she descended the stairs, she wondered what Morgan could possibly want to discuss with her. She'd made it quite clear that she intended to earn her and Timmy's keep while they stayed here, and if he thought he was going to talk her out of it, he had another think coming.

Determined to set Mr. Morgan Wakefield straight, she crossed the great room and front foyer to tap on the frame of the open office door. He held a cordless phone to his ear with one shoulder as he shuffled through several papers lying on top of his desk.

"Is this a bad time?" she whispered.

Shaking his head, he motioned for her to enter the room and sit in one of the two comfortable-looking leather armchairs in front of the shiny walnut desk. "I'll check the breeding records for those two mares and get back with you on that, Brant." Morgan ended the call, then smiling, turned his attention to her. "I think I've come up with a solution to your money worries."

She settled back in one of the chairs across from him and tried not to think about how attractive he looked. Morgan had the nicest smile, and she had a feeling if he set his mind to it, he could charm the birds out of the trees. Fortunately for her, she didn't have feathers.

"You've found a job for me, other than cooking and cleaning?" she asked carefully.

His grin widened as he shook his head. "No."

His gaze held hers, causing her heart to skip a beat and making her feel like a night creature caught in the headlights of an oncoming car. She glanced to the bookshelves beyond his shoulder in order to keep from drowning in the depths of his intense blue eyes.

"What do you have in mind, if it's not a job?"

"Since discovering that your grandfather's place isn't in any shape for you to take up residence, you could sell the land," he said, making it sound extremely simple.

Smiling, she shook her head. "No. That's not an option."

His grin faded and he looked as if it had been the last thing he expected her to say. "Why not?"

"I have plans for that property."

"You do?" He looked extremely interested in what she had planned. It made her feel a little more confident.

Samantha glanced down at her hands resting in her lap as she tried to put her dream into words. "I never got to meet my grandfather because he and my mother didn't get along. He didn't approve of her choice of men, and my mother was too stubborn to admit that he'd been right about my father. To my knowledge he never even knew about me, any more than I knew that he existed." Taking a deep breath to chase away the sadness she always felt when she thought of her father, she raised her gaze to meet Morgan's. "When Daddy left us, my mother refused to come back here and admit that she'd made a mistake. Now she's gone, I haven't seen my father since I was four years old, and I have no brothers or sisters. I know it doesn't make a lot of sense, but that property is all I have that ties me to any kind of family and makes me feel like I belong."

The last thing Morgan expected was for Samantha to have any kind of sentimental attachment to a place that she hadn't even known existed until a few weeks ago. But what was even more baffling about it was that he understood how she felt. The Lonetree was as much a part of him as the blood running through his veins.

"Are you going to try to fix up the house?" he finally managed to ask. He knew full well that she didn't have the funds to do much more than tack a piece of plastic over the holes in the roof.

Nodding, her eyes lit with enthusiasm. "I not only intend to live there, I'm going to open a summer retreat for homeless and abandoned children. I know it will take a while to get things the way I'd like, and I'll probably have to get a job to support myself while I look for financial help to get the camp started, but I'm hoping to have it ready to open next year."

"What kind of job did you have before you left California?" he asked, already anticipating her answer.

"I was a social worker for the county until government cutbacks forced the elimination of several jobs, including mine. It was my responsibility to place abandoned and orphaned children, either with relatives or in foster care." Her pretty face softened as she explained, and Morgan could tell this was something very close to her heart. "I want to continue helping children, who, for whatever reason, find themselves separated from their families. I want to make a place where they can forget, if only for a week or two, the reasons they aren't with their parents."

Morgan didn't know what to say. Her reasons for wanting to hang on to the place were a hell of a lot more noble than what he wanted to do with the property. Helping kids beat raising bucking horses for the rodeo circuit, hands down. He suddenly felt guilty as hell at even suggesting she sell the property.

"Were you put into foster care after your mother died?" he asked, beginning to understand her desire to help children she didn't know.

He watched sadness fill her eyes as she nodded. "When my mother died, I was just like these children. I suddenly found that I no longer had a place where I belonged."

The thought that she'd been alone at such a young age with no one to turn to, tied his stomach in knots. He'd had his brothers when they lost their dad. But

Samantha had been completely alone. He had to fight the urge to round the desk and take her into his arms.

"Were you placed with a good family?" he asked, needing to know that she'd had someone to take care of her.

To his relief, she nodded. "Since I was almost seventeen, I wasn't in the system much over a year. I was fortunate enough to be taken in by a very kind, older couple. They treated me like a granddaughter and I will always be grateful for that. But some children aren't as lucky as I was. Some are taken care of, but not cared for. There's a difference."

"What will you do until you get the camp started?" he asked, mentally reviewing who he knew in county government who might be able to help her get on as a case worker with social services.

"Now that I have Timmy, I'd like to find something that I could do at home, or only be away from him a minimal amount of time."

Morgan could understand her desire to be with the baby. He didn't like the idea of her being away from the little guy either.

His heart slammed into his rib cage. Where had that come from? Why should he care? Timmy wasn't his child.

But whether the baby belonged to him or not, Morgan felt a responsibility toward Samantha and her little boy that defied logic or reason. And it scared him spitless.

Between the sudden urge to help her find a way to

keep the ranch he'd wanted to buy for as long as he could remember, and the protective feelings that were building inside of him at an alarming rate, Morgan suddenly felt as if he couldn't breathe.

Rising from his chair, he grabbed his Resistol, jammed it on his head and rounded the desk. "I...uh, just remembered something I need to do," he said, knowing his excuse sounded as lame as it was. "If you want me for anything, call Frank down at the machine shed. He'll know where to find me."

She rose to follow him. "Do you mind if I look around the kitchen to see what I can make for dinner?"

He turned back to stare at her. She looked so damned pretty standing there gazing up at him that it took every ounce of willpower he possessed to keep from pulling her to him.

Slowly shaking his head, he warned, "Just don't overdo things. You got that?"

She gave him a smile that just about knocked his boots off. "Will do, boss."

"I'm not—" he took a step forward and reached out to cup her soft cheek in his palm "—your boss, sweetheart."

Her easy expression turned into one of awareness, then staunch determination. "You are until Timmy and I leave here."

He shook his head. "No—" he leaned forward to brush his lips over hers "—I'm not."

Turning, he walked from the room, out the front

door and headed for the barn. If he hadn't walked away when he did, he'd have ended up taking her into his arms and kissing her until they both needed CPR.

As he entered the barn he decided checking the fence in the north pasture wasn't a bad idea. He could ride for hours with nothing more to do than try to figure out what the hell had gotten into him, and what he had to do to keep from getting in deeper than he already was.

Saddling his favorite gelding, he led the sorrel out of the barn, then swung up into the saddle. It didn't make a damned bit of sense. He'd only known Samantha for three days.

But with each passing minute, the need to help her and her tiny son became stronger. And every time he looked into her pretty amber eyes, it sure as hell felt like he was about to drown.

Four

After Morgan left, it took Samantha several minutes to bring her pulse back under control. What in the name of heaven was wrong with her? She wasn't interested in Morgan Wakefield or any other man. Between her father and Chad, she'd learned a valuable lesson. Men couldn't be counted on for anything, and only ended up letting a woman down in one way or another.

She'd had quite enough of that, thank you very much. She certainly didn't need to set herself up for more.

The best way to avoid being disappointed by a man was not to become involved with one to begin with. Period. As long as she kept that in mind, she'd be just fine.

With a determined nod, she headed for the kitchen. She'd told Morgan that she intended to cook and clean for him to pay for her and Timmy's keep. Until she gained her full strength back, she'd have to watch what she did. But as long as she didn't do anything too strenuous, and took frequent breaks, the activity would be good for her.

Setting the baby monitor on the counter, she found some paper and a pen to jot down things she'd need from the store, and started taking inventory of what Morgan had on hand. Two hours later, her grocery list filled three full sheets of paper and had her shaking her head. Besides some packages of beef in the freezer, there really wasn't a whole lot to work with.

"Samantha?"

At the unexpected sound of the female voice calling her name, Samantha jumped. Walking out of the pantry, she watched a petite blond-haired woman use the heel of her boot to shut the back door behind her, then hurry over to set two paper grocery bags on the counter.

When the woman turned to face Samantha, her smile was warm and friendly. "I'm Annie Wakefield. I'm married to Morgan's brother, Brant."

"It's nice to meet you, Annie." She smiled and motioned to the list she held. "I was just taking stock of what I could make for dinner."

Annie laughed. "I'm afraid the Wakefield men are rather limited when it comes to their diet. If it didn't moo before it went to the packing house, they don't eat it.''

"I've noticed," Samantha said, grinning. "I've found several steaks and a couple of roasts in the freezer, but that's about it.''

"That's why I brought over a few staples," Annie said, motioning to the bags on the counter. "While he was out riding fence, Morgan stopped by our place and mentioned that he had a guest. I know from past experience how empty that pantry is, so I gathered some things and headed this way.''

Samantha nodded. "I was beginning to wonder what I was going to do with frozen beef, half a loaf of stale bread and a jar of grape jelly.''

Annie frowned as she pulled items from the two sacks. "It's worse than usual. What did you have for dinner?''

Confused, Samantha shook her head. "We haven't had dinner yet.''

"I meant lunch." Annie grinned. "The first thing I learned when I married Brant was that dinner is the noon meal, supper is the evening meal and the word lunch isn't part of the Wakefield vocabulary.''

"I'll have to remember that," Samantha said, liking Annie Wakefield more with each passing second. "Morgan had one of the men bring a couple of sandwiches up from the bunkhouse for lun…I mean dinner, but—''

"Don't tell me he fed you one of Leon's roast beef

and cheddar melts,'' Annie interrupted. She made a face. ''They're horrible.''

Samantha shook her head. ''I lost my appetite after learning my car is in need of major work. I put my sandwich in the refrigerator.''

''Believe me, you don't want to go there.'' Wrinkling her nose, Annie opened the refrigerator door, plucked the wrapped sandwich from the shelf and tossed it in the trash. She placed a half gallon of milk, a tub of margarine and a package of cheese inside, then closed the door. ''Leon means well, but he thinks everything he makes has to be smothered in hot sauce and horseradish.''

Samantha shuddered at the thought of the indigestion she and Timmy would both have suffered from all that spice. ''I'm glad I didn't try it. It wouldn't have been good for my baby.''

Annie gave her an understanding smile. ''Morgan told us what happened. Are you both doing all right? Is there anything I can do to help?''

The woman's compassion touched Samantha deeply. Before coming to Wyoming, she couldn't remember the last time anyone cared if she was all right, or if she needed help.

''We're fine,'' she said, blinking back tears. She'd no sooner gotten the words out than Timmy's lusty cry came through the speaker of the baby monitor. Laughing shakily, she added, ''Well, we will be as soon as he nurses.''

"Then you'd better not keep him waiting," Annie said, smiling back at her.

"I'll be back down as soon as he's finished," Samantha said, picking up the monitoring unit. "Thank you for being so thoughtful. I truly appreciate it."

"I have to admit to having an ulterior motive," Annie said, smiling. "I want to spend some time around your baby to see what I'm getting myself into."

"You're pregnant?"

When she nodded, Annie looked absolutely radiant. "I used one of the early home tests this morning."

"That's wonderful," Samantha said, reaching out to hug her new friend. She grinned. "When I come back downstairs, I'll bring Timmy so you get the full treatment."

"That buckskin and the bay stud would throw a nice colt," Morgan said, pointing across the feed lot to the mare chewing on a mouthful of grain.

His brother, Brant, nodded. "That's what I've been thinking. With those bloodlines, it should buck hard enough to rattle a few brains, too."

Morgan grinned. "Speaking of rattled brains, how did our little brother do this past weekend in Grand Rapids?"

"Colt rode all three of his bulls, but Mitch Simpson won the event," Brant answered. A rodeo bullfighter, Brant worked most of the Professional Bull Riders events that their younger brother competed in. "Colt ended up with a nice hefty check for his efforts, though.''

''Good. Maybe he'll pay me the fifty bucks he owes me,'' Morgan said, turning to walk toward the house.

''What did you two bet on this time?'' Brant asked, falling into step beside Morgan.

''Baseball. He said the Rockies would sweep the four-game series against the Cardinals. I said they wouldn't.'' Morgan grinned. ''He didn't know that the Cardinals took their star pitcher off the disabled list last week. I did.''

Brant laughed. ''Well, you'll have to wait a couple of weeks for him to pay up. Colt went home with Mitch this weekend to help put up a fence.''

''Every time we stretch fence around here, he's as scarce as hen's teeth,'' Morgan said, frowning.

He could understand his youngest brother's desire to help his best friend. Since Mitch and his sister Kaylee lost their parents in a car accident three years ago, Mitch had his hands full keeping the family ranch going, as well as competing at the top level of the Professional Bull Riders organization. But Colt needed to remember there was work to be done around the Lonetree, too.

''The scenery is nicer on Mitch's ranch than it is here,'' Brant said, his grin meaningful.

''Kaylee?'' When Brant nodded, Morgan shook his head. ''How long do you think it will take before the two of them wake up and smell the coffee?''

Brant shrugged. "Who knows? You know how stubborn our baby brother is."

Morgan laughed as they walked across the yard. "About as stubborn as you were when you met Annie."

"Hey, I finally came to my senses and saw the light." His smile fading, Brant asked, "Do you think Tug's granddaughter is really serious about starting a camp for foster kids? Or do you think she'll eventually give up and sell out?"

Morgan shook his head. "I don't know. She doesn't really have the money to do anything, but she's determined enough not to let that stop her."

"You know, we don't really need the land," Brant said thoughtfully.

"Nope." Morgan shrugged. "It would be nice not to have that two hundred acre chunk out of the middle of the Lonetree's western boundary, but it's been that way for the last seventy-five years."

Brant grinned. "So what's another seventy-five? Right?"

"Right," Morgan agreed, returning his brother's easy expression.

As soon as they entered the house, the unfamiliar sight of two women working side by side in his kitchen stopped Morgan short. He was used to seeing his sister-in-law, Annie, make an occasional meal for all of them during calving season or fall roundup. But seeing Samantha with a smear of flour on her chin and her cheeks flushed from the heat of the oven, reminded Morgan of everything he'd wanted, but never hoped to have—a wife, a family and a home filled with love and laughter.

He watched Brant walk up behind Annie, wrap his arms around her waist and kiss her like a soldier returning from war. Remembering the feel of Samantha's soft lips beneath his, Morgan swallowed hard. Why was he having to fight the urge to keep from doing the same thing to her?

Hells bells, what was wrong with him? He really didn't even know the woman.

As he watched Annie laughingly introduce Brant to Samantha, Morgan mentally calculated when he could take time off from the ranch for a drive down to Bear Creek. No doubt about it. He needed to make that trip to Buffalo Gals for a night of good old-fashioned hell-raising. And damned quick. Otherwise, he was going to be as crazy as a loon and climbing the walls by the end of the week.

The baby, sitting in his carrier on top of the table, suddenly let loose with a wail, gaining everyone's attention.

"He probably needs burping again," Samantha said, grabbing a towel to wipe her hands.

"I'll take care of it," Morgan said, clearly surprising Annie and Brant. He ignored their questioning looks as he gazed down at the baby. "You and I have a little experience in this area, don't we?"

Samantha grinned. "Don't forget to place the end of the receiving blanket over your shoulder."

He couldn't help it, he grinned right back. "Good idea. I've only got a couple of clean shirts left." He ignored his brother's gaping expression, carefully lifted Timmy from the carrier and held him to his shoulder. "Come on, little guy. We'll walk around a little and see if that helps." Turning back to Samantha, he warned, "Don't overdo things. If you get tired, sit down and put your feet up."

Morgan caught the questioning looks exchanged between Brant and Annie, and he wasn't a bit surprised when his brother followed him down the hall to the great room.

"Uh, bro, you want to let me in on what's going on?" Brant asked, his smile irritating enough to make Morgan want to bite nails in two.

"There's nothing going on," Morgan answered as he gently patted Timmy's back. "Samantha and Annie are both busy, and the baby needs a little attention. I'm just helping out."

Brant snorted. "Yeah, right. To my knowledge, you've never held a baby before in your life." He pointed to Timmy. "But you sure as hell look like you know what you're doing with this one."

"If you'll remember, I had a crash course in babies a few nights ago," Morgan said, continuing to rub the baby's tiny back. When Timmy burped loudly, Morgan chuckled. "That feels better, doesn't it?"

Brant shook his head in obvious wonderment. "How did you know what to do?"

"I didn't." Morgan transferred the now content

baby to the cradle of his arm. "But earlier this afternoon Samantha was busy and…" He stopped to eye his brother suspiciously. "Would *you* like to tell me why you're so interested?"

Brant hesitated before shaking his head. "Just curious."

Morgan wasn't buying it for a minute. Brant looked like the cat that swallowed the canary. "Is Annie—"

"In due time, big brother," Brant said, turning to walk back into the kitchen. "In due time."

Watching Brant saunter from the room, Morgan figured he knew what his brother was trying to keep from saying—probably under threat of bodily harm from Annie. Morgan grinned. Unless he missed his guess, he was going to be an uncle around the first part of next year, and Annie had plans of making the grand announcement during supper.

Happiness for his brother and sister-in-law filled him, followed quickly by a shaft of deep longing. Morgan had always wanted a family, but he'd have to be content with being the favorite uncle. His thinking that he knew what was best for those he cared for had already cost one life, and he couldn't take the chance of making a wrong decision for anyone else.

He gazed down at the baby in his arms. Raising a child and all the decisions it entailed was an awesome responsibility, and one that he wasn't sure he'd ever trust himself to take on. What if his judgement proved faulty a second time?

No. He never wanted to take that chance again. If

he did and something happened, he'd never be able to live with himself.

"Morgan, is everything all right?" Samantha asked as she walked into the room.

"Couldn't be better," he lied.

"You look rather…grim," she said, placing her hand on his.

A jolt of electric current immediately streaked up his arm at the contact, and he suddenly felt the need to run like hell. The mother of the baby he held was far more temptation than anything he'd had to deal with in the past six years. She was soft, sensual and represented everything he couldn't trust himself to have.

"Here," he said, handing Timmy to her. "I'll be in for supper in a few minutes. I have…a couple of things I need to do before we eat."

Knowing she was staring at him like he'd grown another head, he turned and walked straight to his office. Once inside, he closed the door and walked over to stare out the window at the shadows of evening creeping over the mountains in the distance.

He wasn't at all comfortable with his attraction to Samantha Peterson. But until her car was repaired, he'd be seeing her every time he turned around.

As he watched the cattle grazing in the distance, he came to a decision. There was enough work to do around the Lonetree each day to keep him busy from daylight until well past dark. Until Samantha's car was fixed, and she and her tiny son moved on, he'd work until he dropped if need be. But he was going to keep his distance and contact with her to a bare minimum.

He had to. It was the only way he had a prayer of a chance of keeping what little scrap of sanity he had left.

"I really enjoyed the evening," Samantha said as Annie and Brant prepared to leave.

Annie hugged her. "I did, too. Remember, if you need anything at all, don't hesitate to give me a call." She stepped back and grinned. "And especially if you need someone to baby-sit Timmy."

"I'll do that," Samantha said, smiling.

After Annie's announcement at dinner that she and Brant were expecting, the couple spent the rest of the evening asking questions about pregnancy, birth and the care of an infant. Morgan had remained extremely quiet during the conversation, but not knowing him well, Samantha wasn't sure if that was unusual or not.

"I'll bring that bay stud over tomorrow to meet his new girlfriend," Brant said, putting his arm around Annie as they walked to the door.

"I'm sure Stormy Gal will be happy to see him," Morgan answered, displaying the first genuine smile Samantha had seen from him since before dinner.

Once Brant and Annie left, Samantha returned to the great room to straighten up before she took Timmy upstairs. Now that she and Morgan were alone, she felt a bit awkward. The situation seemed so…domestic.

"I enjoyed meeting your brother and sister-in-law," she said as she straightened the colorful Native American blanket on the back of the leather couch. "You have a very nice family."

"Annie's always nice," Morgan said, walking over to the fireplace to bank the fire. When he turned back to face her, he grinned. "And Brant was on his best behavior."

Samantha could tell that Morgan was very close to his family, and she had to fight the wave of envy threatening to swamp her. She'd always wanted a brother or sister—someone to be close to, someone she could share memories with.

"I'm pretty tired," she said, suddenly feeling more alone than she'd ever felt in her entire life. Being around the Wakefields reminded her of everything she'd never had—siblings who loved and cared for her. "I think Timmy and I are going to turn in now."

Making sure the baby was securely strapped in, she started to take hold of the carrier, but Morgan was suddenly at her side, his big hand wrapping around the handle. "I don't think you should be lifting this thing just yet," he said, gruffly. "It's pretty heavy, even without the baby in it, and you've overdone things today."

"Not really." Her protest would have been a lot more effective if she hadn't had to hide a huge yawn behind her hand.

"Yeah, sure," he said, easily lifting the carrier in one hand as he placed his other hand at the small of her back. "And a donkey can fly."

"You know, I think I saw one soaring over the barn when we arrived today," she said, laughing nervously. The warmth where his hand touched her back was doing strange things to her insides.

He shook his head as he guided her to the stairs. "Nice try, but I'm not buying it. You were on your feet more than you should have been today."

"Oh, really? The other night you told me you weren't a doctor."

As soon as the words were out, she felt her cheeks heat with embarrassment. Her reference to the night Timmy was born reminded her of what had taken place and that Morgan had seen most of her secrets.

But that wasn't the issue here. She wasn't about to admit that he was probably right—that she had come close to overdoing things her first day out of the hospital. "Did you receive a medical degree in the past two days that I'm not aware of?"

"Nope. But I read the rest of that book."

Her cheeks got warmer. "When?"

"After you fell asleep the night Timmy was born," he said, opening the door to her room. He waited for her to walk in ahead of him before following her. Placing the baby carrier in the middle of the double bed, he turned to leave. "Just remember to take it easier tomorrow than you did today."

Reaching out to stop him, she placed her hand on his shoulder. "Morgan?"

She needed to thank him for all that he'd done for her and the baby in the past few days. She'd told him that he was thoughtful, but she hadn't really expressed her appreciation.

When he faced her, she started to tell him how much his generosity meant to her, but the look in his incredible blue eyes took her breath. If she didn't know better, she'd think it was desire. But that was ridiculous, she thought a moment before he reached out to pull her to him.

"Samantha," was all he said as he brought his hands up to thread his fingers through her shoulder-length hair.

Fascinated by the sound of his deep baritone saying her name, she watched him slowly lower his head. Her eyes drifted shut the second their mouths met and she brought her hands up to his chest to brace herself.

Unlike this afternoon when he'd lightly brushed her lips with his, he fused their mouths together in a kiss that seared her all the way to her very soul. He traced the seam of her mouth with his tongue, asking for her acceptance, seeking her permission to explore the sensitive recesses within.

Without a thought of denying him what he sought, she parted her lips and he slipped inside to tease and taste, to explore and entice. He moved his hands to her waist to draw her more fully against him, and Samantha felt as if his big body surrounded hers.

Without a thought to the insanity that seemed to have them both in its grip, she found herself leaning into his strength, melting against the solid wall of his chest.

But as his tongue stroked and encouraged her to reciprocate in kind, the sound of her son awakening to nurse helped to lift the sensual fog enveloping them.

Morgan was the first to move. Lifting his mouth from hers, he quickly stepped back to gaze down at her, his frown formidable. "Dammit, Samantha, I didn't mean for that to happen. I'm sorry."

Doing her best to gather her scattered thoughts, she straightened her shoulders and said the first thing that came to mind. "I'm not."

Dear heavens, what had gotten into her? Had she really said that?

"I mean…that is…"

Her cheeks felt as if they were on fire. What could she say after a blunt admission like that?

But what was more disconcerting than her outspokenness was the fact that she'd really meant it. She wasn't sorry. And that bothered her more than anything else.

His expression softened ever so slightly. "It doesn't matter, Samantha. I'm a thirty-four-year-old man, not a teenage boy with little or no control." He lifted his hand as if he intended to touch her cheek, then quickly dropped it to his side. "Starting tomorrow, you probably won't see me around much. Spring is one of the busiest times of the year on a ranch and there are a lot of things that need my attention. If you want or need something, call the barn or the machine shed and one of my men will see that I get the message.''

Then, without a backward glance, he turned and walked from the room.

Samantha stared at the closed door. Why did she suddenly feel like she'd been abandoned again? And why on earth did the knowledge that Morgan Wakefield clearly didn't want anything to do with her make her feel like she was about to break down and cry?

She shook her head and tried to dispel the all too familiar feeling. She was used to men abandoning her. At the tender age of four, her father had found another woman and walked out on her and her mother as if they'd never mattered to him. Then years later, when social services contacted him after her mother's death, he'd turned his back on her again and refused to take her in.

Picking up Timmy, she sniffed back her tears. But the most devastating abandonment of all had been Chad's response to the knowledge that he was going to be a father. It was one thing for him to cast her aside, but it was an entirely different matter for him to reject their child.

But that didn't explain her reaction to Morgan's dismissal of her. They barely knew each other, and besides, she wasn't interested in him or any other man. Men weren't reliable and couldn't be counted on to be there for a woman when she needed them most.

"These feelings I'm having for Morgan have got to be hormonal," she said aloud. Turning to pick up Timmy, she shook her head. "I'll be glad when this dumb postnatal stuff is over with and I get back on track."

Five

As Morgan left the barn and slowly walked toward the house, he stared up at the starless night sky. Every night for the past month, he'd waited until Samantha had gone to bed before calling it a day. And every morning he'd hauled his sorry butt out of bed and left the house before she came downstairs. He had seen her a few times, but with the exception of Sunday dinners and a handful of visits from Brant and Annie, he'd managed to keep his distance.

But instead of lessening the itch that started the minute he first laid eyes on her, it only seemed to aggravate it. He shook his head at his foolishness. He'd even abandoned the idea of driving down to Buffalo Gals to find a willing little filly for a night of fun and games. Something told him that he'd only end up feeling like he'd betrayed Samantha. Which was completely ridiculous. Hell, they barely knew each other.

"You're seriously screwed up, Wakefield," he muttered as he climbed the back porch steps.

Opening the door, he walked into the dimly lit kitchen and stopped short. Samantha had left the light on over the sink for him, as she always did. But instead of being upstairs in bed, she sat at the table with plans for her camp spread out, and her head pillowed on her folded arms. She was sound asleep.

He swallowed hard. She looked so damned sweet it was all he could do to keep from walking over and gathering her to him. Instead, he squatted down beside her chair to gently touch her shoulder.

"Samantha?"

"Mmm."

"Don't you think it would be more comfortable sleeping upstairs in bed?"

Her long, dark lashes fluttered a moment before she opened her eyes. The slumberous look of her amber gaze sent a shaft of longing right to his core.

He swallowed hard. This was how she'd look waking up beside him after a night of—

"I was waiting for you," she said, sitting up. She pushed her golden-brown hair back. "I need to talk to you about something."

Glancing at his watch, guilt twisted his gut that he'd kept her waiting. She'd have to get up early with the baby tomorrow morning and it was almost midnight now.

"What did you need?" he asked, using his index finger to brush a strand of hair from her porcelain cheek.

"Frank said they've back-ordered that part for my car again," she said, her voice flowing over him like a piece of soft velvet. "And I need to drive down to Laramie in the morning." She looked uncertain. "I wouldn't ask unless it was really important, but would you mind if I borrowed one of your trucks?"

Her expression told him that something was up, and that it had her worried. "Is something wrong? Do you or Timmy need to see a doctor?"

"No. We're both fine. Annie drove us to the clinic for our postnatal checkups a couple of days ago," she said, shaking her head. "But my grandfather's lawyer called this afternoon. He said there's a problem with my inheritance and he needs to meet with me."

"Did he say what was wrong?" Morgan asked, hoping for her sake there wasn't a lien, or someone claiming the property for unpaid taxes.

"I asked, but all he would say was he needed to speak with me in person so he could explain the new terms of the will." She frowned. "He didn't mention anything about there being any kind of stipulations on my inheritance when he first contacted me, or when I called five weeks ago to tell him that he could reach me here at the Lonetree."

Morgan wasn't sure what the lawyer had found, but

he didn't like the sound of it. After old Tug had died, he'd contacted the law firm about buying the property and they'd assured him the place was free and clear, should the heir wish to sell.

"I have to make the drive down to Laramie sometime this week for fencing supplies," Morgan said, thinking aloud. "I could make arrangements to go tomorrow and take you with me. Did the lawyer give you a time to be there?"

"He said any time tomorrow morning would be fine," she answered, yawning.

"What time will Timmy wake up?" Morgan asked, rising to his feet.

She yawned again. "Early."

A warm, protective feeling that he didn't care to dwell on swept over him as he gazed down at her. "Do you think you and Timmy can be ready to leave by eight tomorrow morning?"

When she nodded, he helped her gather her camp plans, then took her hand and led her toward the stairs. At the bottom step, he kissed her forehead. "Go on upstairs and get some sleep, sweetheart. We'll deal with this in the morning."

"I don't know how long I'll be," Samantha said, staring out the windshield of Morgan's truck at the entrance to the brick building housing the law firm of Greeley, Hartwell and Buford.

"Don't worry about it," Morgan said, killing the engine and releasing his seat belt. "Timmy and I will hold down things out here, while you go in and see what the 'suit' has to say."

Samantha nodded, took a deep breath and opened the passenger door. "Keep your fingers crossed that this is something minor."

"Good luck," he said, smiling as he rested his outstretched arm along the back of the bench seat.

It was easy for Morgan to look relaxed. He wasn't the one who'd talked to Mr. Greeley yesterday. The man had been extremely evasive when she asked him if he could tell her what the terms were over the phone. He'd mumbled some kind of legalese that she assumed explained why they'd need to meet in person, and she'd finally agreed. But she didn't have a good feeling about this. Not at all.

After she spoke with the receptionist, she'd barely settled into one of the uncomfortable chairs in the waiting area than a man appeared at the open door of the hallway leading toward the back of the building. "Are you Ms. Peterson?"

"Yes."

When she rose to her feet, the balding little man gave her a nervous smile. "I'm Gerald Greeley," he said, extending his hand. "If you'll come on back to my office, I'll explain the mix-up."

Samantha's stomach suddenly felt queasy as she shook his hand and followed him down the hall. Something told her this wasn't going to be something simple, nor was he going to tell her anything she'd want to hear.

As they entered a small, nondescript office, he motioned to a chair across from his desk. "Please have a seat."

"What's this all about, Mr. Greeley?" she asked, perching on the edge of the seat. "I thought everything was in order."

"So did we." He sighed heavily and sank into the executive chair behind the desk. "But there was a wrinkle that cropped up yesterday morning we couldn't have anticipated."

She eyed him carefully. Sweat had popped out on his forehead and he looked as if he dreaded what he had to say next.

"Why don't you just tell me and get it over with?" she asked, feeling more apprehensive by the second.

"You haven't by any chance gotten married in the past month, have you, Ms. Peterson?" the man asked, sounding hopeful.

She eyed him suspiciously. "No. Why do you ask?"

"Because to claim the land your grandfather bequeathed you, you'll have to be married, and remain that way for the next two years," he said, digging a white linen handkerchief from the inside pocket of his suit coat to wipe the sweat from his brow.

In a daze, Samantha spent the next half hour listening as Gerald Greeley explained the terms of the new will, and why the law firm had been unaware of its existence. By the time she walked out of the office

and back to Morgan's truck, her stomach churned un-
mercifully and she felt a good cry coming on.

When Samantha opened the truck door and got in,
Morgan felt as if he'd taken a fist to the gut. She was
pale and looked like she might be on the verge of
tears.

"Are you all right?"

She laughed, but there was no humor to it. "Not
really."

He watched a tear slip from the corner of her eye,
then slowly trickle down her cheek. The sight of that
single droplet just about tore him apart. "Tell me
what happened, sweetheart."

"I've learned that in three months the Bureau of
Land Management will take possession of my grandfather's ranch," she said, sounding defeated. "And
there's absolutely nothing I can do about it."

"But I thought he left everything to you." The
knot in Morgan's stomach tightened painfully as he
watched her impatiently swipe at a second tear.

"He had another will drawn up a few days before
his death," she said, accepting the bandana handkerchief he retrieved from the hip pocket of his jeans.

"Why didn't Greeley know about it?" He hated
seeing her so utterly dejected.

She shrugged one shoulder. "My grandfather used
the nursing home's attorney because he knew he was
dying and Mr. Greeley was out of town. After it had
been witnessed and notarized, the administrator of the

nursing home accidentally misfiled the will in another resident's folder.'' Her voice broke. ''The mistake…wasn't discovered until the first part of this week…when that man passed away.''

Unable to sit still any longer, Morgan got out of the truck and walked around to the passenger side. Opening the door, he reached inside and wrapped his arms around her.

Samantha immediately buried her face against his shoulder and the flood gates opened. He hated seeing any woman cry, but Samantha's heartbroken sobs were tearing him apart. He wanted to make things better, to fix things for her. But he had no idea where he'd even begin to start on this mess.

When she quieted, he continued to hold her. He enjoyed the feel of her soft body pressed to his too much to let her go.

''Sweetheart, why don't you start at the beginning,'' he finally said. ''Maybe together we can figure out a way for you to keep the property.''

''It's really very simple,'' she said, hiccuping. ''Unless I'm married by September, the Bureau of Land Management will get my grandfather's ranch. And since I don't see that happening—''

''Married?'' Morgan felt like he'd been punched in the gut for the second time in less than ten minutes.

She nodded. ''The will stipulates that I have to be married at the time I claim the property, and that I have to stay married for two years after that before the deed is put in my name.''

"Why in God's name would old Tug do a crazy thing like that to you?" Morgan asked, unable to comprehend the ridiculous terms of the legacy.

"He really wasn't doing it to me," she said, sniffling. "My grandfather wasn't even aware that I existed. Once my mother eloped with my father, she never came back here."

Morgan nodded. "I remember you telling me that he and your mother didn't get along. But in all that time, she never tried to get in touch with Tug?"

"Not that I'm aware of," Samantha said. She sighed heavily as she pulled away from him to open her handbag. Handing him a piece of paper, she added, "Here's the letter explaining his reasoning, although I doubt that I'll ever understand it."

When Morgan scanned the contents of the note, he shook his head in amazement. Tug Shackley's mind must have snapped before he passed on. Either that, or he was the biggest chauvinist the good Lord ever gave the gift of life. At the moment, Morgan wasn't making any bets on which one was the correct answer.

If the heir to Tug's ranch was male, there were no terms to be met, and the property could be claimed immediately. But a female heir had to be married within two years of his death, and stay that way for another two years, before she could claim her inheritance. The letter went on to state that a woman would need a husband to help her restore the ranch to its former productiveness, thus insuring her financial security. But if no heir was found, or a female heir was unmarried by the end of the time limits, the law firm had instructions to donate the land to the BLM in Tug's name.

"Now, I won't even have a connection…to my family through the land, let alone be able to open…the camp," she said, brokenly.

"That's unacceptable." He folded the letter and gave it back to her. "We'll get married this weekend."

As if they were caught in a vacuum, time seemed to come to a complete halt.

He couldn't believe he'd just offered to marry her. But as he stood there gazing into her amber eyes, he realized it was the only thing he could do to help her keep the land that was rightfully hers.

"What did you say?" she finally asked, looking as if he'd taken leave of his senses.

"I said, we'll get married this weekend." He didn't want to dwell on how easily the words rolled off his tongue this time around.

She shook her head. "First it was my grandfather and his stupid stipulations on my inheritance, and now it's you telling me we'll get married." The dubious look in her whiskey-brown eyes left no doubt that she thought his elevator didn't go all the way to the top floor. "Is there something in the water here in Wyoming that makes men go completely insane?"

He placed his hands on her slender shoulders. "Listen to me, Samantha." When he gazed into her amber eyes, he felt as if he might drown. He wanted her. And if they were married…

He swallowed hard and did his best to ignore his wayward thoughts, as well as the sudden tightening south of his belt buckle. "You want to keep your grandfather's ranch to start that children's camp, don't you?"

"Yes, but I can't marry you to do it," she said, her voice shaky.

"Why not?"

"Well, I…that is…" Her voice trailed off and she seemed to be at a loss for words.

"Were there any loopholes?" he asked. "Any way to get around the terms of the will?"

She shook her head. "No. Mr. Greeley said he'd been over it several times, looking for some way for me to keep the land without meeting the terms. But it's quite clear. I have to be married to claim the property."

Morgan gave her shoulders a gentle squeeze. "Then what other choice do you have, Samantha?"

"I…uh, need…to think about this," she said, looking dazed. She massaged her temples with her fingertips. "This is all so bizarre. I have no job, no home and I'm about to lose the only ties I have left to my family, as well as my dream of opening the camp. But if I marry you—"

He could understand her dilemma. If he let himself think about it, he was sure he'd find it pretty unsettling, too. After what happened to Emily, he'd made a vow never to take a trip down the aisle and run the risk of being responsible for another person's well-being.

But this was different. He and Samantha wouldn't be marrying for love, and he wouldn't be responsible for making any decisions for her or little Timmy. They'd lead separate lives, and if they came together from time to time for their physical needs, then where was the harm? They'd be married and it would not only be legal, it would be perfectly moral as well.

"Think about it on the drive home," he said as he stepped back to close the passenger door. Walking around the front of the truck, he got in and started the engine, then reached over to cup her chin in his palm. "We'll work this out, sweetheart. I promise I won't let you lose your land."

Samantha waited until she'd nursed Timmy and put him in the cradle for his afternoon nap before she took a deep breath and headed downstairs to talk to Morgan. Since their discussion in the parking lot, she'd thought of nothing else but the stipulations of her grandfather's will, and the offer Morgan had made to help her meet those terms.

Crossing the great room to the foyer, her legs shook and her insides felt as if they had turned to gelatin. As tempting as it was, she wasn't going to take him up on his offer. She'd learned the hard way not to rely on a man for anything, and she wasn't about to start now. Even if it meant giving up on her dream of starting her camp, she just couldn't do it.

When she reached his office, she took a deep breath and knocked on the frame of the open door. "Are you busy?"

"No." He smiled. "Come in and sit down."

She sank into the armchair across from his desk. "I've reached a decision."

His easy expression faded as he cocked one dark brow. "And that would be?"

"I really appreciate your offer to help me keep the land, but I can't let you put your life on hold for two years," she said, hurrying to get the words out before she changed her mind.

Rising from the chair, he walked around the desk to sit on the edge in front of her. "Samantha, I wouldn't consider it as putting my life on hold. I'd think of it more as helping you, as well as a bunch of kids who got handed a raw deal in life."

Agitated, she stood up to pace. She couldn't let him sway her. "What if you met someone? You'd be tied to me. What happens then?"

"I won't meet anyone," he said, sounding so darned sure that she turned to stare at him.

"You don't know that, Morgan."

"Yes, I do," he said calmly. He crossed his booted feet at the ankles and folded his arms over his wide chest. "You have my word that as long as we're married, I won't so much as look at another woman."

"But the marriage would be in name only," she said, making sure they had that little detail straight.

He shrugged. "That would probably make things simpler."

That hadn't been the answer she'd expected. He was a living, breathing man in his prime. He was going to remain celibate for two years? And how on earth could he be so relaxed about something as important as marriage, even if it wouldn't be a real one?

"Why are you willing to do this for me, Morgan?" she asked, suddenly suspicious of his motives and why he was being so generous. "What's in it for you?"

"Nothing," he said, straightening to his full height. "I just want to see that you and Timmy get what's rightfully yours. And in the bargain, I'll be helping kids who really need it."

"That's it?" She was having a hard time believing that anyone would be that willing to sacrifice their freedom for someone they barely knew.

He nodded, then walked over to take her hands in his. Pulling her to him, he put his arms around her waist. "I want to help you, Samantha. And our getting married is the only way for you to keep your land and start that camp."

She caught her lower lip between her teeth to keep it from trembling. She couldn't believe it, but she was actually thinking about accepting his offer, even though it went against everything she'd vowed never to do again—rely on a man.

As if he sensed she was on the verge of going along with his suggestion, he gave her a smile that curled her toes inside her well-worn tennis shoes. Then, leaning forward, he whispered in her ear, "What do you say, Samantha? Are you going to marry me, keep your grandfather's ranch and help those kids? Or are you going to turn me down and lose it all?"

How was she supposed to think with him this close? His warm breath was teasing her neck, sending wave after wave of delicious heat skipping over every nerve in her body.

"I'm…not sure…what to do," she said, feeling extremely short of breath. His strong hands were splayed across her back, tracing the line of her spine, gently kneading her tense muscles.

"Say yes, Samantha," he commanded, kissing the sensitive hollow beneath her ear.

"But—"

He leaned back to stare down at her, his blue gaze intense. "Yes."

"Y-yes," she finally said, unable to believe she was actually agreeing to become Morgan Wakefield's wife.

Six

Morgan propped his hands on his hips as he looked around the storage area for the old trunk. It had to be here somewhere. His dad had packed all of his mother's things in it shortly after her death, and to Morgan's knowledge it hadn't moved for the past twenty-seven years.

When he spotted the corner of it, he walked over to move several boxes of Christmas ornaments that had been piled on top. Unfastening the clasp, he opened it and gazed down at the contents. The scent of jasmine drifted up from the mementos of his mother's life to flood his senses with memories of the woman who had given him life.

He'd only been seven years old when she passed

away, but he could still remember the feel of her gentle touch when he'd skinned his elbow, the way she'd pressed a soft kiss to his forehead each night when she tucked him into bed, and the smell of her jasmine perfume when she hugged him close. His chest tightened. Even though Hank Wakefield had done a fine job of raising his three sons, and gone out of his way to be both mother and father to them, they'd missed a hell of a lot by not having her with them.

As Morgan dropped down on one knee to begin his search, he felt guilty. It almost felt as if he was invading his mother's privacy. But he somehow knew that she'd approve of what he had in mind and would have probably even suggested it had she been alive.

When he saw the heavy white plastic garment bag close to the bottom of the trunk, he smiled. Removing it, he carefully replaced the rest of his mother's things, then closed the lid and headed back downstairs.

"Samantha?" he called as he descended the steps.

"I'm in the kitchen."

When he walked into the room, she was putting a roast into the oven. Her porcelain cheeks were flushed from the heat and several strands of her golden-brown hair had escaped the confines of her ponytail. He didn't think he'd ever seen her look more attractive.

Handing her the white garment bag, he smiled. "I don't know what size this is, but if it fits, you could wear it on Sunday."

She stared at the bag for several seconds before she gazed up at him. "Was this your mother's?"

He nodded, suddenly unsure about his decision to offer her his mother's wedding dress for the small ceremony they had planned for Sunday afternoon. He knew for a fact that Samantha didn't have the money for a new dress and she'd flat out refused his offer to buy her one. But maybe women didn't like the idea of wearing another woman's dress for their wedding.

"I'll understand if you'd rather wear something else," he said, running his hand over the back of his neck. "I just thought—"

"No, this will be fine," she said, her voice almost a whisper. She lightly ran her fingers over the plastic, as if she touched something precious and fragile. "I would be honored to wear it, Morgan. But don't you think you should save it for after we…that is, when you meet someone else and get married for real?"

"This is most likely the only time I'll ever get married," he said, wishing his statement hadn't sounded quite so blunt.

But he wasn't about to explain his decision to remain a bachelor, or his reasons behind it. It was too complicated, and he didn't think he'd be able to stand the condemnation in Samantha's pretty amber eyes when he told her about his role in Emily's death.

"It will probably be the only time for me, too," she said, surprising him. "I decided after Chad and the choice he made about not wanting anything to do with Timmy, that life alone would be preferable to one filled with heartache. Or worse yet, watching someone disappoint my child the way my father disappointed me.''

It felt as if someone had reached inside his chest and squeezed his heart with a tight fist. How could anyone, no matter who it was, treat Samantha or Timmy as if they didn't matter?

Reaching out, Morgan pulled her into his arms. ''That's one thing you won't have to worry about while you're here at the Lonetree, sweetheart,'' he said. His chest tightened further at the thought of her and the baby eventually leaving to face the world alone. ''I promise I'll never hurt you, or Timmy, and you won't be lonely.''

She stared up at him with guileless amber eyes. ''At least for the next two years?''

''At least,'' he said, nodding as he lowered his mouth to hers.

He didn't want to dwell on the length of their upcoming marriage, or the reason for it. At the moment, the feel of her soft body against his, the scent of her lilac shampoo, and the sound of her soft sigh were sending his libido into overdrive.

Tracing her lips with his tongue, Morgan deepened the kiss to leisurely reacquaint himself with her sweetness, to explore the woman that in two days would become his wife. The thought sent heat streaking through his veins and caused his loins to tighten with need.

When she wrapped her arms around his neck and

leaned into him, Morgan thought his knees were going to buckle. Her firm, full breasts pressed to his chest and the warmth of her lower body cradling the hard ridge of his arousal were almost more than he could stand.

Slowly running his hands up her sides to the swell of her breasts, he cupped the weight of them, then teased the hardened tips through the layers of her clothes. Rewarded by her tiny moan of pleasure, his body responded in a way that made him light-headed. Morgan didn't think he'd ever been as hard in his life as he was at this moment, for this woman.

Knowing that if things went much further, he wouldn't be able to stop, he broke the kiss and took a step back. As he gazed down at her, he decided that wasn't enough distance. She looked so soft, so sweet, that if he didn't move, and damned quick, he'd end up sweeping her into his arms and carrying her upstairs to his bed. And although he was more than ready for it, she wasn't.

"I...really should check on a new colt," he said, turning toward the back door. "If you need help getting that dress ready for Sunday, I'm sure Annie will be more than happy to lend a hand."

Without waiting for her response, he stepped out onto the porch and closed the door behind him. If there had been any doubt in his mind before, it had just been erased.

Taking a deep breath, he tried to get his body to calm down. Their marriage might not be a love match, but the attraction between them was too strong to be denied. There was no way the two of them could live in the same house, day in and day out, without the inevitable happening between them.

It wasn't a matter of if they made love. The question now was, when?

"I knew the first time I saw you and Morgan together that you were made for each other," Annie said, helping Samantha into Morgan's mother's dress.

"You did?" Samantha wondered how on earth her soon-to-be sister-in-law could have gotten that impression.

Annie nodded as she started fastening the tiny buttons that ran from below the waist at the back all the way to the shoulders of the dress. "It's the way you look at each other."

Samantha swallowed hard. She hated that she couldn't tell Annie the real reason behind her and Morgan's decision to get married. But they'd both agreed that the fewer people who knew their marriage was a sham, the better.

As Morgan had pointed out, it wasn't anyone's business but their own. But that still didn't keep Samantha from feeling guilty about not telling Annie.

"Have Colt and Brant made it back from Nashville yet?" she asked, hoping to change the subject. Both brothers had been tied up with a bull-riding event and couldn't make it home until that day.

"They arrived about an hour ago." Annie finished

the last of the buttons and came around to stand in front of her. Tears filled her pretty green eyes. "Oh, Samantha, you look absolutely beautiful."

Staring at herself in the full-length mirror on the back of the closet door, Samantha sighed wistfully. If she'd had her choice of any wedding gown, she knew for certain she would have chosen this one. It was absolutely gorgeous.

With a simple scoop neckline, fitted bodice, cap sleeves, and floor-length skirt flaring from the waist, it was simple, feminine and elegantly traditional. Made of antique white satin overlaid with pure white lace it was everything that Samantha had ever dreamed of wearing for her wedding. That is before she'd stopped dreaming of ever being a bride.

"I think I look scared silly," she said, laughing nervously.

Annie nodded as she arranged a garland of white rosebuds on top of Samantha's head. "I don't think you'd be normal if you weren't nervous." She pinned the headpiece in place, then stood back to admire her handiwork. "Morgan is going to love seeing you come down the stairs in this."

"You think so?" A pang of longing shot through her. Maybe if she and Morgan had met at another time in their lives, and under different circumstances, then things could have been different.

"Absolutely," Annie said, grinning. "He's going to take one look at you and want to carry you back up here before the minister has a chance to perform

the ceremony.'' Before Samantha could find her
voice, Annie reached into the shopping bag she'd
brought upstairs with her when she first arrived. Pulling a box from the bag, she handed it to Samantha.
''Since Morgan was in such a hurry to get you to the
altar, I didn't have time to give you a lingerie
shower.''

Samantha frowned at the Sleek and Sassy Lady
Lingerie Boutique logo on the top. ''What's this?''

Annie gave her a sly smile. ''Oh, just something
to make your evening more...um, shall we say, interesting?''

Opening the box to peel back the layers of tissue
paper, Samantha's cheeks heated. The skimpiest
white lace teddy she'd ever seen lay nestled inside,
along with a book on sensual massage and a bottle of
scented oil.

''Oh, my!''

''I hope you like it,'' Annie said, sounding hopeful.
''I wore one like this on my wedding night, and...''
She blushed prettily. ''I was really happy with Brant's
reaction. Especially when I used the oil and gave him
a massage.''

Annie expected her to wear this for Morgan? Tonight? And to rub scented oil all over his body?

Samantha gulped. She felt warm all over at the
thought, but she couldn't tell Annie that although
they'd shared a few kisses that made her insides feel
as if they'd turned to warm pudding, there wouldn't
be any nights of grand passion.

A lump formed in her throat and an empty vacant feeling filled her chest. She and Morgan had an agreement, and it was best if they stuck to it.

So why did the thought that they wouldn't be sharing everything a husband and wife shared make her feel so sad? So utterly alone? That's the way she wanted it, wasn't it?

"Thank you, Annie." She replaced the box lid, then set it on top of the dresser. "I think any man with a pulse would like seeing a woman in that."

When Colt punched the button on the CD player, and George Strait started singing about crossing his heart and promising that his love was truer than any other, Morgan's stomach churned like a cement mixer gone berserk. What the hell did he think he was doing?

Six years ago, he'd vowed never to get married—never to be responsible for another person's well-being. Yet, here he stood, waiting for Samantha to come down the stairs and join him in front of the fireplace in the great room so Preacher Hill from the Methodist church down in Bear Creek could pronounce them man and wife.

Reminding himself this was the only way to help her keep the land that was rightfully hers, Morgan reached up to put his index finger in the collar of his dress shirt. He gave it a tug in an effort to create a little more space between the restrictive top button and his Adam's apple. Why did a suit and tie always make a man feel like he had a noose around his damned neck?

"Relax, bro. Being married is the best thing that ever happened to me," Brant said as Annie appeared at the top of the staircase, holding Timmy. Grinning he asked, "Have you ever seen a woman prettier than my Annie?"

Morgan opened his mouth to tell his brother he sounded like a lovesick teenager, but the words lodged in his throat. Samantha stood at the top of the steps, her silky, golden-brown hair swept up in a cascade of loose curls, her whiskey-colored eyes gazing at him like he was the only man in the room. Wearing his mother's wedding dress, and carrying a single white rose, he'd never seen her look more beautiful.

He swallowed hard as he stared up at the woman he was about to marry. "Annie's almost as pretty as Samantha."

"I think I'm gonna puke," Colt muttered under his breath. "You two are about the saddest cases I've ever seen."

"Can it, little brother," Morgan said, unable to take his eyes off of Samantha as she and Annie descended the stairs. "You're lucky we didn't make you skip down the stairs scattering flower petals."

Colt snorted. "Yeah, like that would ever happen." He shook his head. "I'm never going to get as moon-eyed over a woman as you two."

"Your day is coming," Brant warned, stepping forward to escort his wife and Timmy over to the fireplace.

Morgan's heart pounded hard against his rib cage and his knees felt as if they might fail him at any second when he moved toward the stairs to wait for Samantha. But the moment she reached the bottom step and trustingly placed her hand in his, a calm swept over him that he couldn't explain, nor did he want to.

"You look beautiful," he said, gazing down into her pretty eyes.

She smiled and Morgan could have sworn it chased the late afternoon shadows from the room. "I was just thinking how handsome you look," she said, touching the lapel of his black western-cut suit jacket.

"Are you ready for this?" he asked, tucking her hand in the crook of his arm.

She took a deep breath and nodded. "I guess so."

Leading her over to where Preacher Hill stood in front of the big stone fireplace, Morgan glanced at the baby sleeping peacefully in Annie's arms, then at Samantha. He was about to take on a wife and child. But instead of striking fear in his heart and sending him running like hell in the opposite direction as it would have six weeks ago, the thought filled him with a deep satisfaction that defied explanation or logic.

"Dearly beloved, we are gathered here today to join this man and this woman…" Preacher Hill began.

As the ceremony progressed, Morgan felt a twinge

of guilt when it came time to repeat the traditional words that would make them husband and wife. He hated to lie about anything, but especially when it came to something as sacred as wedding vows. There was no doubt that he would honor and cherish Samantha. But he'd just promised to love her and stay with her until death.

He swallowed hard. Why hadn't they thought about writing their own vows? They could have skirted around those issues.

But when he heard her promise to love, honor and cherish him in return, a satisfied warmth flowed through him. The thought of having her with him, loving him for the rest of his life lit the darkest corners of his soul. And at the moment, he wasn't about to remind himself that their arrangement was only temporary.

When the stoic, elderly preacher requested the rings, Morgan gave him the wedding bands that he'd made a special trip to Laramie to purchase the day before. Handing the smaller one back, the good reverend instructed him to put the ring on the third finger of Samantha's left hand and repeat the words that would make her his.

"With this ring—" he caught and held her gaze as he slid the shiny, wide gold band onto her trembling finger "—I thee wed."

"When did you get these?" she whispered, her eyes shiny with unshed tears.

"Yesterday," he said, bringing her hand to his mouth to press a kiss to the ring circling her finger.

Preacher Hill handed her the other wedding band, and as she slid it onto his finger and repeated the traditional words, a lone tear slowly trickled down her cheek. "By the power vested in me by God, and the state of Wyoming, I now pronounce you husband and wife," the man said. "Son, kiss your bride."

Samantha held her breath as Morgan reached up to wipe the tear sliding down her cheek with the pad of his thumb, then drew her into his arms to seal their union with a kiss that made her insides quiver and caused her mind to reel from everything that had taken place in the last few minutes.

She'd just promised to love Morgan, to stay with him no matter what. How on earth would she be able to walk away from him in two years after pledging something like that?

"You might want to let her up for air," Brant said, laughing as he slapped Morgan on the shoulder. "Welcome to the world of the blissfully hitched, bro."

When Morgan lifted his head to smile at her, tiny electrical impulses skipped over every nerve in her body. If she didn't know better, she'd think he intended for them to...

"If this big galoot doesn't tow the line, just let me know," Brant said. He pushed Morgan aside to hug her and place a brotherly kiss on her cheek. "I'll be more than happy to kick his butt for you."

"I'll remember that," she said, smiling wanly.

The Wakefields were so nice she really hated deceiving them. But they had no way of knowing the marriage was only temporary, and not an everlasting commitment of love and devotion.

"My turn to kiss the bride," Colt said, shouldering Brant out of the way and making a show of really getting into the act. But when Morgan cleared his throat and sent a dark scowl his way, Colt grinned and lightly pressed his lips to her other cheek. "It's good to meet you, Samantha. Welcome to the family."

When her new brother-in-law mentioned the one thing that she'd always wanted—to be part of a family—she couldn't shake the deep sadness that washed over her. Although her last name had just become Wakefield, it was all pretend. She wasn't, and never would be, a real part of their family.

Morgan must have sensed her discomfort, because he put his arms around her waist to pull her close. "You and Timmy *are* part of us now, sweetheart," he whispered close to her ear.

"Thank you," was all she could manage as she fought to hold back her tears.

Once the minister filled out the marriage certificate, had Brant and Annie sign in the appropriate place as witnesses to the marriage and excused himself to drive back to Bear Creek, Annie took charge. Placing Timmy in his baby carrier, she instructed, "Brant, you and Colt watch the baby while I get everything

ready in the kitchen.'' Turning to Morgan and Samantha, she added, ''You two take a little time to
catch your breath and get ready for pictures and cutting the cake.''

''Pictures?'' Morgan looked as surprised as Samantha felt.

''Cake?'' She hadn't counted on Annie going to so
much trouble.

Nodding, Annie grinned. ''You'll want pictures to
reminisce over when you celebrate your fiftieth anniversary. And it's not official until you smear cake
all over each other's face.''

Before Samantha found her voice to ask if Annie
needed help in the kitchen, her new sister-in-law
breezed down the hall and out of sight.

As Colt and Brant stared down at Timmy like they
weren't quite sure what they were supposed to do,
Morgan asked, ''Are you doing okay?''

''I'm not sure,'' she said honestly. ''It's hard to
take in all that's happened in the last hour.''

He smiled. ''Feels like you've been hit by a train,
doesn't it?''

She nodded, as she watched her two brothers-in-
law gaze down at her son. ''I just hate that we're
deceiving them.''

''Are we?''

Samantha sucked in a sharp breath and turned to
stare at him. ''What do you mean?''

''Everything's ready for the pictures and cutting the
cake,'' Annie said, walking back into the room before

Morgan could answer. "Brant, you get our camera. Colt, you're in charge of the baby."

"Me?" Colt sounded alarmed. "I don't know what to do with a baby."

"Take hold of the carrier's handle and bring him into the kitchen," Annie said, patiently. "Believe me, he won't bite."

"He might," Colt said, eyeing Timmy carefully. "He doesn't look like he likes me very much."

"You end up growing on people. Sort of like a fungus," Brant said, laughing as he picked up the camera from the slate coffee table.

Colt looked insulted. "Thanks a lot. What kind of impression do you think that gives our new sister-in-law?"

"She'll get used to you, just like the rest of us had to," Brant said. "And don't worry about the baby biting. If he does decide to give you a little nip, it won't hurt. He doesn't have teeth yet."

"So now that Annie's pregnant you're an expert on babies, huh?" Colt groused as he picked up the baby carrier and followed his brother down the hall.

Morgan took Samantha's hand. "Come on. Let's get this over with so they'll leave and I can get out of this damned monkey suit."

Samantha didn't budge. "I think we need to discuss the issue of your questioning our deception."

"We'll talk later," he said, giving her a kiss that left her absolutely breathless. "Now smile, sweetheart. This is your wedding day."

Seven

For the next half hour, Samantha felt as if she was living a dream. Morgan played the role of the attentive groom, while Brant, instructed by Annie, snapped so many pictures Samantha wasn't sure she'd ever be able to see again without spots dancing before her eyes.

"Time to cut the cake," Annie finally announced.

"Were you, by any chance, a wedding planner before you married Brant?" Samantha asked as Annie showed her and Morgan where and how to cut the cake.

"No, I was a librarian." Annie grinned as she added, "But one of my favorite books was *How to Plan a Fairytale Wedding.*"

Samantha laughed. "It shows."

Taking the decorative knife, her breath caught and heat coursed through her veins as Morgan covered her hand with his and they sliced the beautiful white wedding cake Annie had bought at a bakery in Laramie. Samantha tried to ignore the feeling.

But when they fed each other a small piece, and Morgan licked the icing from her fingers, there was no way she could dismiss the delicious fluttery feeling deep in the pit of her stomach. Nor could she deny the fact that every cell in her being tingled to life.

She had to get a grip on herself. It was as if she'd forgotten that this was just an act—a show for the benefit of his family.

After everyone had a piece of wedding cake, Annie enlisted Brant and Colt's help, and in no time they had everything put away and the kitchen spotless.

"Colt is spending the night with us," Annie announced as she tugged on his sleeve.

Colt frowned. "I am?"

"Yes, you are," Brant said, elbowing his younger brother in the ribs and treating him to a meaningful look.

"Oh, right." Colt's grin caused Samantha's cheeks to feel as if they were on fire. "Just in case you're tired and want to sleep in tomorrow morning, I won't be back until noon to get my stuff. After that I'll be taking off for Mitch's place."

Annie stepped forward to hug Samantha. "I'd offer to watch the baby for you, but since you're nursing,

I know you can't be away from each other for that long.''

Nodding, Samantha hugged her new sister-in-law back. ''Thank you for everything, Annie. I truly appreciate your thoughtfulness.''

''We're sisters now, and I was happy to do it.'' Lowering her voice, she added, ''Don't forget to wear the teddy. I promise Morgan's reaction will be well worth it.'' Turning to her husband and brother-in-law, she motioned toward the door. ''Come on you two. It's time we left the newlyweds alone.''

No sooner had the three of them walked out the back door, than Timmy let out a wail, indicating that he wanted to nurse again.

Samantha was thankful for the excuse to have a little time to herself, in order to come to terms with all that had taken place. It wasn't every day a woman got married to one of the sexiest men alive, only to plan on spending her wedding night completely alone.

Lifting her son from the baby carrier, she started toward the stairs. ''I'll come back down later and get the baby carrier.''

''I'll get it,'' Morgan said, impatiently tugging on the knot of his tie. ''While you're taking care of Timmy, I'm going to change into something that doesn't make me feel like I'm being throttled.''

''I should change, too,'' she said, hoping Timmy didn't spit up before she could take off her borrowed dress. ''This gown is beautiful, but—'' She groaned as she suddenly thought of how much trouble it would be to get out of it. "Oh, no. I forgot to have Annie help me with the back."

Morgan shoved the necktie in one of the pockets of his suit coat and worked the top two buttons loose on his shirt. "I'll help you once we get upstairs."

Before she could think of some other way to get the dress unbuttoned, he took the baby carrier in one hand and guided her to the stairs with the other. Helping her climb the stairs without tripping on the long skirt, he opened the door to the room she shared with Timmy, then set the baby carrier on the window seat while she laid Timmy on the bed.

When he stepped up behind her, Samantha caught her breath and her stomach felt as if it did a somersault at the first touch of his hands at her shoulders. Having him unfasten the back of her dress seemed so intimate, so husbandlike.

"Damn, these things are little, and there's about a hundred of them," he said, his deep voice sending a wave of longing straight through her.

As he worked the buttons through the tiny loops, his fingers brushed her spine, and with each touch, heat streaked straight to the pit of her stomach. To distract herself, Samantha shook her head and tried to concentrate on what he'd said.

"I think there are only thirty or forty buttons," she said, trying not to sound as breathless as she felt. "But you're right, they are tiny."

When he reached the last few, the ones at the small of her back, his fingers lingered a bit longer with each one. Shivers of excitement shot through her and she found it extremely difficult to draw a breath.

What on earth had she gotten herself into? Had she lost her mind when she agreed to marry him?

Each time Morgan touched her, her body zinged to life and she was in serious danger of melting into a puddle at his big booted feet. How was she ever going to survive two years of living under the same roof with him and not give in to the sizzling tension between them?

"There you go," he said, his warm breath tickling the back of her neck and causing the heat inside of her to intensify.

Holding the dress to keep it from falling off her shoulders, she quickly stepped away from him. "Th-thank you."

His sexy smile and hooded sapphire gaze sent another wave of awareness skimming over every nerve in her body. "Samantha, we need to talk about—"

Impatient for his next meal, Timmy let them know that he was tired of waiting by wailing at the top of his lungs.

"He needs to nurse," she said, thankful for the interruption.

She had a good idea what Morgan wanted to discuss, and she needed time to collect herself. They were going to have to establish some ground rules to keep from doing something that would greatly complicate their situation.

To her surprise, instead of being upset that Timmy

needed her, Morgan leaned down to tickle the baby's stomach. "I'll see you later, little guy." Walking to the door, he turned back to face her. "It's late. Do you think he'll sleep for a while?"

"I—" she swallowed hard "—think so."

Morgan nodded. "Good. We'll have plenty of time to…talk."

Once he'd changed into more comfortable clothes, Morgan carried his boots in one hand as he padded down the hall in his socks to Samantha's door. He'd been so turned on by the simple act of unbuttoning her dress, of feeling her soft skin beneath his fingers, he'd forgotten to tell her to meet him in his office after she got the baby down for the night.

He shook his head. It was important that they get a few things worked out about their arrangement. He needed to make it clear that although they were married, he wouldn't be responsible for any decisions she made concerning her or Timmy's welfare.

Tapping on the oak door frame, he waited a second then opened the door and walked into the room. "Samantha, I'll be down in my office when—"

He stopped short and his boots hit the floor with a loud clunk at the sight of her sitting in the rocking chair holding Timmy. She'd changed out of his mother's wedding gown and put on a pale yellow dress made of soft-looking gauzy fabric. But what held him riveted to the spot was the fact that the dress was open to the waist and the baby was nursing her breast. Morgan had never seen a more poignant sight in his entire thirty-four years.

"Morgan, what do you think you're doing?" Samantha asked, her startled movement pulling her nipple from Timmy's mouth.

The dark coral tip was wet and shiny, and Morgan couldn't have looked away if his life depended on it. "I..." He had to stop to clear the rust from his throat. "...wanted to tell you that I'll be waiting for you in my office."

His evening meal interrupted, Timmy protested loudly.

Morgan swallowed hard as he watched her guide her breast back to the baby's lips, then drape a small blanket over herself and the baby's face. Fascinated, he asked, "Does that hurt?"

She stared at him for several long moments, then slowly shook her head. "It did at first, but that was before I got used to breastfeeding."

He walked over to kneel down beside the rocking chair, then holding her gaze with his, he slowly reached up to move the soft blanket aside. When she didn't try to stop him, he glanced down to see Timmy's mouth working rhythmically to drink his mother's milk.

"I've watched thousands of animals nurse, but this is the first time I've seen a woman nurse a child." He'd never been one for putting his feelings into words, and he figured he should probably shut up now before he made a fool of himself, but the moment was so special, he had to let her know. "It's beautiful."

For the next several minutes they both remained silent as Samantha nursed the baby and Morgan watched.

"He's asleep," she finally said, her voice little more than a whisper.

Without asking, Morgan lifted Timmy into his arms and cradled him to his chest while Samantha covered herself. "Do you want me to put him in the cradle?"

She nodded. "He should sleep until four or five tomorrow morning."

Rising to his feet, Morgan placed the sleeping baby in the cradle that had rocked three generations of Wakefield boys, then waited for Samantha to cover her son with a downy soft blanket. When she turned to face him, he thought he'd drown in the depths of her whiskey-brown eyes.

"Things have changed," he said, taking her left hand in his.

She stared at him for several long seconds before she lowered her gaze to their hands. "This isn't smart."

"Probably not." He ran the pad of his thumb over the shiny gold band circling her finger, reminding himself and her, that she was his.

"We agreed the marriage wouldn't be real," she said, lifting her head to look at him.

"Not really." He took her hands and placed them on his shoulders, then wrapped his arms around her waist to draw her forward. "*You* said the marriage would be in name only."

"And you agreed." She sounded breathless.

"No, I didn't." He leaned his forehead against hers. "I said it would probably be for the best. But technically, I never agreed to those terms."

Before she could respond, Morgan lowered his mouth to hers and once again tasted her sweetness, reveled in the feel of her soft curves against him. The spark that seemed to have been smoldering in his gut since the day they first met, ignited into a flame and tightened his lower body with a swiftness that left him dizzy. He'd never wanted a woman more in his life than he wanted Samantha.

Gently pushing his tongue past her lips, he stroked and explored her inner recesses. He loved the taste of her, the shy eagerness of her response when he ran his hands down to cup her bottom and draw her into the cradle of his hips. Her moan of pleasure at the feel of his arousal pressed to her soft lower belly sent his blood pressure up a good twenty points and had his heart hammering wildly against his ribs.

Lifting his head, he asked, "Can you honestly say we'll be able to live together for two years without making love, sweetheart?"

He watched her close her eyes for a moment, then opening them to stare up at him, she lifted her arms to encircle his neck and tangle her fingers in the hair at the nape of his neck. "We should try."

"Two years is a long time." He pulled her closer,

letting her feel how much he wanted her. "Do you really want to keep this marriage in name only?"

She trembled against him. "I...I've probably lost my mind, but I'm not sure anymore."

"What do you really want, Samantha?" he asked, bringing his hands up to cup her full breasts.

When he teased the tips through the layers of her clothes, she sighed softly. "Kiss me again, Morgan. I want you to kiss me again."

"It'll be my pleasure," he said as he reached up to free her hair from the clip holding it off of her neck. "And I'm going to make damned sure it's yours, too."

Samantha's eyes fluttered shut as Morgan's mouth covered hers in a kiss that robbed her of breath, and what little sense she had left. She didn't want to think about how insane it would be to make their marriage real, or the fact that in two years, it would be over. The need to feel wanted, to be cherished by him as only a man can cherish a woman, was far stronger than the thought of the complications they would face later.

As Morgan ran his hands over her back, shivers of anticipation coursed through her. But when he plunged his tongue past her lips to claim her with sure, confident strokes, her knees began to wobble and she shamelessly clung to his solid strength for support.

Lifting his head to stare down at her with his incredible blue eyes, he smiled. "What do you want now, sweetheart?"

She took a deep breath as she tried to slow her rapidly beating pulse. "I don't think I want you to stop."

His deep chuckle sent a wave of goose bumps shimmering over her skin. "I don't think either one of us want that." He nuzzled the side of her neck, sending shivers of delight coursing to her very core. "Did the doctor put you on any kind of birth control when you went for your checkup?" he asked, his voice low and intimate.

"I...um, no. I hadn't planned on being married...let alone making love." How was she supposed to think with him so close, with his firm lips nibbling tiny kisses at the hollow behind her ear?

He raised his head to gaze down at her, and the look in his eyes sent her temperature skyward. "Don't worry, sweetheart. I'll take care of it." Giving her a quick kiss, he took her hand in his, switched on the baby monitor, then picked up the listening unit. "Why don't we go to my room?"

As she let Morgan lead her down the hall to his bedroom, her heart hammered inside her chest and she had to remind herself to breathe.

Once they made love, there was no turning back. Their marriage would be real and everything would be much more complex. Was that really what she wanted?

And what happened at the end of the two year requirement for her to gain control of her land? Was there a chance she and Morgan would stay together?

"It's going to be all right, Samantha," Morgan said as they entered his room. He switched on the bedside lamp, set the baby monitor on the table, then turned to cup her face with his large palms. "I'm not making any demands on you. If you want to call a halt to this right now, we will."

She searched his handsome features. God help her, she'd probably live to regret it, but she didn't have the strength to take him up on the retreat he'd offered her. Didn't even want to. She wanted his touch, the taste of his kiss and the warmth of his lovemaking.

"No," she said, surprised at how steady and sure her voice sounded. "I don't want to stop."

The heated look in his amazing blue eyes warmed her all the way to her toes as he lowered his head and kissed her with a gentleness that brought tears to her eyes. "I promise you won't regret it, sweetheart."

When he reached up to unbutton her dress, his gaze held her captive and she had to force herself to breathe. "I think I'd better warn you...I haven't lost all of the weight I gained while I was pregnant."

She watched his eyes darken as he shook his head. "I like the way you look. A woman is supposed to have rounded curves."

Figuring he might as well be aware of all of her flaws, she added, "I also have a few stretch marks."

"I've got a few scars of my own, sweetheart." He worked the last button open, then trailed his finger up to her breasts. "You have no idea how extremely sexy you are, do you?"

"I've never—" when he released the front clasp of her bra, she had to stop and force air into her lungs "—thought of myself as sexy."

"You should," he said, pushing her dress and the straps of her bra from her shoulders. "You're the most desirable woman I've ever known."

As he cupped her breasts in his calloused palms, Samantha's heart rate doubled and she felt as if her insides had turned to melted butter. Closing her eyes, she concentrated on the feel of his rough hands on her body, the tingles of excitement that surged through her when he teased her nipples with the pads of his thumbs.

"Does that feel good?" he asked, kissing her fore-head, her eyes and the tip of her nose.

"Y-yes."

She opened her eyes and bringing her hands up to the front of his chambray shirt began to unfasten the snaps. When she parted the shirt to reveal his well-muscled chest, her breath caught. Morgan Wakefield was perfect.

His chest muscles were well developed and the wall of his abdomen rippled from years of physical labor. A fine coating of black hair covered his chest, then thinned out to a fine line arrowing down to his navel and beyond. Samantha's gaze followed the stripe to where it disappeared below the waistband of his well-worn jeans.

"You're gorgeous," she whispered, placing her hands on the hard sinew. She ran her fingers over the thick pads of his pectoral muscles, lingering on the small flat disks that puckered and beaded from her touch.

Glancing up, the heat she saw in his blue gaze sent an answering warmth to the pit of her stomach and had her bare toes curling into the thick carpet. Without a word he lowered his head to kiss the slope of her breasts, then grazed each nipple with his tongue. Threads of desire began to wind their way through her and caused her breath to come out in short little puffs.

"You're the one who's beautiful," he murmured against her sensitized skin. He kissed the tips, then looked up at her. "I want to see all of you, Samantha."

His low, suggestive voice caused a delightful little flutter in her lower belly and made her knees feel as if they were about to fold. "I want to see you, too."

Smiling encouragingly, he slowly pushed her dress downward and in no time at all the loose garment lay in a pool of gauzy cotton at her feet. He placed his hands on her hips to steady her as she stepped away from it.

"My turn?" she asked, bringing her hands to the waistband of his jeans.

When he nodded, she worked the button through the buttonhole, then slowly, carefully pulled the metal tab down over the hard ridge of his arousal. Fascinated by the strength and power straining insistently against his white cotton briefs, she traced her finger along the warm bulge.

"Sweetheart, I'll give you all night to quit that," Morgan said with a groan.

"That sounds interesting," she said, wondering if that throaty female voice was really hers.

"Oh, I can guarantee you're not going to be bored." His low voice and meaningful look held such promise that goose bumps shimmied up her arms.

Before she could touch him again, he stepped back. Shrugging out of his shirt, he shoved his jeans and briefs down his muscular thighs, then removed his thick white socks. Straightening to his full height, he stood before her like a perfectly sculpted statue come to life.

Samantha didn't think she'd ever seen anything quite as magnificent as Morgan Wakefield. With impossibly wide shoulders, muscular arms and lean flanks, he looked like a Greek god. As her gaze drifted lower, her eyes widened and her breath caught. Make that an impressively aroused Greek god.

He closed the gap separating them, then giving her a smile that sent her temperature up a good ten degrees, he hooked his thumbs in the waistband of her sensible cotton panties, and quickly removed the last barrier between them. She suddenly felt shy and extremely vulnerable.

"Could we...turn off the lamp?" she asked hesitantly.

"Why, sweetheart?"

"I'm not exactly—"

He gently touched her cheek with one long, masculine finger. "I've seen you before, sweetheart. You're beautiful."

Samantha felt as if her cheeks were on fire. "You were supposed to forget the night Timmy was born. I wasn't exactly at my best."

Morgan shook his head. "I can't forget. It was one of the most meaningful nights of my life."

His answer shocked her. "It was?"

Smiling, he nodded. "I've always thought women were pretty special. But helping you give birth to Timmy left me with a deeper appreciation of a woman's strength and courage. I'm in awe of you, Samantha."

Before she could find her voice, he pulled her into his arms and the feel of him against her, the contrast of masculine hair-roughened flesh to smooth feminine skin caused her to forget anything she'd been about to say. A current seemed to flow between them, charging her with a need deeper than anything she'd ever experienced.

"You feel so damned good, I think I could stand here like this forever," he said, sounding out of breath.

She brought her arms up to circle his shoulders. "I hope you're strong enough to hold both of us upright because I think I'm about to collapse."

His deep chuckle sent a shiver of anticipation right

to her core. "As good as it feels to hold you against me like this, it's going to feel even better for both of us when I'm inside you."

His candid comment sent a wave of longing pulsing through every cell in her being. Releasing her, he pulled the comforter and sheet back, then lifted her as if she weighed nothing at all, and laid her on his bed.

When he stretched out beside her, he gently ran his index finger down between her breasts, then continued on to her navel. "Are these the places you were talking about?" he asked, tracing the marks left by her pregnancy.

She nodded. "I hope they don't take too long to fade."

He propped himself up on one elbow, then leaned down to press his lips to each one of the uneven lines. "Wear them with pride, sweetheart. They're badges of courage."

The reverence in his deep voice, his firm lips tenderly touching her, caused her heart to fill with an emotion she wasn't quite ready to acknowledge. If she didn't know better, she'd swear she was falling for him.

Before she could fully comprehend the threat that might represent to her peace of mind, Morgan moved to gather her into his arms. His lips covering hers chased away all thought and quickly had her feeling as if the world had been reduced to nothing but this man and this moment.

He slid his calloused palm over her ribs, then down to her hip. A shiver of delight streaked up her spine. But when he moved his hand along the inside of her leg to find the moist heat at the juncture of her thighs, a pulsing need began to pool deep in the pit of her stomach. Parting her, he gently tested her readiness as he deepened the kiss.

Wanting to touch him as he touched her, Samantha ran her hand over his flat belly to his lean flank and beyond. When she found him and stroked him with the same infinite care, a groan of pleasure rumbled up from deep in his chest.

"Easy, sweetheart," he said, his voice strained. "It's been a while and I don't want this over with before we get started."

"Please—"

"Do you want me inside?" he asked, his gaze capturing hers as he continued to tease her.

"Y-yes," she said breathlessly. "Please make love to me, Morgan."

Giving her a smile that caused the empty ache of need within her to intensify, he arranged their protection, then moved over her. "I'm going to try to take this slow, Samantha," he said, propping himself up on his elbows. "But I want you so damned much, I'm not sure I'll be able to." He leaned down to give her a kiss so tender it brought tears to her eyes as he parted her legs with one muscular thigh. "The book said that some women find lovemaking uncomfortable the first time after giving birth." He brushed a strand of her hair from her cheeks with his index finger. "If there's even a hint of discomfort, I want you to tell me. You got that?"

His concern touched her in ways she'd never imagined, and if she could have found her voice she would have told him so. But all she could manage was a quick nod before he pressed forward and she felt the exquisite stretching of his body merging with hers. She bit her lower lip to keep from moaning her pleasure as she savored the feeling of being filled by Morgan.

"You feel so damned good," he said as he sank all of himself into her.

She watched his jaw tighten as he closed his eyes and she instinctively knew he was having to dig deep for the strength to maintain his control.

When he finally opened his eyes, he gathered her into his arms. "Are you all right, sweetheart? Am I hurting you?"

"It...feels wonderful," she said breathlessly.

"Are you sure?"

"I couldn't be more certain," she said, placing her hand along his lean jaw at the same time she tilted her hips into his. She watched his brilliant gaze darken at the movement. "Make love to me, Morgan."

He gave her a smile that made her feel like she was the most desired woman alive as he lowered his mouth to hers. Pulling back, then slowly pushing his hips forward, he set an easy pace and in no time Samantha felt the coil of need inside of her tighten, felt herself tense in anticipation of the mind-shattering release.

Morgan must have sensed she was close because he reached down to touch her tiny pleasure point, encouraging her to take everything that he offered. Without warning she was suddenly tumbling, freefalling through a mist of warm, wonderful sensations.

A moment later, she felt Morgan's big body stiffen, then shudder as he gave into his own climax. Wrapping her arms around his wide shoulders, she bit her lower lip and held him to her as she tried to fight the emotion building deep inside of her.

For her well-being, and for Timmy's, she couldn't allow herself to fall in love with Morgan Wakefield, couldn't let herself count on him returning her feelings. If she did, and he turned out to be like her father, or Chad, she wasn't sure she'd be able to survive the devastation of having him reject her.

Eight

When Morgan finally found the strength to move, he started to lever himself away from her, but she hugged him tighter. "I'm too heavy for you, Samantha."

"I like the way you feel," she whispered against his shoulder.

Chuckling, he held her as he rolled to one side, taking her with him. "I like the way you feel, too." He kissed her cute little nose. "Are you okay?"

The tears filling her eyes scared him as little else could. "I'm...wonderful."

"Then why are you crying?" he asked, wiping a tear from her cheek. He wasn't sure, but he hoped like hell it was one of those times when a woman cried because something was meaningful to her.

"Making love with you was beautiful," she said, sending a wave of relief coursing through him.

He smiled. "You had me scared there for a minute, sweetheart."

The sound of an awakening baby suddenly filtered into the room from the monitor on the bedside table.

"Timmy may need to nurse some more," she said, starting to draw away from him.

Morgan shook his head as he rose from the bed and pulled on his briefs. "You stay here and rest. I'll go get the baby."

Quickly padding down the hall in his bare feet, Morgan entered the room where Timmy was raising nine kinds of hell. He grinned as he lifted the crying baby to his shoulder. Morgan liked the way Timmy smelled, the way his tiny body fit into the palms of his hands.

"Thanks for timing that just right, little guy," he said, gently rubbing Timmy's back.

When Morgan re-entered his bedroom, Samantha was sitting up in bed with the sheet tucked under her arms, her luscious breasts hidden from his appreciative gaze. "He's probably hungry," she said, holding her arms out.

"Wait just a second," he said, handing the baby to her.

She gave him a curious look. "Why?"

"You'll see." He gathered the pillows, propped them against the headboard, then sat down beside her. Pulling her onto his lap, he cradled her to his chest much as she cradled Timmy. "Are you comfortable, sweetheart?"

"Y-yes," she said, looking even more confused.

"Good." He smiled as he peeled the sheet back to reveal her full breasts. "I'm going to hold you while you nurse Timmy."

Tears filled her expressive amber eyes. "You're a very special man, Morgan Wakefield."

"Nah, I just like holding you," he said, settling back against the pillows. He watched as she guided her nipple to the baby's mouth. "Samantha?"

"Hmm?"

"I want you to move yours and Timmy's things in here tomorrow morning," he said, surprising even himself. But the more he thought about it, the more it made sense. He wanted her with him—warming his bed, warming him.

She gazed up at him for endless seconds. "But our marriage isn't—"

"It is now," he said, smiling down at her.

He could tell there were several questions running through her mind. Truth to tell, he was probably asking himself the same things. But at the moment, he didn't have answers for either one of them. All he knew was that it felt right.

When Samantha yawned, he kissed the top of her head. "I'll move the cradle in here tomorrow morning."

She closed her eyes and snuggled against him. "We'll see," she said sleepily.

With his arms wrapped around her, Morgan gazed down at the woman and baby cradled in his arms. Both had fallen sound asleep. A possessive feeling like nothing he'd ever known filled his chest and made him want to protect and take care of them.

He sucked in a sharp breath and his heart began to hammer hard against his ribs. What had gotten into him? He couldn't be responsible for either one of them. He'd proven six years ago that his judgment was faulty. What if he made a wrong decision and jeopardized their welfare?

Closing his eyes, he leaned his head back against the headboard. What had he been thinking when he'd pushed Samantha to make their marriage real? Had he lost his mind and allowed his lust to override common sense?

He forced himself to breathe in, then breathe out. He'd blamed his wanting Samantha on the long, cold winter he'd spent alone in this same bed and the need for physical release. But in the past six weeks, he'd had more than one opportunity to make a trip down to Buffalo Gals, and he'd passed every time.

Swallowing around the fear clogging his throat, he opened his eyes to look down at them. Could he live with this woman and her child for the next two years without getting more involved than he already was?

When he first brought her home from the hospital, he'd tried to keep his distance. But that hadn't worked. He'd only ended up working himself into exhaustion during the day and spent every night lying awake, thinking about her sleeping right down the hall.

Would sharing his days with her, then making love to her every night get her out of his system? Or would it only whet his appetite for the life he'd always wanted, but couldn't trust himself to have? Would it only end up complicating everything in ways that he'd never be able to straighten out?

After Emily died, he'd vowed never to take on the responsibility of having a wife and family, of making the decisions that could mean the difference between life and death for them. He glanced down at his wife and her son. He'd promised to help Samantha get her land, and he'd be damned before he went back on his word. But could he live with them, play the role of husband and father, and still keep from investing himself emotionally?

Unable to come up with any answers, Morgan shook his head. He wasn't sure. The only thing he did know for certain was that he'd have to try. For their sake, and his.

Samantha nibbled on her lower lip as she emptied the dresser drawers in the room she and Timmy had shared for the past six weeks. Had she made the right decision about moving into Morgan's room?

Last night she'd become his wife in every sense of the word, but that would be ending once she met the terms of her grandfather's will. A lump the size of her fist clogged her throat at the thought.

"After we move the rest of your clothes, I'll put your suitcases in the storage room," Morgan said, returning to carry more of her things to his bedroom. He came up behind her to rest his hands on her shoulders. "After Colt finally shows up, we'll move the cradle, then go down to the machine shed and get the rest of your stuff from your car."

A delightful shiver slipped up her spine when he pressed his lips to the nape of her neck. "That's fine," she said, turning to face him. Searching his handsome face, she asked, "Are we doing the right thing?"

She held her breath when he remained silent for several long moments. "Samantha, I can't honestly answer that," he admitted. "I've made no secret of the fact that I want you." He smiled as he wrapped his arms around her waist. "And I can tell you want me. But I want you to know that even though you're my wife, you still have the freedom to make your own choices. I can't decide what's best for you and Timmy. I won't even try."

"I'm not sure I'm capable of that either," she said, bowing her head. She suddenly felt very tired and unsure of everything.

He placed his index finger beneath her chin and lifted her head until their gazes met. "All I can promise you for sure is that I'll provide for you and Timmy, and I'll never intentionally hurt either one of you in any way."

She forced a smile. "At least for the next two years."

His expression suddenly unreadable, he slowly nodded. "At least."

They continued to stare at each other for what seemed an eternity, until the sound of booted feet climbing the stairs, followed by a succinct curse caught their attention. "Hey, Morgan, where the hell are you?" a male voice called.

"Down here in the guest room," Morgan answered. He kissed the tip of her nose. "Do you still want us to move the cradle?"

Thinking of how gently he'd made love to her, how tenderly he'd held her while she nursed Timmy the night before, she found herself nodding. "Yes."

"What are you doing in here?" Colt asked as he walked into the room. He came to a halt, then looking sheepish, shook his head. "Don't answer that. I think I know."

"You don't know squat, little brother," Morgan said, giving her a quick kiss before he released her. "We're moving Samantha and the baby into my room."

"How's my nephew today?" Colt asked, walking over to the cradle. "Still no teeth?"

At the reference to her son being his nephew, Samantha's chest tightened. As long as she was married to Morgan, Timmy had the one thing she'd always wanted for her child—he had a family he belonged to.

"No, he still doesn't have teeth," she said, touched that her new brother-in-law already considered Timmy a part of the Wakefield clan.

"Come on, hotshot," Morgan said, clamping his hand down on Colt's shoulder. "You're going to help me with a couple of things before you take off for Mitch's."

Colt grinned. "Only a couple? You usually have a list of things you want me to do that's at least as long as your arm."

She watched as Morgan ushered his brother toward the hall. "Just wait until you drift in home again," he warned with a laugh. "The list will be twice as long." When he reached the door, Morgan turned back to her. "Where do you want us to put the boxes from your car?"

"I'll need to sort through them," she said, trying to remember what they contained. Her and Timmy's clothes had been brought into the house weeks ago, so they wouldn't need to bring the boxes upstairs. "I think most of what's left are kitchen items. Could you put them in the pantry for now?"

Morgan nodded. "Will do."

"Come on, bro," Colt urged. "You can make moon eyes at your wife after I leave."

"You better watch your smart mouth, kid," Morgan said as he followed Colt out into the hall. "I might just have to kick your butt if you don't."

She heard Colt's laughter as the two brothers walked down the hall. "You and whose army?"

As she turned back to empty another dresser drawer, Samantha couldn't help but smile. She enjoyed listening to the good-natured banter between Morgan and his family.

"Samantha?"

At the sound of her name, she looked up to find Colt standing uncertainly at the door. "Where's Morgan? Is something wrong?"

Colt shook his head. "No, everything's fine. Morgan's on his way to the machine shed."

When he continued to stand just inside the room, she asked, "Was there something you needed?"

He shrugged. "I just wanted to thank you."

"For what?" She couldn't imagine why he thought he needed to express his gratitude. To her knowledge, she hadn't done anything that would warrant it.

"Sometimes Brant and I give Morgan a hard time, but he's a good man with a lot of heart. He doesn't think so, but he is." Colt cleared his throat before he continued. "Anyway, I just wanted to thank you for making him happy again."

Before she had a chance to ask what he meant, Colt turned and quickly walked back down the hall, leaving her to stare after him in total bewilderment.

"Is that the last of your clothes?" Morgan asked.

"I think so," Samantha said, looking around the room. She glanced over at the bright red-and-white striped box from the Sleek and Sassy Lady Lingerie Boutique sitting on top of the dresser.

"What's that?"

"Um…it's just…something Annie gave me," she said, her cheeks growing warm. In an effort to change the subject, she pointed to a box of disposable diapers. "Would you mind taking that to your room while I double-check the closet?"

He walked over, took her into his arms and gave her a kiss that left her breathless. "It's *our* room now, sweetheart."

Her stomach fluttered at the look in his startling blue eyes and the suggestive smile curving his firm male lips. "Right. Our room," she said, nodding.

Releasing her, he picked up the carton of diapers. "After I put these with the other baby things, I'll be down in my office for a while. I need to get some paperwork done."

She nodded. "That reminds me. I need to make a list of places to call tomorrow about building estimates and funding for the camp."

"How's it going?"

"Slow." She sighed. "Everyone is either on vacation, or too tied up with other projects to come out to the ranch and give me estimated costs of renovating the house and barn, and building a couple of dormitory cabins."

"It'll all work out, sweetheart," he said, his smile encouraging.

"I hope you're right."

"I am." He started for the door. "After I get a few

things caught up around the ranch, I'll see what I can do to help you.''

Touched by his offer, she smiled. ''Thank you. I'd like that.''

After he left the room, Samantha stared at the empty doorway for several minutes. Morgan Wakefield was indeed a very special man and nothing like her father or Chad. They were selfish, self-centered men, who wouldn't think of offering to help with anything that didn't benefit them in some way.

But Morgan was different. He was kind, thoughtful and went out of his way to do for others—asking nothing for himself in return. He'd offered her his mother's wedding gown when he learned that she really didn't have anything appropriate to wear for the ceremony yesterday. She glanced down at the gold band on her finger. And he'd gone to the trouble and expense of buying wedding rings, so no one would suspect their marriage was anything but the real thing.

Sighing, she sank down on the edge of the bed. She only wished there was something she could do to show him how special she thought he was—something to make him feel as cherished as he'd made her feel in the past few days.

Samantha glanced over at the box Annie had given her the day before. Did she dare try the book and massage oil?

She rose to her feet and walked over to the dresser, lifted the red-and-white striped top and pushed the tissue paper out of the way. Moving the teddy to the side, she dismissed it completely. There wasn't much more to the undergarment than see-through lace and a couple of satin ribbons, and she didn't think she'd ever be able to work up the courage to wear something that provocative.

But Annie had said Brant loved the sensual massage she'd given him on their wedding night. Would Morgan protest his pretend wife giving him one?

Placing the soft, stretchy lace teddy back on top of the book and bottle of oil, Samantha folded the tissue back in place and put the top back on the box. She'd never in a million years have thought of giving a man a sensual massage.

Suppressing a nervous giggle, she shook her head as she tucked the box under her arm and walked from the room. Maybe if she tried really hard, she'd be able to work up the courage to try it sometime. But she wasn't sure she'd ever have the nerve to wear the teddy.

"Samantha?" Morgan tried to open the door to the bathroom adjoining their bedroom. It was locked. "Sweetheart, are you all right?"

He'd held her while she nursed the baby, as he had every night for the past week. But as soon as she'd gotten Timmy to sleep, she'd put him to bed in the cradle over in the corner, disappeared into the bathroom, and Morgan hadn't seen her since. He checked his watch. That had been half an hour ago.

His concern increasing, he pounded on the door.

"Samantha, if you don't answer me, and damned quick, I'm going to break this door down."

"I'm fine, Morgan. I'll be out in a few more minutes," she said, her voice muffled by the thick oak panel separating them. "And keep your voice down. I don't want you waking Timmy."

He frowned as he unbuttoned and removed his shirt, then shucked his jeans and placed them on the chest at the foot of the bed. Walking around to the side, he sat down on the mattress and stared at the bathroom door. What could possibly take a woman that damned long for something as simple as a shower?

As he sat there contemplating the mysterious ways of women, he heard the lock being released. Glancing up, he watched the door open just a crack.

"Morgan?"

He was on his feet and across the room in a flash. "What is it, sweetheart? Are you sure you're all right?"

"Yes, I'm fine. I want you to do something for me," she said, sounding breathless.

"Name it." He tried to push the door open a little wider, but she held it firm.

"I want you to go lay down on the bed."

"You want me to what?" She had him scared about half-spitless and she wanted him to go lay down?

"Dammit, Samantha, what's going on?"

"Just do it, okay?"

"Women," he muttered as he walked back to the bed, shoved the pillows against the headboard, then leaned back against them.

"Are you lying down?"

"Yes," he said, blowing out a frustrated breath. He had no idea what she was up to, but the explanation had better be damned good.

The light in the bathroom went out a split second before the door opened the rest of the way, and Samantha stepped out into the room wearing a shy smile and a scrap of lace that revealed more than it hid.

Morgan sat bolt upright in bed, his eyes wide, his heart thumping his ribs like a bass drum in a high school marching band. "Wh-where..." He had to swallow around the cotton suddenly lining his throat and mouth. "...did you get that?"

"Annie gave it to me on Sunday, just before we got married." An uncertain look replaced her smile. "You don't like it?"

He grinned. "Hell, sweetheart, if I liked it any better, I think I'd probably have a heart attack."

Her easy expression returned as she walked toward him. "I really had no intentions of ever wearing it, but—"

"I'm glad you did, sweetheart," he said, meaning it more than she'd probably ever know.

He started to rise from the bed, but she shook her head and held up her hand. "Would you mind staying there?"

"Why?"

"Because it's taken me almost a week to work up my courage to do this, I'd like to finish," she said, her cheeks turning a pretty shade of rose.

"What do you intend to finish?" he asked, thoroughly intrigued.

He watched her bite her lower lip, then take a deep breath. "I'm going to give you a sensual massage."

Nine

Morgan's heart took off at a gallop and his libido right along with it. "Sweetheart, are you trying to seduce me?"

Her cheeks colored a very pretty pink. "Well, no...I mean, I hadn't thought of it that way."

"It's fine with me if you are. Although, I don't think you can seduce the willing." Curious to see what Samantha had in mind, he grinned as he clasped his hands behind his head and leaned back against the pillows. "But I'm pretty easy to get along with. Go for it."

Her relieved expression caused his chest to swell with an emotion he forced himself to ignore. He wasn't ready, or willing, to acknowledge anything beyond the fact that his wife was standing before him in nothing more than a wisp of lace and ribbon, and one hell of a sexy smile. And she was looking at him like she fully intended to make him her next meal.

"Keep in mind that I've never done anything like this before, and that I'll have to learn as I go," she said, her throaty admission sending the blood rushing through his veins so fast that it left him light-headed.

"We're breaking new ground here for both of us," he said hoarsely. "You've never given a sensual massage, and I've never gotten one."

She toyed with the tiny satin bow between her breasts. "Do you want me to stop?"

"Hell, no!" He shook his head. "This is just starting to get interesting."

He watched her gaze travel from his face, down his chest to his stomach and beyond. The second she noticed the bulge of his arousal already straining at his briefs, her eyes widened.

"Real interesting," he said, unable to stop grinning. He had no idea what she intended to do next, but he was looking forward to finding out.

When she walked over to the side of the bed, he noticed a bottle in her hand. "What's that?"

"You'll see," she said, her smile sending a curl of heat to the pit of his belly. "But we have to establish a couple of ground rules first."

He made room for her to sit down beside him, then reached for her. "And those would be?"

She drew back. "You can't touch me until I tell you to."

"That's going to be difficult," he said, dropping his arms and feeling as if air was in short supply. "What else?"

"I want you to keep your eyes closed."

This was getting more interesting by the second. "All right. Anything else?"

She gave him a look that sent his blood pressure off the chart. "I want you to concentrate on what I'll be doing to you and tell me how it makes you feel."

He swallowed hard. "You're determined to give me a heart attack, aren't you?"

"No, silly," she said, laughing. "This is supposed to heighten your senses and make you feel wonderful."

"Oh, I'm feeling pretty damned terrific right now as it is," he said, forcing himself to breathe. "And if my senses get any sharper, they could slice granite."

Her smile made the task of lying still all the more difficult. "I hope this makes you feel even better. Now, close your eyes."

When he did as she requested, a pleasant earthy scent drifted around him, followed by something liquid dripping onto his chest. "What is that stuff?"

"Light musk body oil."

"It's…warm." He had to concentrate to keep his eyes shut. "Feels good."

"Mm-hmm. I warmed the bottle in hot water."

She touched him with her soft hands, spreading the

oil over his chest. But when she lightly massaged his pectoral muscles, then circled each one of his flat nipples with the tip of her finger, a shudder ran through him and he sucked in a sharp breath.

"Does that feel good?" she whispered close to his ear.

His muscles flexed and his eyes popped open. "If it felt any better I'd—"

She shook her head. "Close your eyes."

Frowning, he did as she instructed. "Now, I know you're determined to give me a coronary."

He loved the way her hands felt on his body. But he had a feeling before she was finished, he might end up certifiably insane.

As her hands drifted lower over his ribs, to his abdomen and his flanks, she asked, "What are you feeling now?"

Couldn't she tell? Hadn't she noticed how hard his body had become with wanting her?

He had to take a deep breath before he could manage to make his vocal cords work. "I think there's enough electricity running through me right now that I could light up Laramie and probably Cheyenne."

Her throaty laughter only increased the tension building inside of him. "Try to relax."

It was his turn to laugh. "Why don't you ask me to move a couple of mountains while I'm at it?"

"Impossible, huh?"

Shaking his head, he doubled both hands into tight fists to keep from reaching for her. "Never underestimate a man as charged up as I am right now. Just tell me which mountain, when you want it moved and where.''

''I'll give that some thought,'' she said, taking one of her talented little hands away from his lower stomach.

He wondered what she was doing, but the sound of the flip-top cap on the bottle being opened quickly drew his attention. Where was she going to put the oil now?

It didn't take long to find out what she had planned next when he felt the warm liquid dribble over his legs. She placed a hand on each one of his shins, then started spreading the oil upward. His heart stalled. But when she moved her hands over his knees and up his thighs, his pulse took off at breakneck speed and the heat in his lower belly ignited into a flame. If she didn't stop, and damned quick, her hands were going to be dangerously close to—

His eyes snapped open and he swallowed hard. There was no doubt in his mind that she was going to kill him before the night was over. But, he decided as the back of her hand brushed the bulge of his arousal straining against his cotton briefs, he'd leave this world a very happy man.

Unable to lie still a minute longer, Morgan caught her hands in his and drew her up to face him. ''Sweetheart, don't get me wrong. I'm loving the hell out of this seduction business. But I'm about to go into sensory overload.''

Lying across his chest, she smiled down at him. "Don't you want me to finish?"

The air in his lungs came out in one big whoosh and a surge of need arrowed straight to his groin. "If you keep running your hands over me with that warm oil, things will be finished a whole lot sooner than either one of us really wants."

She glanced down his body at the evidence of his overwhelming desire. "Are you trying to tell me that I was successful at giving you a sensual massage?"

If he hadn't been fighting so hard to retain what little control he had left, he might have laughed. "I'd say it was a resounding success, sweetheart." Taking her into his arms, he rolled over to pin her beneath him. "I'll be more than happy to let you do it again any time you want. But would you mind if we put my complete surrender on hold for now and I took it from here?"

"Why?"

"Because I can't take any more of this." He pressed his lower body against her thigh as he lowered his lips to her ear. "I need to be inside of you, bringing you the same pleasure you're giving me."

"I'd like that," she said, shivering against him. Her warm breath teased the side of his neck, sending an answering shudder coursing through him.

The fire in his belly burned brighter, and unable to resist the lure of her soft lips any longer, Morgan traced their fullness with his tongue. When she sighed and wrapped her arms around his shoulders, he deepened the kiss to stroke her inner recesses and coax her into exploring him. Heaven help him, but he was addicted to the sweet taste of her, the way her reserved response quickly turned into passionate need.

Wanting to touch her, to hold her to him and bury himself deep inside of her, he ran his hands the length of her. The scrap of lace she was wearing looked fantastic on her, but he knew beyond a shadow of doubt that he'd like it better off of her. The only problem was, he couldn't figure out how to get her out of it.

He lifted his head to kiss the tip of her nose. "Don't get me wrong. I like whatever this is you're wearing, but how the hell do I get it off of you."

"It's called a teddy." She kissed his chest, sending a shock-wave right through him. "There are two snaps below, at the—"

Before she could finish telling him where they were located, Morgan quickly found and released the tiny fasteners at the apex of her thighs. After he pulled the stretchy lace up and over her head, he removed his briefs and reached for the foil packet he'd tucked beneath his pillow earlier.

"Morgan?" She took the packet from him. "Would you mind if I—"

Blood rushed through his veins when he realized what she was about to ask. "Go right ahead, sweetheart," he said, lying back against the pillows.

He'd never had a woman help arrange their protection before and he found it was more exciting than he could have ever imagined. Her soft touch on his heated body as she rolled the condom into place almost sent him over the edge.

He reached for her once she had the prophylactic taken care of, but Samantha surprised him when she shook her head and moved to straddle his hips. Holding him captive with her smoldering gaze, Morgan thought the top of his head just might come right off his shoulders as her body slowly consumed his.

Closing his eyes, he gritted his teeth and placed his hands on her hips to keep her still. "Don't…move."

Heat and light danced behind his eyelids like some kind of wild laser show as he fought for control. He'd never in his life been this hot, this fast. His body was urging him to allow Samantha to complete the act of loving him, but he ignored it. He wanted this feeling of being one with her to last forever.

The thought might have scared the hell out of him at any other time. But at the moment, Morgan didn't have the strength to fight it. Didn't even want to.

She leaned down to kiss his chest, his shoulder and his chin, then slowly, surely began to rock against him. His senses honed to a razor-sharp edge, he could tell by the tightness of her body and the passionate glow coloring her porcelain cheeks that she was as turned on as he was.

Holding her shapely hips, he helped her set a pace that quickly had them both close to the edge of fulfillment. Only when he felt her inner muscles cling to him, signaling that her release was imminent, did he abandon the last shred of his control and thrust into her a final time. Her moan of pleasure and the rhythmic tremors coursing through her triggered his own climax, and together they hurtled into the realm of complete and utter ecstasy.

The next morning, Morgan shuffled through the stack of files on his desk. When he came across the purchase option he'd had his lawyer draw up for the Shackley ranch, he tossed it aside. He'd have to shred it, along with some other useless papers. But that would have to wait.

He glanced at the calendar. It was time for his annual drive down to the cemetery just outside of Denver to pay his respects to the woman he'd promised to marry.

Every year since Emily's passing, on the day they were to have been married, he'd faithfully placed flowers on her grave and silently begged her forgiveness for his role in her death. But this year would be different. Today, he'd be making the trip to say his final goodbye to her.

He took a deep breath. He'd lain awake most of the night with Samantha nestled in his arms and he'd done a lot of thinking.

Emily was his past and it was time he let her go. She'd been his best friend as well as his lover, and he had no doubt that if they'd married, they would have made it work.

But for the first time in six long years, he felt ready

to move forward and get on with his life. Samantha was his future now. He wanted her with him for the rest of his life, wanted to help her raise Timmy and share her dream of starting a camp for kids of the foster care system.

As he glanced out the window at the distant Shirley Mountains, he sucked in a sharp breath. Good Lord, he'd fallen in love with her.

The thought should have scared the hell out of him. But as the realization settled in, he smiled.

He'd first been drawn to her bravery and pride. She'd faced giving birth to her son in a ramshackle old ranch house with a depth of courage that had astounded him. Then, when she found out that he'd paid the hospital bill, she'd gathered her pride around her like a coat of armor and informed him that she'd cook his meals and clean his house in order to pay him back.

But as he'd gotten to know her better, he'd also learned how kind and caring she was. She was a wonderful mother to Timmy, and even though she had very little herself, she was determined to take her inheritance and turn it into a place where kids could briefly escape their emotional pain.

She'd even allowed him to feel as if he were a member of her little family when she let him hold her while she nursed the baby. And, if she'd let him, he wanted to be a permanent part of it. But he couldn't do that until he made the trip to Denver.

Smiling at the thought of them being a real family,

he slowly rose from his chair and crossed the room. He needed to get on the road. The sooner he bid farewell to his past, the sooner he could get on with his future.

"Samantha?" he called as he walked across the foyer to the great room.

When he found her in the kitchen, he walked up behind her, wrapped his arms around her waist and pulled her back against him. He loved touching her, loved the way she melted against him. Hell, he just plain loved everything about her.

"Sweetheart, I have to go down to Denver today to take care of some unfinished business." He kissed the side of her neck. "Do you need me to pick up anything for you or the baby?"

She turned in his arms to give him a kiss that damned near knocked his size-13 boots right off his feet. "Would you mind picking up a couple of boxes of diapers?"

He shook his head. "Anything else?"

"I can't think of anything." She kissed him again. "How long will you be gone?"

He hated having to leave, when what he really wanted to do was take her upstairs and show her how much she'd come to mean to him, but he needed to say goodbye to an old friend. "I'll be gone most of the day." Giving her a kiss that left them both gasping for breath, he cupped her cheek with his palm. "When I get back, there's something we need to get settled."

She stared at him for several long seconds. "Could I ask what that would be?"

"You'll see." He kissed her again, then set her away from him. If he didn't put some distance between them, he wouldn't even make it as far as the truck, let alone take off for Denver. "I'll call you on my cell phone when I start home."

When he turned to leave, she asked, "Would you mind if I use the computer in your office? It will probably take most of the day, but I'd like to do an Internet search to find contractors for building estimates and possible sources of funding for the camp."

"Sweetheart, the Lonetree is your home now," he said, placing his Resistol on his head as he opened the back door. "You don't have to ask to use my office or anything in it."

Samantha felt warm all over when Morgan winked at her before closing the door behind him. She had no idea what he wanted to talk about, but she had a few things she needed to say to him when he got back.

Her chest tightened and she gave up trying to deny what she knew in her heart to be true. She'd fallen in love with her new husband.

Considering their agreement, it wasn't the smartest thing she'd ever done, but she wasn't sure she'd ever really had a choice in the matter. The question now was could he ever love her in return?

She knew he wanted her. Of that, there was no

doubt. But could Morgan fall in love with her the way a husband loved his wife?

She wasn't sure. But she had every intention of finding out, because there was no way she could remain on the Lonetree Ranch if it turned out that he couldn't.

Strapping Timmy in the baby carrier, Samantha carried him downstairs, along with the folder containing her plans for building the camp. She needed to make some phone calls for estimates on building materials, as well as do an Internet search on Morgan's computer to see what kind of financial aid was available and how to go about obtaining it.

Entering the office, she set the baby carrier on the deacon's bench close to the desk, then settled herself in the big leather desk chair. The first thing she had to do was to start making appointments with an engineer to come out and inspect the existing structures on her grandfather's ranch. If some of them could be renovated, it would cut down on the overall cost of getting the camp up and running.

Glancing over at Timmy, she smiled. "Now, all I have to do is find where Morgan keeps the phone book. Any ideas?"

At the sound of her voice, Timmy waved his little fist in the air and smacked his lips around the pacifier in his mouth.

She laughed. "In other words, you're on your own, Mom."

The pacifier bobbled as if he agreed with her.

"It has to be here somewhere," she said, standing to search the floor-to-ceiling book shelves beside the desk, then the computer center behind it.

Finally spotting the directory under several legal-size files beside the keyboard, she reached to pull the book from beneath the pile. She sighed heavily when the entire stack of folders fell to the floor.

"Morgan will never trust your mommy in his office again," she said to her now sleeping son.

Disgusted with herself for being so careless, she bent to pick up the scattered papers. But her name on one of the documents caught her attention, and straightening, she scanned its contents.

Her heart skipped several beats and a chilling numbness began to fill her soul. Morgan wanted to buy her grandfather's ranch?

Her legs suddenly feeling as if they would no longer support her, she collapsed onto the chair behind the desk. Why would Morgan have a purchase option drawn up? Even before she learned of the new will, and the terms that had to be met to obtain the property, she'd never indicated that she wanted to sell. On the contrary. She'd told Morgan the first day about her plans to turn the ranch into a camp for foster children.

As she thought about the events of the past couple of months, tears filled her eyes, then ran down her cheeks. How could she have been so stupid?

After she'd explained about the camp, Morgan had

avoided her like the plague. He'd left each morning before she got up and hadn't returned until well after she'd gone to bed each night.

But all that changed the day she met with her grandfather's lawyer and he informed her of the new stipulations placed on her inheritance. Once Morgan learned that the land would be turned over to the BLM if she wasn't married, he couldn't get her to the altar fast enough.

Her breath caught on a sob as she glanced down on the gold band circling her finger. What a fool she'd been.

When she questioned him about why he was willing to put his life on hold for the next two years, she'd taken him at his word and foolishly believed that he only wanted to help her hold on to the property. But instead, he'd married her simply because he'd known that once the land was donated to the BLM he'd never get his hands on it.

She scrunched her eyes shut at the emotional pain tightening her chest. Why had she been so quick to believe in Morgan? Hadn't she learned from her father and Chad that men couldn't be counted on for anything but heartache and grief? That they had their own agenda, that didn't include her?

Unable to sit still another minute, she rose to her feet, quickly picked up the remaining files still scattered on the floor and stacked them on the computer center. Turning back to Morgan's desk, she carefully laid the purchase option where he would be sure to see it, then with trembling fingers, removed her wedding band to place it on top of the document.

Tears blurred her vision and her heart felt as if it shattered into a million pieces when she picked up the baby carrier and started out of the office. As she closed the door behind her, the phone started ringing. She ignored it.

She didn't feel like speaking with anyone, nor did she have time. She had to get her suitcases from the store room and start packing to leave.

Morgan let the phone on the other end of the line ring until the answering machine in his office picked up. Frowning, he left another message for Samantha to call him, then depressed the end button. He'd been trying to reach her since leaving the cemetery three hours ago, but she still wasn't answering. Where the hell was she?

She'd told him this morning that she intended to spend the day working on plans for her camp. Fear gripped his belly as he stared out the windshield of his truck at the road ahead. Had something happened to her or the baby?

He pressed down on the accelerator at the same time he pushed the auto-dial on the cell phone. As soon as Annie answered, he asked, "Is Samantha over there at your place?"

"No. I tried calling her a couple of times today, but the answering machine picked up." His sister-in-law sounded alarmed. "Isn't she with you?"

The knot of fear twisting his gut tightened. "No. I've been trying to get hold of her since I left Denver."

"Where are you now? Do you need me to drive over there?"

"I'm only about six miles from home." He turned the truck off the main road and onto Lonetree land. "I'll get there before you could."

"Morgan, if you need us—"

"I'll let you know." As an afterthought he added, "Thanks, Annie."

"When you find out something, let us know if everything is all right." Annie paused. "I...have some bad news, Morgan."

His anxiety increased. "What is it?"

"Colt's friend, Mitch Simpson, was stomped by a bull last night in Houston." He heard Annie take a shaky breath. "He died in surgery a few hours later."

Morgan groaned from the deep sadness filling him. He liked Mitch and his younger sister, Kaylee. Everyone did.

"How's Colt taking it?" he asked, concerned. Colt and Mitch had been best friends since they'd competed against each other at the National High School Rodeo Finals in their junior year. Colt had to be devastated.

"He's taking it pretty hard—" Annie's voice caught. "But he's going to help Kaylee make arrangements for the funeral, then get Mitch's affairs settled before he comes home."

"Was Brant one of the bullfighters?" Morgan asked, knowing that if he was, his brother would blame himself for not taking the hit for Mitch.

"No, he didn't work the event." Annie sighed. "But he's feeling guilty because he wasn't. He said if he'd been there, he might have been able to do something."

It didn't surprise Morgan one bit that Brant regretted not being there. "Are you two driving down to Oklahoma for the funeral?"

"Yes, we'll leave in the morning."

"Take it easy and tell Brant I said to drive safely," Morgan said. "And give my condolences to Kaylee."

"We will. Don't forget to let us know about Samantha," Annie reminded.

"Will do," Morgan said, ending the call.

He tossed the cell phone onto the seat beside him and drove faster. Hearing about Mitch reminded him of how fleeting life was, and if something had happened to Samantha or the baby, he'd never forgive himself for making the trip to Denver, instead of staying home with her.

By the time he skidded to a halt at the side of the ranch house and killed the engine, Morgan already had his shoulder belt unfastened and the driver's door open. Jumping from the truck, he sprinted up the back porch steps, then threw the kitchen door wide. It crashed back against the log wall, splintering wood and shattering the window in the upper part of the door. He couldn't have cared less. All that mattered was finding his wife and son.

''Samantha?'' he shouted.

Nothing.

He rushed down the hall, and taking the stairs two at a time, searched every room on the second floor. They were nowhere to be found.

Going back downstairs, he crossed the great room to the foyer. The door to his office was closed. He hoped like hell she'd taken a break from working on the camp plans to nurse the baby and hadn't answered because she didn't want to upset Timmy, or that she'd fallen asleep.

Morgan knew it was unlikely, but at the moment he was ready to grasp any explanation as long as Samantha and the baby were all right.

But when he entered the office, the knot in his gut tightened. Where the hell could she be?

As he started to leave the room, the late afternoon sun streaming through the windows glinted off something on his desk, causing him to turn back. When his gaze zeroed in on the reflective object, the air lodged in his lungs.

Forcing himself to walk over to the desk for a closer inspection, Morgan's heart felt as if it dropped to his boot tops. Samantha's wedding ring sat on top of the purchase option he'd had his lawyer draw up for her grandfather's land.

Ten

As Samantha cradled her crying son to her, she glanced around the living room of her grandfather's run-down ranch house. Tears blurred her vision once again and she tried not to remember the last night they'd spent here—the night Morgan had helped her give birth to the baby.

He'd been her rock—her source of strength and security that night. And she'd foolishly allowed it to continue, until she'd fallen in love with him.

Her breath caught on a sob. She'd been deeply hurt by her father's abandonment and Chad's refusal to have anything to do with Timmy, but both times she'd gotten over it and moved on with her life. But she wasn't sure she'd ever recover from the devastation of Morgan's betrayal.

Why had she convinced herself that he was everything he appeared to be? Why had she allowed him to convince her that he truly wanted to help her keep her inheritance? And why had she allowed herself to fall hopelessly in love with him?

"What's wrong with Timmy?"

At the sound of the familiar baritone, Samantha turned to see Morgan standing in the doorway, looking much as he had the first time she'd seen him. His wide-brimmed hat pulled low on his forehead, his stance, the rigid set of his jaw, all spoke volumes about his state of mind.

She'd only seen him this way one other time. The night they met. He'd been angry then. He was angry now.

"This is private property," she said, meeting his dark gaze. "You're trespassing."

He shrugged. "So have me arrested."

Shifting the baby from the cradle of her arm to her shoulder, she nodded. "You can bet I will."

"What are you doing here, Samantha?" At the sound of Morgan's voice, Timmy's crying faded to a whimper. "Is the baby all right?"

Samantha detected the concern in Morgan's voice, and no matter how he felt about her, she knew he cared for her son. "He'll be fine. He's fighting sleep."

Morgan walked over to the fireplace to sit down on the raised stone hearth. "When Timmy goes to sleep, we'll talk."

"No, we won't."

"Yes, we will." He sounded just as firm as she had, and from the determination etched on his handsome face, she knew he wasn't going to budge.

Swaying back and forth, she patted Timmy's small back. "There's nothing to say."

"There's plenty to say." Morgan's scowl darkened. "And by damn, Samantha, you're going to hear me out."

Turning to pace the room, she shook her head. "It won't do any good, so you might as well save your breath."

"Look, Samantha, I've had a hell of a day and I don't feel like arguing with you," he said, sounding tired. "Just before I got home and discovered my wife and son had flown the coop, I got word that Colt's best friend, Mitch, died last night after a bull riding accident."

"Oh, I'm so sorry for Colt's loss," she said, her heart going out to her youngest brother-in-law. "Is Colt all right?"

Morgan shook his head. "Annie said he's taking it pretty hard." Rising to his feet, he looked around. "Where's the baby carrier? Timmy's asleep."

"Over by the couch." She kept her voice low, in order not to disturb her son.

Morgan walked over to take the baby from her, then went back to the couch to gently place her sleeping son in the baby seat. When he straightened to his full height, he turned toward her. "Why don't we go back to the Lonetree to talk this out?"

She shook her head. "I'd rather not."

"Why?"

"I don't belong there," she said, her heart breaking. She'd come to love the Lonetree Ranch, almost as much as she loved its owner, and it broke her heart to think she'd never be going back.

Closing the distance between them, he towered over her. "That's bull and you know it. The Lonetree is your home."

"No, Morgan," she said quietly. "It never was."

"How can you say that, Samantha? You're my wife."

He reached for her, but she stepped back. She couldn't let him touch her. If she did, she wasn't sure she'd have the strength to resist him.

"Let's talk about that, Morgan." She folded her arms beneath her breasts. "Let's discuss the reasons behind your willingness to marry me."

His piercing blue gaze met hers head-on. "You were going to lose your inheritance and—"

"And what?" she interrupted, ignoring the pain caused by his duplicity and letting her anger take control. "You were going to lose any chance of getting your hands on the property?"

He shook his head. "No. *You* were going to lose what was rightfully yours and your dream of opening the camp."

Taking a deep shuddering breath, she met his dark

gaze head-on. "Did you, or did you not, want to buy my grandfather's ranch?"

"I did." He had the audacity to smile. "But I don't anymore."

Her anger increased. "How silly of me to forget such an important detail. There's no longer a need to purchase the land, is there? It came as part of the package when you married me."

"Nope. This is your place." He took a step toward her, but she forced herself to stand her ground.

"Not for much longer." Tears filled her eyes again, but she blinked them away. "Once our divorce is final, it will belong to the BLM."

She watched his smile fade and a muscle begin to twitch along his firm jaw. "We're not getting a divorce," he said firmly.

"Yes, we are," she insisted.

"*No,* we're not." Morgan took a step forward. "We're going to stay married, in two years you're going to get the title to your land and start your camp for foster kids."

"I can't do that."

"Why not?"

"Because we aren't going to stay married long enough for me to get the land," she repeated.

He sighed heavily. "This is getting us absolutely nowhere. What do you say we start over?"

Her stubborn little chin came up defiantly. "What's the point?"

As she stared at him, he could see myriad emotions

in the depths of her whiskey-colored eyes. He hated that his carelessness had hurt her and caused her distress, but he had to explain. Their future together depended on it.

Reaching out, he touched her cheek with his index finger. "Just hear me out, Samantha. Please."

"At this point, I doubt there will be anything you could say that will change things," she said, suddenly sounding tired. "But if it will get you to leave, then fine. I'll listen."

"Fair enough." He gave her what he hoped was an encouraging smile. "Do you remember the day you and Timmy came home from the hospital and I suggested that you sell this place?"

"Yes, but I thought you were talking about listing it with a Realtor." She walked over to the hearth to sit down. "You didn't tell me you were the one interested in buying the property."

"No, I didn't." Morgan paused. He needed to choose his words carefully. This was too important to have any more misunderstandings between them. "I had called my attorney to draw up the purchase option before I talked to you about selling it. But once I learned of your plans, I didn't see any reason to mention it. Starting a camp for kids is a much better use for the land than my just wanting to make the Lonetree bigger."

"Then why didn't you destroy the document if you didn't think at some later date you could convince me to sell?" she asked, looking doubtful.

"Because I'm a fool," he said, shaking his head at his own carelessness. "I had the attorney mail it to me so I didn't get it until a week or two after we'd talked. By that time, I was busy working from daylight until well after dark. I was so tired when it arrived, I opened the envelope, saw what it was, then tossed it on a stack of files and forgot about it. Then, when I ran across it this morning, I put it on a stack of papers I need to destroy."

"Okay, I'll accept that. But once you found out about my plans for the camp, you avoided me like the plague," she said, clearly unconvinced. "Then, when you learned that I was about to lose my ranch to the BLM because I wasn't married, you couldn't get me to the altar fast enough. Why?"

Her chin rose another notch and he couldn't help but smile. She was cute as hell when she was angry.

"You don't have a clue about the relationship between ranchers and the BLM, do you, sweetheart?"

"No, I...what does that have to do with anything?" She didn't look quite as certain as she had only moments ago.

"I could have had the land by the first of next year, if I hadn't married you."

"Oh, really?" She didn't look like she believed him. "And how would you have managed that?"

"All I would have had to do was contact the office in Casper and arrange for a long-term lease." He shrugged. "The land would have been mine for as long as I cared to pay for its use."

He could tell she was considering his explanation. "Then you really did marry me to help me keep my land?" she asked, her voice little more than a whisper.

Morgan nodded. "Among other reasons."

He watched the anger and hurt in her pretty amber eyes turn to bewilderment. "What other reasons?"

Taking a deep breath, Morgan knew the time had come to lay it all on the line. "I tried to stay away from you as much as possible because I couldn't keep my hands off of you," he said, hoping she'd understand. "You were everything I wanted, but couldn't have."

"What do you mean I was everything you couldn't have?" she asked, looking more confused than ever.

As he tried to find the words to tell her why he felt the way he had, he rubbed the back of his neck in an effort to relieve some of his tension. This was possibly the most important discussion he'd ever have in his entire life and he hoped like hell that he didn't blow it.

Deciding there was no better way to tell her about his past than straight out, he walked over to sit down beside her on the hearth. "Six years ago, I was engaged to be married. But a week before the wedding, I talked my fiancée into visiting her sister down in Denver while I caught up on chores around the ranch. She didn't want to go, but I insisted." He loosely clasped his hands between his knees and stared down at them. "While they were out shopping, she and her sister were caught in the cross fire between the police and a couple of thugs trying to rob a jewelry store. She…died instantly.''

''Oh, Morgan, I'm so sorry,'' she said, placing her hand on his arm. ''That must have been awful for you.''

He nodded, but remained silent for several moments, drawing comfort from Samantha's warm touch. Covering her hand with his, he finished, ''After that, I vowed that I would never make decisions for another person I cared about. No matter what the circumstances.''

''It wasn't your fault, Morgan,'' she said, her voice filled with compassion.

''Whether it was, or not, I still felt responsible.''

Samantha watched Morgan closely. She could tell that he'd been deeply affected by the loss of his fiancée. ''Do you still feel that way?'' she asked, quietly.

Turning to face her, he shrugged one shoulder. ''I guess I'll always blame myself to a certain extent. But I finally feel ready to move on. It's the reason I made the trip to Denver today. I had to put flowers on her grave and say goodbye.'' He stopped to clear his throat. ''I want us to stay together, Samantha.''

Her breath caught, and for the first time since he walked in the door, hope began to blossom within her. ''Why, Morgan? Is it just because you want to help me get my land?''

''No.'' She watched him glance down at his hands,

then take a deep breath before he raised his head to look at her. "I want to hold you every night and wake up with you in my arms each morning for the rest of my life, Samantha. I already think of Timmy as my own son. I want to adopt him and help you raise him."

Tears filled her eyes and her heart skipped several beats. "Really?"

He nodded. "I also want to help you start your camp."

After all of the things he said he wanted for their life together, she was sure Morgan loved her. But she needed to hear the words. "Why?"

"Because I...love you," he said, his voice rough with emotion. He reached into his shirt pocket to remove something, then taking her left hand in his, he slipped her wedding band back onto her finger.

When he wrapped his strong arms around her and buried his face in her hair, she felt as if her heart would burst with happiness. "Oh, Morgan, I love you, too."

He held her for several minutes before he spoke again. "I can't live without you, sweetheart. Please don't ever leave me again."

She shook her head. "Never."

Releasing her, he cupped her face with his large hands. "I want you to understand that even though we'll be a family, and equal partners in our marriage, I won't make any decisions, or try to persuade you to do anything you don't want to do."

Her chest tightened with emotion at the sincerity she saw in his brilliant blue eyes. He was such a good man, and one that she knew would never do anything to intentionally hurt or disappoint her, or Timmy, if it was within his power to prevent it.

"Morgan, darling, I hate to be the one to break this to you," she said, touching his jaw with her finger-tips. "But you've been making decisions for me since the moment we met."

Frowning, he shook his head. "No, I haven't."

"Yes, you have." She couldn't keep from smiling. "You took charge as soon as you found out I was in labor and told me that I couldn't take myself to the hospital."

"That was different."

"How?"

"You were in no shape to drive."

"That's right. But you didn't give me a choice, did you?" When he slowly shook his head, she contin-ued, "And what about your insistence that Timmy and I stay at the Lonetree with you, instead of coming back here?"

She could tell he considered her words before he finally spoke. "This place doesn't have heat, water or electricity. It wouldn't have been good for you or the baby."

"Once again, you were looking out for our wel-fare," she said, nodding. "You assessed the situation and *decided* it wasn't a good environment for us. You took care of us, Morgan."

He seemed to mull that over for a moment before he grinned sheepishly. "I guess I did, didn't I?"

She nodded. "Morgan?"

"What, sweetheart?"

"There's a few things that I want from our marriage, too," she said.

Giving her a quick kiss, he smiled. "Name it, sweetheart."

"Promise me that you'll continue to watch out for me and Timmy," she said smiling.

Nodding, he ran his thumb over the gold band around her finger as his brilliant blue gaze met hers. "I'll protect you both with my life. Anything else?"

"How do you feel about having more children?" she asked. "I'd like for Timmy to have a couple of brothers and sisters."

His serious expression easing, he laughed. "Sweetheart, I'll be more than happy to give you all the babies you want. Is that all?"

She nodded, the love she felt for him blossoming inside of her with each passing second. "Take us home, Morgan."

He stared at her for endless seconds. "I love you, Samantha. Once I take you back to the Lonetree, I don't ever intend to let you go. This marriage will be forever."

"I love you with all my heart and soul, Morgan," she said, tears filling her eyes. "That's what I want, too."

Giving her a kiss that sent her heart soaring, he

stood up. Then smiling, took her hand in his and pulled her up to stand beside him. "Forever, sweetheart."

She nodded as she smiled back at him. "Forever."

Epilogue

Two years later

"**O**ut, Daddy! Out!"

Morgan smiled as he unfastened the safety straps on Timmy's car seat and lifted him out of the truck cab. "Let's go see what Mommy's doing," he said, setting his son on his feet.

"Mommy! We here," Timmy yelled, racing toward the ranch house they'd turned into an office for Camp Safe Haven as fast as his short little legs would allow.

When he reached the steps, Morgan reminded, "Be careful and hold on to the rail."

Stepping out onto the porch, Samantha laughed

when Timmy knocked his black cowboy hat off when he raised his arm to take hold of the wooden banister. "How are my two favorite Wakefield men?"

"We here," Timmy said proudly.

Morgan grinned as he helped Timmy put his hat back on, then helped him up the steps. "We're doing pretty good. After Timmy coerced Uncle Colt into taking him for a horseback ride, he helped me feed Stormy Gal's new colt, then we went over to visit Uncle Brant, Aunt Annie and little Zach."

"It sounds like you've had a full morning," she said as she lowered herself into one of the rocking chairs by the door, then lifted Timmy onto her lap.

"You feeling all right?" Morgan asked, sitting in the chair beside her.

Nodding, she started rocking Timmy who looked as if he might fall asleep at any moment. "I'm fine." She grinned. "No backaches, no contractions, nothing."

When Morgan placed his hand on her rounded stomach, the baby inside kicked as if telling his father "hello." He laughed. "I see our little football player is still practicing his punting skills."

"He's definitely been active today," she agreed, rubbing the spot where the baby had poked her. "By the way, did you call to see if Kaylee Simpson would be interested in being the riding instructor when camp opens next week?"

"I e-mailed her, but she's not interested." He shook his head. "She said that she hasn't ridden in some time and doesn't intend to. She's out of school now and working as a physical trainer.'' He frowned. "I got the feeling she doesn't want to have anything to do with any of us.''

"Do you think Brant would be interested in the job?''

Grinning, he nodded. "Since Annie is going to be the activity director, and here everyday, I'm betting he'll be here anyway.''

"Go-o-o-d,'' she said, drawing out the word in a way that caused his heart to stall.

"Samantha?''

"What time is it?''

"Was that—''

He watched her focus her gaze on his truck for several long seconds. The hair on the back of his neck stood straight up. Unless he missed his guess, he was going to be a daddy again soon. Real soon.

When she blew out a deep breath, then turned to smile at him, he knew he'd never in his life forget how beautiful she was at that very moment, or how very much he loved her. "Morgan, I think we'd better take Timmy over to spend the night with Brant and Annie.''

Rising to his feet, Morgan took their sleeping son in his arms and helped the woman he loved more than life itself to her feet. "Let's get going.''

She looked absolutely radiant and he was once again struck by her calm, and the depth of her courage. "What's the matter, darling? Don't you want to deliver this baby like you did Timmy?"

"Sweetheart, that was a one time shot," he said, locking the office door and helping her down the steps. "I'm more than happy to be your birthing coach, but that's as far as it goes. This time, you're going to be in the hospital with doctors who know what the hell they're doing."

"I love you, Morgan Wakefield," she said, placing her soft hand along his jaw.

He gazed at the woman who had given him everything he'd ever wanted in life—a family and a home filled with love and laughter. "And I love you, sweetheart," he said, turning his head to kiss her palm. "More than you'll ever know."

* * * * *

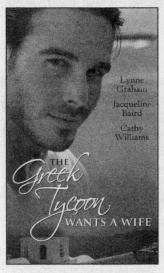

THE ROYAL HOUSE OF KAREDES

Two crowns, two islands, one legacy

8 VOLUMES IN ALL TO COLLECT!

millsandboon.co.uk Community

Join Us!

The Community is the perfect place to meet and chat to kindred spirits who love books and reading as much as you do, but it's also the place to:

- **Get the inside scoop from authors about their latest books**
- **Learn how to write a romance book with advice from our editors**
- **Help us to continue publishing the best in women's fiction**
- **Share your thoughts on the books we publish**
- **Befriend other users**

Forums: Interact with each other as well as authors, editors and a whole host of other users worldwide.

Blogs: Every registered community member has their own blog to tell the world what they're up to and what's on their mind.

Book Challenge: We're aiming to read 5,000 books and have joined forces with The Reading Agency in our inaugural Book Challenge.

Profile Page: Showcase yourself and keep a record of your recent community activity.

Social Networking: We've added buttons at the end of every post to share via digg, Facebook, Google, Yahoo, technorati and de.licio.us.

www.millsandboon.co.uk

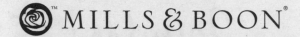